PAHUA
◆ and the ◆
Soul Stealer

by LORI M. LEE

RICK RIORDAN PRESENTS

𝒟𝒾𝓈𝓃𝑒𝓎 • HYPERION   LOS ANGELES   NEW YORK

If you purchased this book without a cover, you should be aware that this book is stolen property. It was reported as "unsold and destroyed" to the publisher, and neither the author nor the publisher has received any payment for this "stripped" book.

Text copyright © 2021 by Lori M. Lee
Introduction copyright © 2021 by Rick Riordan
Spot art copyright © 2021 by Tou Her

All rights reserved. Published by Disney • Hyperion, an imprint of Buena Vista Books, Inc. No part of this book may be reproduced or transmitted in any form or by any means, electronic or mechanical, including photocopying, recording, or by any information storage and retrieval system, without written permission from the publisher. For information address Disney • Hyperion, 77 West 66th Street, New York, New York 10023.

First Hardcover Edition, September 2021
First Paperback Edition, September 2022
10 9 8 7 6 5 4 3 2 1
FAC-025438-22203
Printed in the United States of America

This book is set in Palatino Linotype, Jante Antiqua/Monotype
Designed by Shelby Kahr

Library of Congress Cataloging-in-Publication Control
Number for Hardcover Edition: 2021009212
ISBN 978-1-368-06905-2

Follow @ReadRiordan
Visit www.DisneyBooks.com

SUSTAINABLE
FORESTRY
INITIATIVE
Certified Chain of Custody
Promoting Sustainable Forestry
www.sfiprogram.org
SFI-01054
The SFI label applies to the text stock

For my mom, whose bravery could rival any folktale hero's. And for Matt, one of my earliest partners in imagination.

—L.M.L.

Contents

Be Careful. Some Gongs
You Can't Un-Ring.

I never say this about books, but in the case of *Pahua and the Soul Stealer*, you should start at the end. The author's note from Lori M. Lee offers powerful insights into how this book was created, how challenging it can be to draw on tales from an oral-storytelling tradition when writing a novel, and how much *Pahua* will mean to young readers who have never seen themselves represented in a fantasy adventure before.

I will admit I knew next to nothing about Hmong culture and their traditional stories before reading *Pahua*. Now I understand how much I've been missing. Check out the glossary, also at the end. You'll get a preview of the rich and fascinating world that awaits you, full of secretive gods, brave shaman warriors, ubiquitous spirits, restless ghosts, formidable dragons, magical guardian elephants, multiple realms of reality, and a talking invisible cat named Miv (which, spoiler alert, means *cat*).

But you don't have to know anything about Hmong stories to appreciate this book. If you've ever felt like you don't fit in, like you're too different to belong, you will relate perfectly to the predicament of our young hero, Pahua. Like most eleven-year-olds, Pahua just wants to have a normal life. Alas, she worries she'll never make friends in her tiny adopted hometown of Merdel, Wisconsin. Not only is she Hmong in an overwhelmingly white town . . . Not only is her family struggling to get by since her dad left them . . . Pahua also has a secret she can't even share with her mom or her little brother: She has always been able to see spirits all around her.

Pahua can't even get dressed without having her fashion choices criticized by her cat spirit buddy, Miv, or by the fire spirit who lives in their stove. She can't walk down the street without encountering dozens of dancing mushroom spirits, tree spirits, and air spirits. At least those are friendly. She can't say the same for human ghosts and demons from other realms. . . .

Usually, Pahua is able to steer clear of dangerous apparitions, but one day, when she reluctantly follows some classmates to the local haunted bridge, she makes the mistake of trying to be nice to a little girl ghost. This simple act of kindness starts a domino effect of spiritual mishaps that threatens to tear Pahua's world apart and take her brother, Matt, away forever. Of course, being tough, smart, and brave, Pahua tries to set things right. She grabs her aunt's old shaman tools—a gong for summoning spirits and a dull-edged sword that can only hurt otherworldly entities—and returns to the bridge . . . where she immediately manages to make things even worse.

Bummer. It's going to take Pahua a while to learn to be a true shaman warrior. Unfortunately, she's only got three days to save Matt. Along the way, she'll have to handle a whole lot of dragons, ghosts, demons, and monsters, including a poj ntxoog (tiger spirit) with questionable fashion sense, and a malevolent god who looks suspiciously like Kylo Ren.

I *love* the adventures Pahua has in this book. I also love the sense of humor, the clever plotting, and the fantastic cast of characters. But most of all I love Pahua: her courage, her kindness, and her love for her family. You'll be cheering for her to succeed, even if she does occasionally make mistakes and, you know, summon entities into the human world that could destroy everything she cares about. You always have to be careful with mythological forces, after all. Some gongs you can't un-ring. Once thing I can promise you, though: You'll be glad you made friends with Pahua!

Rick Riordan

1

My Best Friend Is a Cat Spirit

 The day my life changed began like most mornings—with a judgmental cat spirit.

That T-shirt makes you look like an eggplant, Miv said. Despite being a tiny black kitten, he had a lot of opinions. He sat on my dresser, his round eyes watching me get ready for summer school.

Most people would agree that having a talking cat spirit for a best friend is pretty strange. But for as long as I can remember, I've seen spirits. Not in a creepy way (although sometimes in a creepy way—more on that later), but in a normal *Hey, spirits exist, and also, can I borrow some peanut butter?* kind of way. Well, except for the part where no one else can see them but me.

I told my mom about Miv when I was five. She couldn't see him, so she assumed I'd made him up. She'd humored me, patting me on the head and then saying to the seemingly empty space beside me, "Aren't you a pretty kitty?"

Miv had glared at her from his spot on the kitchen counter. *If she even thinks about getting you a real cat, I'll make sure all her rice goes bad.*

Today, I ignored Miv's criticism, as usual. I smoothed down the hem of my shirt. Yeah, it was the color of eggplant, but I liked it. Then I fished out my favorite purple hair clip from the Star Wars tin beside my bed and secured it at my right temple, just above my ear. "Remember what I told you yesterday morning?"

Ramen gives you indigestion? Miv said as he jumped onto my rumpled bed, leaving a ghostly trail of smoke in his wake.

"No." For the record, I did *not* say that.

Pokémon scares you?

Or that. I threw a sock at him.

Stop watching you sleep?

I paused in the middle of wadding up another sock. "*Do* you watch me sleep?"

His yellow eyes glowed faintly. *Let that question haunt you for the rest of the day.*

"No need. *You* already haunt me." Actually, Miv wasn't like human spirits, who are tethered to a specific place or thing. He came and went whenever he wanted.

I tossed the wadded sock into the disaster zone that was my closet. "I told you that I don't take fashion advice from cat spirits."

The look he gave me held a level of disdain only possible in cats. *Clearly.*

I rolled my eyes and then spotted the time on my alarm clock. If I didn't hurry, I would be late for school. My mom made my brother and me take classes every summer because she liked keeping us busy instead of having us "sitting around all day" or whatever. Also, it was free.

With a jolt of panic, I rushed from my bedroom and then nearly ran into my mom coming out of the kitchen. She held two shallow saucers of uncooked rice in each hand.

"Whoa! Careful, Pahua," she warned me. She lifted the saucers over her head as I ducked beneath her arms. She was dressed in jeans and the blue smock she wore at her factory job. Her long black hair was tied back into a tight ponytail.

"Sorry, Mom." I grabbed a granola bar from the kitchen cabinet. A third saucer of rice sat on the counter. I moved it to the back of the stove.

Good morning, squeaked a voice. A spirit shaped like a plump little man climbed out of the nearest electric burner. Dab Qhov Txos, or the spirit of the stove, had red hair that moved like a candle flame and a full beard that flickered and sparked when he talked. He sprawled onto the offering of rice, the hard grains browning from the heat of his beard.

In the dining room, which was just a corner where my mom kept a square table, sat my brother, Matt. He was slurping down a bowl of cornflakes, his mussed black hair in need

3

of a comb. He was small for a seven-year-old, with too-big dark-brown eyes.

"Eat fast," I called over the narrow counter that divided the kitchen from the dining room. Then to Mom: "Still on for tonight?"

"Sorry, honey. Something came up." She went over to the rubber floor mat where we set our shoes and placed an offering of rice for Dab Txhiaj Meej, the spirit of the front door. The last offering went on the family altar for Dab Xwm Kab.

These three guardian house spirits watched over our apartment. I guess that technically made them apartment spirits, not house spirits, but that didn't sound as cool.

"Like a shaman thing?" I asked. Shamans, like my aunt, are spiritual leaders in the Hmong community. Growing up with a shaman for a sister helped my mom pick up enough knowledge to be able to perform minor rituals, like house blessings or simple divinations, for people in need.

But we lived far away from other Hmong families, which meant a long commute—and ditched plans for us— when she did. Tonight was supposed to be our first Friday movie night of the summer, even though it was nearly July already. I plastered on a smile before my mom could see my disappointment, though. It wasn't her fault she had to cancel.

Miv padded into the kitchen and jumped onto the stove beside me. He circled the saucer of rice grains and the rotund little stove spirit. *What do you think of her shirt?* the cat asked with a glance in my direction. *Reminds you of an eggplant, right?*

Wear black and red, the stove spirit suggested in his crackly voice. *Like embers and ashes, in real, wood-burning stoves, back when meals were a sacred time. I miss the smell of scorched bones.*

This was why I didn't seek out the spirits' opinions on my wardrobe choices. I'd rather look like a vegetable than a burned skeleton.

"I have to help a family consult their ancestors about buying a farm," my mom said.

"Do dead relatives give good business advice?" I asked.

She smiled, but her tone was chiding. "Don't joke. The spirits will be offended."

Whatever would we do then? Miv said, watching the stove spirit roll around in the rice some more.

I almost laughed, but my mom was right. All spirits, even good ones like house spirits, have dual natures. They protect your home and bring good luck, but they can just as easily turn on you if they feel they aren't being properly honored. Harsh, right?

My mom lit a stick of incense and placed it across the rice offering on the altar. Hidden between two sheets of shiny joss paper, the small altar spirit stirred. Mom didn't notice. She couldn't sense or see spirits. She just interpreted their messages through tools like bells or horns.

Real shamans can communicate with spirits through rituals and trances, but I wasn't sure how it worked. The only shaman I knew was my aunt Kalia, who my mom didn't get along with. The last time I'd seen her was two years ago during Christmas lunch, and she hadn't given any indication that she'd noticed Miv pretending to drown in the gravy bowl.

"I'll be home late. Love you both." Mom grabbed her lunch box from the table, pausing just long enough to kiss Matt on the temple.

I think he tried to say *Bye, Mom,* but when he opened his mouth, chewed-up cereal dropped into his bowl. Little brothers can be so disgusting.

She blew out the door just as Matt leaped from his chair and announced, "Done!"

After shoving the last of the granola bar into my mouth, I was already slipping on my sandals by the front door. A hissing sound came from one of my mom's sneakers. A second later, the door spirit slithered out. She was a small green snake with black markings around her eyes that made her look like she wore tiny glasses.

You look sssplendid in purple, she said.

I flashed a triumphant smile at Miv, who only turned his head, nose tipped in the air as he disappeared out the door ahead of us.

Outside our apartment building, hedges that had once been square and were now Swamp Thing blobs lined the sidewalk. The neighborhood was mostly other drab brown-brick apartments with yellowing lawns and trees strung with old Christmas lights. The school sat a few blocks down the road, past an open field that led into the woods at the edge of town.

My mom had moved us here three years ago. After my dad left us, a whole parade of gossiping aunties kept showing up to ask too-personal questions and bully her about being a single mother. I always got sent to my room, but that didn't stop me from overhearing things that made me wish I could breathe fire or turn them all into frogs.

Matt and I hadn't gone far from our apartment when a half-dozen mushroom spirits emerged from beneath the hedges. They were each about the size of my fist, with stubby limbs and oversize mushroom-cap heads that made them look like mini Funko Pops. Miv flicked his tail and trotted faster, but I waved as the little spirits darted alongside us.

Matt couldn't see them, but he was used to me waving at empty air. He chalked it up to my imagination. Usually, he played along. He was only four when we moved, so he didn't know that, even within the Hmong community, being able to see spirits—or just talking to seemingly no one—was still considered freaky, unless you were a shaman. In fact, from what I've been able to gather, seeing and interacting with all kinds of spirits the way I could isn't typical even for shamans.

"The troops have arrived," I said to Matt, gesturing to the invisible mushroom spirits. "Are you ready to return to the war front?"

He grinned. "Yes, sir! Ready, set, march!" He began pumping his short arms and legs a little too enthusiastically so that instead of marching, he looked more like a climbing monkey.

I followed him, pretending I was a general leading my brave mushroom soldiers into battle. We were heading into the war zone that was a classroom crammed with hostile, stir-crazy sixth-graders.

Fun fact #1 about me: I like to pretend to be something more exciting than an eleven-year-old who spends all her time babysitting her little brother and talking to invisible spirits. Some would say I'm too old for imaginary games. But some people also like olives, so folks can be just plain wrong.

"Can I pick the movie tonight?" Matt asked. "Since it'll be just us?" He didn't sound disappointed, probably because he was used to it.

The reminder that Mom was skipping out on movie night, though, made my nose wrinkle. When Matt caught my eye, I quickly smiled and nodded. "Anything but *Spirited Away.*"

"Aw, but I love that movie."

"I do, too, but it scares you! You always cry!"

"That's what makes it cool!" Matt laughed and started flapping his arms and hopping up and down, pretending to be the witch.

He was ridiculous. What kind of seven-year-old *liked* being scared? I've always *hated* that feeling—I couldn't even do those cheesy haunted houses around Halloween.

It didn't take us long to reach the school. Merdel Elementary looked like it belonged in another time period. The bricks were red and crumbling, and a rusty flagpole stood out front. A handful of cars were lined up along the curb to drop off sullen-looking kids who'd rather be any-where else.

I walked Matt to his entrance. Before leaving, he planted a sloppy kiss on my cheek and said, "I want ramen for lunch later."

"Yeah, yeah." I mussed his hair, laughing when he smacked my hand away. "Hurry up. You'll be late." I waved as Matt went inside, and then continued to the attached middle school.

Wind spirits sent a sharp gust to tip over the mushroom spirits still trailing after me. This apparently inspired Miv, who flicked a mushroom with a tiny black paw. The small spirit was so top-heavy that they flipped upside down and could only rock back and forth on the speckled red cap of their head, flailing their tiny arms and legs. Miv grinned in satisfaction as the other mushroom spirits rushed to help their friend.

"Stop that," I whispered loudly.

"Who is she talking to?" a kid mumbled behind me.

"Weirdo," another boy said, laughing.

My face went hot, but I pretended I hadn't heard. Although I'm not about to tell people the truth about me, I'm not always good at hiding it, either. As you can imagine, that doesn't make me very popular. But being the only Asian kid in my grade already makes me an outcast. Even though I'm surrounded by a world filled with spirits, sometimes I can feel pretty lonely.

Miv jumped onto my shoulder. "I should use his locker as a litter box."

I smiled but kept my gaze on my feet. You'd think that with only morning classes and fewer kids, summer school would be easier to get through than regular school. But nope. Fewer kids just meant I stood out more. Yay me! So I pretended I was an undercover spy. I had to complete Operation Beat the Bell by reaching my first class as quickly and quietly as possible without attracting the enemy's attention.

I made it to my seat near the windows just as the bell rang. Someone had stuck flower decals on the glass panes but forgotten to remove the plastic snowflakes.

My mom had signed me up for two classes. The first, Intro to Algebra, made my brain feel like it was slowly melting out of my ears. Math should be illegal during the summer. Anybody who attempts to assign math work should be punished by being the last one picked for every team. (I've been that kid. It sucks.)

I slouched low and tried to project my best *I'm a bush, please ignore me* energy. It mostly worked, except for when Miv began peeling off the window decals. Some of my classmates glanced in my direction. I wasn't sure what people saw when spirits messed with physical objects. Probably nothing too bizarre, because they didn't run screaming from the classroom. They only squinted a bit, their eyebrows pinched. I resisted the urge to throw my pencil at Miv's head and sank lower into my desk.

My second class, the Symbiotic Relationship of Plants and Insects, was down the hall, and I had to admit, it wasn't all bad. On cooler days, our teacher took us out to the flower bushes behind the baseball diamond to watch insects. Today, though, just the short walk to school had made my hair stick to the back of my neck. Mom always complained about how cold winters were in Wisconsin, but Wisconsin summers were no joke, either.

As I took my seat there, Hailey Jones, who sat to my right, looked over. She was tall, with long light-brown hair. Her shorts were embroidered with roses. She frowned a little, which she did a lot whenever she looked at me, like I confused her or something. She didn't seem very bright. Maybe that's why she was in summer school.

Since it was too humid to be outside today, we spent the class period doing worksheets about honey bees. Miv amused himself by peeking at other students' papers and declaring punishments like *five minutes of me scratching a chalkboard* for wrong answers. I cringed, but at least he wasn't drawing any attention.

At last, the bell rang. As the other students rushed to escape, relief coursed through me.

Then Hailey Jones pointed at my sleeve. "Ew! Is that *snot* on your shirt?"

2

Human Spirits Are the *Worst*

 Jocelyn, the girl sitting in the desk in front of Hailey, spun around and said, "Gross!" She had curly dark-red hair and freckles.

I checked my sleeve and saw that a few smooshed rice grains had dried and stuck to the fabric. Embarrassed, I tried to peel them off. "It's just rice."

"Are you sure they're not bugs?" Jocelyn's lip curled.

Hadn't they ever seen rice before?

Instead of leaving the classroom, Jocelyn and Hailey continued to stare as I picked at my sleeve. The longer they sat there, the hotter my face grew until I wished I was as invisible as Miv. When it came to dealing with real people, my imagination always failed me. I was only good at pretending to be brave.

"You're not going to eat it, are you?" Hailey asked when the rice finally came off between my fingers. She leaned away, like she thought it might grow legs and start moving. I imagined myself throwing it at her and shouting *Boo!*

Jocelyn smirked. "I wouldn't be surprised. Have you seen what she brings for lunch?"

The two friends laughed. I looked down. My mom usually packed me and Matt leftovers from whatever we'd had for dinner the night before. That could mean anything from cold rice and boiled chicken to tofu and greens or instant noodles. It wasn't exactly the Nutella sandwiches and fruit snacks the other kids brought.

Miv leaped from my desk to Hailey's shoulder. He'd been the size of a kitten for as long as I'd known him, but like all spirits, he could choose when to be solid and when to be permeable. Aside from me, though, people couldn't sense spirits in either state, so Hailey didn't flinch when Miv gave a low growl and pounced at her head.

Drawing courage from Miv, I raised my eyes and met Hailey's blue ones. *Just leave already*, I thought. I usually hung around the empty air-conditioned classroom to wait for Matt. He had a third class, so he wouldn't be out for another forty-five minutes.

Everyone was gone by now except for us and a fourth girl who appeared in the doorway. Hailey and Jocelyn must have been waiting for her.

The girl had short brown hair and pretty gray eyes. I didn't recognize her. She'd probably overheard everything. Ugh.

I expected her to taunt me the way her friends had, but she only frowned at them. "You're being mean. Different people eat different things."

Hailey rolled her eyes. "It was a joke, June."

"Not a very funny one," she said.

"This is boring. Can we go now?" Jocelyn got up and moved toward the classroom door.

I was ready for them to leave, too, but the new girl, whose name was apparently June, looked at me and asked, "Are you by yourself? You want to come with us?"

The question surprised me. I searched her face for signs of a trick, but she only smiled, revealing a full set of braces. She seemed earnest, but the last thing I wanted was a pity invite.

"Why?" I asked.

Really? Miv draped himself over Hailey's shoulder, poking the tip of his tail into her ear. *Someone just asked you to join them, Pahua. No one ever does that!*

My insides squirmed. He didn't need to remind me. When I said before that Miv was my best friend? It's more like he was my *only* friend. So he got the title of *best* by default.

"Uh, I m-mean," I stammered, "where are you going?"

Hailey groaned, but June said, "To some old bridge in the woods nearby."

My stomach flipped, like that feeling you get when your mom drives over a hill a little too fast. "Why would you want to go there?"

Hailey laughed. "Look at her face. She's *scared*."

I twisted the hem of my shirt in my fingers. "I'm not scared." Totally not true. "I was just asking a question."

"Why don't you go home and play with your brother?" Jocelyn said by the door, sounding impatient.

"Yeah, he's the only one who *will* play with you," Hailey added. "And that's just because he has to."

I stuffed my fists into my pockets and tried to hide the hurt that pinched my chest.

"You shouldn't say things like that," June scolded them, surprising me again.

Miv dropped from Hailey's shoulder and wove through June's legs. *This one seems okay. You should go with her.*

"Whatever." Hailey stomped off toward Jocelyn.

Jocelyn let Hailey leave first and then called over her shoulder, "Come on, June!"

June lifted her eyebrows quizzically at me. At her feet, Miv mimicked the look. The idea of hanging out with Hailey and Jocelyn made my skin itch, and I wasn't exactly dying to go to that bridge. But still, June had stood up for me, and she didn't think I was a weirdo just because I didn't look like everyone else.

To be honest, even though I loved my brother and Miv, I wanted a *real* friend. This could be my chance. Would I simply let Hailey and Jocelyn ruin it?

I glanced at the clock on the wall. There were still forty minutes until Matt got out of class, and the bridge wasn't far.

Before I could change my mind, I said, "Okay."

June and I left the school, following Jocelyn and Hailey across the playground toward the hiking trail in the woods.

As we continued down the shaded path, the air grew cooler, and the soft earth muffled our footsteps. Dandelion spirits with tufts of frothy hair emerged from the weeds to trot at my heels, trailing silver fluff. Tree spirits peered out from the hollows of trunks. They had bark for skin, stiff, spindly arms and legs, and nests of leaves and moss for hair.

"Your name is Pahua, right?" June asked. Miv was perched on her head now, doing his best impression of a hat.

"Yeah," I said, surprised. She even got the pronunciation right—*Pah-HOO-ah.* "How'd you know?"

She smiled, flashing her braces. "I pay attention. My dad says I'm good at remembering little details."

I winced at the idea of my name being a "little detail," but she probably didn't mean it to sound rude.

"Are you new here?" I asked, eager to change the topic.

"Yeah! We're from Chicago. My dad is the new manager at Merdel Trucks. They make military vehicles for the army and stuff. Not tanks, though. That would be cool. We've only been here like a month. It's so much quieter than in the city. Our old apartment was next to this bar that played local bands every Saturday, and my dad and I would dance. . . ."

She kept going, and I tried to listen—honest, I did— because I wanted her to like me, but I could tell by the way my stomach grew heavier and heavier that we were getting closer to the bridge.

Almost everyone I knew had a story about this bridge being haunted. To be fair, I didn't know a lot of people, and most of them were adults, like our neighbor Mr. Taylor, who always smelled like wet dog food. Also, the bridge looked like it *should* be haunted, with crooked wooden boards that had black mold and nails eaten through by rust. There was even a sign warning people away. But I was probably the only person in the whole town who could say with absolute certainty that the stories were true.

Yeah, unfortunately, I can see human spirits, too.

All human spirits are creepy—at least they are to me— but most of them are harmless. The recently dead, waiting for the funeral rituals that would release their soul into Dab Teb, the Spirit Realm, just sort of mope around looking depressed. Not that I blame them. The older spirits who, for one reason or another, were never released mostly keep to themselves, scaring the locals only on rare occasions. I don't blame them, either. If I was stuck in one place for all eternity, I'd find my fun however I could, too.

But then there are the genuinely scary ones. They're literally the *worst*. My guess was that the bridge spirit was one of those. I'd never been close enough to the bridge to find out for sure, but I'd always gotten a bad feeling whenever I walked anywhere near it. My mom had warned me to stay away from there, and before today, I'd obeyed.

The sensation gnawed at my insides, made the hair stand up on the back of my neck, and filled me with a cold so intense it burned. People who are attuned to spirits can be affected by them even if they can't see or hear them, and I'm especially sensitive.

I was picking it up already, the awareness of something very old and very angry.

According to folks around town, the spirit who haunted the bridge was a kid who'd died there after her parents abandoned her in the woods. Judging by how I was feeling, I could believe it. I shivered, rubbing my arms where goose bumps had risen.

We'd caught up to the other girls. Hailey glanced at me, her nose wrinkling like she'd smelled something bad.

"Are you cold?" June asked, giving me a funny look. It was the hottest part of the year, and all four of us were in T-shirts and shorts.

"No," I said, dropping my arms. "Maybe . . . Maybe we could just hang out here?" I gestured to an old tree that had snapped in half last spring. It rested at an angle, propped up by sturdier neighboring trees. It would have made a perfect ship, or fallen tower, or drawbridge—

"If you don't want to come with us, then leave," Hailey said.

Jocelyn smirked and whispered loudly, "She's definitely scared."

Of your face, I thought. Miv's whiskers twitched, like he knew what I was thinking.

Even though June gave them both an annoyed look, I could tell she was disappointed in me. That made me feel worse than anything Hailey or Jocelyn was saying. Maybe we weren't meant to be friends. It would be easy to just turn around and go back. By the time school resumed in the fall, June would understand that I didn't fit in and would never try to invite me anywhere again.

But she *had* invited me. And she'd stood up for me—twice! No one but Miv and Matt ever did that. So I stayed.

As we walked, the cat spirit settled onto my shoulder, tucking his head beneath my ear. I put my arms behind my back to hide the way my skin prickled as the chill spread inside me.

Maybe Pahua Moua, eleven-year-old nobody, was scared of a bridge, but I didn't have to be her right now. I'd pretend to be someone braver—a warrior princess setting out to vanquish an evil sorcerer. Or a secret government experiment, part machine and part vampire bat, bent on destroying the mad scientist who'd created me.

My imaginings broke off when we reached the bridge. The trees ended at a steep bank studded with rocks. The tree spirits had gone quiet, and the dandelion spirits had peeled away some time ago. I told myself all that was normal. Lots of earth-based nature spirits didn't like water spirits, which were particularly nasty.

The cold inside me became a sick, sinking feeling, like

the ground beneath my feet had turned to quicksand. There was something here that wasn't right, something that was *not* to be disturbed.

Like an idiot, I ignored it.

3

~

Don't Talk to Bridge Spirits

BRIDGE OUT OF ORDER. DO NOT CROSS.

The ominous message hung from a rusty chain suspended across the entrance. It was written in big red letters, the kind that mean *Pay attention to me! No, really, this is important! Okay, it's your funeral.*

The river was wide but shallow enough to wade into if we wanted (I did *not*). A school of tiny fish moved beneath the surface.

Hailey scooped up a handful of pebbles as she talked about the latest video from some YouTube star. She and Jocelyn started pelting the water with stones, scattering the fish.

"So, what is there to do here in the summer?" June asked me, kicking at a large rock. It clacked down the bank and landed in the water with a dull *sploosh*.

I couldn't answer her. My tongue was stuck to the roof of my mouth. Sitting curled up against one of the bridge posts was a small girl.

The others couldn't see or feel her, but the chill inside me had spread to my fingers.

The girl wore a ragged nightgown, the old-fashioned kind that you see in movies. The hem was frayed and soggy. Her hair stuck out in a wild tangle, like a dandelion spirit's. Her face was buried in her thin arms, the gentle swirl of water drowning out the sound of her crying.

The spirit's misery pricked at my insides like needles of frost. Looking at her made something ache in my chest. She was just a little thing, probably younger than Matt. She didn't seem angry, just terribly sad. . . .

Pahua, don't, Miv warned, and I realized I'd taken a step forward without meaning to.

"But look at her," I whispered.

Fingers touched my arm, and I startled. Beside me, June raised her eyebrows and asked, "Are you okay?"

"I'm fine," I said, too quickly. My thoughts scrambled for something to say. "I was just, uh, thinking about my brother."

At this, the bridge spirit's head twitched upward, and our gazes met. Even though tears streaked her cheeks, when she realized I could see her, her eyes narrowed warily. All the air around her felt like the inside of a freezer. I had to clench my teeth to keep them from chattering before forcing a smile for June.

"What's his name? Is he back at the school?" June peered up at the sky, shielding her eyes with one hand while fanning herself with the other. She didn't sense the cold.

"Matt," I said. "And yeah, but he should be out soon."

The ghost girl listened, distrust pinching her mouth.

"June, come look at this!" Hailey called. She and Jocelyn were crouched at the edge of the water, poking at something with a stick. Probably a frog.

June gestured for me to follow before joining the other girls. When I stayed where I was, Miv shoved both paws against the side of my head.

Pahua, he began. But then a soft child's voice interrupted him.

You can see me? the bridge spirit asked.

Don't answer her, Miv said.

The girl glared at the cat spirit. Her anger vibrated around us, intensifying the chill. I quickly shushed Miv.

My mom had told me that people should never speak to human spirits outside of a shamanic ritual. Sure, some of them might *seem* harmless, but if they latch onto you, there's no telling what might happen. You could get sick or attract the attention of an even worse spirit and accidentally curse your whole family line with bad luck. Can you imagine your descendants blaming you for all eternity every time they stubbed their toe or a bird pooped on their shoulder?

But I couldn't ignore this little girl. How long had she been bound here, alone, trapped by terrible memories? People like to ignore things that make them uncomfortable, as if not talking about something can make it go away. Feelings don't work that way, though. Something about the spirit tugged at me, like a hook sinking into my stomach.

Why are you here? the spirit asked. She sounded suspicious but curious as well.

"To visit," I answered, my feet seeming to move forward on their own. Actually, I was only here because June had seen me as more than an awkward kid who didn't fit in. Maybe that's what this spirit needed, too—for someone, anyone, to acknowledge her rather than pretend she wasn't there, screaming to be heard.

Will you stay with me? she asked, head tilting. Those dark eyes remained fixed on my face, like she was anticipating my answer.

Miv batted the side of my head with his paw and tugged my hair with his teeth. I barely felt it. I was near enough to the spirit now that my shadow fell across her feet, tiny and streaked with dirt.

"Pahua," June said loudly.

I glanced over to see all three of them watching me. Hailey and Jocelyn were snickering behind their hands. I went still as I realized how I must look, speaking to a bridge post. June must have called my name a few times.

Looking away, I pretended to fix the hair clip above my ear as I quickly whispered to the bridge spirit, "I can't. My brother is waiting for me, but—"

I knew it. The little girl's eyes shone with hurt even as she snarled, *You're just like everyone else. No one ever stays.*

"Wait—" I began. I'd been about to promise that I would come back later, alone, but it was too late. The spirit's face twisted with fury before she uncurled from her post and lunged at me.

Terrified, I threw up my hands. Miv hissed and launched himself off my shoulder at the spirit. Something jolted through me, like a shock wave that began in my chest and surged outward through my arms and into my fingertips.

An explosion of wind hurtled down the length of the bridge, screaming in my ears and stinging my skin. I gasped as frost collected in my hair. My heart pounded with fear. Ice bloomed at my feet, crackling down the rocky bank before spearing over the water's surface.

The other girls screamed and hopped up and down. They slapped at the frost on their heads. June rushed over, tugging my arm, but when I didn't move, she let go. Then they took off, all three of them fleeing into the woods.

It was only because my hands were still up in front of me that I saw a spiral symbol flash beneath the skin of my forearm. I blinked, and it disappeared. Had I imagined it?

The wind settled as quickly as it had come. When I finally lowered my arms, the spot where the bridge spirit had been was empty. Confused, I turned in a circle. I found only Miv, crouched low like he was about to pounce on an unsuspecting mouse. He was looking toward the woods, but the spirit

25

was definitely gone, as well as the ominous feeling that had accompanied it.

Miv settled onto his hind legs. *What in the worlds* was *that?*

"I have no idea." I sucked in a deep breath and released it again. I was used to strange things, but the ghost girl had been beyond weird. Maybe that was why you weren't supposed to talk to human spirits—because the universe completely flipped out on you! "Was that normal?"

Not in my experience, Miv said.

I'd known the cat spirit all my life, and I often got the impression that he'd been around for a long while before that. He never talked about it, though, even when I asked.

I took one last look around, but I really was alone now, aside from Miv. The humidity had returned, and the ends of my hair, which had been frozen a moment ago, sent streams of cold water down my bare arms.

Remembering that I had to get back to Matt, I hurried down the trail to the school.

What a bunch of cowards, Miv muttered as he trotted beside me. A dandelion spirit had caught the cat's tail and was riding it, waving their tiny arms like they were on a roller coaster.

It did annoy me that all three girls had just left me there. What if I'd been in danger? But I wasn't surprised. "They were scared," I said. "What did you expect?"

I cringed thinking of what they would tell their friends. Now I wasn't just Pahua the weirdo who talked to herself and had tan skin and monolids. I would also be Pahua the weirdo who summoned a ghost in the middle of the woods. *Great.*

Miv sniffed. *You were scared, too, and you stood your ground.*

I swelled with pride at his words, even if they were undeserved. I hadn't moved because I'd been paralyzed with fear. But it made me happy that he saw a version of me that was better than the truth.

Wouldn't have happened at all, though, if you'd listened to me. But noooo, you just had *to say something.*

"At least no one got hurt. Where do you think that spirit went?" I asked. Maybe she haunted more than one spot—a two-for-one deal, like at the supermarket.

I'd always thought that human spirits who weren't properly released into the Spirit Realm stayed tied to one place or thing. Or a particular moment. I knew a little about that— there were times in my life, too, that I didn't think I'd ever be able to escape. Like the day my dad left us.

Sometimes I couldn't stop replaying that moment over and over in my head. If I'd just said the right thing, or done something different, or gone after him . . . would he have stayed?

A nearby shout made me startle. Was that Matt? Miv shot off ahead, his tail a black streak, as I ran toward the sound. My sandals, damp from the frost, nearly flew off my feet as they crusted with dirt.

Miv reached him first. Matt was on his butt just beyond

the playground, looking a little dazed. He was rubbing his elbow, which he must have jarred when he fell.

I helped him up. "What are you doing out here?"

"Class ended early. A teacher said you went into the woods with some girls. She told me to wait, but I snuck out to find you." He brushed off the bottom of his shorts. "I thought I heard someone call my name, and I figured it was you, so I answered, but then something flew out of the trees and came right at me. I didn't see what it was, though."

Chills raced down my spine. It was probably nothing. Maybe one of the other girls had run into him, not seeing him in their panic. He was pretty small.

"Why'd you leave without me, dummy?" he asked.

He was lucky I loved him.

"Because you need a bath, and I wanted to escape the impact zone of your smelly feet."

Matt grinned. He gave me a playful shove before taking off through the trees toward our apartment. "I'm going to put my shoes in your bed!"

I gasped and raced after him. "Don't you dare!"

It didn't take us long to get home. We waved to Mr. Taylor, who was reclining in a lawn chair out front. He was a thin, bald man with skin like crumpled paper. I didn't know why he smelled like wet dog food. He didn't have any dogs.

After lunch (ramen, as requested, fancied up with a boiled egg), we binged *Voltron* episodes all afternoon. Even if it was true that Matt was stuck playing with me, he didn't seem to mind. When we got to his favorite parts of the show, he'd grin, grab my arm, and demand that I "Watch, watch this part. Pahua, are you watching?!"

And pretending was more fun with him, because he liked to add his own embellishments. If I were a superhero, he would be my car that could transform into a robot sidekick. If I were a witch, he'd be the frog I'd cursed to only say words that began with the letter G.

Anyway, he was happy, and he was way better company than those girls. He'd never abandon me in the woods, that was for sure.

That evening, as I washed dishes and Matt ate ice cream and watched *Spirited Away* for the two thousandth time, a high voice squeaked from the direction of the stove.

Something's wrong with him.

Wisps of fiery hair glowed beneath the coils of the burner. The stove spirit had been hiding ever since we'd gotten home. He hadn't even poked his head out when I was cooking. Most days, he perched along the back, reminiscing about real wood-burning stoves and how he'd enjoyed taking naps in the hot embers.

"Who, Miv?" I looked around for the cat spirit, but he'd disappeared. He liked to wander through the apartment building and spy on what the neighbors were doing. Later, he'd come back and tell me about Miss Masi's latest Chinese TV drama or who had the best designs that week on *Project Runway.*

I realized then that I hadn't seen the door spirit since that morning, either, and the only sign of the altar spirit had been the rustling of joss paper. Why were they all hiding?

What have you done, Pahua? the stove spirit squeaked. *You've brought something wicked into the house. This is not good. Not good at all. Consequences will be paid.*

My thoughts went immediately to what had happened at the bridge. Even though my hands were covered in hot, soapy water, I shivered. But that couldn't be it. If the bridge spirit were anywhere near me, I'd feel her. Right?

The house spirits weren't usually so cryptic. Normally, all they did was whine about the good old days, eat our offerings of rice, and hide things, like second socks.

"What are you talking about?" I asked, but the stove spirit didn't reply. He had disappeared beneath the burner again.

It wasn't until I put Matt to bed that I noticed he looked a little flushed. The house spirits were good about detecting illnesses entering the apartment. They must have sensed something.

When I touched his forehead, though, something jolted through me. I snatched back my hand. Matt didn't notice. He was busy adjusting his blanket around him in just the way he liked.

He was burning up. But more than that, I'd felt . . . something else—a tug like a string pulled taut.

From the front of the apartment came the sound of the

door opening and my mom's voice. Relief flooded through me. She'd know what to do.

But when she checked on Matt, all my mom did was give him some Tylenol.

"Are you sure it's just a fever?" I asked. I rubbed my palms against my shorts, wondering if I'd imagined that strange sensation when I touched him.

"It's nothing a good night's sleep won't cure," my mom assured me as she put him back to bed. "We'll see how he feels in the morning."

"But don't you think you should, I don't know, do some shaman thing to make sure?"

My mom paused in adjusting the blanket around Matt's shoulders. She got a funny look on her face, like she was remembering something unpleasant. Then she frowned at me and asked, "Why would you think he needs a 'shaman thing'?"

My shoulders tensed. I didn't want to admit that I'd disobeyed her by going to the bridge, so I only said, "I just think it's weird. He got sick out of nowhere. He was fine this morning."

The line between my mom's eyebrows disappeared, and she smiled faintly. "People get sick for all kinds of boring reasons, Pahua."

Times like these, I wished she could see spirits the way I could. When I was little, she'd believed Miv was an imaginary friend, because seeing animal spirits was unusual, even by shaman standards. I'd never told her the truth. She would believe me if I really needed her to—what worried me was what she might do about it.

When we'd been around Aunt Kalia in the past, I'd noticed that she was only able to see a limited number of human spirits. What would Mom do if she knew I could see and speak directly to *all* spirits? Would she freak out and have a shaman try to "heal" me to make the ability go away? In her effort to protect me from evil spirits, she'd block the good ones, too. I didn't want to lose my best friend, even if no one else could see Miv.

Or worse, she might want me to become a shaman like Aunt Kalia. I definitely wasn't cut out for that. Mom said it took a lot of focus and study to learn the rituals. I was terrible at concentrating. My mind wandered *all the time*, cooking up adventures more exciting than my current life.

And on top of that, I didn't need to stand out even more at school. I was already that Hmong girl who talked to herself because she didn't have any friends. I wasn't about to also be that Hmong girl who rang a gong and chanted at altars. *No thanks.*

~

That night, I had a dream.

I stood before an enormous banyan tree. Its limbs stretched into the clouds, and the roots tunneled deep into the earth. Instead of leaves, the branches held thin strips of white cloth. Thousands of them. Hundreds of thousands.

The tree stood at the top of a mountain. All around was vibrant green forest. Rice paddies cascaded down hillsides and disappeared into mist.

From behind me, there was a *thwack*.

I turned. Nestled among the roots was a vegetable garden. A woman wearing knee-high red rubber boots was bent over a row of cucumbers, jabbing a hoe at the weeds. A thick black braid fell over her shoulder as she worked.

Suddenly, she paused, and her head tilted, as if listening for something. Then she reached up and pulled a strip of white cloth from thin air. It glowed a little as she turned it in her hand.

I stepped forward to get a closer look. My foot kicked a root. At the sound, the woman whipped around and peered straight at me.

I froze. Even though this was only a dream, I felt a moment of panic. It was like that time two girls at school used the bathroom to talk about finding zits in weird places, not knowing that I was in the last stall. Like then, I was somewhere I wasn't supposed to be.

The woman's golden skin was strange—puckered with seams and knotted like the bark of a birch tree. Her eyes, pale and watery like sap, widened at the sight of me. Maybe she was the banyan tree's spirit?

"You!" She had a voice like dry kindling. Her skin cracked a little. "You're the one who escaped." She hurled her hoe to the ground and stalked out from between the cucumbers. She was very fast for someone made of tree bark.

"I—I think you've got the wrong person," I said, edging away from her.

She smacked her papery lips. "I had you for nearly four millennia. I'd know you anywhere. Get back here!"

My heel bumped a root, and I gasped, falling backward. I hit the dirt with a pained *oof*, and then my eyes opened.

I was in my bed again, staring up at my ceiling, which was already streaked with early-morning sunlight. My heart pounded. I half expected the tree woman to burst from my closet. But I was alone, with only the echo of her words ringing in my head.

4

Continuing the Tradition of Making Bad Decisions

 Since I was awake, I got up to check on my brother. Matt's red pajama top was bunched up around his chest, and he'd kicked his dinosaur-print blanket to the foot of the bed.

I reached out to fix his shirt and then stiffened at the heat emanating from his skin. Holding my breath, I rested the back of my hand against his forehead. Then I leaped away like I'd touched a burning pan. I may have felt that other strange sensation as well, but it'd been too quick to be sure.

Shaking out my hand, I counted to five and reached for his forehead again. I could only hold the touch for a few seconds, but it was enough. I recognized that angry feeling from yesterday. The bridge spirit was inside my brother!

I leaned over, grabbed his shoulders, and shook him. "Matt, wake up."

He didn't move. He didn't groan or flutter his lashes. I

shook him again, hard enough to rattle his teeth. But Matt still didn't wake or even twitch.

Panicking, I ran from the room and threw open my mom's door. At the racket, she lifted her head from her pillow. Hair was stuck to the side of her cheek. "What?" she mumbled.

"Mom, wake up!" I leaped onto the edge of her bed and ripped off her blanket.

"Oy! Pahua, koj xiam hlwb lawm los? Are you trying to scare my spirit from my body?" She squinted at the clock on her nightstand. "It's five twenty a.m. What's wrong?"

"It's Matt—he won't wake up."

The urgency in my voice finally broke through her sleep fog. Instead of me tugging at her, she pulled me into Matt's room.

Five minutes later, she had retrieved three sticks of burning incense from the altar. She chanted words I didn't understand as she swept the incense smoke over my brother's small body. I sat on the floor in the corner and hugged my knees. The stove spirit had warned me, but I'd ignored him. My mouth opened to confess what happened at the bridge, but I hesitated.

Telling my mom wouldn't just mean admitting I'd disobeyed her warning to stay away from there. It could also mean revealing my secret about seeing spirits, and I wasn't ready to share that. But then again, this was my brother. . . . Did I have a choice?

This looks ominous, drawled a voice beside me.

My eyes suddenly felt hot and stinging as Miv jumped into my lap. I hugged him, burying my face in his fur.

Not so tightly, please. I'm not a pillow.

I released him with a huff and left the room to be out of earshot from my mom. She didn't even notice me go.

"This is all my fault," I said to Miv when we were in the kitchen.

How's that? he asked. He jumped onto the stove and prowled around it, sticking his front paw under the cold burners. He liked scaring the stove spirit out of hiding and then pretending to eat him.

"I think the bridge spirit collided with Matt in the school playground. Mom always says that contact with bad spirits can make your own spirit sick. If I hadn't gone to the bridge, Matt wouldn't have tried to follow me." Then I gasped and smacked my palm against my forehead. "Do you think she went for him on purpose? He said he heard someone call his name. . . ."

You did *mention it right in front of her,* Miv said. *You make a good case. This is definitely your fault.*

"Is that all you can say?"

I'm sure your mom will figure it out. It's not like this is the first time someone's ever gotten sick because of a nasty spirit. If it's serious, she'll talk to her sister about it.

Would she, though? They'd barely spoken since we moved here. Aunt Kalia had been furious with my mom about our moving away from the community, and they'd had a rocky relationship even before that. The weirdest thing was that some of their fights had been about me. Before the move, I'd occasionally heard my name whispered hotly between them, along with hissed warnings for Aunt Kalia to mind her own business. My mom had been so mad that I hadn't dared to ask what they were talking about.

"But how will Mom know if it's serious?" I asked Miv in a small voice. "She couldn't even feel the spirit in him last night."

I remembered what the stove spirit had said. *You've brought something wicked into the house.*

I didn't have any experience with spirits that could make you sick. The only spirits I dealt with, aside from Miv, were the protective house kind and friendly nature ones. Everything else I ignored, and they were happy to ignore me right back. That was my best coping method for, well, life.

I couldn't ignore this, though. I checked in on Matt and my mom again. There was no change, so I decided to wash up and get dressed. As I pulled on my clothes, I made a decision. Since I was the only person here who could talk directly to spirits, I should at least try to reason with the ghost girl.

Miv had abandoned tormenting the stove spirit and was now in my room, sprawled on top of my dresser.

"I need to go back to the bridge," I said, fixing the purple hair clip above my ear. I didn't know how or if I could reach her through my brother, but he was unconscious anyway.

"See if I can find that ghost and tell her to leave Matt alone. I could *feel* her connected to him. That can't be normal."

Talking to her is what caused this in the first place, Miv reminded me.

"But this time I'll be more careful."

Once I was dressed in a rainbow T-shirt and khaki shorts, I slipped into my mom's room and opened her closet. Tucked against the back wall was a large gray chest, like the kind pirates dug up that were always filled with long-lost treasure. Except my mom's chest didn't hold jewels and gold—it contained Aunt Kalia's old equipment from when she was training to be a shaman.

I had no idea why this stuff wasn't at Aunt Kalia's house. Most of the tools could only be used by a shaman. But the chest had been in the closet for as long as I could remember.

What are you doing? Miv asked, peeking over my shoulder.

"I can't confront an angry spirit unprepared, can I?"

The tools were neatly wrapped inside thick blue-and-green towels. I pulled them out one by one, unfolding each to check out my options.

Do you even know what these do? Miv asked, poking at a set of split water-buffalo horns.

Nope. "I have . . . a rough idea. . . ."

In the end, I chose the small hand gong, which was supposed to summon nearby spirits (in case the ghost hadn't gone back to the bridge yet), and the short sword. The blade was dull and wouldn't cut anyone. My mom said it was only meant to hurt spirits. Shamans had to carry them when they crossed into the Spirit Realm in case they ran into evil creatures.

I strapped the sword belt around my waist. The scabbard was a little long on me and kept knocking into my knee. The gong and attached hammer I had to stuff into my backpack.

It wasn't until I was putting on my sandals that it fully struck me what I was about to do. I paused with only one shoe on, fear worming through me.

I could handle this. All I was going to do was talk to a spirit, and I did that every day. *Pretend it's a game,* I told myself. I was a shaman warrior setting out to negotiate with a wicked ghost. The idea of pretending was familiar enough that it unstuck my legs.

Before long, Miv and I had crossed the playground and were on the trail through the woods. The sword's leather sheath smacked my thigh with every step, making my skin turn red and itchy. I had to be the most pathetic shaman warrior ever.

A cluster of mushroom spirits waved to us as they darted through the tall grass. Wind spirits flickered through the air, swirling around Miv's head. The cat spirit hissed and swatted them away. It felt like a normal day, which was both weird and comforting.

But I had to keep my guard up. Unless they were tied to the mortal world by very strong emotions, I couldn't usually feel the presence of human spirits. The bridge spirit was powerful enough that she could be felt even by regular people.

When we reached the bridge, everything looked like last time, except the ghost hadn't returned. I wondered if that meant she'd left for good or if she frequently wandered off. The idea of a malevolent, disease-causing spirit roaming around wasn't very comforting.

Even worse . . . what if she was stuck inside my brother?

The warning sign still hung from its rusty chain across the bridge's entrance. The river and fish seemed to have recovered from being frozen yesterday.

I shrugged off my backpack and pulled out the gong. "I guess I'll try summoning her."

Are you sure? Miv sat on a flat stone, licked his paw, and groomed his face with it.

"Blegh. You know you're just wiping spit all over yourself, right?"

Don't compare my high-quality spirit spit with your sixth-grade spit.

"I'll be in seventh grade in two months."

Doesn't count yet. And, for the record, I think this is a terrible idea.

I held out the gong with one hand and the hammer with the other. "Well, if you're done licking yourself, then maybe you could come up with a better idea, O Elevator One."

Miv gave me a withering look. *The word is* Elevated.

"Whatever. This is partly your fault, you know. You told

me to go with June, so unless you're going to be more helpful today, go lick yourself somewhere else."

He stuck his tiny nose in the air and rose from the rock. *Excuse me for wanting you to have friends.*

Miv scampered away, trailing wisps of black smoke. I sucked in my cheeks, annoyed. For a spirit, he could be awfully moody. I hadn't meant to yell at him. But I was worried about Matt, and I wasn't going to sit around all day waiting for a spirit that might not show up.

I moved to the spot where the ghost girl had been yesterday. Then I took a deep breath and rang the gong.

The sound that issued forth was much louder than I'd expected. Maybe I'd hit it too hard. Low and resonant, the note echoed across the bridge and down the bank to the water's edge. It lingered in the air way longer than was probably normal.

Something splashed in the river. Bubbles rose from beneath the surface, and a moment later, slick, webbed fingers rose from invisible depths.

I took several giant steps away from the bridge and the rocky bank. Water spirits can't leave their liquid home, so as long as I wasn't close enough for this one to grab me, I would be fine. Water spirits are *nothing* like earth-based nature spirits. They mostly ignore people, unless a person pollutes the water by littering or washing clothes or something. In that case, the spirit might get angry enough to drag the human in and drown them.

Now you've done it.

Miv had wandered back. His ears were high and alert, and his tail flicked back and forth in agitation, but it didn't seem to be because of the water spirit. He smacked the surface of the river with his paw. Water splattered the bank, and ripples spread outward. The webbed fingers curled, sharp claws flashing in the sunlight, and then disappeared into the depths. Once again, there was only the shallow rock bed.

"Done what?" I asked. "Nothing happened."

Having seen way more movies than the average eleven-year-old (bored babysitter, remember?), I should have known better than to say that. The universe *always* makes you regret it.

5

Shaman Warriors Are
Real and Also Rude

 A figure emerged from the woods at the other end of the bridge.

I clutched the gong to my stomach. The creature had the rough shape of a person, but its arms were too long and thin, like they'd been stretched. It was covered in thin patches of dark fur. Beneath the fur, its skin was bone white. Both feet were *backward*, and long, stringy hair fell over its face. It wore a pair of ripped skinny jeans and a T-shirt with a lightning bolt beneath the words I WOULD RATHER BE A SATYR.

The thing looked a bit like someone in a half-finished undead-werewolf costume. I would have laughed, except the creature opened its mouth and snarled, revealing rows of unnaturally sharp teeth. My stomach turned to jelly.

All this would have been bad enough, but the worst part?

Miv, who was one of the bravest beings I knew, leaped onto my shoulder and shouted, *Run!*

I didn't need to be told twice. When I reached the cover of trees, I looked back.

It was fast for a creature with backward feet, but not as fast as I expected. Actually, I think the skinny jeans were slowing it down. Still, it crossed the bridge quickly. Planks of wood fell beneath its weight, splashing into the water below. Within seconds, the monster had bitten through the metal chain with the warning sign.

Come on! Miv shouted.

I couldn't move as nimbly as the cat, and I stumbled on a root. Something smacked hard into my thigh. The sword!

I dropped the gong, which hit the ground with a dull ringing sound. I cringed, hoping it wouldn't summon any more spirits. But there was no time to worry about that, because the hairy monster-thing was speeding right at me, skinny jeans and all. I drew the sword and swung it.

The blade bit into the creature's spindly arm just as its heavy body rammed into me. I went flying, and my back hit the dirt hard.

Miv jumped between me and the creature. *Stay back, demon.*

"Get out of the way, Miv!" I shouted, but he didn't move. The cat was the size of that thing's palm—he didn't stand a chance.

A few feet away, the creature was frowning down at its arm. A long black line split the fur-covered skin—the dull blade had actually cut it! Instead of blood, though, the wound leaked black smoke.

"Little shaman," it growled in a low voice. Now that it was closer, I could see that its eyes were sunken and completely black. "The young ones give me indigestion, but you're a sacrifice I'm willing to make."

I scrambled to my feet and thrust the sword out in front of me. "I'm not a shaman. You've got it wrong!"

"Oh, there's no mistake." The monster's nostrils flared wide as it took a long, deep sniff. "I can smell the spiritual energy on you." It curled its fingers, claws drawn, and lunged.

Miv leaped at the monster just as I thrust the sword. The demon howled when the cat spirit clawed its face and my weapon sank into its shoulder at the same time. With a roar, it tore off Miv and threw him aside.

"No!" I shouted right before the creature's huge hand caught me on the side of the head. I fell again, stars exploding in my vision. My fingers lost their grip on the sword.

"You ruined my shirt," the demon said, pulling the sword from its shoulder. Smoke billowed out of the wound. "I am so going to enjoy eating you."

Because I was about to die, I didn't point out that his jeans were already ripped, so a few holes in his shirt shouldn't matter. But then the demon shuddered as something long and thin pierced its chest. We both looked at the projectile, confused. It appeared to be a crossbow bolt.

A second later, a short figure barreled out of the woods with a screaming battle cry. The demon staggered back, arms windmilling as a second bolt struck it. Its attacker tossed down their crossbow and drew a gleaming shaman's short sword.

I watched in awe as the figure swung the weapon in a shining arc and took off the demon's head. The creature disintegrated into a swirl of black smoke.

Nearby, still lying in a tiny heap, Miv groaned. I crawled over to him, relieved when he stirred. He lifted his head, blinked at me, and mumbled, *How in the worlds are we alive?*

I motioned to the person who'd saved us. Now that we weren't in danger, I was able to get a closer look at our rescuer. I was shocked to see she was a girl. A Hmong girl, like me.

She sheathed her sword as I stood cradling Miv. The girl regarded me with a curl of her lip. She had to be around my age, but she was shorter and had light-brown skin. Her shiny black hair was cut in a straight line at her jaw, which made her look even fiercer.

"Who are you?" I asked as I bent to retrieve my own sword. I tried to sheathe it the way she had—in one smooth motion—but I missed the first time and had to fumble to fit the sword tip into the scabbard. My face went hot.

The girl's eyes narrowed. I knew that expression. She

was adding up the sum of my parts and deciding that it wasn't enough. That's how it was at school, too. I didn't fit other kids' expectations with how I looked, what I ate, how my family talked. Even though I was used to it, the scorn felt especially hurtful coming from another Hmong girl, one who'd just beheaded a demon no less.

She obviously wasn't from Merdel—I hadn't seen another Hmong kid in town since we'd moved here. But then, where had she come from? And what was she doing out in the middle of the woods?

"Never mind that," the girl said. "Are you the one who freed the bridge spirit yesterday?" Her voice was kind of nasal, which suited her, because she talked down her nose at me.

She wore a jean jacket over a striped green-and-purple T-shirt dress and had on black high-tops. Shiny pins decorated the front pockets of her jacket. On her shoulders hung an oversize backpack, which she unzipped so she could shove her crossbow inside. She would have looked like a completely normal kid if not for the weapons.

"I don't know what you're talking about." I wasn't about to admit anything to this stranger, and anyway, how did she even know about that? "This has all been *really* weird."

The look the girl gave me made me want to disappear into smoke like the demon had.

"I knew it." She threw up her hands. "I knew it had to be

an accident. No one could botch a spirit release *that* badly on purpose."

"Why would anyone botch a spirit release on purpose?" And was she implying that *I* had broken the spirit's tether to the bridge? That was ridiculous.

I thought about the weird sensation that had swept through my arms and snapped at my fingertips like a painless static shock. Then there'd been that even more bizarre rush of wind and ice.

Had I done that? Panic fluttered in my gut, but I pushed it down. No way. It couldn't be possible.

"Don't play dumb," the girl said. She began searching the ground around us.

Was she looking for the creature? Luckily, it hadn't left pieces of itself everywhere. But that wasn't it, because a moment later, she strode over to the metal gong I'd dropped.

"You didn't do anything right. You were supposed to guide the little girl into the Spirit Realm for reincarnation, but all you did was unleash her from the bridge. You are *so* lucky she got to the Spirit Realm on her own. The shaman elders sent me to check out what happened, but I wasn't expecting to find a demon."

Wait. Something suddenly occurred to me that made my breath hitch. "How were you able to see that thing?"

Her lips pursed like I'd asked a really stupid question. "Apprentices at the school are trained to sense evil spirits from the moment we're assigned a shaman mentor. But only the best apprentices can develop their spiritual energy enough to eventually *see* them."

I didn't really understand what she meant. Becoming a shaman was what my mom described as "a calling." You couldn't just *decide* to be one. So what did this girl mean by "school"?

Before I could ask, she walked up to me and thrust the gong into my face. "Are you an apprentice? How were *you* able to see the demon?" She sounded suspicious.

I resisted the urge to step back as I took the gong from her, careful not to let the hammer hit the metal. "I . . . don't know," I said pathetically. "I've just always been able to. I'm not an apprentice."

"Great," she muttered. "An untrained shaman. This just figures."

"I'm not a shaman at all," I insisted. What was going on? I felt overwhelmed.

"Well, you must have *some* spiritual energy if you could see that demon," she said. But she'd seen the demon as well. Did that mean she could see other spirits, too? Was she like me?

I glanced at Miv, whose whiskers twitched. His large eyes glowed. He must have been wondering the same thing, because he stared intently at the girl and said, *If you can see or hear me, say, "Miv is my lord and master, and I will do everything he tells me to."*

The girl didn't react.

Disappointed, I said, "Lucky you were close by. What are you doing here?"

"Trying to figure out what happened yesterday," she said. "I need to go scope out the bridge."

"I, um, left my backpack by the river."

She waved at me, like she was giving me permission to come along. As we retraced my steps, she held out her hand. "I'm Zhong."

I looked from her hand to her serious eyes. Only adults introduced themselves with a handshake, and Zhong was shorter than I was. Still, I shook it.

"I'm Pahua. What was that thing back there?" That had definitely been a different kind of spirit than anything I'd ever come across before.

"Poj ntxoog," Miv and Zhong said at the same time. But Zhong added, "Better fashion sense than others. It shouldn't even be in this area, but you called it when you rang the gong. You can't just go around hitting that. Don't you know anything? You're only supposed to use it during a ritual so you can summon *good* spirits to help you. Otherwise, it's dangerous."

"Yeah, I figured that out," I mumbled. I touched my temple where the poj ntxoog had hit me and winced at the bruise that was forming. Hopefully, it wouldn't look too bad.

Miv climbed onto my shoulder. *I don't like her, even if she did save your butt.*

I wasn't sure I liked her, either, and I didn't know whether to believe her story about being a shaman warrior. But I wanted to. The way she'd attacked that demon had been *epic*. It was everything I'd only ever imagined doing.

"Poj ntxoog," I repeated slowly, sounding out the word. *Paw . . . zong.* I'd heard that phrase before. If I was remembering correctly, it had to do with tiger spirits.

In the dab neeg (or traditional Hmong folktales) my parents used to tell me, tiger spirits were always evil. Maybe the big cats got stuck with the bad rep because they were such a danger to jungle settlements back in Laos.

Anyway, tiger spirits supposedly lurk around villages and can mimic human voices. I know—super freaky. They use that talent to lure victims into the forest so they can eat them. The spirits of the people who get killed become twisted and vengeful and return as poj ntxoog.

Or at least that's what I thought *poj ntxoog* meant. I wasn't completely sure, though.

Fun fact #2 about me: My Hmong is terrible. I used to speak it when I was little. But when some kids at school heard me using it with my mom, they'd made fun of me by yelling random sounds that didn't mean anything. It had made me feel small.

That's when the whole pretending thing began. I couldn't change the fact that I was different from everyone else in real life, but in my fantasy life, I could make myself unique in more exciting ways. Then it wouldn't matter what anyone else thought.

The pretending had started small—I'd imagined myself as a Girl Scout, or a ballerina, or a world-famous ventriloquist. You know, attainable things. But Mom hadn't had the money or time to make those dreams real, and I never would have fit in anyway. So my daydreams grew from there until I was riding dragons in my backyard, usually with Matt as my copilot.

Matt, who was currently lying unconscious in our apartment. Worry for him gnawed at my insides.

"A poj ntxoog is an evil spirit that was once mortal—a person who got stolen by another evil spirit and was turned into one themselves," Zhong explained.

So the folktales had it about right. Why would a poj ntxoog be around here?

We'd reached the bridge. Everything was quiet again. My backpack was where I'd left it. I stuffed the gong back inside and then waited as Zhong poked around the area.

"Were you hunting that thing?" I asked. That seemed like something a girl who went around with a crossbow and sword would do.

"No," she said, squashing the fantasy. Her nasal voice had that tone people use when they think they're more important than you. "The shaman elders sent me after they dreamed of the little girl's spirit last night. They knew something important must have happened here."

Shaman elders? I didn't get it, but the whole universe-flipping-out-at-me thing that happened yesterday *had* been really strange. Even Miv had agreed it was out of the ordinary.

"Wait, so what are you again?"

She rolled her eyes and turned away from the bridge, apparently deciding there was nothing there that interested her. "I'm a shaman warrior."

I tilted my head, intrigued. Shaman warriors were *real*?

Miv swatted the side of my head with his tail. *I don't trust her, Pahua.*

I ignored him as we returned to the path. My fingers danced over the plain hilt of my aunt's old shaman sword. Zhong's sword was polished silver and etched with pretty swirls and sunbursts, the same kind of designs as my mom's traditional Hmong jewelry.

"What is that, exactly?" I asked. "What does a shaman warrior do?"

"We track down evil spirits and send them to the Spirit Realm," Zhong said. "They're usually restless mortal souls, though, like the little girl, not demons like that poj ntxoog. Why were you out here ringing a shaman's gong anyway? Any spirit in the area could have shown up."

I flushed, feeling dumb now that she'd put it that way. Even Zhong, a shaman warrior who went around with a crossbow in her backpack, thought I was weird. But although I could see and talk to spirits, she seemed to know a lot more about this stuff than I did, so it couldn't hurt to get more information from her.

"I did see the bridge spirit yesterday," I confessed. I

decided to leave out the part where I'd approached the little girl because I'd thought, stupidly, that I could help her.

"Did she speak to you?" Zhong's eyes narrowed like she knew I was hiding something.

"She was just surprised I could see her. But then she looked at me like she hated my guts and jumped at me. There was this freak windstorm, and ice, and the spirit must have escaped into the woods, because the next thing I knew, I heard my brother shouting. He said something flew out of the trees at him."

"You're telling me you didn't do anything to release the spirit?"

I hesitated, recalling again that moment right before she disappeared from the bridge. "I . . . I wouldn't know how," I said, twisting my shirt around my fingers. Anxiety turned my stomach. "If I did, I didn't mean to. Then last night, Matt got a fever, and this morning, he wouldn't wake up." My voice caught at that last part.

To her credit, Zhong's hard look softened. But when she spoke, it was to say, "You really messed up. Luckily, the bridge spirit is gone now."

"But if your, um, shaman elders think she's in the Spirit Realm . . . how come I could feel her when I touched my brother's forehead?"

I looked at Miv. He was busy glaring at Zhong and mumbling about how he'd like to leave hair balls in all her shoes.

"The shaman elders were certain the spirit had crossed

over, and they're rarely wrong." She scrunched up her eyebrows. "But if you can feel her connected to your brother, that's not good. It means the bridge spirit took his soul with her into the Spirit Realm."

My feet stopped. I stared at her, her words echoing inside my skull. "She what?!"

Zhong was chewing on the corner of her lip. She seemed worried . . . except when she caught my eye, the look faded, replaced with that smug tilt of her nose. "She took his soul—"

"No, I heard you," I cut in. Fear made my heartbeat quicken. "But how? He was fine all afternoon yesterday."

"It's a gradual thing. When a living soul leaves its body, it's like a battery slowly draining. They might seem fine at first, but then they become sick—and the longer the soul is away from the body, the worse it'll get."

"But you just said that spirits stolen by evil ones turn evil themselves." Panic ballooned in my stomach, and I shouted my next question. "Is that going to happen to my brother?"

I began to pace, my body suddenly restless even though there was nowhere to go. This was my fault. What was I supposed to do now? Why was I so *useless*?

Miv pressed his paw against my cheek. *Calm down. These things don't happen overnight, Pahua. You have some time to fix this. I'd guess a week at least.*

I took a deep breath, the panic deflating a little, but it was replaced by a needling worry in my gut. A week wasn't much time, and what could I even do? Wouldn't I need a shaman to fix this? Except what did it mean that even Zhong, a shaman warrior who'd just killed a demon, looked worried?

But then Miv continued. *Time passes differently in the Spirit Realm, though, so it's probably more like three days.*

"THREE DAYS?!" I shouted, startling Zhong.

On reflex, she went for her sword. "*What* are you shouting about?" Her fingers tightened around the hilt, like she wanted nothing more than to draw it on me.

"My brother has three days before he becomes a demon." I tried not to hyperventilate.

It's not an exact science, Miv said.

That was *not* helpful.

Zhong crossed her arms and scowled. "We don't know anything for sure. We need more information about this bridge spirit if we're going after it, like how dangerous it might be."

Her words surprised me. "*We?* You're going to help me?"

She sneered. "It's my job as a shaman warrior to stop evil spirits from hurting innocents. Besides, I was sent here to fig-ure out what's going on, so that's what I'm doing. Come on."

6

~

Flying by Elephant Statue

 Zhong waited outside my apartment while I dropped off the gong. I didn't want to make any more accidental demon calls, and I figured the fewer shaman-scented tools I carried, the better. I kept the sword, though, and grabbed the cell phone my mom had gotten me for emergencies.

I also checked on Matt, who hadn't woken yet. Mom was on a call with someone, probably a nurse or something, because her voice was low and urgent. The incense was still burning on a saucer beside the bed. *Three days to fix this.* My stomach twisted in fear. If I didn't succeed, Matt would never wake up.

Now that I knew what was going on, there was no way I could tell my mom about the bridge spirit. First of all, she wasn't a shaman, and the knowledge would only worry her even more, especially if she knew I'd seen the ghost girl or that I'd tried to summon her and gotten a demon instead. Second, this was my fault. Even though I hadn't meant to, I must have released the spirit from the bridge, and the first thing she'd done was go after my brother. This was my problem to fix.

I scribbled a quick note about forgetting something at school and left it on the dinner table. Guilt pricked at me for leaving her to care for Matt alone. She shouldn't have had to stay with him by herself, and for a brief second, I let myself wonder what it would be like if my dad were still here.

But then, if that were the case, we wouldn't be living so far from all the people my mom had grown up with, in a tiny town with a haunted bridge.

I don't trust that shaman girl, Pahua, Miv kept insisting.

"I don't have any other choice."

Even Miv couldn't argue with that. I didn't know the first thing about demons or going after spirits in the Spirit Realm. Zhong was the best person to help me.

After the stop at my apartment, Zhong led me into town. We walked down Main Street, which was only a few blocks of tiny stores crammed together. It was a warm day, so people were out shopping or hanging around a bronze elephant statue that stood in a green at the center of town.

"Why are we here?" I asked.

"We need to talk to Shao."

"Who?"

We stopped in front of the statue. Three teenagers sat

against its bronze base. Their T-shirts said MERDEL HIGH SCHOOL PING-PONG CLUB. One of them had his hair dyed in rainbow colors, as if a unicorn had vomited on his head. They'd left burger wrappers and empty soda cups everywhere.

"Shao is the elephant statue?" I asked. Maybe I'd been wrong about Zhong. Maybe she was completely bananas and had made everything up, and now my brother was going to die because I had the worst judgment in the history of the world.

Zhong gave me a look like I was a fly in her rice. "No, Shao is a hermit. Master shamans sometimes seek out his wisdom. Elephants are guards and guides between important gateways."

Even though she said all this confidently, the way she kept twisting the charm bracelet around her wrist made me think she wasn't as calm as she sounded. Normally, I would have liked to know someone who pretended the way I did. But right now, for my brother's sake, I needed her to be the shaman warrior she said she was.

Zhong rummaged in her backpack. I rose onto my toes to get a look at what else was in there besides her crossbow, but before I could, she snapped it shut again. In her hand, she held a miniature reed pipe.

I recognized it as a qeej, a traditional Hmong musical instrument. It had a straight body dotted with finger holes and seven pipes that stuck out at the bottom in a bow-like curve. Usually qeej much larger than this one were played at festivals and funerals. I'd always thought it was weird for an instrument to symbolize two completely different things—celebration and death. But my mom once told me that when a shaman played the qeej, the music could communicate with the spirits in a language forgotten by humans. Or *mortals*, as Zhong would say.

Zhong held the tiny mouthpiece to her lips. Her fingers danced over the holes. I stiffened as each note vibrated through me. Unless I was imagining it, I thought maybe the statue was vibrating, too.

She lowered the instrument and announced, "Zhong Vang, School for Shamanic Arts and Spiritual Mastery. Code Name: Sailor Moon. 'In the name of the moon, I will punish you.'"

The teenagers began laughing and pointing at her. Zhong's face turned bright red. But she kept her chin held high as she told me, "My mentor makes all of us use his travel code."

I was about to tell her that Mercury was the best Sailor Scout when the elephant's bronze trunk began to sway. I yelped, startling back. On my shoulder, Miv made a small *hmm* sound.

"Destination," came a loud, clear voice.

My eyes went huge. The elephant blinked. Its mouth somehow formed a smile beneath its mini tusks. I quickly looked around, but the teens didn't seem to notice.

"People who can't see?" Zhong said. "Well, they can't see."

I nodded. It was like how spirits went unnoticed by everyone except me.

Zhong cleared her throat. "The Echo, please."

"Business or pleasure?" the elephant asked cheerfully.

"Business."

"Wonderful. Remember: no foods, liquids, or cursed relics allowed between realms. Enjoy your flight!"

The elephant tapped its base once, twice, three times with its trunk. The plaque on the bottom began to grow until it became a door tall enough for us to step through. A moment later, the door swung open.

I gaped. On the other side was an entirely different world. It looked like no city I'd ever seen before. There were brick houses in every color imaginable. Far in the distance, enormous buildings loomed, their doors and windows built for giants.

"Let's go," Zhong said, stepping through. The doorway shimmered gold.

"Wait!" I shouted. But it was too late. She was gone. I stood there, dumbstruck, staring at where she'd been. Then, closing my eyes tight, I stepped through as well.

~

Now I knew why the elephant had said *Enjoy your flight*.

I was falling through complete darkness. I would have screamed, but I was too afraid to do even that. Frost pricked my face. Miv's small body was tucked tight against my neck.

After a moment, I realized we weren't technically *falling*. It was more like floating. Through blackness. With no end in sight. Yeah, still terrifying.

"What is this place?" I squeaked. I blinked the melting frost from my lashes and was relieved to see a Zhong-shaped figure a short distance beneath me. I didn't know what I would have done if I'd lost her.

"The Echo." Amazingly, she sounded bored. "One of the first things apprentices learn at school is how to cross into the Echo. It's the least regulated of the six realms. Plus, it helps prepare apprentices for the Spirit Realm."

She had a funny way of talking. Like she thought she was an adult. "What you said to the elephant . . . You called it the School for Shaman . . . Artists?"

"The School for Shamanic Arts and Spiritual Mastery. You wouldn't have heard of it."

Even though I couldn't see her, I could imagine perfectly the way she was sticking her nose in the air.

"Where is it?"

She took a few seconds to answer. I wondered if she was trying to come up with a lie.

At last, she said, "In Minnesota. Ish."

The summer before we moved, my mom had driven my aunt, Matt, and me to St. Paul to visit the Hmong Village Shopping Center. We ate beef pho and eggrolls stuffed with pork and bean thread noodles, and drank boba tea with chewy tapioca pearls. Aunt Kalia bought an entire crate of fresh vegetables that made the car smell the whole ride back.

The drive had taken *ages*, especially because we'd had to make half a dozen bathroom stops for Matt. He'd refused to sleep, instead alternating between singing the same song over and over again and pointing out every single cow we passed. In Wisconsin, there are a lot of cows.

What I wouldn't give to hear him nagging me again.

Swallowing the lump in my throat, I asked Zhong, "How'd you get to Merdel? That's a whole state away." Maybe she'd taken another magical shaman portal or something.

"The night bus."

"Oh." That was less exciting. "By yourself?" I instantly cringed at my words. Zhong had just killed a demon with a sword. Riding a bus was a lot less dangerous, although my mom would ground me until I was sixty if I ever left the state on a bus by myself.

Probably best if she never found out I'd left the entire *realm*.

Before Zhong could make a rude retort, I added, "But my aunt is a shaman, and my mom grew up with her. Wouldn't they know about this school?"

"Maybe they do," Zhong said, which made me frown. "Most shamans don't have the spiritual energy to become a warrior. Those who do are invited by the elders to enroll."

I scrunched up my nose. It sounded like those snobby clubs at school that didn't want you unless you were supersmart or superrich or superpopular. No wonder Zhong was unbearable.

The longer we floated in darkness, the more anxious I became. So I did what I do best—I pretended I was someone and somewhere else. I was an astronaut soaring through space on a hunt for new planets. But I couldn't hold on to the fantasy. Maybe because Matt was usually with me, and I kept expecting him to chime in with something like *I'm an alien searching for intelligent life. That's not you, Pahua,* and then crack up at his own bad joke.

Or maybe because, for the first time in my life, my reality was more bizarre than anything I could've imagined. I had just walked through a doorway between realms that was guarded by a talking statue, with a shaman warrior as my guide.

None of this should have been happening. If I'd just left the bridge spirit alone, my brother's soul wouldn't be in danger. My eyes began to sting, and I squeezed them tightly shut.

"How long is this supposed to take?" I asked. "Talking to Shao, I mean."

"I'm not sure, but we won't even know where to begin looking for your brother unless we do this first."

So we didn't have much choice, then. Fortunately, my feet touched solid ground a moment later. I opened my eyes to see that we stood beside another elephant statue, this one made of stone, on a paved path between great rolling hills. A city sprawled in the distance, colorful and strange.

"What is that?" Zhong shouted, making me jump. She pointed over my shoulder.

"What?" I spun around, expecting to find another demon like the poj ntxoog. But there was only the empty road and a blue sky speckled with clouds.

"*That*," Zhong said again. She drew her sword and thrust it toward me.

I threw up my hands. "What are you talking about?"

"Right there!" She shook the tip of her blade at what I realized wasn't something over my shoulder but *on* my shoulder.

"I think she's talking about me," Miv drawled, licking his paw.

Zhong's nostrils flared, indicating that she could not only see him, but she could hear him as well.

"Oh!" I beamed. "You can see him now!"

"You *know* this creature?"

"Sometimes I know things you don't. Weird, right? Put down your sword."

She didn't. "Has he been with you this whole time?"

"Yes?" It came out a question, because I wasn't sure I wanted to tell her the truth when she was pointing a sword at my best friend.

"You do know it's never a good thing when a spirit

latches onto you, right?" She was using that annoying tone again, like she thought I was an idiot.

She did sheathe her sword, though. I began to relax. But then she pulled a slip of paper from her bag. It was bookmark-shaped and looked a bit like joss paper.

"I can exorcise him for you," she said, as if that were a good thing.

"No!" I backed away and cradled Miv to my chest. "He's been with me since I was four. He's my best friend. Don't you dare hurt him!"

Zhong looked exasperated. "The paper talisman won't hurt him. It just subdues him so I can send him back to the Spirit Realm. It's like the shaman equivalent of tying up a soul with rope, although it does only work on the less powerful ones."

"I don't want that, either!"

"Well, you can't keep it."

"*It* is right here and can speak for himself, thank you very much." Miv's whiskers tickled my neck as he turned to hiss at Zhong.

"What kind of spirit are you?" she asked. "You don't look like a normal cat spirit. Are you a shape-shifter? A demon?"

"If I told you, I'd have to pluck out your tongue so you could never repeat it." He stuck his little nose in the air in a perfect imitation of Zhong.

Her eyes narrowed dangerously.

"Calm down, both of you," I said. "Miv, you're not pluck-ing out any tongues. That's disgusting—why would you say that? And, Zhong, you're not sending him anywhere."

Zhong's mouth twisted to one side. After a second, she grudgingly put away the paper talisman. I glimpsed a whole stack of them in her bag. She *really* came prepared.

"Miv? You named your cat spirit *Cat*?" she asked flatly.

I hunched my shoulders. "I was four, okay? My imagina-tion wasn't so great yet."

Besides, Miv didn't seem to mind. He even thinks it's funny how the word sounds like a cat—*mee*.

"Whatever." She stalked down the road, heading away from the city in the distance.

She seemed to know where she was going, even though nothing but green hills stretched along either side of the road. But past those hills I got glimpses of things I wanted to ask about—the colorful city was one of them, but also forests with leaves that glimmered like crystals, and a frothing lake that looked like boiling water. Those would have to wait, though.

I hurried to catch up to Zhong, afraid of being left behind in this unfamiliar place. The road veered to the left, up and over a hill too high to see what lay beyond it.

"Why is it called the Echo?" I asked.

"Because it's a copy of the mortal realm. As the mortal realm changes, so does the Echo. The spiritfolk who live here learn to adapt."

"Spiritfolk? Is that like human, I mean mortal spirits?" I

couldn't quite connect what I already knew about spirits—which was apparently very little—with what Zhong was telling me.

She made an impatient sound, like she couldn't believe I didn't know something so basic. "There are four kinds of spiritfolk: beast, nature, guardian, and mortal."

"And they all live here?"

"No. Mortal souls only go to the Spirit Realm for reincarnation after they die."

My gut tightened. Matt's soul was trapped there with the ghost girl, but the only mortal souls that should be there belonged to the dead. I glared down at my feet. He wasn't going to die. Not if I could help it.

"Other spiritfolk can travel between all the realms," Pahua continued, "but it's strictly regulated. Some realms are closed off to outsiders, even with the proper paperwork. Shamans can enter the Echo and the Spirit Realm because of an ancient pact we made with the gods, but any travel outside of that requires a special license."

"What gods?" I asked. "Do the Hmong have gods?"

Her eyes went wide. "Of course we have gods! If you value your life, don't ever say that again. Their spies could be anywhere. The four oldest and most powerful of them sit on the Council of Elder Gods. They basically run the six realms."

I'd never heard of any council, but I decided not to say that.

"It's really pitiful how uneducated most Hmong people are about our own stories," Zhong continued. "For centuries, everything was passed down orally, and almost nothing is recorded in writing."

"You sound like my aunt," I muttered. Aunt Kalia used to lecture my mom about how Matt and I didn't know enough about Hmong customs. Whenever she heard me speak to Matt in English, she snapped at me to use Hmong, but she never bothered to actually teach me the right words.

"Well, it's true," Zhong said. "The school has tried to archive what they can, of course, but still, so many stories have been lost, and those we did record have a dozen different versions, because the details change between every person who tells it."

"I'd hate to be the librarian," Miv drawled, which earned him a glare.

Just then, a cart passed us along the road. I gawked, first at the bird-faced spiritfolk driving the cart, and then at the two striped horses pulling it. My mom had described these zebra-like spirits to me before—I knew they helped shamans—but she'd left out the part where the horses had cloven hooves like deer.

Zhong didn't even give the cart a second glance. She seemed perfectly comfortable in this extraordinary place. I had to admit, even though I still didn't like her much, I was a little in awe of her.

"This is all *so* weird," I said. "Also, who is this Shao

again?" If we couldn't look for my brother until we spoke to Shao, then he had to be someone pretty important.

"He's a hermit oracle. A thousand years ago, back when travel between the realms wasn't as regulated, Shao tried to follow in the footsteps of the first and greatest shaman, Shee Yee, and earn the favor of the gods. Shao wanted to study in the coral library of the Dragon Emperor and dine with the Sky Father in his palace of storms."

"Sounds like a noisy dinner," Miv remarked.

Zhong's gaze twitched in his direction, but she continued. "Somehow, Shao survived the treacherous journey into the Sky Kingdom, the home of the gods, and presented himself to the Council."

"Are they nice gods?" I asked hopefully.

"Define *nice*," Miv said.

"*Anyway*," Zhong continued. "Unlike Shee Yee, Shao wasn't family. The Sky Father had seven daughters, and Shee Yee was the son of his youngest and favorite. Shao was just some random shaman who wanted fame and glory."

"This doesn't end well, does it?" I asked Miv.

He gave me a flat look. "Does it ever?"

"Can I finish?" Zhong said. "The gods didn't know whether to reward Shao's bravery or punish his insolence, so they did both. They granted him immortality and the powers of an oracle, but they exiled him to the Echo, where he would be bound to help any traveler who sought his wisdom."

"That . . . sucks," I said.

"Majorly sucks," Miv echoed.

"Yep," Zhong said, surprising me. It might have been the first time she'd agreed with me about something. "The Echo changes with the mortal realm, but there are a few corner-stones that remain the same no matter what, like the Bamboo Nursery, where Shao lives."

We'd reached the top of the hill. I held my breath, expect-ing to see a fantastical landscape, something plucked straight from my imagination, like an enchanted forest or herds of spirit-beasts. Instead, spread out before us was a clothing store.

"Huh," I said.

Zhong's mouth fell open. "Noooo, this can't be right. The Bamboo Nursery should be here." She hurried down the road toward the parking lot.

Miv and I shared a confused look, but we followed. The store was tall and boxy, like department stores in the mortal realm. The glass storefront displayed mannequins dressed in everything from boring business suits to glittery dresses to blue jeans. Above the automatic doors, curly capital letters spelled out THREAD AND NEEDLE.

"How are we going to find the Bamboo Nursery?" I asked, eyeing the empty parking lot. The bright lights inside the store seemed to indicate it was open. Why wasn't anyone here?

"The Nursery shows up in a few different locations,

depending on where you are and how urgent your need is. Based on where we arrived, this is where it should be."

"Maybe the Echo thinks we need new clothes more than we need wisdom right now?"

Zhong didn't seem to think that was funny. She marched up to the front doors. They opened just before she would have smacked her forehead into the glass. Inside, aisles split off in three directions between endless racks of clothes. Signs hanging above each section declared unsettling things like BUSINESS CASUAL MURDER and FORMAL EVENING TORTURE.

"Zhong, what are we doing here?" I whispered. It was eerily quiet. We hadn't seen anyone else yet, not even a store employee. This didn't feel right, and we really couldn't be wasting time wandering around a store.

"This is one of the Bamboo Nursery's fixed points, so it's here somewhere. We just have to find it. And after we've spoken to Shao, I'm filing a complaint with the manager. This layout is too confusing."

We passed an aisle of accessories and a sneakers display. I paused. A tag on the silver necklaces read PERFECT FOR THAT LITTLE BLACK DRESS OR FOR STRANGLING YOUR ENEMIES. On the shoes display, the sneakers looked wrong. The laces were in the back where the heel was instead of down the front. Was this some weird Echo fashion trend?

Then something else caught my eye. Ice-blue gloves shimmered from the center of a rack. They were oddly labeled

NEUTRALIZERS. I reached for them. The slick fabric was as fine as the whorls of frost that painted our windows in winter. But when I slipped my hand into the first glove, subtle waves of warmth spread up my arm.

The attached tag read FOR THE NEUTRALIZATION OF SPIRITUAL ABSORPTION.

"What do these do?" I asked, trying to find a price tag.

"You have more problems than I can fix if you don't know what gloves are for."

I frowned at the back of her head. Normally, I would've let the insult go. I'd had worse things said to me. But the empty store made me uneasy. I was starting to think I'd made a mistake by trusting Zhong, and it was my brother who would pay for it.

"Why do you have to be so rude?"

To my surprise, Zhong's ears turned pink. But her voice was still as obnoxious as ever when she said, "If you don't like hearing the truth, then don't ask me questions."

I held up the gloves. " 'For the neutralization of spiritual absorption.' I bet you have no idea what that even means."

Zhong spun on her heel to face me. "It means that when you cross between realms, the gloves will neutralize the spiritual energy pulled from your body so that you don't freeze."

"Why didn't you just say that, then, instead of being a jerk about it?"

"This *jerk* saved your life, and now I'm trying to save your brother's."

Miv stood up on my shoulder, his chest puffed with outrage. It gave me the courage to say, "Saving my life doesn't mean you get to treat me like I'm an idiot."

Zhong looked down her nose at me again. But instead of arguing, she gave me a grudging nod. "Fine. I guess you're r—" Her voice broke off as her eyes focused on something behind me.

I turned. On a corner display, floral dresses hung beneath a poster board featuring a creature that looked very much like the demon that had attacked me in the woods. A poj ntxoog.

"Oh no." Zhong's gaze darted around the store as if she was seeing it for the first time. "Oh no, no, no." She grabbed my wrist and began running back the way we'd come.

"I don't get it," I said. My feet kept slipping over the polished floor tiles.

"This is a store for demons," she hissed.

7

Killer Fashion

My eyes went wide. "They have whole department stores just for poj ntxoog?"

Zhong made an impatient sound that was a cross between a snort and a cough. "Poj ntxoog are obsessed with mortal fashion. It's because they know they were once mortal, but they can't remember what it was like to actually *be* mortal. So they can only mimic the superficial parts."

Even though a poj ntxoog had tried to kill me that morning, part of me felt sorry for them. They were trying to connect with something they'd lost. For years, I'd kept a note my dad had written me on my seventh birthday. Nothing special, just a scribbled message and drawing on a Post-it that he'd stuck to the fridge before heading to work. It had said *Love you, birthday girl!* alongside a doodle of him waving and holding a cake.

That was the last time he'd ever wished me a happy birthday, because he'd left a month later. I still don't know why he did, but afterward, I'd held on to that note like those words could keep me warm through all the days without him.

But really, all I'd been doing was holding on to a piece of paper. I threw it away last year.

Zhong pulled me around a corner into the shoe aisle and then skidded to a stop. A figure blocked our path. It was fur-covered and tall, maybe seven feet, with gangly, too-long arms and legs. Its greasy black hair fell over a bleached, snarling face. It wore a spandex jumpsuit, like a really bad supervillain costume.

"Where are you going, shamanlings?" the poj ntxoog growled.

Miv hissed. "Nice outfit. You forgot your cape."

"Capes are actually a terrible idea," I said. "They get caught in everything."

The demon pointed at me. "Yes! Thank you! Someone who gets it."

"Does that mean you'll let us go?"

"Nope." It started forward.

We turned to run down a different aisle, but another demon cut us off. This one wore a bright-yellow sundress. If you've ever wondered whether demons' fur extends to their legs, I can tell you that it does.

Miv jumped from my shoulder to land between us and the sundress-wearing demon. Zhong had already drawn her sword and was facing the spandex-clad one. They were both so brave when all I wanted to do was either curl into a ball and cry or run away as fast as possible.

Instead, I made myself draw my own sword. I could pretend I was a shaman warrior like Zhong. I could act confident and courageous and cool, even though my hands shook. I could do that much for Matt.

I shoved the neutralization gloves into my back pocket for the time being. The spandex demon closed the distance between us—at least ten feet—in one easy leap. Zhong met the poj ntxoog with her sword. The symbols on the blade glowed, infused with spiritual energy. I looked at my own sword, shiny but plain and not even sharp. It was a ceremonial sword that wasn't meant for *real* battle. I gulped.

"That's a pretty hair clip," the second demon said to me. "Did you get it in our store?"

"Uh, no. It's an old gift."

"Ooh, vintage! I want it!" The demon swung for me, barely slowed down by the cat spirit clawing at its leg.

Something inside me awoke, like a flash drive had been plugged into my brain, giving my body access to new information. I dodged the demon's attack as if I'd done it a hundred times before. Eyes wide, I sidestepped again, ducking beneath its arm to get behind it.

"Stay still, you!" the demon growled.

I swept my sword downward. I missed the demon's leg, but the blade tore through the sundress. The fabric had a cute print—large sunflowers accented with clusters of yellow daffodils.

The demon gasped sharply. "My dress! Do you know how hard it is to find a seamstress willing to work with a poj ntxoog?"

"I'm guessing hard?" I tried not to think about what my body was doing. If I focused too much on how my hands were maneuvering the sword, my fingers would grow awkward again.

Sometimes, on evenings when I let Matt stay up to wait for Mom, we'd sit out front with Mr. Taylor and search the sky for constellations. Some stars, though—the really faint ones—you couldn't look at directly. If you tried to focus on them, they'd melt into the black sky. But if you looked at the space around them and relaxed your eyes, they always twinkled and made themselves known.

Fighting the demon was like that—as long as I relaxed my body, it seemed to know what to do. With another swipe of my sword, I drove the demon backward. It rammed into a rack of knee-high boots. Now I knew why the shoes looked wrong. They were all designed for huge backward feet.

The demon roared. It slashed at me with both claws, nearly slicing my throat. My heart pounded. Fear shot through me, making me clumsy. I barely deflected the blow.

"Don't kill her, you idiot!" the other demon screeched as it fought Zhong.

The sundress demon shouted back, "I'm not going to kill her. But he never said I couldn't maim her a little."

I didn't like the sound of that. And who was "he"?

The creature knocked me into an aisle tower with a sign declaring FIRE-BREATHING VITAMINS, HALF OFF! ONLY MARGINAL BURNING REPORTED! I would have fallen, but my hand caught the edge of a nearby glass jewelry display. My arm bled where the demon's claws had caught me.

Miv leaped off the demon's leg, where he had left a mass of scratches. Zhong was still preoccupied with the spandex demon.

I had to do this myself. I pushed away from the display case. Pahua Moua was a nobody. The only interesting thing about her was that she could see and talk to spirits, a gift that had only ever gotten her labeled a weirdo. But right now I wasn't her. I was a shaman warrior.

I raised my sword and said, "I've seen sixth-graders with better fashion sense than you."

And honestly, I had. But this seemed to infuriate the demon. It threw its head back and roared. Then it charged, claws and teeth flashing. I stood my ground, fighting the urge to run until the very last second. Then I flung myself to the side.

The demon barreled into the display case. The glass shattered. Broken shards and jewelry went flying.

Nearby, Zhong kicked the spandex demon hard in the

stomach and then plunged her sword through its chest. It melted into black smoke.

She met my eyes. We must have been thinking the same thing, because we both took off without any further prompting. Behind us, I could already hear the poj ntxoog cursing as it disentangled itself from the display case. It screeched, *"You ruined my dress!"*

"Where in the worlds is the exit?" Zhong shouted, taking another turn at random.

As we fled, a sign caught my eye: OUTDOOR SPECIALTIES. It was nearly hidden behind the much larger SPORTING GOODS sign.

"This way!" I grabbed Zhong's wrist before she could make another turn. We weaved through the racks, staying low to keep hidden. "This has to be where demons obsessed with fashion would put the Bamboo Forest."

Fashion is as much about the overall look as it is the attention to detail. Who knew that listening to Miv's weekly recaps of *Project Runway* would come in handy someday?

Zhong's face lit up. When she smiled at me, it felt almost like we were friends.

The clothing rack we were hiding behind was suddenly shoved aside.

"There you are, you sneaky shamanlings," the sundress demon said. Smoke leaked from a dozen cuts in its face and arms, courtesy of its meeting with the glass case.

"The dressing room!" Miv said, and streaked across the tiles. Zhong and I bolted after him.

The demon lunged for us. Miv reached the dressing room first and nosed the door open. On the other side, a lush bamboo forest waited.

Behind me, the demon grabbed for my legs. With a kind of grace and dexterity I'd never had before, I twisted around and slashed my sword across the demon's knuckles. A breath later, Zhong and I burst through the door. Miv slammed it shut, cutting off the demon's shriek of outrage.

8

Sleep Is for the Weak

 We landed on a bed of ferns so soft I could have closed my eyes and fallen asleep right then and there.

Zhong had other ideas. She was on her feet again within seconds. Then she grabbed my arm and hauled me up as well. *"Never* lie down in the Bamboo Nursery."

Before I could thank her, she fisted my shirt and got right in my face. I sucked in my breath and went cross-eyed trying to see her expression. Miv jumped onto my shoulder and smacked her cheek. She glared at him but eased back so she wasn't breathing on me.

"Who are you?" she demanded, giving me a small shake.

I didn't know what she was talking about. Whatever warrior instincts I'd had while fighting the demon had abandoned me, because I fumbled my sword and dropped it. My fingers felt slow and clumsy. In fact, my entire body felt slug-gish, as if the fight had drained me.

"Let me go." I pushed at her arm.

Zhong's eyes narrowed. Her cheeks were red. I wasn't sure if that was from the fight or because she was suddenly angry. "I saw the way you fought that poj ntxoog. I can't believe I let you trick me into thinking you haven't had any training."

"I haven't! My body did that on its own."

"It's true," Miv said, brandishing his tiny claws at her. "She's never used a real sword before today. I've seen her trip on stairs, flat surfaces, and her own feet."

My face went hot. *"Thanks."*

Zhong let go of my shirt, but the suspicion in her face didn't fade. "The poj ntxoog at the bridge shouldn't have even been there, certainly not close enough to hear your gong. And now the store? You're hiding something."

"Well then, why don't you tell me what that is, since you think you know *everything*?" I was really tired of having to defend myself to her. Actually, I was really tired, period.

"Those demons put that store there on purpose. It was a trap. The demon said 'he' told them not to kill you. Who is 'he'?"

"How should I know? I don't get why any of this is hap-pening or who 'he' is or what we're even doing here. I just want to save my brother, and you said you'd help." I rubbed my eyes and yawned.

"Stop that," Zhong snapped. She crossed her arms and

somehow managed to look like she was towering over me even though I was the taller one. "Shao will know the truth. Once we find him, he'll be able to tell if you're lying."

She ended her threat with a yawn of her own. Her eyes widened. She looked briefly furious. Then she spun away and stalked through the bamboo trees.

"I told you we couldn't trust her," Miv said, sulking against my neck.

I sighed and bent to retrieve my sword. I stuck it clumsily back into its scabbard and then reluctantly followed Zhong. "We need her help."

Besides, she wasn't wrong that there was something more going on here. Those demons had not only been waiting for us, they'd been trying to capture me. For a few seconds, fear restored my focus, burning away the exhaustion like droplets of water on a hot pan.

But it wasn't long before my eyes began to droop again. My legs felt like there were weights strapped around my ankles. Had those demons done something to me? I yawned so deeply that my jaw ached and my eyes watered. Maybe I could just sit for a—

My foot knocked into something heavy. I looked down and jerked to a stop. A fallen statue lay in the ferns that grew beneath the slender bamboo trees. It looked like a man, his body curled on his side with one arm tucked beneath his head. I leaned over for a closer look, which was when I realized the statue was breathing.

I almost swallowed my tongue as I backed away, eyes wide. He wasn't a statue at all. Plants had grown around and over him, coating his skin in a fine layer of dirt. He looked like he'd lain down for a nap and never gotten back up.

My heart leaped against my chest. Horror jolted me awake.

Zhong glanced over her shoulder, catching the look on my face. When she saw the body sleeping at my feet, her lips pinched. "*Never* lie down in the Bamboo Nursery," she repeated.

I gripped the hilt of my sword, although it wouldn't do me much good. How could Shao live here? Was the Bamboo Nursery part of his curse, or was it a test to prove us worthy of his wisdom? I imagined him as a giant floating head, like in the Wizard of Oz, complete with a light show and green smoke.

Then again, Zhong had said he was a thousand years old. Maybe he could live here because he was now a dried-out husk, like those mummy exhibits at the museum. I shuddered.

As we walked beneath the shadow of the trees, I craned my head up to watch sunlight filter through the forest canopy. It was quite beautiful. The leaves formed a lattice of green shoots and sunbeams. But it was too quiet. Not even the nature spirits were immune to the enchantment here.

Still, if consulting Shao would help me save my brother, then his information was worth the risk. Oracles were sort of like fortune-tellers or psychics . . . but if his powers had

come from the gods, did that mean Shao knew *everything*? I
shuddered at the thought of some withered mummy spying
on my every move.

We passed several more sleepers. Some of them had been
here for so long they were barely distinguishable from the
underbrush. I thought of Sleeping Beauty, cursed to sleep for
a hundred years until she could be awakened by True Love's
Kiss.

But real life wasn't a fairy tale, no matter how hard I pretended it was. No one was coming for these people, and if I
fell asleep here, no one would come for me, either.

"We should talk." I cringed at how loud my voice sounded
in the quiet. Even though I was terrified of falling asleep, my
body still wanted to lie down. "It'll help keep us awake."

"I don't need help," Zhong muttered. But I knew she was
fighting the enchantment as well. She was scowling so hard
I half expected the trees to jump out of her way in apology.

"Everyone needs help. We fought pretty well together
back there, didn't we?" That moment when she'd smiled at
me for figuring out where the Bamboo Nursery was hidden
had made me feel . . . I don't know, *proud*, I guess. And we
had fought well together, even though I wasn't sure how I'd
done it.

Her shoulders tensed, but she didn't argue, which I took
as a good sign.

"Listen, we need to keep each other awake, or we're both
dead. And my brother, too."

She drew an exasperated breath. "Fine. The Bamboo Nursery is a dangerous place to be without allies. We'll watch each other's backs and stay awake. What do you want to talk about?"

Even though I was exhausted and scared, I felt strangely happy, too. *Allies* didn't mean friends, but it was something. "You mentioned a Council of Elder Gods. Who are they?"

"Ugh, you really don't know anything, do you?"

"I know I'll drool all over you in my sleep if you don't start talking."

She huffed. "There's Ntuj, of course, the Sky Father. He was the eldest son of the very first man and woman, who crawled out from the core of the world. He was born holding a blade in one hand and a bottle of life-giving elixir in the other."

"And all I got was a tail." Miv draped himself over my shoulder and sighed.

Zhong ignored him. "Ntuj pushed up the sky and placed four pillars at each corner to hold it up. Then he created the six realms before climbing into the sky to rule over them. His brother, Xov, was the god of thunder, destruction, and wrath."

"Hard for a little brother to compete with the creator of all realms," Miv said.

"Xov also fathered the first demons. His wife gave birth to an egg—don't ask, gods are strange—but when the egg cracked open, a horde of demons poured out. They killed their mother and then chased Xov across the Sky Kingdom. To escape, he opened the gate between realms, releasing them into the world along with illness and strife. Xov was eventually imprisoned by Shee Yee, his brother's half-mortal grandson.

"Next on the Council is Huab Tais Zaj, the Dragon Emperor of Zaj Teb, the Land of Dragons and the source of all rivers. He's the Sky Father's son-in-law."

"So it's a family council," I said.

It always is. The Hmong are separated into clans according to our last names. Every Hmong person with the same last name is considered family, regardless of whether they actually share any blood. Within each clan, a council of ruling heads makes decisions for their local community. I guess it makes sense that our gods are no different, except their "community" is a whole lot bigger—all six realms.

"Keep going." I tried and failed to stop myself from yawning.

"Shall I scratch you?" Miv asked drowsily.

"That might help, actually." I winced as he stabbed my neck with one tiny claw.

One side of Zhong's mouth curled up. "Next is Xiav, another dragon, who took over as thunder god after Xov's imprisonment. Last is Nhia Ngao Zhua Pa, the shape-shifter goddess. She's a trickster who loves to mess with mortal men. . . . Oh, thank the gods."

We stumbled on exhausted legs into a clearing. At its

center stood a small single-story cottage that would have looked like a cute bed-and-breakfast if it hadn't instead gone for the "abandoned haunted house" aesthetic. Peeling paint revealed gray wood beneath. The shutters hung crookedly from broken hinges. Half the roof tiles were missing, and dead bamboo leaves littered the front step.

The run-down cottage was not helping to disprove my idea of Shao as an ancient talking corpse. Also, I *really* hate haunted houses.

I hugged my arms and blinked away the heaviness in my eyes. Since we weren't directly beneath the trees anymore, my head began to clear. The enchantment was still there, but it wasn't working as quickly. I had to push Miv off my shoulder so he'd stop stabbing me.

Zhong shoved open the front door, covering her mouth as dust billowed around us. The condition on the inside wasn't any better. But the most alarming thing in the room wasn't the thick layer of grime and cobwebs that coated every surface or the bowl of what might have once been rice porridge on the counter. It was the man slumped in a chair at the dining room table.

"Is he dead?" So Shao wasn't a mummy, but he could still be a corpse. He looked like a middle-aged man with short salt-and-pepper hair. He wore cargo shorts and what might have been a bamboo-print shirt, but it was hard to tell beneath the dust.

"Of course not." Zhong pulled out a chair at the table.

She swiped her hand across the seat before sitting. The dust was so thick that it came off in a single gray sheet.

An old-fashioned radio sat on the table in front of Shao. She flipped a switch on its side. White noise filled the silence as she began turning the dials. Instead of FM/AM, the letters CW sat above the radio dial along with the words COSMIC WAVES.

"What are you doing?" I asked before checking on Miv. He sat outside the door, grooming himself. He'd mumbled something about the dust not agreeing with him.

"I have to find the right station to wake him up," Zhong said, blinking rapidly. The sleep enchantment continued to tug at the frayed edges of our willpower. "It changes depending on whatever cosmic frequency he's tuned into. I have to find the right one to find *him*."

As she fiddled with the dial, I kept a cautious eye on Shao. He didn't *look* very intimidating, but if master shamans sought out his help, then he had to be powerful. He would tell us where to find Matt. But even though I knew every minute spent messing with the radio was a minute wasted, I was almost afraid to find out what would happen when he woke up. Was I supposed to bow? Cower?

My eyes drifted shut. My head drooped, and I snapped awake again with a gasp. Groaning, I scrubbed my face with my hands. "What's wrong with this place?"

Zhong continued working her way through the radio stations and their programs, none of which sounded familiar. A production of *A Midsummer Night's Dream* with spirits instead of fairies. Live tracking of a locust swarm, with interviews of the locusts. *Ask the Moon-Emperor Hour.*

"According to the story," she said, "a powerful warrior died here after spending a hundred days and nights searching for his lover, who'd been stolen away by tiger spirits. Although he finally found the spirits, he couldn't defeat them. The only thing he had left of his beloved was her bamboo comb, which he was holding when he died. From the comb sprang the bamboo forest, and from his heartbreak, the sleeping curse."

"Wow," I said, wishing I hadn't asked. My fingers curled into a fist. Hopefully that story had taken place before Shao was exiled here. Because if not . . . how would Shao help us find Matt if he couldn't help the shaman who'd died looking for his lover?

The radio settled on a loud old-school pop song. *"Wake me up before you go-go. . . ."*

Shao suddenly bolted upright, nearly startling me out of my skin.

9

Let Me Cosmos-Google
That for You

Shao reached up with painful slowness, his clothes stiff with dust, and rubbed at his eyes. When he yawned, I heard his jaw creak.

"Esteemed One," Zhong said in a tone that was surprisingly respectful given the way she talked to me. "We've come to seek your council. We—"

"Don't I know you?" Shao's voice croaked from disuse. "Or could that have been your mother? I can never tell. You'd think that with infinite knowledge, there'd be *some* way to keep track of time, but that's the gods for you. Phenomenal cosmic powers—"

"Itty-bitty living space," I finished with a grin.

Zhong glared at me for interrupting the "Esteemed One," but Shao only looked surprised to see another person standing at his door. After a moment, his expression cleared and he said "Aaaah" as if he'd found the answer to a question no one had asked.

"Actually, I was going to say 'Phenomenal cosmic powers, but no one arrives on time.' Nhia Ngao Zhua Pa showed up twenty years late to a baby shower for Huab Tais Zaj's grandson and was nearly exiled from Zaj Teb for complaining that the eggrolls had gone cold."

"So, is the cosmos like the gods' version of the internet?" I asked.

Zhong cut her hand through the air—a universal sign for *ignore her*—and said, "I visited you six months ago with my mentor. His name is Master Bo, from the School for Shamanic Arts and Spiritual Mastery. He's one of the elders there, and he's visited you before on his own."

"Oh, that's right. Master Bo is always a delight to talk to. He brought me some haw flakes to try once, and for weeks afterward, I dreamed I was a screaming berry getting picked off a fruit tree."

Zhong blinked. "I'll . . . let him know to bring something else next time."

"Excellent. Let's begin, then. Bring me the vial and lighter in that drawer, child." He looked at me and pointed to the crooked drawer next to the sink.

Begin what? I wondered as I crossed into the kitchen. Was there a ritual to this, or could I just go straight to asking about my brother? Inside the drawer were random bits of things: colored paper clips, coins, half-burned birthday candles crusted with stale frosting, a glass vial with a rubber stopper, and a lighter with the words SHAO'S FOREST SUITES. FREE LODGING FOR ALL ETERNITY on it.

Weirded out, I picked up the lighter and vial and set them on the table. Shao caught my expression and explained, "Some centuries ago, I tried making the Bamboo Nursery an appealing tourist stop. But people would check in, fall asleep, and never leave. Customer satisfaction plummeted. The Echo Tourism Information Center refused to put me back on their brochure."

I wonder why, I thought.

Shao unstoppered the vial. The liquid inside was clear, like water. "Do you know the name Shee Yee?" he asked me.

"I think he was a shaman?" Besides what Zhong had said earlier about Shao wanting to follow in Shee Yee's footsteps, I was sure I'd heard his name in the folktales my parents used to tell me.

"Not just *a* shaman," Zhong said hotly, as if I'd personally insulted her. "Shee Yee was the *first* shaman, and more powerful than any who came after him. He mastered magic, swordsmanship, and shape-shifting in Zaj Teb under the tutelage of his aunt and her husband, the Dragon Emperor. He defeated hordes of demon children that his uncle Xov unleashed across the realms and then vanquished Xov himself. He's a *legend* at the school."

"Oookay. So he's a Hmong folk hero." What did any of that have to do with rescuing Matt?

Shao's eyebrow twitched at Zhong's outburst. "Yes, his exploits are quite legendary. To defeat Xov's children, he used his many skills, skills that I myself also happened to master."

I didn't know why he was talking about Shee Yee. Maybe he was still bitter about not winning the gods' favor?

"Um, we came here because we need your help," I said, trying to redirect the conversation. "It's about my brother."

"We'll get to that. Shee Yee's skills included shape-shifting, like when he transformed into a woman to trick nine demon brothers and infiltrate their camp, and sorcery, like when he summoned storm clouds to strike a wicked dragon from the sky." Shao lifted the lighter. With a flick of his thumb, a small flame erupted from the tip.

I looked nervously at the vial he still held in his other hand. "What's the water for?"

"Oh, this isn't water." He placed the flame to the lip of the vial. "It's oil."

Zhong's eyes went wide. Then she launched herself at me and shouted, "Get down!"

Flames exploded above our heads as we hit the ground hard. My ears rang. Zhong recovered first, dragging me into the living room. A dozen lines of fire raced across the ceiling, as if following invisible fuses. Then the orange lines split into a dozen more that shot down around us until Zhong and I were completely trapped. Suddenly, we were inside a prison, except instead of metal bars, our cage was made of flames.

The air grew stifling and hot. Panic pounded through me as Zhong and I squeezed tight together. Zhong looked bewildered and betrayed. Part of me was terrified, but another part of me was furious. I couldn't believe we'd survived a demon attack and suffered through the Bamboo Nursery just for this.

"Shao!" I shouted. "You're supposed to help us!" That was what Zhong had said—Shao had to help anyone who sought him out. It was his curse for trying to be Shee Yee's equal.

But Shao just continued as if nothing had happened. "Another of Shee Yee's skills was summoning fire. Shaman fire is quite effective, you know." He gestured to our fiery prison. "For exposing evil spirits."

I sucked in a dry breath that made my lungs burn. Sweat poured down our faces. Whatever magic Shao was using to imprison us didn't create smoke, so at least we wouldn't suffocate. Instead, we'd only burn to death. *Great.*

"Are you out of your mind?" I shouted.

"Quite frequently. When I don't have visitors, my mind is always somewhere in the cosmos. Feels weird returning to my body. Confining. Also, I can't remember the last time I used the bathroom."

"Why are you doing this?" Zhong asked. The outrage in her eyes faded to hurt. "We're not evil spirits."

"Maybe not, but consider this a test. I need to be certain of something."

I couldn't tell if he was narrowing his eyes or just falling asleep. Either way, we were in big trouble. I felt like I was being roasted alive. Even my *eyeballs* hurt. Worst of all? The Bamboo Nursery's enchantment was still working its magic, making even my fear feel sluggish.

"What will you do, young shaman?" Shao asked. He was looking at me, not Zhong.

"I'm not a shaman." But then I remembered that the poj ntxoog at the river had called me a shaman, too. What did it mean?

"Yes, we know. Focus," Zhong snapped. If we weren't about to die painful, fiery deaths, her tone of voice might have annoyed me. As it was, it was hard to argue her point.

"What do you know about shaman fire?" I asked.

She swiped the back of her hand over her forehead, eyes closed in frustration. "In ancient times, it would expose evil spirits hiding within a home, but the practice died out because houses back then were made of wood and thatch, and the shamans didn't exactly have Shee Yee's control. They just ended up burning everything down."

"Well, that's comforting. So what do we do?"

She looked around as if expecting a pitcher of water to magically appear. "I don't know. I haven't learned much about shaman fire yet. That's next year!"

I looked at Shao. "What 'something' do you need to be certain about? I thought you knew everything already."

" 'Everything' is a bit of an exaggeration," said the hermit.

"I know *most* things, but it takes a while to organize it all in my head. As I mentioned, there's no concept of *time* in the cosmos. It's like putting a book back together after all its pages have been torn out. I need the complete story in order to understand."

He wasn't making any sense, and I was more concerned about becoming a girl-shaped ash stain on his carpet than about the details of his curse. His eyes were nearly closed. If he fell asleep before we escaped this prison, there was no way we were getting out of this alive. Which meant Matt was doomed, too.

"I've got it!" Zhong shrugged off her backpack and began rummaging inside. "Master Bo once said something about sealing elemental magic. It's supposed to be like binding a spirit. I just need to find a talisman and a container."

As she dug through her backpack—how much stuff did she *have* in there?—I looked out the open window for any sign of Miv. Had he fallen asleep? My eyelids were so heavy. Zhong kept shaking her head, her fingers clumsy, like she couldn't focus.

Part of me wanted nothing more than to lie down, close my eyes, and just let the fire burn me away so I could get some shut-eye. That scared me enough to redouble my search for Miv, even though I wasn't sure what a tiny cat spirit could do to help us.

The sky outside was a clear, brilliant blue. What I wouldn't give for some rain.

Then the strangest thing happened—even stranger than an immortal hermit imprisoning us in a cage of fire. The heavens began to darken.

Something stirred inside me. I could sense the wind quickening and clouds gathering into a roiling mass. The bamboo trees swayed sharply as leaves were stripped from their branches.

Zhong jumped, looking up from her backpack as the wind howled through the open window. The flames flickered wildly. "What's going on?"

But I only half heard her. As in that strange moment at the bridge, everything seemed far away. Even the heat from our prison felt less painful, the sleep enchantment less pressing.

Without warning, rain blasted into the room. A maelstrom of wind and water doused the flaming bars of our prison, freeing us and soaking everything. Lightning flashed, followed by the deafening crash of thunder. Zhong cried out and threw her arms over her head.

Then, just as suddenly, everything stopped. The wind died. The clouds dissolved. The sky brightened, restored to its previous calm. Whatever had opened inside me slammed shut.

Zhong and I looked at each other. Her face had gone paper white. Miraculously, we were both dry. The rain hadn't touched us.

"What just happened?" I whispered.

She opened her mouth, but then her eyes lowered, as if drawn to something. "Your arm!"

A spiral shape glowed underneath my skin, bright and golden. It was the same mark I'd seen appear when I freed the bridge spirit. I hadn't imagined it after all!

"What is that?!" I rubbed frantically at the spot where the mark was now fading. Then I glared at Shao. "What are you doing to us?"

If it were possible to be both sleepy and stunned at the same time, that was how Shao looked. Unlike us, he was drenched, but he hardly seemed to notice. "What you just did wasn't shaman magic. It was something else entirely."

The Bamboo Nursery's enchantment returned with a vengeance, as though it was angry that it had been briefly pushed aside. It took all my energy not to collapse on the spot.

"Don't try to do it again, though," said Shao. "If you haven't already, you'll rouse the attention of the Sky Father. He won't allow you to command his domain a second time, not until you come into your full strength."

"Command his domain? What are you talking about?" I was too tired and angry for his half answers, and too confused about what had just happened.

Zhong pressed her fingers to her temples and muttered, "I can't believe I'm going to have to give you a bad review on RateYourOracle-dot-spirit-dot-com."

Shao only continued: "Of all Shee Yee's exploits, his greatest victory was trapping his uncle Xov within a prison of gold, silver, and ivory. But the act gave the Council of Elder Gods pause. Let's just say they were less than enthusiastic about a mortal with the strength to defeat a god."

"Why are you going on about Shee Yee again?" I asked. Shao *really* needed to let this go. Wasn't being punished for all eternity enough to make him get over the guy?

Zhong put on her backpack and stood, pulling me up with her. My legs barely held.

"When Shee Yee died," Shao said, "the gods decreed that his spirit be bound to the Tree of Souls so he could never reincarnate. His powers were simply too great to allow to be reborn. Over the millennia, the blood of his line grew thinner and thinner until . . ." He gestured to me.

My tired brain took a second to understand what he was implying. But when I finally put it together, I gave him an incredulous look. "Are you saying I'm his descendant?"

Even Zhong muttered, "You have *got* to be joking."

"That spiral on your arm is the mark of the gods. The center of the coil symbolizes the ancestors, and each spiral represents a successive generation. It was branded into Shee Yee's soul when he was blessed by his grandfather Ntuj. You're not his descendant, Pahua Moua. You are Shee Yee himself, reincarnated."

Apparently, it *was* possible to be sleepy and stunned at the same time. I stared, waiting for him to elaborate. Instead, he only slouched into his seat as if he hadn't just said something completely ridiculous. His eyes were half-lidded and his clothes dripped rainwater.

"That can't be right," I said. Judging by the redness in Zhong's face, she agreed with me. Or maybe that was just from nearly burning to death a moment ago.

Shao's chin dipped. His eyes slowly closed. I rubbed furiously at my own eyes. Then I marched over to him and kicked a leg of his chair. Instead of startling him like I hoped to do, it only made his eyelids flutter open.

"You can't just try to kill us and then fall asleep," I said.

"I wasn't trying to kill you. I'm prohibited from killing anyone. That was mild torture at most. I needed to see what innate skills you'd reveal in your escape." His lids began to close again.

"Tell me why you think I'm . . . what you said." The idea that I was a reincarnated shaman was too impossible to speak out loud. If not for the sleep enchantment, my heart would have been racing. Shao had to be mistaken. Even if it *did* kind of explain why I've always been able to see spirits . . . and why I'd suddenly been able to use a sword against those demons. . . . But no, this sort of stuff just didn't happen in real life!

The hermit shook his head, the barest of movements. "Your powers are a threat to the Elder Gods. You must have come to their attention when you set that bridge spirit free. They can't leave the Sky Kingdom, but they have many creatures at their command who can. The gods will want to stop you from growing stronger. . . ."

His voice grew weaker with every word. A small snore escaped his lips. I gave him a rough shake. Even though Zhong had to be angry with him, too, she gasped at my disrespect. He was still an immortal oracle, revered by her school. I didn't really care about that right now, though.

"My brother," I said quickly, when his eyes cracked open. "We've wasted so much time coming here, and after what you just put us through, we deserve answers. My brother's spirit was taken into the Spirit Realm. How do I save him? Can a shaman do a ritual and get him back?"

The slivers of Shao's eyes went glassy, as if he were searching the cosmos-internet for an answer. Either that or he'd fallen asleep. But then he said, "If only it were so easy. The bridge spirit is powerful. Unnaturally so. Facing it would be too dangerous for even a master shaman. It must be you. Use your gifts." His eyes slid shut again. "And remember . . . to avoid . . . the ivory . . . gates. . . ." The last word came out in a whisper, followed by a deep, contented snore.

"Wait!" I said, shaking him. He didn't stir this time. I looked at Zhong and gestured to the radio. "Can't you find his frequency again?"

She was half-slumped against the dripping wall.

"Zhong!" I shouted.

She lurched awake and looked around, frowning and disoriented. Then she straightened, swaying on her feet, and stumbled toward the door. "We've stayed too long. We have to get out of here."

We dragged ourselves out of the house. My legs nearly folded underneath me, and my head spun with exhaustion. Miv was lying beneath a lawn statue of a frog using a leaf as an umbrella. Eddies of water from the sudden downpour swirled around him. Thankfully, he was awake and alert, doing a much better job of resisting the enchantment than we were.

When he spotted us, he scurried around puddles and stopped at my feet. "Talk about your isolated thunderstorms." Then he saw our faces and added, "We should hurry."

I thought I nodded, but I wasn't sure. I felt disoriented and dizzy. The bamboo trees blurred into streaks of green. I tried to focus on what Shao had said. *Use your gifts.* What gifts? I didn't know anything about Shee Yee or his powers. And what did he mean by ivory gates? I needed to save my brother, but how . . . ?

My eyes closed, my mind went blank, and I fell face-first into the grass.

10

~

Meeting Grandpa, Ruler of All
the Realms. No Pressure.

 I sat in a garden. Except *garden* felt like too small a word.

Life-size topiaries shaped like elephants, dragons, monkeys, and tigers adorned the grounds. Every few seconds, they changed poses. The elephant's tail flicked at a cicada, the dragon stretched its neck, and the monkey scratched itself. Clusters of bamboo trees hugged stone pavilions whose arches and columns were draped in white magnolia blossoms.

Mango trees heavy with golden fruit lined a cobblestone walkway that led to a vibrant pink grove. A gilded bridge arced over a clear pond where lotus blossoms floated like lanterns.

Directly before me, waterfalls cascaded from the clouds into a shimmering pool whose reflective surface somehow remained perfectly still. At either side of the mirror pool stood two elegant posts, one made of silver and the other of gold. A lantern hung from a hook at the tip of the silver post, its light a soft glow.

In the Hmong creation story that my mom used to tell, the Sky Father, Ntuj, fashioned two celestial lanterns—the sun and the moon—and ordered his servants to carry them across the sky to divide the days. The golden lantern was missing from its hook now because it was on its daily journey.

"Please tell me I'm not dead," I murmured. Panic fluttered in my gut. But if this was the afterlife, it could definitely be worse.

"You're not dead," said a voice to my right. "You're dreaming."

I startled, surprised to find a man sitting on the stone bench at my side. Had he been there before? He wore a robe— not the fancy silk kind you'd expect from someone who lived in a place like this, but a fluffy blue bathrobe. He had warm brown skin and gray hair, and a clipped beard that gave him a grandfatherly look. On his feet were fuzzy white slippers that could have been fashioned from clouds.

I must have looked as confused as I felt, because the man smiled kindly and closed the book in his lap. It was *A Game of Thrones*.

"Are you a reader?" he asked.

"Uh . . ." I began. Adults were always telling kids not to talk to strangers. But what was I supposed to do in a dream? "I'm more of a TV and movie watcher, actually."

"Ah, technology. Most of my daughters switched to digital readers, but I like the feel of paper and ink. Besides, the signal up here is terrible, and unlike my daughters, I can't make trips down to the mortal realm for the free Starbucks Wi-Fi."

"This is a dream . . ." I said, repeating the only words he'd said that made any sense.

"Oh yes," he confirmed with another smile. "It's truly wonderful to see you again. It has been a very long time."

I rubbed my forehead. What had I been doing before I fell asleep?

"We've missed you—my youngest, Gao Pa, especially."

"Do I know you?" Something about him seemed familiar, but I knew we'd never met.

"At one time you did, yes. And if we're lucky, perhaps you will again someday. But time runs short, and you need to get back. I can't let you do that trick with the rain again, though. It'll attract far too much attention, and you should stay as inconspicuous as possible. Since I gave my word long ago that you shouldn't be reincarnated, I can't offer you any more assistance." His thick gray eyebrows drew together. Storm clouds gathered behind his eyes, complete with the ominous flicker of lightning. "But I can give you a warning: You cannot trust *anyone*, Pahua, not even those close to you. You're in danger."

His words made my skin prickle. *Danger?* The image of a demon in a floral sundress flashed through my mind.

There'd also been a man, his hair gray not from age but dust, and . . . a forest of bamboo trees. I jumped to my feet. *The Bamboo Nursery!*

The man touched my arm. The spiral symbol rose against my skin, shimmering with golden celestial light.

I realized then who he had to be. "Ntuj?"

He clasped rough, weathered hands around mine and said gently, "I cannot help you. But fortunately, you already possess the power to help yourself."

The spiral on my arm glowed brighter. Heat seared my skin. I gasped and wrenched my hand away—

~

I jolted awake, sitting up straight in the Bamboo Nursery. My heart thundered and I was breathing hard, as if I'd just run a mile.

Miv leaped onto my shoulder and pressed his face into my neck. "Thank the gods," he said. He'd been on my chest, shouting my name.

I hugged him back with trembling arms. Overhead, the bamboo trees loomed, both beautiful and somehow threatening. "How long was I asleep?"

"Not long. Maybe thirty minutes. I've been trying to wake you, but nothing would work. Sorry." He nosed my palm, where there was a kitten-size bite mark, next to other scratches from my fight with the poj ntxoog. Now that he'd pointed out the punctures, I felt a dull throb there.

Zhong lay on her backpack a few feet away. Her legs were splayed and her arms thrown over her head like she'd tried making a snow angel in the dirt. I would have found it funny if we weren't in so much danger. Even though I'd awoken from the sleep enchantment, it still tugged at my consciousness, coaxing me back into its embrace. My head felt woozy. My body begged me to lie back down. But terror was a strong motivator, and I somehow found the strength to stand.

The symbol on my arm had faded, but I could still feel its burn. I'd dreamed of the Sky Father. Had it been only that—a dream? Or had it been real? He'd said he missed me, but he hadn't meant *me*. He'd meant the part of me that was once Shee Yee.

Had Shao been telling the truth? It was still hard to wrap my mind around it. If the oracle was to be believed, Ntuj was my grandfather. He'd mentioned his youngest daughter, Gao Pa. Shee Yee's mother?

I thought of my own mom back home. Right now, she was probably still praying to the ancestral spirits over my little brother. Matt was dying, his soul lost somewhere in the Spirit Realm, because of me. So much for me being a powerful shaman.

I hung my head in shame and my hair clip nearly slipped off. It was an ugly shade of purple with the letter *P* outlined in rhinestones. Most of the stones had fallen out, but it was still one of my most precious possessions. The clip was the first thing my mom had gotten me after my dad left. I couldn't lose it.

Once I had resecured it, I went over to Zhong and grabbed her shoulders. I shouted into her ear, "Wake up!"

She didn't so much as twitch. I would just have to carry her out of this place. Except, for someone shorter than me, Zhong was a lot heavier than she looked. I couldn't get her onto my back, and Miv wasn't any help.

"Sorry about this," I said to Zhong as I grabbed both her arms and began dragging her through the underbrush. I winced every time her head bumped a rock or a fern slapped her face. Dirt stained her clothes and backpack. Twigs disappeared into her hair.

Miv contributed by riding on my shoulder and shouting encouraging things like "You need to build your upper-body strength." And "You can do it, because if you don't, you'll both die." And "What would Shee Yee do?"

I wrinkled my nose. How could anyone think I was some reincarnated hero after how badly I'd messed up with the bridge spirit? But then, there was that dream with the Sky Father. And the glowing mark on my arm . . . I definitely hadn't made that up.

Assuming we survived this, I would have time to figure it out later. I grunted and strained, growing more exhausted with every excruciating step. The bite on my hand and the claw scratch on my arm stung. My various bruises ached. I nearly tripped more than once, but somehow I kept my feet under me each time. I knew that if I fell again, I wouldn't be getting up. At last, the forest thinned, and I glimpsed a road beyond the last stretch of trees.

I could have cried with relief as we finally broke free of the Bamboo Nursery. The demon department store was gone. Now there was only a long stretch of road past the tree line and rolling hills on either side. I collapsed into the grass, gasping for air. My back and arms throbbed. But even as I lay there, energy surged back into me.

Zhong's eyes opened. She frowned up at the sky. I could tell she was trying to remember what had happened. Then her eyes went huge, and her face paled. She sat up, looking frantic until her gaze found mine.

"I fell asleep!" she whispered, horrified.

"I did, too," I admitted, still trying to catch my breath. "But I woke up again, and look"—I gestured limply to the open sky—"we made it out."

"How . . . ?" She trailed off as she touched the matted tangle that was her hair. With a cry of alarm, she stood, brushing leaves and debris from her clothes. Dirt cascaded off her in a mini landslide. When her fingers touched a spot on her head that had bumped into a rock, she winced and demanded, "What did you do to me?"

"I had to drag you," I said, rubbing my aching arms. "I couldn't wake you up."

"You couldn't have done it more gently? And you lost

some of my pins!" She patted frantically at the pockets of her jean jacket, counting the pins that were left. A bug fell from her hair. "Ugh!" Disgusted, she flicked it back into the Bamboo Nursery.

"You're welcome," I said stiffly. We'd nearly died, and she wanted to yell at me for not saving her life more *gently*? Unbelievable!

I shoved myself to my feet and stalked away. We wouldn't even have been in the Bamboo Nursery in the first place if not for Zhong, and what had we learned from Shao anyway, other than that I was Shee Yee's reincarnation? Okay, fine, that was kind of a major deal, but what about Matt? The oracle hadn't told us where to find him or how to defeat the bridge spirit, just that I had to "use my gifts."

Miv was quick on my heels. "We should have left her behind," he said.

I huffed and looked around, wondering where in the Echo we might be. Remarkably, I recognized the road as the same one we'd arrived on. Where Thread and Needle had been, there was only the Bamboo Nursery, exactly where Zhong had said it should be. The demons must have cleared out when their trap failed to snare us.

I glanced back at Zhong, who was still picking dirt off her jacket, and felt suddenly overcome by a wave of hopelessness. Taking a deep breath, I tried to calm the panic twisting my stomach. I couldn't remember the last time I'd been away from Matt for this long outside of school. He was like my second shadow, always at my side, and I was so worried about him that it hurt.

After a moment, Zhong stepped up beside me, her arms crossed over her chest. "I'm sorry."

My eyebrows rose. Had she really just apologized?

"And thank you." She looked me up and down, eyes narrowed, like she was seeing me again for the first time. She smiled, but I could tell that it was forced. "I guess he wasn't kidding about you. Who else would be able to wake themselves up in the Bamboo Nursery?"

My shoulders tensed. "Don't do that."

"Do what?" she asked, her lips still fixed into that terrifyingly fake smile.

"Look at me like that. Stop it. You're creeping me out."

Her smile transformed into a scowl, which was more like it. "It's just weird, okay? I grew up on stories about Shee Yee, and now he's . . . you. I don't know if I should be bowing or—"

"Please don't."

"That was the last thing I expected Shao to say, so I'm not sure how to deal with it yet."

"Well, neither do I! So just . . . don't be weird about it, okay?" I turned away, arms crossed tight. "Nothing's changed about me."

Zhong stuck her nose in the air again. "Fine, then." But I caught her glancing at me out the corner of her eyes, like she was still trying to square what she knew about Shee Yee with the skinny kid standing next to her.

"Anyway, why did we even come here?" I asked. "Why would anyone from your school ever risk going into that forest?"

"Shaman masters have the spiritual focus to resist the sleep enchantment long enough to speak with Shao. Sometimes they bring their apprentices. I came here once before, with Master Bo."

My eyes narrowed. "You said you're a shaman warrior, but you've only been here once, with your mentor?"

She winced and pretended to inspect her nails. "Technically, I'm . . . not a shaman warrior . . . yet."

I sucked in a furious breath. "You lied to me! You could've gotten us both killed!"

Miv made a small, judgmental *harrumph* and then trotted off ahead. Without a word, Zhong and I followed him. I should have known something wasn't right with her story, but she talked with so much confidence, and she always had a good answer for everything. At least when I pretended to be something I wasn't, I never tried to pass it off as the truth or risked anyone's life.

Part of me *did* want to leave her behind. But the way back home likely went through the elephant statue, and I still needed her help in getting the door between realms to open.

"Since I'd been here before, I thought I'd be strong enough." Zhong's hands curled into fists. "I was fine with

Master Bo. I should've been able to do this without him!"

"You should have told me the truth. You kept accusing me of hiding something, when you were the one who was lying." I felt like an idiot.

I wasn't just furious that she'd put our lives in danger; I was disappointed, too. I'd been so awed by her, a warrior who was everything I wasn't—brave, powerful, confident. But she was just a better pretender than me, and I was the biggest pretender I knew.

Now that I was supposed to be the reincarnation of the first and most powerful shaman in Hmong mythology, did that make me a super pretender? Demigod of pretending? Pretender Supreme?

For once, I didn't have to imagine I was someone more interesting. Except . . . it didn't feel real. It felt less real, actually, than all the times I'd pretended to be someone else. Being told you're supposed to be some big-shot shaman isn't the same as making something up yourself.

And besides that, in my dream, the Sky Father had said that he and the other gods agreed that Shee Yee shouldn't be reincarnated. Shao had said the same thing. But . . . I was here. So what did that mean?

"I shouldn't have lied," Zhong said, glowering. If she was going to be sorry, she could at least look it. "But I'm on a quest for the school. The shaman elders sent me to investigate what happened with the bridge spirit and to ensure it reached the Tree of Souls for reincarnation. It's my only chance to prove myself so I can earn the blessing of the school's guardian spirit."

"Your only chance? What happens if you fail?"

Her lips pressed into a firm line, the way mine sometimes do when I'm trying not to cry during the sad parts in a movie. Miv always teases me for it, and Matt sits in my lap to make me feel better.

"Then I don't pass my year," she said, "and I have to leave the school. I'll never become a shaman warrior. Without the guardian spirit's blessing, I'll be an outcast."

If there was one thing I understood, it was being an outcast. Even though it was hard for me to trust her, I couldn't abandon her.

"I need to save my brother. You need to finish your quest. And both involve the bridge spirit. So let's do this, then. Partners?" I stopped walking long enough to hold out my hand.

She gave it a suspicious look—either that or she was grossed out by my grimy fingers and dirt-encrusted nails. But she must have decided she didn't have any more choice than I did, because she finally shook it.

"Okay, so what's our next step?" I asked as we continued walking.

"I'll have to perform the ritual to project our spirits into the Spirit Realm. We'll need a secure place where we won't be disturbed."

"My room back home?" I suggested. My door had a lock. I wasn't actually allowed to use it, but I figured this could be an exception.

"I'll have to scope it out first."

There wasn't a lot to "scope out" other than the fact I hadn't made my bed that morning, but I nodded anyway. "And then what? How do we find my brother in the Spirit Realm? He's got less than three days."

"I have a spirit friend who'll be able to help us search, and she's really fast. It should be fine."

It wasn't much of a plan, but I reminded myself that Zhong had a lot on the line as well. Her entire future was riding on us defeating the bridge spirit. If she was confident her friend could help, then I had to believe it.

Hopefully, we wouldn't run into any more demons, either. Speaking of which . . . "I've been thinking," I said. "The name of the poj ntxoog's trap was Thread and Needle."

"Because it was a clothing store."

"Yeah, and I might be wrong, because my Hmong is kind of terrible, but isn't the Hmong word for thread—"

"Xov!" she shouted, before clapping her hands over her mouth and looking around anxiously. "Oh no. The god of destruction *would* have poj ntxoog working for him. The demons did mention a 'he,' and it would make sense. If Shee Yee was the one who imprisoned him, he'd want revenge."

Specifically, revenge on *me*. I cringed. I was hoping she'd tell me I was wrong, but now a cold dread shivered along the back of my neck. Covering my face, I groaned into my hands. "Ugh, *why* is this happening?"

"But the demons said he'd told them not to kill you. Why would he want you alive?"

"I don't know—to torture me probably!" As if things weren't bad enough with my brother's stolen soul, now I had an angry destruction god after me, too. What was I supposed to do with that? Dodge demons and hide away for the rest of my life?

I dropped my hands from my face and took a deep breath. No, running really wasn't an option while my brother was lying unconscious, waiting for his sister to fix her mistake.

"I suppose I could do some research at school for warding off poj ntxoog," Zhong said. "But that'll take time we don't have at the moment."

"Right," I said. Xov and his demons would have to be a problem for another day. For now, Matt was the priority. "Let's worry about him *after* we save my brother. Shao said to use my gifts, but I don't have any idea what those are. You know a lot about Shee Yee. What do you think?"

Zhong nodded. I wasn't sure what she was agreeing with—probably the part where I said she knew a lot.

"Shee Yee had powers that most shamans outside of the school no longer possess," said Zhong. "Like the ability to transmute objects or transform himself into other creatures, and the ability to send souls into the Spirit Realm without shamanic tools or rituals. You obviously used that talent already. You're not very good at it yet, though, so you should probably not do it again until you get trained."

"I didn't do it on purpose!" I argued, but she continued as if I hadn't spoken.

"I'm not sure about your magical skills yet, either, although you did summon that rainstorm. . . ." Her eyebrows rose briefly, like she was grudgingly impressed. "But that wasn't shaman magic, and anyway, it was way too flashy. You should be trying not to draw attention."

"I didn't do that on purpose, either," I muttered.

"I'm not great at using magic without shamanic tools, so I can't help you with that," Zhong admitted, "but I could show you how to control your spiritual energy. That's the first thing shaman warriors have to learn."

"You would do that?" I asked, eyes narrowing.

Her chin jutted out. "What? I'm not good enough to teach you now that you're Shee Yee?"

"That's not what I meant! I'm just . . . surprised you're offering."

"Well, you should know how to do *something*."

"Wow, thanks," I said flatly. Then a thought struck me. "Is spiritual energy like the Force?"

She snorted. "Don't be ridiculous. We can't move things with our minds. Even Shee Yee didn't have that ability."

"What about weapons?" I asked. "Did he have a cool shaman sword, or—"

"Yes, he was a master swordsman and archer," said

Zhong. Then she suddenly brightened, as if remembering something else. "Oh! His uncle, the Dragon Emperor, gave him a lightning ax. It was said to be able to split a tree with a single strike. That's what Shee Yee used to defeat Xov."

"Sounds awesome!" I said.

A weapon like that could not only defeat the bridge spirit, but it'd also be protection against any other godly henchmen who had a bone to pick with Shee Yee's spirit—which apparently happened to be inside me.

A lightning ax was a weapon of legends. Could I really wield something so powerful? Every part of me that had dreamed of being something *more* screamed *Yes!*

"Where is it?"

Zhong's shoulders slumped. "I have no idea."

My heart sank.

"I know where it is," Miv announced.

We'd reached the stretch of road where we'd first arrived, and there was the elephant statue. Miv had climbed onto its trunk and was sprawled against the warm stone.

I tilted my head at him.

"No need to look so skeptical," the cat spirit said, licking his paw. "I haven't always been with you. You'd be surprised by the things I know if you ever bothered to ask."

"Well?" I said impatiently.

He grinned, his cat eyes filled with mischief. "It's in the Spirit Realm, buried deep within the Tree of Souls."

11

~

I Wouldn't Even Mind if
He Called Me *Dummy*

 The moment we returned to Merdel from the Echo, my phone began to vibrate in my back pocket. (By the way, floating upward through complete darkness instead of drifting down? Still terrifying.)

We arrived through the bronze elephant on Main Street. There were more people sitting around the statue now, eating lunch and staring at their phone screens. Even though we'd just walked out of a glowing magical doorway in the middle of a crowd, no one paid us any attention. It was super weird.

Nobody even looked up when the bronze elephant swung the door shut with its trunk and remarked cheerfully, "My, looks like you two had quite an adventure!"

I shook the frost from my hair and pulled my phone from my pocket. Something else fell out—the gloves from the demon store. Frowning, I picked them up. I hadn't meant to keep them, but I didn't feel too bad about it. The only reason the store had been there was to capture me. It had almost worked, too.

I stuffed the gloves back into my pocket and checked my phone. I had three missed calls and a text from my mom. She must have noticed I'd taken the phone and gotten worried when she saw my note.

I bit my bottom lip, recalling Zhong's suggestion that maybe my mom and aunt knew about the shaman school. I didn't know how it could be possible, but on the tiny chance that it was—did that mean they also knew about me?

Was that what they had argued about when they'd whispered my name between them? That I was the reincarnation of Shee Yee? But my mom had never given me any reason to believe she was aware I could see spirits, much less that I was some kind of mythological hero. And being a shaman herself, my aunt would have said *something*, right?

When I read my mom's text message, though, all my questions were shoved aside.

"My brother's in the hospital," I told Zhong. I pressed the button to dial Mom.

"That's not going to do him any good," Zhong said. I knew that already, but I guess she had to make sure.

The phone rang only once before my mom picked up. "Pahua?" She sounded frantic. I was flooded with guilt for worrying her. "Where are you? Why didn't you pick up?"

Miv sat on my shoulder with his ears perked so that he could hear my mom's side of the conversation as well.

"Sorry, I went to the school and then decided to play in the woods. Maybe the signal is bad there." I didn't usually lie to her, but telling her the Echo had bad reception wouldn't go over well. If my mom didn't know about me being Shee Yee, then I couldn't give her one more thing to worry about. I had to keep her safe as well.

There was a burst of static in my ear as she sighed. "Please don't wander off. I'd feel better if I knew you were safe at home."

"How's Matt doing?"

Silence hung on the line for several seconds. I felt certain my heart had stopped beating. When Mom finally answered, I didn't recognize her voice. It was so quiet, and it shook a little. "I don't know what's wrong. He won't wake up."

My eyes stung. I rubbed them before Zhong could notice. "What room are you in? I'll be right there."

"There's no point," Zhong said after I hung up. "We should get to the Spirit Realm as soon as possible. That's the best way to help your brother."

"I have to see him." I wasn't sure how to explain it to her. Even though time was short, I had to be completely certain that, at least for now, his body was still okay. I wouldn't be able to go to the Spirit Realm until I did.

"Fine," Zhong huffed.

Since I didn't have any change for the bus, I began walking, and Zhong stepped in line next to me.

After a while, Miv said, *It's a pity Zhong can't see me in this realm.* He didn't sound the least bit sorry about it. In fact, he looked pretty pleased as he made faces at her.

Zhong must have noticed me glancing at my shoulder, because her eyes narrowed. "Is he talking about me? I still don't think he's a normal cat spirit. There's something strange about his aura. Are you sure I can't exorcise him?"

I leaned away protectively. "Yes."

Miv jumped onto Zhong's shoulder, pressed both paws against her head, and shouted into her ear, *Hellooooo in there!*

"But you can answer something for me," I said.

She waited until we crossed a street and then nodded like a queen allowing her subject to speak. "Go ahead. Shee Yee's reincarnation really shouldn't be so clueless. It's insulting."

I gave her a sour look. "Anyway, back in the Echo, you said something about neutralizing spiritual energy so that people don't freeze every time they cross between realms." I fingered the edges of the gloves sticking out from my pocket. If I'd remembered I had them, I would have put them on before going back through the elephant doorway. My hair was still damp from the frost. "But what does that mean? What's with the ice when you cross between realms?"

"Passing between realms requires spiritual energy, even for spiritfolk. If you've got too little, then you can hurt yourself trying to cross. It's why it wouldn't even work for normal mortals without a really strong neutralizer, and even then, they're not always reliable. You don't have to worry, though. You've got plenty of spiritual energy."

"Why was there frost at the bridge, then, with the girl?"

"You broke her connection to the mortal realm—"

"By accident."

"—and opened a temporary path for her to cross into the Spirit Realm. Dead mortals don't usually need to worry about spiritual energy, because their guides protect them."

"Their guides?" I repeated. I didn't like having to ask her so many questions about how things with the spirits worked, especially since I'd been seeing them for as long as I could remember. But at least she'd stopped talking to me like I was an idiot.

"Elephants, of course," she said, like it should be obvious.

Okay, so at least she'd stopped talking to me like I was a *complete* idiot. That probably had more to do with her respect for Shee Yee than me, though.

"Elephants guard all the gates between realms and guide the dead into the Spirit Realm."

Guards and guides. She'd said that before. I hadn't really thought about what it meant.

"How come you don't freeze?" I asked, looking her over.

Her hair was dry. And while my clothes were spotted with damp from melted ice, hers looked fine. Well, maybe not fine. The back of her striped T-shirt dress was streaked with grass stains, and dirt caked the seams of her jean jacket. There were empty spaces on the pockets where some of her pins had fallen off.

She pulled up a sleeve to reveal a woven red string tied around her wrist. "A protection charm from the school. It keeps me from losing too much spiritual energy when I travel. We should get you one. It'll be a while before you learn how to focus your spiritual energy into a shield. Even I haven't mastered it yet, which is why I have to wear this."

"So once I can 'focus my spiritual energy,' I won't need a charm or a neutralizer? And I can start doing shaman magic?"

Zhong nodded. "Right now, your energy is too uncontrolled and all over the place. That's normal for untrained shamans." She gestured to the gloves sticking out of my pocket. "Those should help with crossing between realms. But we still need to get you a protection charm for binding your spirit to your body." She raised her wristband again. "This does that, too."

The possibility of my own spirit getting taken hadn't even occurred to me. I really was an idiot.

If only Matt had been wearing a charm like that, it would have protected him from the bridge spirit.

I studied Zhong more carefully, wondering what other tricks she had up her sleeve. "You said you could teach me how to control my spiritual energy."

"You'll have to learn how to sense it first. Here, I'll show you now," Zhong said, surprising me. She turned neatly on her heel so that she was walking backward and facing me. "It's easy, but it does take practice to get it under control."

She was being way too nice.

"You'll probably need a *lot* of practice," she added.

That was more like it.

"Watch. This will be quick," she said, pausing on the sidewalk next to a lamppost.

I stopped alongside her, scooting to the side to let a woman with a dog in a stroller pass by. Even Miv returned to my shoulder to observe.

Zhong closed her eyes. "Imagine your spiritual energy like a whole separate respiratory system." She drew a slow, deep breath and raised her hands in front of her like she was pretending to lift her stomach. It was like a move out of a xianxia movie. "You should be able to feel it, like air filling your lungs, except instead of air, it's energy, and it's flowing all throughout your body."

I mimicked her, closing my eyes and taking a deep breath. But I didn't feel anything other than an itch on my knee. I scratched it and said, "I don't think I'm doing this right."

Zhong gave me a look like *Shee Yee would be ashamed.* But she only said, "Practice. You'll get it." Her words were friendly, but her tone was almost like a threat—I had better get it, because her hero's reputation was on the line.

"I'll keep practicing," I said, hurrying along again. Even if she was only helping me because of her quest and her admiration for Shee Yee, I was still grateful. "By the way, I'm sorry about your pins. Were they a present from someone?"

Keeping pace with me, she looked down at the glossy badges on her jacket. I could tell by the way she touched them that they were important to her.

"Most of these are marks of achievement. We get them at school when we've learned a new skill, or passed a test, or overcome something difficult." She pointed to a bronze pin in the shape of a short shaman sword. "This one means I achieved my second rank in swordsmanship. When I pass the test for third rank, I'll get a silver pin."

There were other shapes, too: a crossbow, a qeej, and an open book. I didn't recognize most of the rest.

"How about this one?" I pointed to a circular badge, like a shaman's cymbal, containing a pair of two connected spirals, which was a common Hmong pattern that my mom called an elephant foot. Three vertical stripes were drawn over the top. Something about the whole design looked familiar.

"That's the school's emblem," said Zhong. "The three stripes show how many years I've been there." She gave me a resentful look. "My first- and second-year pins fell off in the Bamboo Nursery."

I grimaced. "I was trying to get us out of there without falling asleep."

She sighed. "I know. It's not your fault, I guess."

"So, three years, huh? Is it like a boarding school?"

She pursed her lips, like she was considering how much

to tell me. Then she shrugged and said, "We call it a school, but it's more of a community. The apprentices take some classes together based on their year, but most of the time we work independently with our shaman mentors, learning the trade by going out and exorcising spirits and stuff. Master Bo is one of the toughest elders at the school, but I'm glad for that, because it means he knows I can do better. He's the one who recommended me for this quest."

Meaning if she failed, she would not only bring shame upon herself but on her mentor as well. I winced.

"In the summer, we hold sword-fighting tournaments with games and challenges," Zhong continued. "On weekends, we play capture the spirit. It's like capture the flag, except you have to trap the other team's spirit mascot while protecting your own."

"Spirit mascot?"

"Usually just a nature spirit who volunteers to play."

It sounded pretty incredible. It also sounded like a fancy, exclusive academy for the rich and powerful, but I didn't say that. I could never belong in such a place. I didn't even fit in at normal school.

"How many more years until you're officially a shaman warrior?"

"Four. I still have a lot to learn about shaman magic, like transmutation or forming protection shields. And I've got a few ranks to go before I'm considered a master swordsman or archer."

After three years, Zhong was already a pretty impressive fighter. What would she be like in four more?

"But if you don't complete this quest, you'll get a do-over, right?"

She shook her head, the corners of her lips drooping. "If I don't get the blessing of the school's guardian spirit, then there's no point."

That seemed harsh. "How come you never told me all this stuff about the Spirit Realm and shaman schools?" I asked Miv, who was once again perched on Zhong's shoulder.

It took a second for Zhong to realize that I wasn't talking to her. With a shout, she began flailing her arm and slapping at herself. "Get off me!"

I covered my mouth and laughed. Even though her hands passed right through him, he still hissed and jumped off.

Even after all these years, I didn't get how spirit physics worked. I mean, I didn't get how physics worked *at all*, but spirit physics seemed extra confusing. Miv could sit on Zhong's shoulder, but her hands went through him. It made no sense.

The hospital was on the other end of town. Luckily, it wasn't a very big town. We stopped at a gas station on the way and washed up in the restroom. I cleaned my wounds— all minor—and then straightened out my clothes so I wouldn't look like I'd been raised by feral raccoons.

When we reached the hospital and found Matt's room, Zhong said, "I'll be over there," and pointed to the waiting area. It was one of those awkwardly narrow rooms with ugly chairs and magazines about diseases with names not even adults could pronounce.

Do you want me to go with her? Miv asked.

I shook my head quickly. "Stay with me?"

He rested his head beneath my jaw, and I relaxed a little. Having him with me always made me feel stronger.

Mom was in a chair next to Matt's bed, frowning in concentration as she sewed a protective charm. I'd seen this kind before. It was a simple red pouch, stuffed with various dried herbs and then either tucked beneath a mattress or secured on a bedpost. My chest felt tight as I spotted my brother, who seemed too small against the white sheets.

When I reached his other side, Mom looked up, startled. Her face was pale. She looked more tired than I'd ever seen her, even after she'd worked a double shift at the factory. Her eyes were puffy and red, and she'd pulled her hair back into a messy ponytail. She was still wearing the sweatpants and T-shirt she'd slept in.

"Pahua," she whispered in relief. She rose and rounded the bed to pull me into a tight hug. "I'm glad you're safe."

"Of course I am," I said. She was already so worried about Matt; I didn't want her worried about me, too. "What did the doctors say?"

She shook her head and returned to Matt's side. I didn't know what that meant. Were the doctors confused? Or maybe Mom hadn't understood them. The doctors on TV always used really complicated words, so it wouldn't surprise me. Plus, she was so anxious that she hadn't even noticed the bruise on my forehead. Not that I blamed her.

As my gaze fell on the red protection charm, I wondered again whether my mom knew about my secret or about Zhong's shaman school. I couldn't ask her directly, not if she really was clueless, because it might freak her out. But she might reveal something if I asked in a roundabout way.

I cleared my throat lightly. "So then what do *you* think is wrong with him?"

Mom bent over to press a kiss on Matt's forehead and smooth down his hair. "If the doctors don't know, how can I? They're still running tests."

As she found her seat again, I said, "I mean spiritually."

Her fingers stilled around the charm pouch and needle. She didn't answer right away. Instead, when she looked up at me, there was a question in her eyes. "Pahua, why did you think Matt might need a 'shaman thing' last night?"

I stuffed my hands into my pockets and looked at my feet. How much should I say? Even if she was aware that I was Shee Yee's reincarnation, if she found out that I'd left the mortal realm and nearly died—and that I would have to leave again to save Matt's spirit—she probably wouldn't handle that well.

"I don't know. Like I said, I was just worried, because it happened so quickly," I said, hoping she'd buy the lie.

She watched me for a few uncomfortable seconds. Then

she finally sighed and went back to sewing her charm. "A shaman might say his soul is lost and needs to be called back."

"Does that . . . Does that actually work?" I asked. I watched Matt's little chest rise and fall. I was relieved to see him alive, but the stillness in his face, which was usually split into a huge grin, left me unsettled.

Even though I knew he wanted Mom to be home more often, he rarely complained. He usually tried to distract *me* from being sad about it. And lately, when he scraped his knees or bumped his elbows, when he was hungry or needed help with his homework, it was me he went to first, even when Mom was around.

My shallow breaths grew shaky. There was still time to fix this, I told myself.

Mom gave me a small, tired smile. "I shouldn't have worried you. Your brother will be okay. If the doctors can't come up with anything soon, I'll think about reaching out to a shaman as well."

I frowned a little. Shamans were expensive. A little over a year ago, my mom had helped out a couple with a blessing for their newborn, and then word spread that she could do small things for cheap, which was why people from neighboring towns called her instead of their local shaman.

"What about Aunt Kalia?"

Mom's lips twisted to one side, and she didn't look up from her sewing. "Maybe. We'll see."

"Aunt Kalia would want to help, and she wouldn't make you pay." If Shao had been telling the truth, then I was the one who had to face the bridge spirit. There probably wasn't much another shaman could do. Still, I felt kind of bad fishing for information by bringing up her sister.

Mom's fingers fumbled a little with the needle. "Not money, but she'd want something else."

I blinked, surprised. "Like what?"

She shook her head. "Promises that aren't mine to make." Her eyes lifted, and her voice softened. "Go home soon. Get some rest, and don't go anywhere, okay?"

Although she spoke gently, I could tell she was done talking about this. Her answers only left me with more questions, though. My mom had never said much about Aunt Kalia, even when the two had been on speaking terms, but it was now clearer than ever that she was hiding something from me. Once Matt was safe, I'd have to try and get it out of her.

Miv jumped onto the hospital bed and settled on my brother's stomach. He folded his stubby kitten arms and rested his head on them as if intending to stay awhile.

I watched them for a moment—the boy and cat spirit who'd always stuck by me. I'd told my brother about Miv. The first time was when Matt was five, young enough to believe me. He used to ask constantly about what Miv was doing, what he was saying, where he was sitting, and if he could pet him. For a year, I'd been able to share my best friend with him.

But then something changed. The more I talked about Miv, the less Matt believed in him, until one day, he'd told me to stop acting like Miv was real, because it was weird.

Hearing the *weird* label come from my own brother hurt way more than it ever had from the kids at school. And after that, I'd never mentioned Miv again.

If only Matt could see how the cat watched over him now.

I sucked in a deep breath. It was deceptive how peaceful Matt looked, like he was only asleep and he might wake at any second to complain about how hungry he was. My fingers flexed at my side, but I knew what I had to do. Squaring my shoulders, I rested my palm on my brother's forehead.

His skin wasn't burning the way it had before, probably thanks to whatever medicine the doctors had given him. But that didn't stop my teeth from clenching. A tempest was building inside him, with angry winds that seared and cut. The bridge spirit's presence within him had grown stronger. Matt was still in there, too, but his spirit felt far away, like a kite caught in a thunderstorm. Its string could snap at any moment. I lifted my hand, afraid my touch might make things worse.

How many times had I wished for my mom to hire a babysitter? How many times had I wanted just one weekend by myself, without having to worry about him? I would take it all back if he'd just open his eyes. I wouldn't even mind much if he called me *dummy*.

I curled my fists around Matt's blanket. *She can't have you,* I thought fiercely. *I'll find you and get you back. That's a promise.*

Mom's eyes had closed. Her head rested on the back of her chair. It didn't look very comfortable, but I didn't want to wake her. Her hands cradled the unfinished charm in her lap. I moved the needle to a table so she wouldn't prick herself in her sleep.

I found Zhong near the nurses' station instead of in the waiting area. When she saw me, she rushed over to my side and hissed, "I've been listening to the nurses talk. Another case was just brought in—that makes *five* kids falling into comas, all within the last twenty-four hours."

My stomach dropped. "Do you think the bridge spirit is taking more spirits? Why? How?"

"Don't know. But we have to go. We need to get that lightning ax so we can put a stop to her."

I nodded, even though the idea of having to face the presence I'd felt inside my brother made my legs turn into pudding. How were two kids and a cat spirit supposed to get a celestial weapon from the heart of the Spirit Realm and take on a vengeful ghost? I barely knew how to use a kitchen knife, much less a magical ax.

Zhong looked ready to do battle right there in the hospital, though. It made me feel pathetic in comparison.

I supposed, if we were going after a powerful spirit, I should pretend to be one, too. Yes. I was an avenging dragon, and the mere sight of my shadow sent evil running in the opposite direction. . . .

It was a good distraction until Miv jumped onto my head and said, *Is it time to get ourselves killed now?*

12

~

Dragon Spirits Need Fashion Tips. A Sword Tip Works, Too.

With a renewed sense of urgency, we hurried back to my apartment so Zhong could check out the space. Supposedly, she would perform a quick ritual that would project our spirits into Dab Teb while Miv and the house spirits watched over our bodies.

On the way, I practiced trying to sense my spiritual energy, but Miv kept distracting me by saying my concentration face looked like my *I just smelled Matt's sock drawer* face.

Outside the apartment building, Mr. Taylor called a greeting from his lawn chair. I smiled and waved before heading inside, eager to get started.

Except when I opened our front door, the apartment looked like a tornado had blown in through the window. Dishes were scattered across the kitchen floor, along with the dish rack. Our sofa lay on its side, the cushions missing. The end table had been knocked over as well, and the lamp had rolled into the hallway. The altar on the wall had been completely torn down. Stubs of burned incense and rice grains littered the carpet.

The culprit stood in the center of the chaos. He looked like a man with blue hair, but I knew better by now than to think he was human. There was a slick sheen to his skin, like fish scales, and he had golden slitted pupils, like a snake. He wore oversize jeans, a purple silk blouse, a scale-patterned cloak, and snow boots, as if he'd thrown on the first mortal clothes he could find.

His arms were down at his sides, but his face was red. The veins in his neck and forearms bulged like he was fighting against invisible chains.

And he kind of was. On either side of him, two of the guardian house spirits glowed as they restrained him. The little stove spirit was literally on fire, his hair a torch of red-and-orange flames. The door spirit shone a bright yellow like an exploding star. I was disturbed to see the altar spirit, who looked like a tiny elephant with twelve tusks, lying motionless atop a pile of silver and gold joss paper on the carpet nearby.

When we walked in, everyone sort of froze and stared around in surprise for a few seconds. I had no idea how the man had gotten into our apartment or who he was, but after Shao's warning about the gods sending their servants to find me, as well as the run-in with the poj ntxoog, I could hazard a guess as to why he was here. Knowing this, however, didn't make my stomach feel any less queasy when the man's eyes focused on me. He blew two trails of white smoke through his nostrils.

With a burst of strength, he broke free of the guardian spirits. The stove and door spirits cried out as they were flung backward by the force of his spiritual energy.

Zhong kicked the door shut behind us, and we both drew our swords, which we'd put back on after leaving the hospital. She didn't consider herself safe without a sword at her hip, and I was beginning to feel the same way.

Miv launched off my shoulder, his tiny claws flashing. He was too small to do much damage, though. The man batted him aside. Then, before either of us could attack, he began to transform. His body lengthened and grew. His skin turned blue and scaled.

I flattened my back against the door, petrified. He hovered over us now, an enormous serpent with four clawed feet and a long scaly body. His head was wide and frilled with two thin whiskers. He wasn't just a serpent. He was a *dragon*.

"What is happening?!" I shouted.

"You're coming with me," the dragon growled. His voice was low and gravelly, like scraping rocks.

Zhong recovered from her shock before I did. With a battle cry, she leaped forward. The dragon's tail whipped around, but she ducked, slashing at his exposed back. My eyes widened as the tail sailed right at my face.

I dropped to the floor and almost lost my sword. *Come on, Pahua,* I told myself. *You're a dangerous snake charmer. No, a dragon hunter.*

Uttering a shout that I hoped sounded fierce and not like a deflating balloon, I jumped to my feet and threw myself onto the dragon's lower half. His talons swiped at me. I somehow avoided them as I held on for dear life. Zhong was still battling his upper half, so I aimed my sword for the dragon's thrashing tail.

The blade bounced off the thick scales without even leaving a mark. With a snarl, the dragon bucked me off. I fell hard onto my side.

"Watch out!" the door spirit shouted.

I rolled out of the way as the dragon's heavy tail slammed down where I'd been lying. With a sinuous twist of his long body, he threw Zhong over the upended sofa.

The dragon rose above me, baring sharp fangs. White smoke curled from his wide nostrils. "You will come with me, even if I have to carry you in my belly."

I backed away, holding up my sword despite the fact that whacking at his scales wouldn't get me anywhere. "I'm sure that's a five-star accommodation, but I'm going to have to pass."

I flinched, hands shaking, as the dragon's head came close enough for its hot breath to blast my face. It smelled like rotten fish and unwashed feet. The dragon could see my fear. His eyes narrowed, and he actually retreated a little.

"I thought you'd be more impressive," he said, his voice low and rumbling. He sounded a bit disappointed and kind of reluctant as well. "But you're just a child after all."

I wanted to shout, *Seriously? Sending a dragon after an eleven-year-old? Talk about overkill!* Instead, I latched onto the hope that maybe he didn't really want to hurt anyone and said, "You seem like a reasonable dragon." Those were words I never thought I'd say outside of my imagination. "How about we just, uh, talk about this first? Who says we have to be enemies, right? Maybe Miv could share some fashion advice. You seem like you could use a few tips."

"I could, actually," he said, head tilting thoughtfully. "I'm usually in armor."

"You're a warrior," I said quickly, lowering my sword. "Being sent after a kid is probably way beneath you."

"Pahua!" Zhong shouted. She'd risen from behind the sofa, crossbow primed and ready. As she aimed, I threw up a hand in a signal for her to wait.

But at the sudden threat, the dragon reared back, his mouth opening so wide that I could see down his throat. I raised my sword again and swung it hard, smashing the blade into one of his sharp teeth. The dragon's head whipped against me, knocking me into the wall. A portrait of Matt on his previous birthday smashed to the carpet.

"Together now!" the little stove spirit squeaked. He began to burn again, bright and red. Nearby, the door spirit did the same.

The dragon's tail whipped back and forth as he fought against the house spirits' hold. Zhong aimed her crossbow again. He roared as the bolt pierced the roof of his mouth. His outer scales were like armor, but his insides were vulnerable.

"Now, Pahua!" Zhong called, climbing over the back of the sofa.

I leaped onto the dragon's exposed belly and then paused with the tip of my sword pressed against the soft flesh within the dragon's mouth. Zhong's crossbow bolt looked like a toothpick beside his large teeth.

"I really don't want to kill you," I said, because it was the truth. He was just following orders, after all, and he'd hesitated when he saw I was afraid. "You're a warrior, right? If you leave now, then you don't have to die at the hands of two kids."

The dragon snarled, still fighting against the house spirits' restraining powers. Yet I could see that he was thinking it over.

"Fine. *I'll* do it," Zhong said, raising her sword.

"Okay!" the dragon said quickly, and with difficulty, considering my blade was still shoved into his mouth. "You've got a deal."

The dragon burst from the house spirits' hold. Zhong shouted my name as I tumbled off its belly onto the carpet, jarring my elbow. Bracing for the dragon's attack, I swung my sword at empty air. But no attack came. Instead, the door flung open and the dragon escaped, transforming into a human.

Zhong rushed after him, pausing in the hallway to make sure he had really fled, and then she rounded on me. Her face was flushed with fury. "What is your problem?! Why didn't you kill him?"

Gasping for breath, I collapsed onto my back, my heart still pounding. "Because I didn't want to. I don't think he wanted to kill us, either."

"So what?" Zhong nearly screeched. "Who knows if he'll be back with more dragons next time!"

I winced, because she had a point. "Are all dragons evil? Like poj ntxoog?"

"Not usually." Zhong strode past me to shove her cross-bow into her backpack. "But that doesn't mean anything. Just because someone isn't inherently evil doesn't mean they won't still hurt you. You can't risk your life hoping they can be talked out of it."

"Better than just killing everything we meet," I muttered. Seeing spirits had always been the only cool thing about my life, and before the ghost girl at the bridge, I hadn't run into many bad ones.

Maybe it was true that some folks were terrible through and through, but it was better to believe that they had redeemable qualities. Then at least you could convince them not to capture you, like I did with the dragon.

I wasn't stupid, though. I knew that, sometimes, the reasons people did awful things were complicated. My mom had never told me why my dad had left us—she promised to when I was older—and it would be easy for me to blame it on him just being a bad person. But . . . I remember him from before he left, and that's the version of him I miss.

He'd been a good dad. At bedtime, he would tell me Hmong stories, like how a great hero shot down all nine suns so the people's crops would no longer burn and the rivers would stop boiling, and how the rooster won its crown by singing one of the suns back into the sky. Those were some of my favorite memories.

He would often help me with my homework while Mom prepared dinner, and the summer before he left, he taught me how to ride a bike and took me fishing in the afternoons.

Before marathoning TV shows became a thing Matt and I did, it was something Dad and I had enjoyed on weekends. Mom would start watching along with us, with Matt playing on the floor, but then she'd wander off to read or garden. In the evenings, she always went to bed when Matt did while Dad let me stay up late, laughing every time I insisted, "One more episode!"

More than once, I'd wished he was a terrible dad just so I could be glad that he left.

The hand that wasn't gripping my sword balled into a fist, and I rolled onto my side. Thinking about him always made my chest ache and my stomach burn, the sadness and anger battling behind my ribs. It was better to focus on our current dilemma, which was that my apartment wasn't as safe as I'd thought.

My gaze fell on the joss paper littering the floor, and I suddenly remembered the tiny altar spirit. I hurried over to retrieve the elephant from where they had fallen. I returned the upended altar to the wall and placed the elephant on it. Then I rushed to the kitchen to fill a shallow saucer with uncooked rice. My mom kept a sack of it beneath the sink.

"What are you doing?" Zhong sounded annoyed as she zipped her backpack and dropped it beside the door, which she'd shut and locked. "We need to talk about what to do next."

"In a minute. The house spirits need help." I set the rice on the altar. The tiny twelve-tusked elephant lifted their trunk, groping for the hard grains. I smiled and lit a few sticks of fresh incense. I placed those on the altar, too. "Thank you for protecting our home."

I sank to my knees and touched my forehead to the carpet. I made the same gesture of respect to the door spirit. Finally, I bowed to the stove spirit, who was lying between the burners while Miv tried to put out his hair flames.

"You can really see *all* spirits?" Zhong asked, watching me. Her anger seemed to be fading, and she raised one eyebrow in curiosity. "Even the shaman masters at my school can't see all spirits all the time, and that's after decades of developing their spiritual energy."

I shrugged as I finished placing offerings before the stove and door spirits. "I've always been able to. I guess now I know why."

"It's . . . pretty cool," she said grudgingly, although the way her nose wrinkled made me wonder if she really meant it. At least she wasn't yelling at me anymore.

We both went still as a knock sounded on the door. Zhong drew her sword again, but I waved her away.

Maybe the dragon came back, Miv said, lowering onto his paws, preparing to pounce. *Or it's a demon.*

"A demon wouldn't knock." Then again, before yesterday, I also would have said demons don't wear spandex. I drew my sword, too, just in case. Then I called out, "Who is it?"

"Mr. Taylor. I heard a commotion. Everything okay?"

Relief swept through me. "Uhhh. Yep. I'm just . . . redecorating? Sorry about the noise."

I waited until I heard the sound of his footsteps shuffling away and then smacked my palm to my forehead. What if he said something to the landlord?

"Pahua." Zhong grabbed my arm and pulled me around to face her. "You know what this means, don't you?"

"I'm going to get us kicked out of our apartment?" Dread filled me. How was I going to tell my mom? Couldn't I do *anything* right?

"No," Zhong said, shaking me. "It means we can't take the shaman routes into the Spirit Realm. The gods' servants will be looking for you. And if we leave your body here, even with the house spirits as protection, you risk being possessed or killed. Your spirit would be lost to either wander the Spirit Realm forever or get stuck on the Tree of Souls for another four thousand years."

Oh. That sounded a lot worse than being evicted.

"So I can't leave my body to travel into the Spirit Realm, but I can't stay here, either," I said. "What you're saying is that, basically, I'm doomed?" And if *I* was doomed, then what did that mean for my brother?

"I'm saying that we have to cross over physically. It'll take longer, but it might be safer."

"Well, how do we do that? The Echo again?"

"The Crossroads is our best option," said Zhong. "I've never been there before, though. Does your cat friend know the way?"

Miv, who was now tossing rice grains into the altar spirit's open mouth, looked up with a twitch of his whiskers. *Of course I do. All paths lead to the Crossroads.*

That sounded kind of vague. "I think so?"

"You don't seem sure," Zhong said.

"Well, I trust Miv, so you're just going to have to trust him, too."

She didn't look very happy with that answer, but she mumbled, "Fine."

We needed more supplies and protection, so we raided my mom's trunk. I didn't touch the gong again, but I took a simple cloth mask made of red cotton. It was old and smelled a little musty, but Zhong told me that shamans have to cover their faces when crossing into the Spirit Realm to hide the fact they aren't dead. Miv explained that even though Dab Teb is just like any other realm for spiritfolk, it's unique for mortal spirits, because it's our resting point between death and whatever comes after.

Zhong stuffed a whole stack of silver and gold joss paper into her backpack. Apparently, it turned into real money in the Spirit Realm. If that was true, I couldn't wait to see it.

"Aha!" Zhong withdrew a bundle of woven red string and small sewing scissors. She snipped a short length of the string, which she then tied around my wrist. Her eyebrows pinched in concentration as she whispered words that didn't really sound Hmong.

"What were you saying?" I asked when she finished.

She knotted the string twice and then clipped the loose ends. "It's a protection spell to keep your soul firmly in your body while we're in the Spirit Realm. I don't know what the words actually mean. It's an ancient dialect."

I decided not to ask what *dialect* meant.

Miv peeked over my shoulder. *The mask only works against the elephant-spirit guides. They're a bit dim. The gods, though, will likely have servants watching the Crossroads. If you want to avoid being recognized by anyone like our dragon friend just now, you'll need more of a disguise.*

I perked up at the idea. Wearing a costume was like

playing pretend. Besides, I did need to change after our morning's adventure.

Even though Zhong's clothes were a mess from her being dragged through the Bamboo Nursery, she refused to change, saying I was the only one the gods were after. She was probably still mad about losing her pins. Now that I knew what they'd meant to her, I understood. I would have been mad, too.

I kept eyeing the one with the school's emblem. It really did look familiar, but maybe that was because the elephant foot was so common in Hmong designs. I wish I'd remembered to ask my mom about it at the hospital.

I dug through my closet. What sort of disguise would work among spiritfolk? I spotted my brown hooded cloak and pulled it off the hanger. My mom had sewn it for me last Halloween. It was supposed to be a Jedi cloak, but she'd made it too big, so I'd ended up looking more like a hobbit. I put it on over a pair of galaxy-print leggings and a simple green dress. It was my favorite dress, because it had big pockets.

Next, I filled my backpack with as many snacks as I could find—mostly ramen packets and half a box of granola bars.

Miv had said time passes differently in the other realms. A day in the Spirit Realm might only be a couple of hours here, which was why instead of a week, we now only had two and a half days to save my brother. We couldn't afford to lose any more time.

We left the apartment as it was. Hopefully Mr. Taylor wouldn't tell the landlord, and I could clean up after we got back. My mom wasn't going to stray from Matt's side until he woke up anyway.

"Are you sure you know the way?" I asked Miv, who led us down the road toward the field.

All paths lead to the Crossroads, he said again. What did that even mean?

"What's a crossroads, anyway?" I asked Zhong.

Her mouth twisted, like she was holding herself back from saying something rude. Progress!

"The Crossroads is the intersection of nine paths that lead almost anywhere in the six realms. It's the only way I know to reach the Spirit Realm aside from the shaman paths and, you know, dying."

"Yeah, no to the dying part."

Focus, Miv said. *Actually,* unfocus. *Unfocus your eyes and imagine that feeling you get when you cross between realms.*

I repeated Miv's instructions to Zhong. Then I did as he ordered and ended up tripping on a maintenance-hole cover. Zhong made a strangled sound that made me think she was mentally screaming.

Looking ahead again, I unfocused my eyes and squinted a bit so that the houses all went a little fuzzy. A tingling sensation began in my fingers. It turned into numbness, like frost spreading over my knuckles. I shivered.

Remembering the gloves, I slipped them on. Warmth

immediately thawed my skin. I relaxed a little, but my stomach still felt unsettled. My body went weightless, like I was floating through that dark space between realms. The sound of a car down the street transformed into the clatter of wheels and cloven hooves. Houses with overgrown bushes distorted into rolling hillsides.

I blinked to focus my vision. We were no longer at the end of my street. Instead, we stood in the middle of a dusty road, surrounded by the bustle of strange traffic. I gasped and turned in a circle, unable to believe my eyes, even after everything else that had happened today.

13

~

Traffic Jam at the Crossroads
of the Realms

 "Welcome to the Crossroads," Miv said. He looked smug, which, for a cat, was pretty normal.

"Wow," I said. The place was like a painting. Or a scene from a fantasy movie.

Even Zhong, who supposedly had experience traveling with her mentor, seemed a little awestruck.

A rainbow of wildflowers blanketed the surrounding hills. Nature spirits with hair like thistles and crowns of woven grass giggled as they blew pollen at passersby to make them sneeze. I had to jump to see beyond the travelers walking in front of us, but I caught a glimpse of what lay ahead: nine roads, all converging at a single point.

"Keep it moving!" someone shouted. We were blocking a wide assortment of spiritfolk headed toward the Crossroads. Some of them looked completely mortal, like me and Zhong. But others were a bizarre mix of mortal and animal. Beast spiritfolk. A man with scaly skin grunted as he elbowed his way ahead of us. He pulled a large wooden cart filled with leafy vegetables, their dirt-encrusted roots still attached. I caught a whiff of soil just as his cart nearly rolled over my foot.

"Watch it!" Miv shouted. The man turned and flicked his forked tongue at us. The cat spirit hissed in response. "Lizard shifters. They think they're so important just because they're distant relatives to dragons. I should steal his relic."

"Relic?" I asked, only partly paying attention. I shuffled forward, gawking at everything around us. A pack of tigers in leather jackets prowled down the opposite lane. We passed a turtle in mismatched socks making slow and steady progress.

"His cloak," Miv said.

Now that he mentioned it, everyone who looked mortal was wearing a peculiar-looking cloak. Some were covered in feathers of midnight black and flame orange, royal purple and peacock green. Others had luminous silver and baby-blue scales. There were cloaks of fur and quills and leather. I even saw a woman wearing a tortoiseshell slung over her shoulders like a backpack.

All these human-looking people—they were actually shape-shifters?

"That is *so cool*," I whispered.

Miv rolled his eyes. "They wear the relic as a cloak when

they're in their mortal form, and as skin when they shift back into animals."

I thought about the dragon we'd met in my apartment. Before he had transformed from man to beast, he *had* been wearing a scaled cloak. I'd just assumed it was part of his questionable fashion sense.

"My mom used to tell me this folktale about a peacock princess," I said. "When she took off her cloak of feathers to go swimming, she turned into a beautiful woman. A man saw her, fell in love, and stole her cloak so she couldn't change back." She'd ended up marrying him, but he kept her cloak hidden. When she found it years later, she abandoned him and their children to return to her home in the sky.

That story had stuck with me. The man was the worst for taking her cloak and trapping her into marriage, but she wasn't so great, either. What sort of person just abandons their kids like that? I could never understand it.

"The princess was one of the Sky Father's grand-daughters," Zhong said. "So I guess that would make her Shee Yee's cousin."

Did that make me royalty, then? I almost laughed. Princesses were definitely not awkward eleven-year-olds who only had invisible friends.

Parked along the side of the road was an entire mini market. Vendors shouted over the clatter of traffic and voices, adding to the din. A woman sitting on a brightly colored bamboo mat held out a basket of metal bracelets fashioned with tiny bells, like the kind Hmong women put around their babies' wrists and ankles. She shook the basket, and the sound of tinkling bells rose into the air.

Another seller had arranged bushels of fresh fruits and vegetables over vibrant banana leaves. My empty stomach grumbled, even though I couldn't smell them over the mixed scents of too many bodies, dust, and grass. Beside the vegetables, a monkey spirit carefully measured bags of spices in vibrant reds and yellows.

I pulled a granola bar out of my backpack as a rooster with a badge and a notepad squawked at a seller.

"No permit, no selling!" the rooster was saying. I was so focused on figuring out how the rooster was holding that pen that I ran into someone's back.

"Ow," I said, rubbing at my nose where it had bumped into a stiff bag.

We were close to the intersection of the Crossroads now, but that meant traffic was almost at a standstill. The person I'd run into turned around. He was a bulky man with huge bull horns and broad nostrils that smoked faintly. His shadow alone was bigger than me. I swallowed hard.

"Um, sorry," I said. Miv arched his back, his fur standing up as he hissed. I pressed my palm to the cat spirit's head to settle him down. If he wanted to, the man could squish Miv into paste with one fist.

Next to the huge bull man, a short woman with a small

horn on either side of her head jabbed her elbow into his side. "Stop towering over her like that, Choj."

The man grunted but turned back around. The heavy bag hanging from his shoulders—the one I'd run into—nearly whacked me in the temple.

"Don't mind him. That's his usual expression," the horned woman said with a laugh that ended in a distinct *moo*. "Life is hard when you look like a bull about to charge."

I was so grateful for the friendly smile that I bowed my head. "Thank you, Niam Tais."

Niam tais is the Hmong term for an aunt on your mom's side. Obviously, she wasn't really my aunt, but it's a polite way to address older women you don't know.

"Call me Aunt Chan," she said. She had large brown eyes with thick lashes, and even though her face was mostly human, her arms were covered in short brown fur with white spots. She wore a long green dress with triangles printed along the hem. "What's your name?"

After I introduced everyone, Aunt Chan's eyes narrowed as she looked me up and down. I recognized the expression immediately as the Asian Auntie Critical Eye.

She made a disapproving *moo*. "You're very thin. And short. Which realm are you from? What are your parents' names?"

I mentally groaned. *Who are your parents?* is usually the first question out of older Hmong people's mouths. Hmong communities are so intertwined—and the gossip networks so advanced—that pretty much everyone has heard of everyone else. My mom moved us to Merdel to get away from it all, but honestly, I thought she missed it sometimes. It isn't always a bad thing when everybody knows who you are and you're all part of the same community.

But when Dad left, the way our Hmong neighbors treated my mom changed, even though it hadn't been her fault. Right before we moved, she'd told me that, sometimes, it was hard to change the minds of people who'd already decided to judge you. I certainly knew all about that from school.

As I struggled with how to reply to Aunt Chan, my stomach saved me by growling again, despite the granola bar I'd just finished.

Frowning, she dug into the leather pack that hung from her shoulder. "Have you had anything to eat?"

"No, no, we're fine," I said.

"I could eat something," Zhong said. When I looked at her in surprise, she added, "What? It'd be rude to refuse."

Aunt Chan pulled out three green sticks. I recognized them as sticky sweet rice wrapped in banana leaves. They were a treat that my mom only made around the New Year. Matt could eat three of them in less than two minutes.

"Thank you." Zhong used the same respectful tone she had with Shao. Basically it was nothing like how she talked to me. But I was grateful for that. I'd told her not to be weird about the fact I'm Shee Yee's reincarnation, and so far, she'd listened.

I pulled off my gloves and accepted the snack. Then I turned away and whispered to Miv, "Is this okay? Me eating the food here?"

"You'll be fine," Miv drawled, waving away the stick that was offered to him.

As Aunt Chan put it back into her pack, I peeked inside. There were some folded clothes, wrapped possessions, and a bundle of dried seaweed. I was baffled. Where was she getting these rice sticks from?

She noticed my bewilderment. While I watched, she withdrew a strip of seaweed. As she held it, the seaweed grew plump and greener in front of my eyes, and the air sweetened with the scent of coconut.

"How did you do that?" I asked, amazed.

"Haven't you ever seen transmutation before? Of course, it's especially tricky with food. Few people master the skill." She said this like she was proud to count herself among them.

As I stuffed my mouth with sticky rice, I had to admit she was a master. Zhong had mentioned that Shee Yee had the power to transmute things. Maybe I could learn how to transform food, too. Then Matt and I wouldn't have to eat eggs and ramen all the time. An ache began in my gut. He and I might never share a meal again if I didn't hurry up and find that ax.

I gestured to the traffic jam up ahead and asked through a mouthful of rice, "Was there an accident?" We didn't have time to stand around.

"Oh, no," Aunt Chan said. "It's always like this. I have to account for the congestion on my daily commute. You two look unfamiliar. Are you new here?"

"Yeah," I said at the same time Zhong said, "Not at all."

Aunt Chan's head tilted in confusion. Glaring at Zhong to stay quiet, I added, "This is our first time at the Crossroads by ourselves. Our, uh, parents don't usually let us travel alone."

She patted my arm. "Choj and I would be happy to watch over you while we're together."

Zhong frowned at the idea, but I didn't mind. Aunt Chan collected our empty banana leaves and stuffed them back into her bag.

As we inched closer to the intersection, I noticed statues on either side of the road. They stood behind the mini market where sellers kept shouting unlikely things like "Get a glimpse into your future! Pay only two memories!"

But the statues commanded more of my attention. They were bigger than life and incredibly detailed: dragons with curling whiskers and clawed feet attached to serpentine bodies, tigers with their teeth bared, and boars with raised tusks. Thick weeds and wildflowers climbed up their bases, as if they'd been there for a long time.

"These statues were once the guardian spirits of the Crossroads," Aunt Chan said, noticing my interest. "They were turned to stone after demons tricked them in order to gain access to the Sky Kingdom." She pointed upward. "Through those stairs."

Sure enough, shrouded by wispy clouds, a staircase rose into the sky. High up, there was a huge gap between the steps, like a giant had smashed a hammer into the stairway. The chasm was an uncrossable distance.

"What happened?" I asked.

"The shaman Shee Yee destroyed the stairs with his powerful lightning ax to prevent the demons from reaching the Sky Kingdom," said Aunt Chan. "Ever since, no one has been able to go there without the gods' assistance. You can't even imagine the paperwork involved. And the wait time? Might as well not bother."

Zhong's expression brightened at the mention of Shee Yee's past exploits. Even though the folktales made him out to be a hero, which Zhong clearly believed, it sounded like he'd caused a lot of trouble. Destroying the stairs to the Sky Kingdom? Hunting down every single one of Xov's horde of demon children? Imprisoning a god? No wonder there were demons and dragons after me! Shee Yee sounded reckless and brave. *Nothing* like me. I wasn't even sure I would come back from this trip alive.

I didn't know how I was going to save my brother. I only knew that I had to do it, and not just because his current condition was my fault. Like me, Matt didn't really have anyone else. If his big sister couldn't look out for him, who would?

But what if Shao was wrong about me having any sort of gifts to use against the bridge spirit? Maybe all that time he'd spent in cosmic space or whatever had messed up his brain frequencies, and he'd mistaken me for someone else.

Except that wouldn't explain the mark on my arm. Or the sudden rainstorm in Shao's cottage. Or me not impaling myself with my own sword in the demon store. Shao had said something else, too, which I hadn't had a chance to think about in between trying not to die. Something about an ivory gate . . .

"Aunt Chan," I began. I paused, fumbling for what to say. "You seem to know a lot about . . . spirit stuff."

"Smooth," Miv said.

My face went hot. "I mean, obviously you do, because you're spiritfolk. Like me. I'm spiritfolk, too. Ha-ha-ha."

"Oh my *gods*," Zhong said, covering her face.

Aunt Chan's brow rose. "You seem tired, dear. Here, take some more." She shoved a half dozen more transmuted rice sticks at me.

I sighed heavily, dropping the food into my backpack as Miv laughed. I *was* tired, but that was beside the point. I decided to ask my question straight out. "Do you know anything about ivory gates?"

Her look of concern turned into one of puzzlement. "You can't mean the first seal holding the old thunder god?"

Of course! Relief washed over me at having at least one mystery cleared up. Shao had warned me to stay away from Xov's prison because the god of destruction hated Shee Yee for trapping him. Well, Shao didn't need to worry about that. I wasn't going anywhere near that guy. I was more concerned about keeping Xov's minions away from *me*.

"Why would you want to know about that?" asked Choj, the bull man. He must have been eavesdropping. When he turned around, everyone squished back to make room for his bulk.

"Um," I said, scrambling for something that made sense. "So I know how to avoid it?"

"No one knows where his prison is except the gods. What's wrong with you, girl?" Aunt Chan clucked her tongue. It was the same sound my mom made when she wanted me to clean my room. (And hey, if I know where all my stuff is, then it can't be *that* messy.)

"How does the curse go again?" Choj asked. He tapped a finger the size of a hot dog on his chin.

> *"Bound in ivory, silver, gold,*
> *The god of wrath will prison hold.*
> *By victor's hand the gate undone*
> *When sky bridges earth for love of gum."*

"You got that last bit wrong," Aunt Chan said. "It's 'love of *fun.*'"

"Wait, wait, we're both wrong," said Choj. "I'm pretty sure it's 'love of *bun.*'"

As they argued, I turned to Zhong. "So Shee Yee was also a poet?"

"Not a very good one, obviously," Miv said.

Zhong stuck her nose in the air. "I've never heard of any curse before."

A loud whistle made me jump. Choj faced forward again. I accidentally stepped on Zhong's foot to avoid getting brained by his pack. Then I had to jump up to see what was happening ahead. I was used to being one of the shortest people around, but it still sucked at times.

At the center of the intersection, a crossing guard in a bright-orange vest stood holding a big STOP sign. From the neck down, he almost looked human. But his torso was twice the normal size, because it supported three furry badger heads, all facing in different directions. Each head blew an ear-piercing whistle whenever someone tried to cross out of turn.

Behind him, looming over the entire Crossroads, was a tall stone pedestal topped by a statue of a massive eagle. The bird was evil looking and super disturbing.

Each of the roads led somewhere different in the six realms. This close to the intersection, I could see the ghostly impressions of those different places. The road immediately to our left was surrounded by thick jungle. From vines hanging over the travelers, monkeys hurled papayas at their heads. The next road over was framed by sheer cliff walls.

I wanted to blink and rub my eyes to clear them. It was kind of like looking at a double-exposure picture, like the computer-manipulated photos of "ghosts" a boy had shown me back in third grade. He'd said the ghosts lived in his house and would kidnap me if he told them to. So I told him that ghosts only haunted people who they knew were about to die and join them in eternal torment. He started crying, and I got detention and a note sent home to my mom.

"Which road are we taking?" I asked Miv. That restless feeling in my stomach got more persistent the longer we were stuck there.

He pointed one small paw to the right of the eagle statue. "The Dragon's Veins."

That road was narrower than the others and ended at a sandy gray riverbank where numerous small rowboats were moored. Spiritfolk were boarding the boats and pushing off into the river. The "water" was dark red, like cranberry juice.

Farther down the bank, new boats sprang from the water. They bobbed to the surface, completely dry and ready for the next passengers.

Large shapes waded through the river as well. Elephants, pale and gray and semitranslucent, moved with steady grace, their trunks swaying. Mortal spirits sat on their backs. My skin prickled. They were like taxis for the dead. Now *that* was a crummy job.

"So we have to take a boat?" I asked.

Miv said, "Unless you'd rather swim."

I groaned. Fun fact #3 about me: I can't swim. I wasn't sure if you could drown in a magical river of . . . whatever that was. Hopefully not actual blood.

When I was little, my parents took me swimming at a local lake. I hadn't known then to avoid water spirits. So when I saw one, I waved to them and called them a mermaid. The moment my dad's back was turned, the water spirit got hold of me and pulled me under. I almost drowned. I don't actually remember much of it other than the water spirit's big fishy eyes, their slick fingers around my ankle, and a feeling of intense fear. I do, however, remember what happened afterward.

My dad had held me tightly, his big hand cradling the back of my head while his voice called my name. Even though I'd been afraid moments earlier, I'd felt completely safe in his arms. Now it seemed like a stupid memory, because my dad had ultimately let me go. In the past four years, I'd never gotten so much as a card from him.

Anyway, I'd never really cared for swimming after that.

I didn't have much experience on boats, either, but that part didn't worry me as much as the fact there didn't seem to be any life jackets available. Butterflies flailed in my stomach.

Zhong suddenly grabbed my arm. "He's demanding travel permits."

She pointed at the crossing guard, who was handing a

card back to a long-legged crane. The bird spirit shook their feathers and continued down the road toward the waiting boats.

"I've been watching, and every single person taking the Dragon's Veins has had to give him a physical permit." She twisted the bracelet around her wrist. I'd noticed she did that when she was nervous.

"So, we can't use your mentor's code?" I asked.

Zhong shook her head and rubbed her face. "I should have expected this. The Spirit Realm isn't as tightly regulated as the Sky Kingdom or Zaj Teb, but it's still pretty restricted."

"We could tell the crossing guard you're Shee Yee and demand celebrity treatment?" Miv asked.

I gave him a deadpan look.

He shrugged. "I'm out of ideas, then."

I crossed my arms, frustrated. We couldn't give up. I *had* to get into the Spirit Realm, and this was our only path there. We had no other options.

Zhong was already gripping her sword anxiously, as if she expected us to fight our way to the Dragon's Veins. I didn't want it to come to that, so we'd have to think of a better idea. I'd always been good at using my imagination to pretend myself out of a situation, but that had only been in my head.

Well, I was about to find out if it would work for real.

14

The Guardian of the Crossroads
Is a Stone-Cold Screamer

 You'd think, with the amount of time I spent pretending, I'd be a good liar. But I really wasn't. I made things up in my head, and they usually stayed there.

I tapped Aunt Chan's arm. "Auntie, I think someone stole our permits. Or maybe they fell out of my pocket while we were walking. Anyway, they're gone, and now I don't know what we're going to do."

Zhong's eyebrows rose. I hoped it was because she was impressed. But since it was Zhong, I doubted that was the case.

"Pahua's an idiot," Miv added helpfully. I glared at him.

Aunt Chan's lips drooped in concern. "Where are you headed?"

I drew a deep breath, my fingers clutching my cloak. "To

the Spirit Realm. Our uncle lives there, and he sent a message for us to visit."

"Sent it by turtle, since it's the cheapest way, you know, so it took two months to reach us," Miv said.

Turtle mail must have been a thing, because Aunt Chan nodded sympathetically.

"It's been so long since we've seen him," I said. "And he's getting so old—"

"Nearing two hundred," Miv interrupted again.

"And we've come all this way already . . ." I gave her as pathetic a look as I could manage. It wasn't too hard. I already felt pretty pathetic.

Aunt Chan's face softened. She patted my cheek. "Oh, you poor kids. Leave it to me and Uncle Choj."

"Are you sure about this?" Zhong hissed as we finally reached the front of the line.

"Just thinking outside the box," I said, trying to sound confident even though my heart was pounding.

The crossing guard's head—the one that was facing us— had two enormous buckteeth and deep bags under his large round eyes. But even though he wore a blinding orange vest and had three heads, my gaze kept returning to the stone eagle watching over the intersection. I couldn't shake the feeling that it was looking at me. It freaked me out.

We waited as the crossing guard allowed what felt like all eight other lines to go before it was finally our turn. He blew a short sharp sound on his whistle and waved us across. All three faces began asking for permits and nodding in turn as travelers showed them.

"Pahua," Zhong whispered as we approached the crossing guard. I grabbed her wrist before she did something hasty like challenge him to a duel.

Aunt Chan was on it, though, because she stopped next to the three-headed badger-man and exclaimed loudly, "Look at you! So thin and pale. You must be exhausted. A few extra hours of sleep will clear those dark circles away. If you need an eye-cream recommendation, I've got you covered. Have you eaten today? Here, have some rice. I insist."

I could have kissed her. She was unleashing the power of the Asian Auntie.

"Keep moving," said the crossing guard's first face.

"You're holding up traffic," said the second face.

"What kind of rice?" said the third face.

Aunt Chan was already taking out a stick of transmuted rice. She rolled back the banana leaves, revealing the sweet, sticky contents. The scowl melted from the first badger's face.

"That does look good."

"Smells good, too," said the second face.

"I can't see!" said the third face.

"Don't worry, there's plenty for everyone." She handed the rice stick to the crossing guard, who took a bite with each of his faces. "Have another. Eat until you're full." She took out a second stick and gave me and Zhong a meaningful look.

We tried to appear as innocent as possible as we headed for the path that led to the docks.

"You work so hard. That's good! Your mother would be proud. But remember to take a break every now and then, too," Aunt Chan said. She *moo*ed in disapproval as she looked him over.

He nodded, digging into the sweet rice now as Aunt Chan peeled a third one. "You'd think the gods would have come up with a better road-management system by now," he said between bites. "Traffic lights, turnstiles, more workers . . . something to give me a break!"

"Completely unethical," Aunt Chan agreed. When one of the crossing guard's faces frowned at us, Choj stepped directly into his line of vision, blocking us from view.

"Faster," I muttered, shoving Zhong. We walked as quickly as we dared toward the docks. With the crossing guard distracted, no one else seemed to care that we hadn't shown him any permits. They were too busy shouting about the delay.

"Hurry it up!" yelled an angry woman with leopard spots along her arms.

"Keep it moving!" others chimed in.

"Shut it!" the crossing guard shouted back. "I've been here two thousand years. You can wait five minutes!"

"Two thousand *years*?" I repeated incredulously.

"He was probably assigned the post as punishment for something he did in a past life," Miv explained.

At last, we reached the riverbank. I breathed a sigh of relief as my sandals sank into the sand. The shore's gray color was strange, but the tiny grains sliding between my toes didn't feel any different from walking on a beach. Then, from behind me, came the sound of grinding rocks.

"Uh, Pahua . . ." Miv said.

I turned to look and froze. The eagle statue's head had moved. It was staring straight at us! With the scrape of stone against stone, the eagle's wings slowly unfurled.

My stomach rolled over as we scrambled toward the first boat. The eagle leaped from its perch atop the pedestal, cutting a dark shape over us as it released a sharp cry. It sounded like a dozen birds shrieking at once.

A strange feeling sneaked beneath my skin. I fell to my knees in front of the boat and gripped the wooden hull. Zhong stumbled as well, gasping.

Behind us, panic erupted. Spiritfolk screamed and ran in all directions. The crossing guard dropped the stick of rice, all three faces shouting for order. When that didn't work, he began blowing desperately on his whistle. Everyone ignored him.

Overhead, the eagle made a second pass. Its mouth opened, revealing not just one tongue but nine. Each of them was a different color. The eagle let out another screech. Again, it sounded like multiple birds, but the sound was a different pitch this time.

I sucked in a breath as my arms and legs grew sluggish.

It was like being back in the Bamboo Nursery. My body felt heavy, and it was hard to think.

"Miv, what's happening?" My tongue was thick in my mouth, and it sounded more like *Miv, wahammy?* I swallowed and tried again, getting the words out right this time.

"Eagle demon." The cat spirit sounded strained, like his mouth wasn't working right, either. "Get in the boat." He flopped on my shoulder and stabbed his tiny claws into my neck.

The pain jolted me back into focus. With my teeth clenched, I tightened my grip on the hull. Somehow, I found the energy to get my leg over the edge and tumble inside. I landed on top of Zhong, who'd dragged herself in a second before me.

She grunted and probably would have shoved me off if she'd had the strength. Instead, I slid off her, mumbling, "Sorry, sorry," every time my elbow jabbed her ribs. Then I could do nothing but lie there for a few seconds, gasping for air. The eagle swooped over us once more.

"Cover your ears!" Miv ordered.

I tried, but it didn't completely block the sound of the eagle's third cry, in yet a different pitch. It must have been leading with a different tongue each time.

My body grew even heavier, like someone had stuffed rocks beneath my skin. Groaning from pain, I closed my clumsy fingers around the grip of my sword. It took a couple of tries, but the blade finally slid free of its sheath. This was one of those times when it was probably better to fight first and ask questions later. Beside me, Zhong seemed to agree, because she'd gotten her crossbow out of her backpack and was struggling to notch the bolt. (But then, Zhong's first reaction always seemed to be to fight.)

Even though it felt like I was carrying a hundred pounds on my back, I managed to get my body to sit up so I could see over the side of the boat. The Crossroads was pure mayhem. Shifters threw on their relics and fled, leaving behind carts and wagons. Market wares were scattered all over the place. Spiritfolk ran around with hands covering their ears. Others lay on the ground, moaning. The crossing guard was still frantically blowing his whistle, even though no one was listening. I couldn't see Aunt Chan or Choj. I hoped they'd gotten away safely.

The eagle was circling back around. Desperation gave me the strength to lean over the hull. With my palms flattened against the sandy bank, I gave a mighty shove. The small boat only moved an inch.

"Argh!" I shouted as I pushed harder.

Zhong threw herself into the space beside me, grunting as her body hit the wood a little too hard. Her arms flopped stiffly as she tried to help me. But, together, we managed to get the boat into the river.

Luckily, we didn't need to paddle—the boat seemed to know the way. I groped for my sword again. Zhong reached for her crossbow, which she'd somehow managed to load. I searched the chaos of the Crossroads, looking for anything or anyone who might help. But all I could make out were the other statues—the guardians who'd paid the price for allowing themselves to be tricked.

At that moment, I realized what was happening to us. With each eagle cry, we were being turned into stone. Once the count reached nine, we'd be dead.

Nearby, Miv lay on his side, unmoving except for his quick frantic breaths. Sweat broke out on Zhong's brow as she raised the crossbow, waiting for the eagle to get in range.

I struggled to my knees. My arms felt so heavy I could barely lift them.

The eagle swooped low over our boat. Its beak opened, the nine tongues a weird prism of colors. The bird only got out half a cry before I surged to my feet and swung my sword. At the same time, Zhong loosed her crossbow bolt.

The tip of my sword caught the eagle's foot, and the bolt sliced through a few stone feathers. All nine tongues screamed in fury before the eagle lifted higher into the air and cried a fourth note.

Zhong dropped the crossbow and collapsed onto her back, panting. She was turning gray. So was I, for that matter. My skin felt rough and dry. I held my sword tight and my stiffening fingers molded around the grip. I was still on my knees, but just barely.

We would never make it like this. What could I do? I squeezed my eyes shut.

I wasn't Shee Yee—he was a legendary hero. I was just an eleven-year-old kid. But I was also an eleven-year-old kid with a brother who needed saving, and I wasn't ready to give up yet.

Think brave thoughts, I told myself. I was a master hunter going after her greatest prey. I would be an elf assassin with perfect, deadly aim (an elf like from the Lord of the Rings, NOT Elf on the Shelf, which was creep city—*so* glad that wasn't a Hmong thing).

The eagle swooped through the clouds, circling high above us. I had to wait until the demon bird was closer, though I didn't think we'd survive another cry.

I sucked in as much air as I could, which was really hard when your body was petrifying. Then I shouted, "Hey, birdbrain! You're not an eagle. Flying up there where nothing can reach you? You're a chicken!"

The eagle's eyes flashed red as they fixed on me. I swallowed the words that bubbled up in my throat: *Just kidding, sorry. Go ahead and finish killing us now.*

With a rush of air, the eagle dove toward us. Then it flapped its huge wings and landed on the prow of our small boat. It looked even bigger up close.

It took all my strength to lift the sword. I honestly wasn't sure how I managed it. My heartbeat should have been pounding in my ears. Instead, it was slowing down.

The eagle demon spread its stone wings, red eyes gleaming like rubies. "Not tho brave now, are you, little thaman?"

It had a lisp. Talking with nine tongues probably wasn't easy.

Thanks to the size of the boat, the eagle was within reach of my sword. Now, if only I could get my arms to work.

"You're like a chicken that puffs up its feathers to look bigger," I said, gasping for each breath.

If an eagle could snarl, it definitely would have. Stone feathers rose around its chest as it opened its mouth again, tongues vibrating.

With a burst of strength, I swung my sword in a wide arc. Some inner power must have guided my hand, because the tip of the blade sliced through two of the eagle's tongues. The eagle screamed.

It was a painful discord of sound, like when I passed by the music room at school during orchestra rehearsal. Have you ever heard a bunch of sixth-graders with violins? Ow.

The eagle flapped wildly. It jumped up and down on the prow, making the boat dip. "Wretched thing! Wicked creature! How dare you?"

I had to use my sword like a cane to keep from falling over as the boat rocked beneath me. The two tongues had landed in front of me, one red and one violet. I gagged.

Stone feathers molted from the furious eagle. They shattered against the boat and sank into the red water. Then the demon bird paused, spying its missing appendages. "My tongth!"

I dove for them at the same time the eagle did. *Dove* might be too strong a word. I mostly just fell and let gravity do its thing. My fingers snatched up the tongues before the eagle could grab them. Then I rolled away, avoiding a vicious peck of its sharp beak.

I collided with the side of the boat and flung out my arm, holding the tongues over the water. "Stop or I'll drop them. They'll sink to the bottom, and you'll never get them back."

The eagle squawked furiously, hopping from talon to talon. "Give them to me! Give them to me, you loaththome urchin!"

I had expected the tongues to be slimy and disgusting. But they just felt like rocks. "You can have them back when you reverse whatever spell you cast on us."

Seven tongues shrieked in protest. "I'm the guardian of the Crothroadth. Did you think you could thlip path my notith? I thee all. You're no thpiritfolk. You're *thamanth*."

"So what? We need to get to the Spirit Realm. If you want your tongues back, turn us back to normal and let us go."

"Aagh, detheitful mortal." It flapped its wings, dislodging more feathers. With an angry shake of its head, it released a cry. The pitch was similar to the last one but softer.

Immediately, the gray began to fade from my skin. With each of its cries, this time in reverse, my body felt lighter. I could breathe easier. My skin returned to its normal tan color. Nearby, Miv and Zhong stirred.

"Now." The eagle demon spat out the word. "Give me my tongth, detethtable child."

"Deal's a deal," I said, and tossed its tongues at its feet. The eagle snatched them up with its beak. *Blegh.*

The tongues rejoined the other seven in a vibrant rainbow of colors inside the bird's gray mouth. Then the eagle lifted off from the bottom of the boat and hovered over us.

"Very well then, thamanling. Go to the Thpirit Realm. You will find that a far worth fate awaith you there." With that, it swept around and returned to its pedestal at the Crossroads.

15

~

Death by Cursed Frog

 "I can't believe we're alive," Zhong said. She was sitting up and flexing her fingers like they were still a little stiff.

"Me neither," I said, fanning my face.

"That was pretty smart, Pahua," Miv said, who climbed onto my shoulder only to drape bonelessly against my neck. He had the nerve to sound surprised after I'd just saved our lives.

"See?" I said to Zhong, exhausted but thrumming with relief. "We don't have to kill everything that attacks us. We can survive by bargaining with something they want. We just have to figure out what that is."

Zhong rolled her eyes. "I'd rather bargain with my sword."

"Is that what they teach you at your fancy school?" I asked as Zhong began rummaging through her backpack.

Her ears turned pink just as Miv said, "Put your masks on."

Up ahead, the river was taking us toward the mouth of a tunnel. Zhong found her mask quickly. Getting to mine was a little awkward with my cloak in the way. But I managed to shrug off my backpack and dig it out.

The mask wasn't the kind you could get at a Halloween specialty store. The material was simple red cotton and looked like the cut-off hood of a sweater, except instead of going over the back of your head, it went over the front and hung loosely over your face. With the mask on, I couldn't see a thing, so I occasionally cheated and lifted it to peek out.

"They teach us a lot of things," Zhong finally answered me. She'd shifted on the boat so that we were sitting next to each other. "History, magic, spiritual tools, that kind of stuff. Fighting just happens to be what I'm good at."

"And you're not good at that other stuff?" I asked. I hadn't seen her do any shaman magic, aside from using her qeej to open the gateway into the Echo. While I was curious, I also wanted to keep talking to fill the uneasy quiet. We'd entered the tunnel, and the walls gleamed with clusters of crystals that gave off an eerie red light.

"I know what my strengths are," Zhong said, sounding defensive.

"I'm not very good at much, either."

She scoffed, which surprised me. But then I remembered that she was probably thinking about how I was Shee Yee, and he was supposedly the best at everything to do with shaman warriors.

She surprised me again by saying, "You're good at some things." She said it grudgingly, though, which made Miv hiss at her. I ran my fingers along his soft fur as she continued. "You did just save us from the guardian of the Crossroads."

Even though she was complimenting me, she sounded angry about it. Almost like she was . . . jealous? But that couldn't be right. Zhong was an amazing shaman-warrior-in-training on a quest to earn the approval of her school's guardian spirit.

"Thanks?" I mumbled, uncertain.

"But sometimes, the only solution *is* to fight," she insisted. "Like against the poj ntxoog."

"We did manage to get away from them. But I know what you're saying." I drew my shaman sword from the scabbard. "It might be a good idea to learn how to use a weapon properly." I lifted my mask to inspect the new nicks and dents in the blade. I didn't even want to think about what my mom would do to me when she saw its condition. "Will you teach me? What if we're in another life-or-death situation, and my Shee Yee Fighting Skills file doesn't open?"

"Shee Yee Fighting Skills file?" She sounded amused.

My face grew warm. "I've been thinking of it like I'm plugging into Shee Yee's backup files. Or . . . I don't know. Like I'm downloading a 'how to fight' guide straight to my brain. It's hard to explain."

"I guess I see your point. This boat is too small to allow us to do much, but if we get a chance, I'll show you a few moves." She pulled up her mask and frowned at the way I was clutching my sword tightly with both hands. "Here, hold it like this." She withdrew her own sword to demonstrate. "One hand, so you can swing it with your wrist. And your grip has to be just right—if you hold it too tight or too loose, your palm will blister."

I copied her, swishing the sword around until she nodded in approval.

"Once you can sense your spiritual energy, you'll need to learn how to control it by focusing it toward a single part of your body—usually your hands. That's the foundation for most shaman magic. The easiest way to practice this is by using a spiritual tool, like your sword, to hold the energy." She held up her sword, and the symbols on her blade began to glow.

I bit my lip and nodded. "I'll keep practicing."

Our boat glided so smoothly through the river that it barely felt like we were moving. But we were going fast, easily passing the slower elephant guides. I couldn't help lifting the edge of my mask even higher to check one out as we sailed by. It was the size of a house. Like the altar spirit back home, this elephant had twelve tusks, but these were each as long as a grown man's height. It was definitely an animal you wouldn't want to make angry.

The spirit riding on its back was a girl, maybe Matt's age.

She had a dark tangle of hair and sad eyes that made me think of the bridge ghost. My fists clenched as I thought of whatever she might have done with Matt's soul.

"Put that down." Miv batted at my hand, and the mask fell back into place. "If the elephant notices you're not dead, it might try to kill you to fix the problem."

"Being alive isn't a problem."

"It is for mortals trying to enter the Spirit Realm."

Hard to argue with that. For such big animals, the elephants didn't make a sound. And whatever liquid the river was made of, it didn't act like water. It didn't slosh against the side of the boat or spray our clothes. It smelled a little like incense, and when I dipped one finger into the red water, it didn't even feel wet. All that happened was a slight tugging sensation, like the river was a drain trying to suck me down. I quickly withdrew my hand.

"We're getting close now," Miv murmured. "You should put your gloves on."

I'd stuffed them into the side pocket on my backpack. Now I pulled them out and slipped them over my hands. Zhong scooted a little closer to me. Maybe with her mask on she couldn't tell that her backpack was already digging into my shoulder. Or, I realized suddenly, maybe she was just as scared as I was.

That was as difficult to imagine as Zhong being jealous of me. She was one of the bravest people I'd ever met. She'd rushed into fights with demons and dragons without hesitation. Even though she was only here because she needed to complete her quest, I wouldn't have gotten this far without her. Actually, without her I'd probably already be dead, considering the poj ntxoog I'd summoned with the gong.

A rushing sound interrupted the silence, growing louder and louder. I lifted my mask to see what it was. Zhong did the same. Up ahead, a waterfall spilled red liquid over the mouth of a tunnel that was large enough to fit several elephants.

Where the waterfall poured into the river, the surface remained smooth and undisturbed. It reminded me of the mirror pool in Ntuj's garden. Maybe that hadn't been real water, either.

I dropped the mask over my face again. The roar of the waterfall was the only sound. My heart sped up. Without thinking, I reached over and linked my arm with Zhong's.

I expected her to shove me away, but she didn't. Instead, her arm tightened around mine. Despite how scary all of this was, I couldn't help feeling comforted. Like having Miv on my shoulder, knowing Zhong was beside me made me feel a little braver.

We sat perfectly still and waited as our boat reached the waterfall. With a jolt, I felt the strange liquid rush over my head. It didn't soak through my hair or clothes.

But it did feel cold—the kind of chill that steals your breath. Frost spread across my skin. Zhong and I pressed closer, both seeking any kind of warmth.

The string Zhong had tied around my wrist began to vibrate. It felt . . . fragile, somehow, like it was about to snap. I slapped my hand over it. That probably wouldn't help, but I didn't know what else to do.

Then, all at once, it was over. We were through!

With a gasp, I flopped onto my back, shivering even through my cloak. Frost crystals fell from my hair and clothes. Without the gloves, would I have even made it? The thought chilled me even more.

Then the bottom of our boat scraped land, and I bolted upright again. Flipping up the edge of my mask, I saw that we had reached a grassy shore. A slope rose before us, beneath thick white clouds. Ghostly elephants and spiritfolk had formed a winding line in the large space. Skinny trees and low shrubs created aisles for those who were waiting, like the velvet-rope dividers that theaters put up when a big movie is out.

Sheer cliffs enclosed us on all sides. I didn't like the feeling of being trapped.

"Where are we?" I asked. "Is this the Spirit Realm?"

Miv jumped onto the shore first. "It's like the Spirit Realm's waiting room."

As soon as we left the boat, it slid back into the river. Then it sank beneath the surface with barely a ripple. My guess was it would return to the bank of the Crossroads, ready to be used by its next passengers. Hopefully, they'd have an easier time than we did.

Miv yelled at me to drop my mask and then told us to follow his voice. I tripped over him twice. Zhong had to hold on to the back of my cloak. When Miv announced that we'd reached the back of the line, I peeked underneath my mask and almost leaped onto Zhong. I was looking straight up at an elephant's behind. Its tail swished and nearly poked out my eye.

I took a big step backward and didn't care when Zhong elbowed me for stepping on her foot.

I quickly learned, though, that standing behind a guardian elephant isn't so bad. For one, they don't smell. I don't know what real elephants smell like, but it can't be great. And two, no one could see when I lifted my mask. Unfortunately, that also meant I couldn't tell where this line was taking us, especially since we were at the bottom of a hill. I could hear a strange sucking sound nearby, though, like water going down a drain, which made me nervous.

Slowly, we followed the winding line back and forth up the slope until the ground began to level out. If it always took this long to reach the Spirit Realm, no wonder some human spirits chose to just stick around in the mortal realm. As we waited, I tried to relax by attempting to sense my spiritual energy, but Zhong was right that I'd need a lot of practice, because all I could feel was my stuffy breath inside my mask.

How much time had passed since we'd arrived at the

Crossroads? What was happening to Matt while we stood here waiting? Was he even aware that his soul had been stolen, or was he unconscious in this realm, too? The selfish part of me hoped it was the former so that by the time I rescued him, he would have learned that all the spirits I spoke to were real. But the protective part of me wanted it to be the latter so he wouldn't ever have to know how much danger he was in.

Once I figured we were near the front of the line, I lifted my mask again and peered around the elephant to see what awaited us.

The cliffs we'd seen when we arrived were encircling a large pond. It looked like normal water this time, but it was hard to be sure. All I could tell was that it wasn't red, and it swirled a lot, like it was being stirred with a giant invisible spatula. Water lilies gathered at the edges, where the pond met the granite wall. In one wall, there was a tunnel half-submerged by water. Light shone through it, which meant it was our only way out of here.

A flat rock jutted out at the far-right end of the pond, and on it sat the biggest frog I'd ever seen—the size of a horse. The creature was slick and green, with eyes like enormous marbles. On a smaller rock beside it sat a toad, not as big, with spotted brown skin and warts. The toad sported a hat like the kind mall security guards wear. In their webbed fingers was a leafy tree branch.

"Hurry it up!" The toad whacked the frog's rock with the branch. Leaves flew off in all directions. "The queue is getting backed up."

The frog grumbled unhappily. Then they lowered their head to the water to take a drink. Or at least I thought they were taking a drink. Instead, the frog began to suck up the water like a vacuum. My eyes went huge as the frog inflated the more they drank, until I was sure they had to be the realm's biggest water balloon. Before long, they had guzzled all the water in the pond, leaving behind a muddy crater and a slick stone path that led directly to the unobstructed tunnel entrance.

"Now that's funny," Miv said with a dark laugh.

The frog must've had super hearing, because their marble eyes rolled until they found the cat spirit. I imagined the angry frog spitting the pond scum at him, and us, like a giant water cannon.

"Don't laugh," Zhong said, slapping at the cat spirit. She'd lifted her mask, too, so she could see what was going on. Miv moved too quickly, though, and she hit my shoulder instead. "Don't you know the story?"

"Okay, move it, move it, move it!" the toad shouted in a deep, croaky voice.

Five elephant guides and a few spiritfolk hurried across the muddy bottom of the pond. The frog, now the size of a pond itself, watched their progress. Their stomach was stretched to bursting. A long, thin line cut across the frog's stomach, like an old scar.

"What's the story?" I asked.

I could tell by the way Zhong's chin lifted that she was going to use her *I know more things than you* voice. Funny thing, though? I didn't mind it so much anymore.

"The shape-shifter goddess, Nhia Ngao Zhua Pa, likes to trick mortal men into falling in love with her. She usually targets terrible, shallow boys who think girls are only good for being wives, so I never really feel bad for them."

"Ooh, ooh, I like this story!" called an old woman with two fox tails and fluffy ears. She was two elephants behind us in line. "Tell it louder, dear!"

Zhong stood a little straighter. Even though she'd let the mask cover her face again, I knew she was smiling underneath. Attention usually made me want to shrink into myself and wish I was invisible. Zhong was the opposite—she knew she had skills, and she liked it when people noticed.

"Once, Nhia Ngao Zhua Pa disguised herself as a beautiful mortal maiden. She waited on the side of a dirt path, pretending to be lost and hungry, until a young man passed by and took pity on her by giving her a meal and a place to sleep. To repay his kindness, she offered to help him harvest his fields. She amazed him by clearing an entire field of rice with nothing but a small sickle in the time it took a single incense stick to burn."

"It's a knife in my mom's version," the fox woman muttered loudly to a man standing behind her.

Zhong continued as if she hadn't been interrupted. "The man decided to make her his wife. But on the day of their wedding, the bride didn't show up for the ceremony. The goddess had instructed one of her servants to claim that Nhia Ngao Zhua Pa was the daughter of a dragon and had been taken to the bottom of a lake."

"My mom tells it with a river," the fox woman mumbled.

"Anyway," Zhong said pointedly, "she'd wanted the groom to dive in after her and drown. But instead, he sat on the shore, crying, as he truly believed that his bride had been abducted. A frog overheard the man's laments and offered to help him rescue her by drinking all the water in the lake. It gave the man one warning—'Do not laugh'—and the grateful groom swore he wouldn't."

"Let me guess," I said. "He broke his word."

"Shh, don't ruin it!" the fox woman hissed.

"As the frog slurped up the water, it grew so big that the man couldn't help but laugh. The poor creature's stomach burst open, and all the lake water flooded back out. Fortunately, the frog survived, and when the man pleaded once more for help, the creature's kind heart couldn't refuse him. So the man sewed up its stomach and the frog drained the lake a second time, revealing Nhia Ngao Zhua Pa at the bottom."

I thought about the scar I'd seen on the frog's stomach and winced.

"The goddess was furious with the frog for interfering. In punishment, she cursed it to be stuck here forever, forced to repeat its act of kindness over and over."

"So tragic," the fox woman whispered, looking way too happy about it.

I'd never liked sad stories. I'd always thought of books, TV shows, and movies as like playing pretend. They were supposed to be better than real life, weren't they? Otherwise, what was the point?

"Looks like the goddess is punishing everyone else, too, by making the spiritfolk wait for the frog," I said. Nhia Ngao Zhua Pa had a cruel sense of humor. It was probably best not to say that out loud, though, in case any of her underlings were around. The gods already hated me for being Shee Yee's reincarnation. Insulting them on top of that wouldn't get me on their good side.

As soon as the last elephant disappeared into the tunnel, the frog's mouth opened. All the pond water gushed out in a crushing wave of algae, fish, and mud.

"Gross," I said. I dropped the mask over my face and pinched the fabric over my nose.

The process repeated several more times until, at last, we were in the group that would go through the tunnel next. The frog dipped their head to the pond and began vacuuming up the water again. Their stomach ballooned and stretched and looked so ridiculous up close that it was kind of funny. I bit the inside of my cheek to keep from laughing.

It wasn't the frog's fault. They had only wanted to help someone, and now they were cursed for all time. Harsh.

Once the pond was cleared, the toad shouted, "Okay, folks, keep it moving!"

Miv returned to my shoulder to avoid getting his paws muddy. We hurried across, stepping from stone to stone. They were slippery, so we couldn't move as fast as the elephants. I was paranoid of getting trampled, especially since I could barely see. I had to keep lifting the edge of my mask to make sure I wasn't about to step into a mud puddle.

I heard Zhong mumbling something in Hmong. She was having the same trouble I was. When I glanced over at her, though, I noticed something behind her. At the far left end of the pond, almost hidden in the muck and mud, there was a hole in the side of the cliff, like the narrow mouth of a cave. It led into pure blackness.

"What is that?" I asked, nudging Miv.

Miv's small body stiffened against my shoulder. "I'm not sure, but I've heard there are tunnels beneath the Spirit Realm. Probably a good way to get lost for all eternity."

"Hurry it up!" shouted the toad.

We'd somehow ended up at the rear of the group, and we were only halfway across. The elephants and other spiritfolk were quickly leaving us behind.

"I can't see with this stupid mask on," Zhong said, holding it up over her face so that one eye was visible.

The toad began to smack their branch furiously against the rock. I couldn't move any faster, though. My sandals kept slipping on the algae-covered stones. Then the toad started hopping and looking frantically between us and the frog, whose stomach had begun to tremble.

"Forget this." I ripped off my mask and started running, but it was too late.

Unable to hold in the water any longer, the frog opened their mouth. Water poured out, throwing up mud and plants. All of it rushed toward us in a terrifying wall of frog-flavored destruction.

Please don't fall, please don't fall, I thought as Zhong and I sprinted across the stones. But we had no chance of withstanding the torrent.

Scummy pond water crashed over us, taking my feet out from under me. Miv clawed at my shoulder to avoid getting swept away. I barely even noticed, because I was too busy being terrified. I didn't know up from down as the waves battered me from all sides. My cloak tangled around my legs, pinning them together.

This was it—I was going to drown in frog backwash. It just figured.

16

~

If There's a Booby Trap,
It's an Evil Lair

 My back slammed into something solid and rocky. Pain lit through me, but my hands found a jut of stone. I clung to it as tightly as my cold fingers could manage.

Someone grabbed me under the armpits and tugged. My head surfaced, and I wheezed in air. Lungs burning, I collapsed onto dry ground.

"Pahua!" Miv pounced on my face as I lay there.

"Agh!" I shouted, rolling over to make him fall off. Being suffocated by a wet cat doused in frog drool on top of nearly drowning is *not* my idea of fun. After a couple of tries, I managed to get my arms free of my sopping cloak, and I flung them limply over my head as I caught my breath. Squinting in the gloom, I saw that we were in some kind of cave. My mask was long gone, washed away with the pond debris.

Miv held out his front paws and looked at them with

disgust. "This is so gross. I don't even want to clean myself right now."

"Wiping . . . saliva . . . on your fur," I gasped out. "Already gross."

He glared at me. But I could barely see his eyes through the wet strands of hair plastered over my face. I pushed the streaming mess from my eyes, patted my head to make sure my hair clip was still in place, and then tried to look around.

It was too dark to see much. Only the dimmest of light came from the opening behind us, where the pond water still sloshed.

Zhong, who must have been the one who'd pulled me to safety, was sprawled on her back beside me. Her mask was missing as well. I nudged her foot to make sure she wasn't dead. She turned her head to squint daggers at me. Not dead, then.

"Thanks," I said sincerely. "I can't swim."

"It was my turn," she said, sounding exhausted.

If I thought about it too hard, it was pretty disturbing how many times we'd almost died today. I untied my cloak, grateful that it hadn't choked me in the water, and dropped it at my feet. I removed my gloves and backpack next and then wrung out the hem of my dress.

"Where are we?" Zhong sat up, wiping her eyes. She shrugged off her backpack and gave it a good shake.

"Nowhere good," Miv said.

Our voices didn't echo, so we couldn't be in too big a

space. I could make out the rocky ceiling overhead but not much else. I gulped loudly.

"Can we go back?" I pointed to the underwater entrance. I startled when the water began to quickly recede, allowing in more light. The frog was drinking up the pond again. "We can make a run for it."

Miv shook his small head. "We're still too far from the tunnel. I'm afraid we'd never make it in time before that ridiculous frog released the water. We'd either get swept right back in here or smashed against the cliff."

Frustrated, I rubbed both hands down my face and then gagged, because my hands smelled like frog, too.

Zhong opened her backpack and rummaged inside to check the contents. I frowned.

"How are your things still dry?" I asked. I gathered my hair around my hands and squeezed. Thick streams of water splattered the stone.

"Waterproof spell." She lifted one shoulder, a little embarrassed. "My roommate is friends with a water spirit, and she owed me a favor. We're technically not supposed to interact with that kind of spirit until we start venturing into Zaj Teb, where most of the realm is underwater."

"That sounds cool. Maybe my uncle will let me visit it someday—if he and the other gods stop trying to kill me, that is. And I guess I should learn how to swim first." I gestured to her backpack. "You wouldn't happen to have any spare masks in there, would you?"

"I do, but I doubt we'll need them. Those were just for the elephant guides. We'll have to keep a low profile, though, to avoid any henchmen the gods have sent to look for you."

To my surprise, Zhong pulled out a flashlight and flicked it on. That girl had left her school seriously prepared, and I could have hugged her for it. The light illuminated the dark maw of a tunnel, large enough for a few people to walk through. Besides the watery entrance, there was nothing else around us but dusty gray stone.

Somehow, our narrow beam of light only made the darkness beyond our small circle seem even more ominous. I inched a little closer to Miv.

Fun fact #4 about me: I'm afraid of the dark. Which I know sounds dumb, but remember, I can see spirits. I know what sorts of things tend to hide in the shadows.

"There's another way out of here, right?" I asked Miv.

He gave me a look like *How should I know?* But out loud, he said, "Y-y-yes?" He didn't sound very confident. "There has to be."

"Ugh, why do these things keep happening to us?" I said, tugging at my soaked dress. At this rate, I would never find the ax or my brother in time. I wanted to kick a rock, but I couldn't see any in the dim light.

"Well, there's no way but forward." Zhong smoothed her short, wet hair away from her face.

We took a few minutes to assess ourselves for any injuries. Miraculously, we were all generally okay. My backpack was soaked, but my granola bars and ramen packets were in a plastic bag, so those were fine. Even Aunt Chan's rice sticks seemed okay. Banana leaves were no joke. The bad news? My phone, which wasn't waterproof, was completely dead. My mom was so going to kill me when she found out.

I wrung out my cloak and then put it back on. It wouldn't keep me warm, but it also wouldn't dry if I stuffed it into my backpack with my gloves.

When we were ready, we set off into the darkness. I might have stuck a little too closely to Zhong's side, because she elbowed me. But I couldn't help it. This place was like a tomb. There weren't even any nature spirits down here— everything was dead or abandoned. The only positive was that it wasn't wet or cold, so at least we didn't have to worry about dying of hypothermia.

The smell down here was a little moldy, though, and a lot frog-breath-y. Fortunately, the stench faded the farther we traveled.

"Shouldn't we have come across a door or an exit sign by now?" I asked.

Something brushed the top of my head. I shrieked and dropped into a crouch, hands covering my hair. Miv yowled, and Zhong drew her sword.

After a tense moment, during which nothing leaped out of the darkness to eat me, Miv smacked my cheek with a wet paw.

"It was just a root," he said, annoyed.

Embarrassed, I straightened. Tugging at my damp dress, I peered up at the ceiling. Roots and bits of earth had broken through the stone and dangled low over our heads.

"That's a good sign," Miv said. "It means we're getting closer to the surface."

We continued. My hands felt restless, and my back kept itching like we were being watched. I knew it was just my imagination, but I couldn't wait to get out of there. I reached up and unclasped my hair clip. Holding the familiar shape helped calm me a little. Zhong glanced over as I clipped it back in place above my ear.

"What's with the hair clip?" she asked.

"What do you mean?"

"You keep touching it like you're afraid to lose it."

"Because I am. My mom gave it to me."

She pointed to the front of her jean jacket. It was too dark to see the pins clearly, but she said, "I get it. Most of these are from the school, but a couple are from my parents. It would suck to lose them."

I wondered if that was another dig about me losing her pins in the Bamboo Nursery, but she didn't sound mad or anything. That was the first time she'd mentioned her family, though.

"What do your parents think about this whole shaman-warrior thing?" I asked.

When she answered, her voice was quiet. "I don't see them a ton, but we do get two-week breaks every three months to go home."

"Do you miss them?"

"You get used to it. My sister goes to the school, too, so I get to see them when they visit her."

It was strange how she'd worded that—when her parents visited her sister, not when they visited *her*.

"That's cool that you have an older sister at the same school. Shaman-warrior siblings. Is that normal?" I wondered if Matt was a typical mortal or if he had any hidden abilities, too.

"We're not very close," she said quickly. "And no, that's not normal, but my family has pretty strong spiritual energy."

I couldn't imagine not being close to Matt, although that might have been because I had to watch him all the time. Once I got him back, I would let him pick out everything we watched for the next year, even if it was *Spirited Away* on repeat.

The ability to become a shaman wasn't an inherited thing, according to my mom. It wasn't about your blood—it was about your spirit. For Zhong's family to have numerous shaman warriors in it was pretty impressive.

"Are your parents shaman warriors, too?"

"My dad is." Her voice was devoid of any enthusiasm.

"But he doesn't work for your school?"

"He's a graphic designer. The shaman-warrior thing is just part-time for him, though Dad is good enough that he could be a mentor at the school if he wanted."

"My aunt is a shaman," I said.

"You said that before. Does she know you can see spirits?"

I shook my head. "I've never told anyone but Matt. Although . . ." I frowned and looked at her. She was holding out the flashlight, her face cast in shadows. "Can I ask you something?"

"You're always asking me something," she said.

I took that as a yes. "My mom and aunt used to argue a lot—I'm not sure what about, but sometimes I overheard my name. One time my mom was so mad that she told her own sister to get out of the house." I frowned into the darkness. "Do you think they know that I'm, you know, Shee Yee's reincarnation?"

"I should have listened in on their fights," Miv mused, sounding less like he was sympathetic and more like he was sad to have missed out on juicy gossip. "But there's always something more interesting happening than mortals bickering."

I poked him with one finger, which he pretended to bite.

"I doubt they know," Zhong said, answering me. "Unless you're an oracle like Shao, there's no way to tell who a person was in a past life without performing a special ritual, and the shaman doing it would need to have really strong spiritual energy. At most, your aunt probably knew you were meant to be a shaman. That would've been easy enough to find out with some divination."

"But I don't know why my mom would get so mad about that. . . ."

"Why don't you just ask her?"

I wrinkled my nose. "We don't talk about that kind of stuff." Mom wasn't home enough for us to talk about much besides what we did that day. Also, she'd been through a lot with Dad leaving and then our moving away from the Hmong community. I felt guilty asking questions that made her think about those things. "She works a lot to take care of me and Matt. I don't like making her sad."

Zhong sucked in her cheeks, like she was annoyed, but I didn't know what I'd said wrong. She didn't explain, either. She just said, "What about your dad?"

My shoulders climbed up to my ears, and I mumbled, "He's not around anymore."

Miv shoved his paws against my neck so I'd relax and stop squishing him. Luckily, Zhong got the hint that I didn't want to talk about my dad and she fell silent.

When she'd said her dad was a graphic designer, it had made something jump in my stomach. Mine had been an artist as well, and he'd had a big imagination.

Back before I'd learned that having an invisible friend wasn't normal, I used to talk about Miv with him. Dad would draw little pictures of us, like me on a tire swing with a black kitten in my lap, or me reading in bed with a black kitten curled on top of my head. I'd loved the drawings so much. I'm not sure what happened to them after we moved.

Zhong and I walked on for another few minutes before we came across anything, and it was the worst thing possible—a fork. Two dark tunnels split in different directions, and neither looked very welcoming.

"The left one is bigger," I said. Maybe it was a trick of the shadows, since our only light was Zhong's flashlight, but it did look wider. I really didn't want to have to squeeze through the smaller right tunnel. It would feel even more like we were being buried alive. No thanks.

Miv cocked his head. "I vote for the right."

I rolled my eyes. Smaller spaces didn't bother him—he was the size of a cereal bowl. Not to mention that cats, including the spirit variety, are made of Jell-O and can squeeze through just about anything.

"I think Pahua is right, actually," Zhong said. She squinted into the tunnels and flicked her flashlight back and forth.

"No," Miv said. "The right one is the right path. Right is right."

"Have you been here before?" I asked.

"Of course not. But my gut tells me I'm right."

"Your gut also tells you to spread spit on your face, so it probably shouldn't be making decisions for us," I said. "It's two against one. We're going left."

Miv huffed and stuck his little nose in the air. "Yes, let's listen to the two children over the wise and powerful cat spirit. That'll end well."

The walls in the left tunnel were dry and musty, and the roots had disappeared from the ceiling. That worried me. The farther we walked without any sign of an exit, the more anxious I became that we'd gone the wrong way.

"At least there aren't any booby traps," I said.

Zhong frowned and gave the stone walls a wary look, like she hadn't considered until now that spikes might start growing out of them. "Why would there be booby traps?"

"I don't know. Isn't that what always happens in movies? The heroes find a mysterious tunnel and walk into a bunch of booby traps because it turns out to be the villain's evil lair."

Zhong sneered, her shoulders relaxing. "I really don't think the bridge spirit has an evil lair. She was stuck in the mortal realm for however many years? That wouldn't even make sense. And anyway, an evil lair shouldn't be so easy to"—she froze, her eyes going big—"find."

Her flashlight shone on an engraving in the stone. She swiped the light in a wide arc to reveal that the walls and ceiling of the tunnel ahead were completely covered in elephant-head designs. Not only that, but every single one had two sharp stone tusks poking out of it.

"Is this what a booby trap looks like?" Miv said.

I gulped. "Maybe we should have taken the other path."

Even though I was already turning around, Zhong moved forward, looking fascinated. "What is this place?"

Since she had the flashlight, and I didn't want to stand in a pool of growing darkness, I sighed and followed her. She ran her finger over the smooth grooves that formed an elephant's ear and then down the length of one tusk. I had to admit, the images were kind of awesome in a really eerie way. Who had created them? And why were they here, hidden beneath the Spirit Realm?

"Someone is way too obsessed with elephants and sharp pointy things," I observed. We had to step carefully to avoid getting jabbed by a tusk. But the ones sticking down from the ceiling made me especially nervous.

Then I felt something. It began as a cold lump in my stomach. I edged away from Miv and Zhong, taking slow steps into the gloom. The cold lump grew heavier, filling me with ice and the absolute certainty that something was waiting for me ahead. Something very old and very angry.

"Pahua?" Miv asked from behind me. I'd left the circle of light.

Spinning on my heel, I hurried back. "Do you guys feel that?" I whispered.

"Kind of?" Zhong pulled herself away from the engravings. She rubbed her stomach, looking a little unnerved. "It's uncomfortable."

No, it was *unbearable.* Even though she was a shaman warrior's apprentice, it seemed I was more sensitive to spiritual energy than she was. That explained why she couldn't see Miv in the mortal realm and why she couldn't feel the bridge spirit's presence the way I could.

"She's here," I breathed into the silence. My heart raced with fear, and goose bumps rose on my arms. I pulled my still-damp cloak tighter around me.

"Are you sure?" Zhong asked, reaching for her sword.

Then my whole body stiffened as I realized something. "If the bridge spirit is here, then so is my brother's soul."

Without thinking it through, I drew my sword and charged into the darkness. Miv pounced on my head and dug his claws into my scalp.

"Ow!" I shouted. I reached up to pull him off, but Miv had already retracted his nails. "What's your problem?"

"You're not ready to face her yet." He jumped out of reach before I could strangle him.

"But Matt—" I gasped as the weight of the bridge spirit's presence suddenly intensified. A shock of cold swept through me, prickling my skin like a thousand tiny needles. My knees almost folded. Instead, I bent over, sucking air into my seizing lungs.

Zhong swayed on her feet and nearly fell into the stone tusks. "What *is* that?" she whispered, sounding horrified.

"She's too strong." Somehow, she'd grown even more powerful since leaving the mortal realm.

How was I going to beat *this*? For my brother's sake and the sake of all the other kids she had stolen, I knew I'd have to try. But right now, as the spirit's power tried to wrench me to my knees, I also knew I'd fail.

"Matt . . ."

Miv latched onto the hem of my cloak, digging his claws into the cloth to hang there like a scruffy Christmas ornament. "He still has time."

"Less than three days," I said through my teeth. I stabbed my sword into the ground to steady myself before I backed up through the tunnel. I could barely stand.

Things couldn't get any worse. I scrubbed my hands through my hair. Then I winced, because even though it was mostly dry now, it was tangled and felt clumpy and sticky.

I needed Shee Yee's lightning ax. It was my only chance. If I tried to face the bridge spirit now, it would be a massacre. Of me.

Suddenly, a blast of wind shot down the corridor. Zhong and I flinched and threw up our hands to shield our faces against the rock dust. I tugged my cloak over my nose and mouth, even though the sour, scummy pond-frog smell made me want to set it on fire.

A soft, girly voice echoed all around us. "Have you come to stay with me?"

"We need to get out of here," Miv said.

Zhong's voice shook. "No kidding."

I sheathed my sword. Then we turned and rushed back the way we'd come.

"Where are you going?" the voice asked, pitched higher

with what almost sounded like panic. A chorus of other childlike voices suddenly joined her, quieter but just as chilling. "Don't leave us. Come back. Come back!"

I stumbled, my feet stalling. "Matt," I whispered. I had begun to turn toward the voices when Miv yowled for me to keep moving. Gritting my teeth, I obeyed. *Hold on, Matt. I promise I'll come back for you.*

The combined voices grew louder with each word. The tunnel began to rumble around us. "Stay with me," the bridge spirit called. "Stay with me! *Stay with me!*"

The ground shook. I gasped as a stone tusk broke from the ceiling and impaled the exact spot where I'd been about to step. For a second, I could only stare at it, shocked at how close I'd come to losing my foot.

Then Miv detached himself from my cloak and shouted, "Keep going!"

Zhong grabbed my arm, and we started to run. More tusks fell, nearly spearing us.

"Come back!" wailed the bridge spirit. *"Come back right now!"*

I gasped as a tusk caught the tail of my cloak. It pinned the cloth to the ground like a thumbnail through paper, jerking me backward. For a heartbeat, I thought about throwing off the cloak and leaving it behind. But I couldn't—my mom had made it for me. So I bunched my fingers around the cloth and ripped it free. The tearing sound was swallowed by the rumble of rocks and earth.

Soon, we reached the plain stone walls of the tunnel, and the bridge spirit's voice faded. All around us, the earth went still.

With a deep breath, I collapsed against the wall. My hands trembled. I buried them in the cloak.

"Well," Zhong said. She sounded unsteady, too. "At least we know where to find her once we've got that ax."

I nodded. My stomach wanted to heave at the idea of my brother's spirit stuck down here with her. But I couldn't face her yet. If I tried, we would all die, and that wasn't going to help anyone. "I'm ready to get out of here. Come on."

We traveled the rest of the way back to the fork in silence, all of us caught up in our own dark thoughts.

"Please let this one lead us out," I said as we squeezed single file into the smaller tunnel.

Within minutes, I knew we were on the right path. The roots over our heads grew thicker, crawling down the walls. They reminded me of snakes, but they were a lot better than sharp elephant tusks. After some time, the ground began to slope upward.

At last, light glimmered ahead. Even though I was exhausted, I picked up my pace.

"Finally," Zhong murmured. "I'm pretty sure we've made it to the Spirit Realm."

The sun had just set and was now only a distant golden glow. Still, the last light of day shining through the exit felt glorious. The opening was only wide enough for one of us to crawl through at a time, so Miv went first, then Zhong. I climbed out last onto thick green grass. We'd emerged at the edge of a lush forest, which explained why there'd been so many roots underground.

I shut my eyes and drew in a deep, calming breath. We'd escaped the tunnels, and now that we were safe, we could plan our next steps toward rescuing my brother.

Just as I was about to exhale, Zhong slapped her hand over my mouth. I tried to push her away—we both really needed a bar of soap—but her grip only tightened. Then she whirled me around and pointed.

It was a good thing she had me muffled; otherwise, when I saw what she was motioning to, I would have screamed.

17

~

Running for Our Lives—A Theme

The beast wasn't as big as the elephant guides, but it was still terrifying. With a dark-brown coat and a wide snout, it should have looked harmless as it grazed, just your everyday water-buffalo spirit, but its eyes shone red in the deepening night. On top of that, instead of two large horns curling over its head, it had *six*.

It was close enough to where we'd emerged that any sudden movement on our part would attract its attention. And there were more buffalo foraging in the plain beyond or resting in the shallows of a muddy stream.

I had to bite my lip to keep from whimpering. Why were all the animals in the Spirit Realm so freakishly scary?

Miv jumped onto my shoulder without a sound. "Very slowly, very quietly," he whispered, "move into the forest."

Zhong and I backed away with measured steps. The water buffalo's tail twitched. I held my breath. Tall blades of grass tickled my ankles. My nose began to itch. I quickly reached up to pinch it closed, but the sneeze escaped before I could.

"Ah-choo!"

The water buffalo's head snapped up, ears twitching. Its nostrils flared as those vivid red eyes fixed on us.

"Oh, good," Miv said. "Now we get to run for our lives again."

With a furious huff, Zhong grabbed my wrist and yanked me around. My heart pounded in my ears as we shot through the grass into the forest, the sound of grunting and heavy hooves tearing through the earth behind us.

"Pahua, I could kill you!" Zhong shrieked, chancing a look over her shoulder.

Miv clung to the side of my neck, his claws digging into my skin. "Get in line! We might as well sell tickets."

"Can we focus, please?" I said as we weaved through the trees. I couldn't handle being terrified *and* annoyed at the same time.

As we ran, Zhong held the flashlight in one hand, but in her other, a strange white light began to form. It wasn't very steady, though. It was wavering and dim.

"What are you doing?" I asked, breathless.

"Condensing my spiritual energy into a shield." Then, to

my surprise, she spun on her heel and threw up her hand. I skidded to a stop as she surrounded us with a white glow. But just as quickly, it vanished. Her eyes widened as she tried to bring it back, light sparking from her fingers.

"Move!" I screamed, ramming into her. We crashed into some low ferns just as the water buffalo thundered past. The beast had been a heartbeat away from either trampling us or turning us into shaman kebabs.

"It's coming back around!" I yelled, pulling her to her feet.

"I had it!" she shouted. The beam of her flashlight wavered wildly as we darted in another direction.

"You really didn't!" I shouted back. It was becoming difficult to see in the twilight, and I nearly smacked my forehead on a low-hanging branch. Miv leaped from my shoulder and onto the tree.

"Climb!" he ordered as he darted nimbly into the shrouded branches.

He had a point. There was no way we were going to outrun that thing, so our best option was to escape upward. Zhong sprinted for the nearest tree.

As I spun away to do the same, I spotted something in the flattened underbrush. The creature looked like a tree spirit, but they were several inches larger than the ones I was used to seeing in the mortal realm. Curls of vine-like hair trailed out from beneath a cap of green moss. They rubbed their head with twiggy fingers, like they were dazed. Maybe the spirit had fallen from a branch when the water buffalo barreled through.

"Pahua!" Miv shouted from somewhere overhead.

The ground beneath me trembled as the beast closed the distance between us. Without thinking it through, I scooped up the tree spirit and draped them around my neck, hoping they would know to hold on, and lunged behind a tree trunk. The whole tree shuddered as the water buffalo's horns scraped past.

I was panting, and my heart felt like it was trapped in my throat as I quickly grabbed the nearest branch. My sandals slipped against the bark, but somehow I managed to haul myself upward just as the water buffalo turned again, its red eyes fixed on my pathetic attempt to climb a tree. My fingers fumbled, and I gasped as I nearly fell.

Now would have been a *great* time for Shee Yee's instincts to kick in, but it seemed I was on my own. The tree spirit was now wrapped around my head, snagging my hair with their sharp little knees and elbows. With another heave, I pulled the rest of my body onto the branch.

I rose unsteadily to my feet, holding on to the trunk to keep my balance, and made it several feet higher before the water buffalo paused beneath me. The massive spirit stomped its hooves, nostrils snorting and huffing. It waited for several long minutes, its red eyes like two hot coals.

Then, at last, the beast grew bored and turned to head back to the rest of its herd. Not today, Ferdinand!

~

Once we were certain the water-buffalo spirit wasn't coming back, I left the tree spirit in the branches and climbed down.

"We've only been in the Spirit Realm a few hours, and I'm already dreaming about leaving," Miv said, returning to his place on my shoulder. "Gods, I hate it here."

"It's usually not this bad," Zhong said. She jumped from her perch and landed nimbly, even with that giant backpack upsetting her balance. "Although I've never been here physically before, only through spiritual projection."

Now that the frenzy of panic and fear was past, I looked around at the thick forest, marveling that we had actually made it. We were in the Spirit Realm. Despite nearly being turned to stone, almost drowning in frog backwash, and then narrowly escaping death by horns, we were somehow alive and mostly unharmed.

I thought about Matt's soul trapped in that dark, stifling place underground, and a sick feeling yawned inside me. As amazing as it was to be here, we had a purpose, and we needed to get moving.

"That thing you did back there with your spiritual energy . . ." I said to Zhong. "What was that?"

"You mean that thing she *tried* to do that nearly got her impaled?" Miv asked.

"I was trying to form a shield," she muttered. Her voice was harsh, but that was probably due to embarrassment. "Shaman magic isn't . . . I'm not the best at it yet."

"Will I be able to do that once I figure out how to use my spiritual energy?" I asked, flexing my fingers in front of me and imagining a white glow.

"Probably," she snapped, stomping ahead.

I wasn't sure if she was mad at herself or me, but since she had the flashlight, I quickly followed. We headed deeper into the forest to put more space between us and the water-buffalo herd.

As we walked, I brushed dirt and leaves off my leggings and tried to untangle my cloak. After a time, Zhong found a spot for us to make camp. I wanted to keep moving, but I knew it was pointless. Without food and rest, we wouldn't be getting very far.

Miv scampered off into the darkening forest without a word. He always runs off at night. I don't think he sleeps. I would have said he doesn't eat, either, but he insists that he does. He just does it when he's alone. I imagined him chasing spirit mice through the weeds and criticizing their escape plans. *No, you dumb creature, go left. Your* other *left. Oh, never mind, just come here so I can eat you.*

Zhong must have learned how to build a fire at her super-exclusive shaman school, because she didn't have much trouble making one. Except for when she went looking for kindling and got pummeled by acorn-throwing mushroom spirits and whacked in the head by an angry tree spirit.

Like the one I'd rescued, the tree spirits here were different from those in the mortal realm. They had spindly arms and legs, with patches of moss at their knees and elbows and lichen sprouting from their shoulders or the sides of their heads. The one who hit Zhong had pine needles for hair so that they looked like a green hedgehog.

They were all variety of sizes as well. Some were small enough to cup in my palms, while others were taller than us—which actually wasn't that hard to be.

One of the larger tree spirits emerged from the trunk of a thick pine just as Zhong finished building our fire. My eyes went wide as the spirit approached, but they didn't seem hostile, just curious.

"Hello, strangers," they called in a soft, melodic voice. A bright-red flower grew from their head, right above their ear. Nestled in the petals sat a fat, fuzzy bumblebee, dusted with pollen.

Zhong scrambled to her feet, bowed politely, and introduced herself. I followed her example.

"I am Nplooj, queen of the nature spirits who call this forest their home," the tree spirit said. I wondered if the tree spirits back home had a leader as well, or if this was just a Spirit Realm thing. I decided I would find out when I returned with Matt safely by my side.

"Sorry about the kindling," Zhong said, gesturing at our fire. "We should have asked first."

Nplooj waved away the apology. A bracelet of woven red and blue flowers circled her wrist. "I know you don't mean the forest any harm. I was told that you saved one of us from the water buffalo."

I winced. "It was my fault in the first place."

"Even so," Nplooj said, "you have our thanks and our help, should you ever need it."

To prove her words, the tree spirit led us to a stream where we could wash off the stink from the frog's pond. We had to clean up quickly, though, because it was dark, which meant we wouldn't be able to see any water spirits sneaking up on us.

Zhong unearthed travel-size bottles of shampoo from her backpack. I was beginning to suspect that pack had more than just a waterproof spell on it.

We took turns at the stream. While Zhong was washing, I peeked inside her backpack. (Look, it wasn't one of my prouder moments, but I had to know.)

I almost fell in. Literally. It *was* spelled to be bigger on the inside. There were so many pockets and compartments that I didn't know how she kept everything straight. Plus, it weighed a ton. How had she been carrying this on her shoulders all day?

Sometime later, we sat around the fire chewing granola

bars, Aunt Chan's sweet rice, and ramen I cooked over the fire with a pot Zhong had pulled from her bottomless backpack. Fire spirits flickered around the flames. They looked like sparklers, the kind we lit on the Fourth of July, except with tiny arms and legs. Their long red tongues licked at the heat. Some of them launched embers at one another like flaming snowballs.

Zhong had brought extra clothes, because of course she had, and she loaned me a T-shirt dress while my own clothes dried nearby. I'd doused them in the stream.

"You okay?" she asked.

I'd been staring blankly at the fire spirits, thinking about what still lay ahead of us. I turned to her in surprise—had I heard her right?

For a second, she looked embarrassed. Then she shoved her nose in the air and asked, "What? I can't be concerned?"

Without my permission, my mouth curved into a smile. At some point between the Bamboo Nursery and our nearly getting gored by a water buffalo, I'd stopped thinking of Zhong as just an ally. Whether she agreed or not, we'd saved each other's lives too many times by this point to not be friends.

"I'll be better once we save Matt. What about you?"

"Fine," she said. "But that bridge spirit isn't going to be easy to defeat. Even after Shao said you were the only one who could take her on, I wasn't sure what to expect. She was just a mortal spirit before. . . . They never get that powerful."

"She did feel different from when I first met her. Way stronger."

Zhong stared at the fire, like she was mulling something over. "The souls of dead mortals are supposed to be met by an elephant guide when they cross between realms. But that doesn't seem to have happened with the bridge spirit."

"Do you think it's because of me? Because I'm the one who freed her?"

She shrugged one shoulder. "Maybe. Or maybe she's always been that strong, and you just didn't realize it. If she's able to resist the pull of the Tree of Souls and steal other mortal souls, she definitely isn't normal. And the fact you still want to face her is . . . well, it's brave of you. Not every shaman warrior would do the same."

The compliment warmed me almost as much as the fire, and she didn't sound upset this time. I must have misread her on the boat. She couldn't have been jealous of me—that would be ridiculous.

"I'm not brave," I said, rubbing my forehead to hide my embarrassment. "Not like you and Miv. But I don't have any choice. He's my brother."

A line appeared between her eyebrows as she tossed a twig into the flames. Then she pulled her knees to her chest and said, "That doesn't mean anything. Plenty of sisters wouldn't go this far for their siblings."

I recalled what she'd said about not being very close to

her sister. After a few seconds of listening to the nature spirits shuffling through the underbrush, I said gently, "Sometimes family means different things to people." To my dad, it had meant nothing, apparently.

She cast me a sidelong glance. I had no idea what she was thinking. Finally, she tucked her hair behind her ear and said, "We're going to beat that bridge spirit. I know we have a lot to do yet, and it probably won't be easy, but we *will* win."

Zhong trying to cheer me up was so weird that it almost worked. "Thanks."

It all seemed so impossible, though. By morning, we would only have two more days to get to the Tree of Souls, find the lightning ax, and hightail it back to the tunnel to save my brother. I wished the Sky Father hadn't made that stupid promise not to let Shee Yee be reincarnated. It meant we had to do everything alone when we really could have used the gods' help.

Zhong had to feel the same way. Our chances of winning were as likely as me sprouting wings. But she was still here with me, trying anyway. That counted for something.

As Zhong lay down on her side, pulling a thin blanket around her shoulders, I remained sitting. I straightened my spine and closed my eyes. Then I drew a slow breath. With my elbows out and palms up, I raised my hands like I was imagining lifting my stomach. The heat from the flames warmed my skin, and the grass poked my legs.

I drew another breath, listening to the crackling fire and humming grasshoppers. *Like inhaling oxygen,* I told myself, focusing on the sensation of my lungs filling with air. I repeated this several times before, all at once, I became aware of a strange sensation.

It was like a painless current of electricity flowing outward from my center and swirling through my limbs. As I took an even deeper and slower breath, the current seemed to strengthen, growing from a stream into a river.

My eyes flew open and my face broke into a grin. I was about to shout Zhong's name when I saw that she was already fast asleep. I swallowed my excitement and closed my eyes again, feeling the spiritual energy course through me.

~

I dreamed of a cage. I stood outside it, close enough to touch the metal bars that stretched up and up until they were swallowed by the dark sky.

The bars had that freckly look of tarnished metal, like the silverware Matt and I used to help my aunt polish before every Hmong New Year. A paper talisman hung from each bar, along with a small red pouch. My mom had been sewing something similar in Matt's hospital room. It was a sort of charm. I didn't know what these were for, but I didn't think it was protection.

Inside the cage, shrouded in blackness, something prowled. The *clink, clink, clink* of its chains echoed as it moved.

I squinted, but I couldn't make out its shape. Then two spots of light appeared through the dark—eyes. They burned white-hot, like lightning.

If the presence of the bridge spirit had been bad, this was a thousand times worse. Its magic slammed into me like an army tank. All the air rushed out of me as I dropped to my knees. My throat made dry gasping sounds.

A low, rumbling voice filled my ears, as if talking right into my mind. *At last, you come before me again. Your face has changed, but I know you. I know you, defiler of gods. Your magic awakens, and soon you will free me from this prison. Then I will devour you, most unworthy one.*

That doesn't sound like a very fair trade, I thought. Panic was making my head go fuzzy.

The voice hissed in my ear:

> *Bound in ivory, silver, gold,*
> *The god of wrath will prison hold.*
> *By victor's hand the gate undone*
> *When sky bridges earth for love of sun.*

Sun! That was the last word of the curse, not *gum.*

The chained prisoner, who I now knew had to be Xov, said, *Soon, defiler. Soon.*

I tried to stand, but it was like an elephant was sitting on me. My back bowed, and my ribs felt ready to snap. How had Shee Yee faced this deity? How had he defeated him? The thunder god was as old as creation. My nails dug into the dusty stone floor and my eyes squeezed shut as I gasped for air, the weight of all that power crushing me.

Then soft hands gripped my shoulders and yanked me to my feet. My head spun from the sudden relief. Air filled my lungs again. I felt the brush of a kiss at my temple. The scent of jasmine teased my nose. . . .

My eyes flew open and I gasped, my heart pounding, every part of my body aching and vibrating with dread.

But I was back in the forest with Zhong, lying next to our cold fire.

18

~

Equestrian Rentals

 A fire spirit was building a tiny fort from the ashes of our campfire.

Sunlight barely peeked through the trees, which stood around us like the bars of a cage. I shuddered. It was still early. Even though I knew it was just a dream, it had felt as real as when Ntuj pulled me into his garden. And those lines the voice had spoken—the curse Choj and Aunt Chan had recited—what did they mean?

I could still smell the scent of jasmine, as if the person who had helped me had been right here. . . .

"You seek the Tree of Souls," came a quiet voice.

I looked up to find the tree spirit Nplooj sitting in the branches over my head.

"How do you know that?" I asked.

"I listened to your conversation last night." She didn't sound the least bit embarrassed about eavesdropping.

"Nyom is the queen of the nature spirits in the hills around the Tree of Souls."

"So you've been there? You know the area?"

Nplooj shook her head, making the dry thicket of her hair crackle. "I cannot travel outside my forest. But that doesn't mean I can't communicate with my siblings in distant groves. All tree spirits are connected."

"Siblings," I echoed, smiling despite a pang of sadness and fear.

"Yeah, like the kind that pull off your leaves just to annoy you," chirped a new voice. A second tree spirit hung upside down from a neighboring tree. Their large green eyes blinked owlishly. "Or pick at your bark or steal your fruit and spit on your roots while calling it rain."

I made a face. Still, I knew all about annoying siblings. And I wanted mine back more than anything in the world.

"Do you mind?" Nplooj asked.

"Sorry, sorry," the other tree spirit said brightly. They didn't sound very remorseful, but they did leave.

Nplooj released a sigh. She scratched a patch of moss on her cheek. "Anyway, if you find yourself in Nyom's forest, she will help you if she's able."

"Thank you," I said, but Nplooj had already slipped back into the tree.

I went to wash up at the stream. When I got back, Zhong was awake. Kind of. She groaned and shambled past me like a zombie for her turn with the water. Miv had returned and was curled into a tiny black ball on top of my clean cloak.

"Where'd you go?" I asked. Back home, I always figured Miv was being a creep by poking around in other people's apartments. As a cat spirit he could go right through locked doors. (Like I said, total creep.) Here, though, it was just a lot of trees.

"Scouted ahead." He sniffed at a tower of berries that a wildflower spirit was building next to my dried clothes.

The wildflower spirit had sharp thistles growing out of their arms, which they smacked into Miv's nose. He hissed and knocked over their tower.

I shook my head. "So, what did you find?"

"Well, there's good news and there's bad news." He rolled onto his back. "Let's wait until Zhong's here so I don't have to say everything twice."

By the time Zhong returned from the stream, I had my stuff packed and ready. I was back in my green dress, along with my galaxy-print leggings and Jedi/hobbit cloak. The wildflower spirit let me eat their berries, and the tree spirit I'd saved the night before even brought me a handful of nuts, which I gave to Zhong.

"Guess what I did last night?" I said, grinning at her.

Her nose wrinkled. "Don't smile at me like that. You look maniacal."

I rolled my eyes. "I felt my spiritual energy! You were right. It's like a current flowing through my whole body."

Zhong's expression transformed into surprise, and then

she was smiling, too. "That's awesome! Congratulations. Keep practicing to learn how to control the flow and volume. Once you're comfortable with that, you can begin trying to direct it to your sword."

As we beamed at each other, Miv drawled, "Well, aren't you two chummy. I leave for one night and our whole team dynamic shifts."

"Don't be dramatic," I said, offering my hand so he could climb up my arm and onto my shoulder.

We thanked the nature spirits for letting us sleep in their forest. Then Miv pointed our way forward. "The good news is that we're not far from the main road."

He was right. It wasn't long before the trees began to thin, and I spotted a dusty orange thoroughfare.

"So what's the bad news?" I asked when he fell silent.

"You'll see in a second."

That sounded foreboding. But when we stepped out of the forest, I didn't know what he could be talking about.

The road continued along the edge of the trees before it curved into an enormous valley between two mountains. Villages made up of squat thatched huts dotted the lush mountainsides between tiers of green rice paddies. Huge banana trees lined the pathway, their large, broad leaves stretching over the dirt.

The sky was a dusky pink, the sun not yet visible. Colorful nature spirits, so many that I couldn't identify them all, flicked in and out of sight among the trees and tall grasses.

My mouth fell open as something moved overhead. Impossibly, a cloud in the shape of a massive crab hovered over the valley. Its fluffy pincers opened and closed. When it raised its arms, rain poured from the crevices of its shell right where its armpits were, spilling over the trees in a shining cascade. Far past the mountains, obscured by mist and distance, the shapes of other enormous spirits moved against the horizon.

All of it reminded me of my dream, the one with the tree and the gardener. But if that had been a real place, then what I'd seen about Xov's prison might be real, too, and I didn't want to think about that.

Wind spirits laughed as they blew over our heads. They sent a sharp breeze to tangle my cloak around my legs. In the mortal realm, wind spirits were normally shapeless creatures with only the faintest impression of a face. Here, they looked like translucent leaping deer. Then, before my eyes, they transformed into a swarm of tiny glass-like dragonflies. They changed again into a flock of long-legged cranes before vanishing over the treetops.

"Wow," I breathed. "It's incredible." Matt would have loved every aspect of this place. It was like our imaginings brought to life. But instead of being out in the open air with the nature spirits, he was trapped in the dusty darkness below with a vengeful ghost.

Miv cleared his throat. "Yes, it's all very pretty. The bad news is that the Tree of Souls is located at the center of the

Spirit Realm." He pointed to a distant mountain range, barely even visible. "Past those mountains."

All my wonder turned to dread. "What? How are we supposed to get all the way there and back again in two days?"

"Exactly my point."

"How do shamans travel in the Spirit Realm?" Zhong asked me like a teacher addressing a student she didn't think was very bright. Even though I didn't mind that tone of voice much anymore, I still wanted to throw the berries in my pocket at her.

"Spirit horses," I said, gesturing down toward the valley, where a pair was pulling a wagon along the road. "But I don't see any standing around, waiting for riders. Are we supposed to steal some?"

"Not a good idea," Miv said. "The horse would just kick you and neigh for help. They're notoriously rude."

This, coming from a cat who liked to tell me how terrible I was at everything and how I didn't have any friends.

"We're not stealing anything," Zhong said louder, and with an annoyed look at Miv. "As a shaman's apprentice, I have a contract with a spirit horse."

Miv casually flashed his claws as he said, "You've had a spirit horse at your disposal this whole time?"

"You can put away the kitty back-scratchers. We came here physically, so I'll need to call her from a rental agency." She nodded to the town at the bottom of the valley. "There's probably an office down there."

"Is a horse going to be fast enough?" I asked before the two could keep at it. I didn't know much about traveling over long distances, but those mountains looked *really* far away.

"Don't worry," said Zhong. "She's as fast as the wind."

Since we'd moved away from the Hmong community, I hadn't seen many real shamans at work. The last time was years ago, during the New Year, when my aunt had blessed our family and renewed the house spirits' powers. But when a shaman goes into a trance, projecting their spirit into Dab Teb, they sometimes sit on a wooden bench. The bench symbolizes the horse familiar that carries them through the Spirit Realm. I'd never thought about how a horse and rider actually meet up on the Spirit Realm side.

Also, I'd never ridden a horse, and now I was supposed to get on one "as fast as the wind"? "Will we all be able to fit on her?" I asked nervously.

"It won't be a problem. We'll make it to the Tree of Souls in no time."

What was that look on Zhong's face? Anticipation?

Eventually, traffic on the road grew busier, and a town opened up past the banana trees. I pulled the hood of my cloak lower over my face, but no one looked twice at us, except for a grumpy badger-woman pulling a cart of turnips and mumbling about "spirits these days."

Aside from the spiritfolk, though, the town didn't seem all that unusual. Dusty buildings were topped by chimneys spouting gray smoke. Awnings of brightly patterned fabrics in pink, yellow, and green hung over outdoor shop displays where tables were piled high with vegetables or buckets of freshly clipped flowers. On one corner, we passed a tower of fat squash where a nature spirit in a dress of moss and spiderweb perched at the top like a queen on a throne.

"Don't stare," Zhong muttered, giving me a small shove.

Right. I was supposed to be blending in. We didn't know where Xov's henchmen were, or if any of the other gods had sent their servants to find me. I doubted they'd expected us to end up in the tunnels beneath the Spirit Realm, though, so I hoped that meant they weren't looking in this particular area.

"There it is," I said in relief. I pointed to a red barn with a horse painted in white above the large double doors. It sported a hanging sign that read EQUESTRIAN RENTALS: WHATEVER THE NEED, WE'VE GOT YOUR STEED.

Inside, a striped brown-and-black stallion spirit wearing a monocle and tie looked up from a bucket of apples. I saw a horse once at a carnival, but only from a distance. I was pretty sure this one was bigger than normal.

There was a desk against the wall, but it looked more like a messy snack bar. It was littered with pulpy bits of chewed-up paper and clumps of hay. On a small metal plaque was the name SUAB NAG.

"How can I help you?" asked the horse spirit, who I assumed must be Suab Nag. It was a little hard to under-stand him, because every other word ended in a whinny.

"I need to contact a friend," Zhong said. "Her name is Spike. Could you call her for us?"

Suab Nag tossed his mane of thick brown-and-black hair. "Impossible. She could be anywhere in the realm."

Zhong crossed her arms and said haughtily, "Spike has a shaman contract. That means she must be reachable during all hours in case she's summoned by her shaman."

"How do you know that?" the horse spluttered, spraying bits of apple on us.

"Oh, come on, I just washed this!" I grabbed a handful of hay from the desk and rubbed the horse spit off my cloak.

Neither of them paid any attention to me.

"Because I'm a shaman, and Spike is my spirit horse."

"Then why didn't you summon her when you crossed over? Ha!" If he'd had fingers, Suab Nag would have pointed one accusingly at Zhong.

"Because I'm here in my physical form," she said, as if Suab Nag were an idiot for not noticing. "Now either you call her, or I'll put in a complaint with the Imperial Equestrian Offices."

The horse whinnied and stomped his front hooves. "Shaman contracts aren't binding unless you're here on shaman business."

"We *are* on shaman business, you donkey."

"How dare you!" The horse began to rear up. Zhong reached for her sword.

"Whoa, whoa!" I shouted, grabbing Zhong and dragging

her out of harm's way. "What have I said about trying to solve everything with a sword?"

Suab Nag made a sound that was half whinny and half *harrumph* and stomped his hooves again.

"Open your backpack," I told Zhong, who still gripped her sword and looked like she was imagining the horse with a severe haircut.

At my words, her glare shifted to me. "Why?"

"So I can admire your crossbow and count your talismans. Would you just do it?"

She did. But halfway through unzipping it, she seemed to realize my plan, because a sly smile pulled at her mouth. She rummaged through the endless compartments and then brought out a short stack of silver bills. The silver and gold joss paper that we'd taken from my mom's trunk had transformed into spirit money, just like she'd said it would.

Zhong handed me the stack, and I set it on the desk without a word. Suab Nag's eyes narrowed. It wasn't a very effective expression, though, because the monocle made one eye look twice as big as the other.

"Are you trying to bribe me?" the horse asked, sounding scandalized. "Because I happen to be a horse spirit with *principles*."

Zhong gave me another handful of silver bills. I set them on top of the first stack.

The horse began to look nervous. "I have . . . um, principles," he whinnied.

Zhong took out several gold bills this time. I added them to the pile. Suab Nag shifted from hoof to hoof, tail swishing. Then he coughed and trotted over to the desk.

"Well, they're loose principles." With one hoof, he swiped the silver and gold bills into a drawer, which he swiftly locked with his teeth. "I'll call for Spike, but it's not my fault if she doesn't pick up."

He disappeared behind a set of swinging doors.

"Nicely done," Miv said, hopping onto my shoulder. "Your mom would be proud."

"That I just bribed a horse?"

He considered that. "Never mind, she'd be horrified."

"Thinking outside the box, *hmm*?" Zhong said, like she was finally beginning to accept the possibility that she didn't have to resolve every conflict with her sword.

"At least Zhong didn't have to stab anyone," Miv continued.

"I'm sure she'll get another chance."

I wasn't sure we could trust the horse to make the call, though. But he was true to his word, because we only waited ten minutes before the barn doors burst open. A beautiful white-and-blue horse with a braided mane pranced in. Her cloven hooves were painted with sparkly silver glitter.

"Spike!" Zhong grinned and threw her arms around the mare spirit's neck.

For the first time since we'd met, Zhong looked really happy. It was kind of strange. Not bad, just strange. I was used to her looking like she'd smelled something off and then realizing it was everyone and everything around her.

"You're lucky I was in range," Spike said.

At my confused look, Zhong explained, "Horse spirits are free to cross boundaries without waiting in line, and calls from small towns like this usually can't reach other realms."

"Why didn't you just come through one of the shaman routes?" asked Spike. "I would have gotten an alert and met you at the usual spot."

"It's a long story," Zhong said. "But we could really use a lift." She quickly explained our situation, about how we had to get to the Tree of Souls in order to save Matt's life.

"Of course I'll help." Spike flashed me a wide, horsey grin and said, "I bet you've never been on a spirit horse before. Get ready for the ride of a lifetime."

19

Friendship Upgrade

Within moments, three of us were mounted on the horse spirit. Zhong sat in front of me, with her enormous backpack hanging down like a saddlebag. Spike suggested I take off my cloak in case a wind spirit tried to grab it and rip me off her back. I was happy to oblige. Miv had to ride squished between us so he would be secure once we started moving.

My stomach flipped whenever Spike shifted beneath us. At least Zhong seemed to know what she was doing. She told me to hold on tight, so I did, flattening Miv against her spine. He clawed at my ribs to ease up, but it was a good thing I didn't. Spike took off a second later. It was only my death grip on Zhong's waist that kept me from tumbling right off the saddle.

Fun fact #5 about me: I love roller coasters. After my dad left, my mom would take Matt and me down to Six Flags

Great America in Gurnee every summer. We'd go on rides and eat greasy burgers and deep-fried desserts until we were sick. Not literally . . . though I did throw up once because I'd eaten a whole funnel cake by myself right before a really twisty roller coaster. Still, those were some of my best memories. Not the throwing-up part. The part where my mom gave us her full attention for an entire day.

We didn't get to go last year, because she'd had to work overtime at the factory, and she was busy every weekend with shaman-related jobs. She hadn't mentioned it this year, either, and we were already a month into summer. I hadn't wanted to ask, because at least then I could keep hoping that maybe she'd surprise us.

Anyway, riding Spike was like being on a roller coaster if the ride had just finished five energy drinks. The horse was literally *flying* without wings. She rode on currents, helped along by wind spirits. She soared so fast over the valley and trees that I was glad I hadn't eaten much that morning. Wind spirits laughed in our faces as my hair whipped my eyes and stung my cheeks.

We passed whole villages in a flash. Far to the right, beyond a mountain thick with mist and trees, I spied a shining fortress. Its towers shifted in and out of focus like a mirage. That had to be the palace of the Spirit Emperor, ruler of the Spirit Realm. When the mountain moved and blocked my view, I realized it was an enormous turtle spirit, an entire forest sprouting from the shell.

Against the distant horizon, the hazy shapes of monstrous spirits stood as massive as thunderheads. I pointed and shouted, "What are those?"

When Zhong looked, her entire back went rigid against me. Then she quickly faced forward again. "Those are the lost peaks. It's all fog and barren mountains over there. Something about that place draws lost souls, so when a living mortal loses their soul, that's usually where they end up, and shamans have to go retrieve them."

My mom said that our souls could be frightened out of our bodies, like from a serious accident or even from just a bad prank. If someone's soul can't find its way back to their body, then the person falls sick, and a shaman has to be called. I shuddered at the thought.

"The spiritfolk who live there are . . . particularly wild," Zhong continued. "Before we ran into her in the tunnels, I figured that was where we were going to find the bridge spirit."

The tunnels were no walk in the park, but I was grateful we wouldn't have to go searching through stark mountainsides inhabited by ginormous spirits.

We traveled for a few more hours before Spike began to descend. We hadn't reached the Tree of Souls yet, but she needed to rest. The stop was understandable, even though my heart did that anxious aching thing whenever I thought about my brother waiting to be rescued.

We landed smoothly in a small clearing. After climbing

down from the horse's back, my legs felt like jelly. Miv wasn't in much better shape. His fur stood on end, and he seemed to be permanently attached to my dress.

Zhong removed her backpack so Spike could be free to graze and rest. She offered me a rice stick, but I shook my head. I was still trying to convince my stomach to climb back down my throat.

"That was wild," I said, steadying myself against a tree. "But really cool. And you get to do it every time you come to the Spirit Realm?"

"Not every time," Zhong said nonchalantly, but I could tell she was pleased by my admiration.

Past the trees that enclosed our small clearing, we were surrounded by forested peaks. The thatched roofs of huts peeked out from beneath leafy canopies on distant mountainsides, and glimmering waterfalls churned mist that clung to the branches.

"You know, you keep surprising me with how well you're handling everything." Zhong settled down at the base of a tree to munch on dry ramen. She was wearing her freshly washed jean jacket, and her pins flashed in the sunlight. "I wouldn't have said this when I first met you, but you'd make a decent shaman warrior."

"Really?" I paced, trying to work some feeling back into my legs. Miv had finally released me and was currently sprawled in the grass, hugging the ground. "Because I'm Shee Yee?"

She snorted. "No. If you were Shee Yee—the fully trained version—this adventure would be over already. But you did get that donkey to let me call Spike. And not many apprentices could face down a demon eagle and live."

I couldn't tell if she was insulting me or complimenting me. Maybe both.

Still—and I wouldn't have said this either when I first met Zhong—she could be surprisingly nice. But only when she wanted to be. She hid that part of herself behind a tough-shaman-warrior act. When I pretended, unless I was playing with Matt and Miv, it stayed in my head. When Zhong pretended, she made it convincing enough to seem real.

"I don't remember if I've said this yet, but . . . thank you." It felt awkward to thank Zhong for something she would have done anyway, but it still needed to be said. "I know you're only here because you have a mission to complete, but I'm really glad for your help."

"I wish I hadn't been chosen," she said. Before I could feel hurt, she added, "This is a really dangerous quest, and your brother's life is on the line. Not to mention all the other kids the bridge spirit stole, too. A shaman master should have been sent to look into this."

She had a point. We were just two kids and a spirit cat. It was a miracle we'd made it this far.

"I think we're doing all right." It was better to be optimistic than to wish for the help of shaman masters. That wasn't going to get us any closer to rescuing Matt, and I already felt scared enough that we wouldn't succeed.

Zhong pursed her lips. "We are, but there've been a lot of lucky close calls."

"You call it luck. I call it using my head." So far, we'd bribed, bargained, and threatened our way out of some pretty tough situations. I could feel proud of that, right? Really, all we had to do was figure out what a person or spirit wanted and go from there. Everyone had a motive.

"You won't always be able to use your head."

"That reminds me," I said, gesturing to my sword. "We can't go anywhere until Spike is ready, so can you teach me some shaman stuff?"

Nodding, she set down the packet of ramen and rose to her feet. Excitedly, I drew the sword from the scabbard, bouncing on my heels as I moved to stand where she indicated.

Now that I could sense my spiritual energy, she showed me how to focus it into my sword. After several attempts, I finally got the blade to flicker weakly.

"Good," Zhong said.

Then it exploded into a light so bright that Zhong cried out in alarm. I dropped the sword, shaking out my hand.

"Okay, you need to work on that," Zhong said, still shielding her eyes. "You're going to hurt yourself and others if you can't control it."

"Sorry," I said, embarrassed.

"Here, I'll show you some fighting moves. No using spiritual energy, okay?"

She taught me some basics first, like how to plant my feet so I wouldn't get knocked over as easily, and how to hold my sword so I wouldn't accidentally stab myself. Then she demonstrated the motions for slashing and stabbing and how to block.

"Want to try dueling?" she asked.

Honestly? Not really. I was tired just from swinging the sword around a few dozen times. She hadn't let me stop until I got the motions right. I wouldn't have guessed it, but Zhong was a pretty good teacher.

Still, I didn't think she'd let me say no, so I nodded.

She disarmed me with one move.

"Ow," I said, cradling my wrist.

"Try it again." She grinned. She was enjoying this!

She knocked the sword out of my hand five more times, although I felt a tiny spark of pride when it took her two moves instead of one.

"This is pointless," I said. "I'm pathetic."

"I *was* thinking about being your cheerleader, but this is too sad even for me," Miv remarked from his place in the grass.

Scowling, I bent over to pick my sword back up. Then I lowered my center of gravity like Zhong had shown me and raised the blade. *Come on, Pahua. No pretending. Just do it.*

I took a slow breath and felt a rush of satisfaction when

I immediately sensed the spiritual energy flowing through me. It surged outward from my chest, a current invigorating my limbs.

When Zhong next attacked, my arms moved reflexively. I blocked her thrust, twisted my wrist, and forced her to drop her weapon.

She gaped at the point of my blade now directed at her chest. Beaming, I backed off and stabbed my sword into the sky. I'd done it! I'd controlled Shee Yee's abilities!

Zhong didn't smile back, though. Instead, she retrieved her sword and shoved it into the scabbard.

"If you want to learn how to fight, then take it seriously," she snapped. "You tricked me just so you could show off."

I sheathed my sword. "I wasn't showing off—I was trying to fight back. Isn't that the whole point?"

"You asked me to teach you, not be your sword-fighting dummy." She turned on her heel and stalked off in the direction Spike had gone.

I threw up my hands, cast Miv a *Can you believe this?* look, and went after her.

"Why are you so mad?" I called to Zhong's back. "Isn't it a good thing I can use Shee Yee's skills?"

Zhong whirled around so fast that I almost walked into her. "You. Are. *Impossible!*"

"And you're not making any sense!"

She covered her face like she was trying to calm herself down.

I thought again about that moment on the boat when she'd seemed jealous and wondered if I'd been right after all. Why did she think it was so terrible to lose a fake duel to me? She didn't need to be the best at everything or have all the answers or always be prepared. I mean, it wasn't bad to be those things, especially when we were being attacked by demons, but this was just practice swordplay. Why was she acting like I'd kicked her cat?

We'd been getting along so well since we got out of the Bamboo Nursery. I didn't want to ruin it. So I stayed quiet instead of telling her she was acting like a brat.

"I'm sorry, okay?" she said stiffly. "It's not about you, and I don't want to talk about it." She slumped against a tree.

I shrugged. "Fine." I stepped over a rock and sat next to her so that our shoulders bumped. My hair clip was sagging over my ear. I pulled it off, examined it, and groaned.

"What is it?" Zhong asked, glancing over.

"Nothing. Just lost another rhinestone." I sighed and fixed the clip at my temple.

"Why doesn't your mom buy you a new one?"

"She's not really around much."

Zhong frowned. "Oh. Sorry. I forgot that you said she works a lot." She bit her lip. I remembered how she'd said she didn't see her parents much, either. "So, you watch your brother? Are you guys close?" There was a hint of wistfulness in her voice.

"Yeah, he's great. We get along really well." If I had to

talk about personal stuff, then it was only fair that she did, too. "What year is your sister in? You said she goes to your school?"

Her lips tightened. She looked away. "Three years ahead of me."

"Is she a good shaman warrior?"

"Why do you want to know?"

"Because you're a good shaman warrior. Your sister must be pretty good, too, right?"

She was quiet for several long seconds. Just when I figured she was ignoring the question, she finally sighed. It was a weary sound, like she was tired of always having to act tough. "Not just pretty good—she's a prodigy. The elders don't allow for early graduation, but she's basically a shaman warrior already. Her mentor sends her out on solo jobs all the time, and my parents think she's the best thing ever."

I could understand how it would be hard to live up to that. "Is that why you're mad I beat you just now?"

She huffed. "You're really nosy, you know that?"

I looked down, my shoulders hunched. Normally, I was really good at minding my own business. It was easy when you didn't have any friends. But I considered Zhong a friend now, so wasn't I supposed to care about her? Clearly *something* was upsetting her besides just losing to me in a duel.

"Remember when I said my family has really strong spiritual energy?" Zhong said, surprising me. She turned her back, like pretending I wasn't there made it easier for her to talk. "My dad is a shaman warrior, and so are his sister and their parents. My family expects nothing but the best from me. There's a *lot* of family honor riding on me being able to finish this quest."

I frowned in confusion. "But you've been amazing! You defeated the poj ntxoog, and you knew how to get us to the Spirit Realm, and you saved me from drowning in the frog pond. And you ride a spirit horse!"

Even though I was praising her, every word made her cringe. "I have some physical skill, and knowing how to travel between realms is basic information any shaman warrior would have. I told you—fighting is what I'm good at. The other stuff doesn't come as naturally to me. I should be several levels into learning shaman magic without spiritual tools, but I'm not. I couldn't even make a spiritual shield, which my sister mastered in her first year."

"You said most shaman warriors can't use magic without spiritual tools."

"But I'm not supposed to be like most shaman warriors. I'm supposed to be like my sister. And then I meet you, the literal reincarnation of the greatest shaman who's ever existed, and you just *instantly* know how to be better than me without even trying, when I've been working at this for *three years*. Most of the situations we've gotten into, you've been the one who got us out." She made an exasperated groan and covered her face again. "You don't even seem to realize the advantage you've got."

This explained a lot about Zhong. She pretended she was better than everyone else because she came from a family of powerful shaman warriors. But she felt like she wasn't good enough for them, so she had to pretend even harder to fit the part.

"It sucks to have that kind of pressure on you," I said. "But I'm not sorry for having whatever powers I got from Shee Yee if they'll help me save my brother. Also, you might not care what I say, but even if you can't do magic, I still think you're really cool."

It was impressive how she could both look over her shoulder and down her nose at me at the same time. "I never said I didn't care what you say."

Her words made me feel less anxious, so I continued. "Trust me, I know what it's like to feel not good enough. Or just not . . . enough, period. When my mom moved us to Merdel, none of the kids in my class had even heard of Hmong people before, which wouldn't have been bad, except they never let me forget that I was different. And before that, when my dad left, it felt like . . ." I touched the hair clip.

"Like what?" Zhong asked. She finally turned to face me.

It was only because she'd asked gently, without any judgment in her voice, that I was able to answer. I'd never said it out loud before, not even to Miv. "Like even my own dad didn't want me the way I was."

Dad had always encouraged me to imagine myself as someone exciting and heroic. He'd often played along. After he left, I couldn't help wondering if maybe it was because being myself hadn't been enough for him.

"He sounds terrible." Zhong said it so flatly and confidently that I almost laughed.

"I guess. But then why can't I stop being sad about it?"

She rested her head against the tree. "You don't look sad."

"It's all on the inside. I don't want Matt or my mom to notice. Mostly, I can just ignore it, and it's like it's not even there. Other times . . ."

"Yeah," she said softly. "I get it. I don't like letting my parents see how mad I get at them, either."

"So you don't think I'm, you know, stupid for feeling this way?"

"I think you're stupid for a lot of reasons, Pahua, but not for that."

I glared at her, but she only laughed. It was a nice change from her scowling. Against my will, my mouth started to smile, too. "I still think you're pretty cool, but you're also stuck-up and a know-it-all, so I guess we're even."

She laughed again. But it also looked like she wanted to tackle me, so it was a good thing Spike chose that moment to come back.

We retrieved her backpack and Miv, and then we were off. We flew higher and higher into the mountains. Before long, Zhong nudged me with her elbow and then pointed ahead.

I peered over her shoulder. If my stomach hadn't already been doing somersaults against my spleen, it would have flipped.

We were headed directly for the crest of one particular mountain. At its peak stood the biggest banyan tree I'd ever seen in my life. Its branches twisted into the clouds, and instead of leaves, it bore thousands upon thousands of white strips of cloth. It was the tree from my dream.

The Tree of Souls.

20

~

Sacred Ground, No Trespassing, Will Be Cursed

 Spike landed well beyond the wide-spreading roots of the banyan tree.

Nearby, white wooden spears stabbed the ground, like the posts of an unfinished fence. They looked as though they might encircle the entire tree.

"Can't get any closer than this," the horse spirit said while chewing on a granola bar that Zhong was shoving into her mouth. "Inside that boundary is sacred ground. But I'll keep an eye out and try to catch you if the arborist throws you off the mountain."

"Um, thanks." I left my backpack and cloak on the saddle. There was no one to recognize me here, and all our supplies fit in Zhong's magic backpack. "What's an arborist?"

"Protector of the Tree of Souls."

I thought about the gardener-woman I'd seen in my dream the night after I released the bridge spirit. *You're the one who escaped,* she'd said to me. Come to think of it, the bird's-eye (horse's-eye?) view of this place as we descended was exactly as it had been in my dream—a vista of vibrant green trees and rice paddies climbing the sides of mist-shrouded mountains.

Zhong finished feeding her horse and then wiped her hands. "It's incredible. I've always wanted to see the Tree of Souls, but Master Bo said it was bad luck to come here before your time."

"Hopefully he was wrong."

The white cloths on the branches fluttered in a silent wind that blew across the mountaintop. When I stepped past the boundary, voices began to whisper around me. I covered my ears, but it didn't help.

"I shouldn't have run away."

"I never got to say good-bye."

"Did I leave the oven on?"

I shook my head. I was hearing the voices of souls that were bound to the tree as they waited for reincarnation. How long they lingered probably depended on the life they'd lived. Some people would be stuck here a very long time. Although not as long as Shee Yee, who was never supposed to have been reincarnated. What had happened to change that?

"I don't like it here," Miv said. He'd had to disentangle himself from my dress again before climbing onto my shoulder.

"Me neither." I waved my hand around my head, like I could swat the voices away.

Zhong joined me inside the boundary, her backpack on her shoulders again. With a wary nod, we approached the tree. It looked weathered and ancient. I couldn't help feeling a little awed thinking about how long it must have stood on this mountain. Without leaves, the tree could have looked dead, but it didn't. I felt its presence like a living, breathing spirit.

"You said the ax is buried inside?" I asked Miv.

We picked our way through the tangle of the tree's limbs. We had to climb over roots that both dove down and climbed up through the earth. Just trying to reach the main trunk was like going through an obstacle course.

"*Deep* inside," Miv said.

"Well then, how do we get in?"

One time last summer, I'd wedged myself into a hollow trunk while pretending to be a tree spirit. It had been tight, scratchy, and kind of spooky in there. Ants had crawled up my legs. Matt had said I looked like a squashed banana and Miv, sitting on his shoulder, had nodded in agreement. I didn't think going inside the Tree of Souls would be like that.

Except maybe the spooky part.

Suddenly, a hidden door in the banyan's trunk swung open. A woman walked out, holding a garden hoe and wearing bright-red rubber boots. A green handkerchief covered her black hair. Her skin was a warm brown but weathered and knotted, like the bark of a birch tree.

It was the woman from my dream. Her gaze flew to ours before we could even think to hide. She shook the garden hoe at us. "Trespassers!"

She clearly had way more practice getting around the tree's roots and branches than we did, because she crossed the distance between us with amazing speed. Miv hid beneath my hair. I exchanged a look with Zhong. Were we supposed to run away? I hadn't been afraid of the woman in my dream, only startled, because of how strange the whole thing had been. For some reason, I didn't think she would hurt us.

The woman paused, squinting to get a better look at me. Her eyes were watery and clear, like tree sap. She pointed one knobby, twig-like finger. "*You*. I'd know your soul anywhere."

I stood up straighter. It hadn't made any sense to me in the dream, but now I knew that she was talking about Shee Yee's spirit. "My name is Pahua."

"I know what your name is." She smacked the hoe into a large root. The root sank into the earth, clearing a path for her. I gulped and stepped back. Maybe I was wrong about her not hurting us. "If you were anyone else, I'd curse you and throw you off the mountain. This is sacred ground."

Spike *had* mentioned that. I wiped my palms on my dress and asked, "Are you the banyan tree's spirit?"

She gave a single, harsh laugh. It sounded like the scrape of sandpaper. "Ha! The tree already has plenty of those, don't you think? I'm Yeng, the arborist."

"You care for the tree and the souls here." I glanced over my shoulder at where Spike still waited beyond the boundary. The horse spirit was flailing her front hooves. She could have been performing an elaborate dance ritual or telling us to run away before Yeng killed us.

But I still didn't think we had anything to fear from the arborist. It wasn't because she wasn't threatening looking. That garden hoe seemed pretty sharp. It was because she was a caretaker of souls. Something in her eyes reassured me. They had a warmth to them.

Also, she'd just said she wouldn't curse me.

Yeng glared at Zhong and Miv as if deciding whether to curse *them* instead. "Cat spirits aren't welcome in a waiting place for mortal spirits. As for you," she said, gesturing to me and Zhong, "are you so eager to die? All mortal souls eventually come into my care, but few of them come so willingly."

With that, she turned away, grumbling under her breath about trespassers, mortals without any sense, and weeds.

Zhong made a shooing gesture to indicate I should follow Yeng. The door in the tree had closed. If anyone could help us get inside, it'd be the arborist.

"Wait!" I called, hurrying after Yeng. Geez, she was fast. "Since you know who I am, then you must know why I'm here."

"Oh, I certainly do, little shaman. You're after the lightning ax, a celestial weapon of the gods. What destruction do you plan to unleash in this lifetime?"

We picked our way around the tangle of roots and branches, she more easily than me and Zhong, until we arrived at her garden.

"I'm not going to unleash any destruction," I said. "I just want to save my brother." My sandals weren't made for walking through rich, moist soil. I waited beside a row of cabbages as the arborist continued between small bushes of red chili peppers.

She made a skeptical *hmm* sound. "And what about that one?" she asked, looking past me at Zhong.

My friend bowed over the cabbages and said, "I'm on a quest for my school. Our guardian spirit has always spoken well of you. It's an honor to meet such an esteemed one."

"Is your quest worth your life?" Yeng asked, leaning on her hoe like a cane. "If the Tree of Souls decides to levy such a toll?"

Visibly swallowing, Zhong gripped the hilt of her sword and glanced at me.

"I can go alone, if—" I began, but Zhong cut me off.

"We've already come this far," she said. "My future is worth the risk. Besides, if we succeed, I'll be the first shaman at the school to pass through the Tree of Souls while still alive. It'll be a mark of achievement. The guardian spirit will have to take that into account."

Yeng snorted and then abruptly stiffened. She tilted her head, listening. Her dark braid fell over her shoulder. Slowly, she lifted her hand and pulled from the air a thin strip of white cloth. It glowed a little, casting her brown fingers in soft light. She caressed it with her thumb, nodding and whispering something under her breath.

"A new soul," she said louder, glancing over at me. "You can hear them, can't you?"

"Hear what?" Zhong asked, looking between me and Yeng.

I nodded. The voices of the souls had been distinct at first, but the closer we got to the main trunk, the more the voices began to blur into an unintelligible hum. There were simply too many of them to make out.

"That's a rare gift," Yeng said. "But unsurprising for Shee Yee, who was favored by the Sky Father. Where should I place it on the tree?"

The question surprised me. I looked up. Every visible branch was covered end to end with white cloths. So many souls, so many stories, so many regrets. And Shee Yee had been stuck here for four thousand years. "I wouldn't even know where to begin."

Yeng's mouth twisted into a mocking smile. She held the cloth up to the tree. The branches creaked and groaned as they parted, revealing a smaller branch lowering itself to meet her short reach. She passed her fingers over the white cloths already tied to the branch. I flinched as the din of their voices flickered through my head. I couldn't catch any words, but I felt enough of their pain and regret that I didn't want to know what they were saying.

"Some spirits fall from the tree on their own when they're ready, like leaves in autumn. Others must be coaxed." She rubbed the end of one cloth between two fingers, considering. "This one has been here awhile." She leaned her ear close to the cloth. Her eyes grew glassy as she listened. "Petty thievery, lying, never changing the toilet-paper roll. You can go, I guess."

She gave the cloth a gentle tug. It instantly unraveled from the branch. After inhaling deeply, she blew the soul from her hand, releasing it to the wind. Within moments, it vanished, and she tied the new one in its place. When she was finished, the branch returned to its original position, high out of sight.

There were so many questions I wanted to ask her. Right now, though, there was only one answer I needed. "So, can I have my ax?"

She gave that bark of laughter again. "Oh, you can have it. If you can get to it. Can you face your own soul, Pahua Moua?"

"What does that mean?"

Ignoring me, she turned to Zhong. "Make sure your quest is worth it. Are you certain you're meant to be a shaman warrior?"

For a heartbeat, doubt flickered over Zhong's face. Then that familiar superiority settled over her, and she nodded firmly. "I am. Whatever it takes."

Yeng clucked at the tree. Another hidden door swung open. A set of stairs made of roots descended into darkness. Why did it always have to be darkness? Why couldn't it have been a tunnel full of daisies and sunshine? In my pretend adventures, I always liked imagining dangerous stuff— labyrinths full of monsters, goblin caves with booby traps, flesh-eating plants that spit venom. But those things were a lot less fun in real life.

"I don't suppose you have a map?" I asked.

Yeng tapped the side of her head and gave me a grin that didn't seem entirely sane. "Nope, it's all up here. But I guess I can give you this."

She pulled at a chain around her neck that I hadn't noticed before and drew the necklace over her head. At the end of it hung a flat silver locket the size of her palm. She opened it, revealing a single vivid green leaf. Without a word, she held out the locket to me.

I accepted it, waiting for an explanation. The leaf was glossy and leathery, its shape long and rounded.

"That is the only leaf the Tree of Souls has ever grown," Yeng said. "It will help get you where you need to go. Or, if nothing else, it'll prevent the tree from swallowing you."

I tried not to gulp at the way she smiled when she said

this. It was just a leaf, after all. Before I could thank her, she turned away to lean over her chili peppers.

"Does the leaf turn into a boat?" Zhong asked.

"Why would it do that?" I put on the necklace, tucking the locket with the leaf inside the collar of my dress.

Zhong shrugged like that hadn't been a totally random thing to ask. "Because, you know, the story about how the Hmong ended up in Southeast Asia."

"No?"

"Geez, Pahua. Didn't your mom teach you anything about our mythology?"

"She taught me plenty! But what does that have to do with a leaf?"

"The Hmong originally lived in China, but when they were persecuted for not fitting in with the culture, they had to migrate. A great shaman created a boat from a pile of leaves, and a benevolent spirit blew a powerful wind that carried them south into what's now Laos and Vietnam."

"Oh. That's cool."

Zhong looked annoyed, like she'd expected a more enthusiastic reaction. She nodded toward the open door. "Come on, then."

I hesitated. Yeng was still crouched over her peppers, picking off the bad ones and tossing them over her shoulder. Tiny nature spirits ran screaming from the garden. She cackled in delight.

"Excuse me," I said, approaching her cautiously. "Can I

ask . . . How did you lose Shee Yee's soul? Didn't the gods want him bound to the Tree of Souls forever?"

She lifted her head to glare at me. The bark of her forehead puckered, peeling in one spot. When she spoke, it was in a furious hiss. "It wasn't me. A trespasser entered this sacred ground and laid hands upon the branches."

"Where were you?"

She snarled. "In my weekly yoga class. It's not easy staying limber when you're made of wood, you know."

"So, someone just stopped by and pulled his spirit free? Just like that?" I asked, looking up at the cloths.

"Don't be an idiot. If it were that easy, human souls would be flying all over the place and making a nuisance of themselves. Shee Yee was magicked free with a power greater than my own."

That sounded pretty worrying. Power greater than the arborist's? "But whose?"

"That's the million-dollar question, isn't it?" she said, and spat a wad of sap into the dirt. I tried not to gag. "Get going. Aren't you supposed to be short on time?"

"Right. Thank you for the leaf," I said, giving her a quick bow.

She cackled. "Don't thank me yet, girl."

Feeling unsettled, I joined Zhong by the doorway. Miv, who was still curled into a ball on my shoulder, whispered, "I don't think she's all there."

"Looks like we'll have to find the ax on our own," I said

to Zhong. Maybe there would be a sign inside. FOR DEFEATING VENGEFUL GODS AND PESKY BRIDGE SPIRITS, AND FOR SUPER-SPEEDY WOOD-CHOPPING, CHECK OUT THE CELESTIAL AX IN AISLE 12.

"I'm right here with you," Miv said.

I smiled gratefully, some of my worry fading. Miv wasn't the best at delivering motivational speeches or saying nice things in general. But like Matt, he'd always been there for me, for as long as I could remember. He gave me confidence. "Thank you." I looked at Zhong. "You, too."

Even though Zhong's ears turned pink, she rolled her eyes and handed me the flashlight. "If you two are done being mushy, let's get this over with."

"Right." I shone the light before us. It didn't reach very far. The bottom of the stairs was still shrouded in complete darkness.

Right, I repeated to myself. I was a daring treasure-hunter searching for long-lost gold. I was a warrior archaeologist on a dig for an ancient artifact.

With a nod, I descended into the tree.

21

~

Knowledge Hurts

 At the bottom of the stairs, we found ourselves in a circular chamber with three separate doors.

Great. It hadn't gone so well the last time we'd had to pick a path. Tree-shaped lanterns hung from the walls between the doors. Inside of each sat light spirits, looking bored. They were basically identical to fire spirits, except they shone white. One of them had joined their friend in a neighboring lantern to play Pictionary in the dusty glass.

The first door was black and engraved with roots that looked like snakes all twisted together. It made my skin crawl.

The second door had flowers carved along the bottom of it, with blossoms of purple and blue. The brown frame had been painted to look like it was covered in green moss, and it was rendered in such detail that I could imagine the spongy feel against my fingers.

The third door displayed tree branches in the full bloom of summer, pale brown with rough strokes of green representing leaves, set against a sky-blue background. It looked cheerful and bright, even in the gloomy chamber.

"Which one should we take?" Zhong asked.

I wanted to say that the last door looked like a good choice. But my brother's life was on the line. We couldn't afford to get it wrong.

I joined her in front of the first door. "Are those words up there?"

Scrawled into the wall above the door were the letters CAG NTOO. The second door was labeled CEV NTOO. The third was CEG NTOO.

"What do they mean?" I asked, a little ashamed that I couldn't read the Hmong words.

"*Roots, trunk, branches.*" Zhong pointed to each as she read them.

"That does make sense," I said, indicating each door's design. It was nice of the tree to supply visual aids.

"I like the sound of *branches,*" Miv said. "Maybe that one will lead aboveground."

"Who put the ax in here, anyway?" I asked. "Was it Shee Yee?"

Miv answered, "Supposedly, it was his mother. After he

died, she placed it here so that it would remain with his soul. Neither of them was ever meant to leave the tree."

Zhong crossed her arms, drumming her fingers against her skin. "So then maybe she put it in the branches, because if he was never supposed to be reincarnated, she would want him to eventually move on to the realm of the ancestors."

"Like I said, *branches*," Miv said, throwing up his paws.

It did make sense. But something Yeng had said bothered me.

Can you face your own soul, Pahua Moua?

My soul, not Shee Yee's.

And why would that be difficult? My life was already pretty pathetic. My best friend was an invisible cat, I didn't fit in at school, my dad was gone, I hadn't spoken more than a few sentences to my mom for weeks because she was barely home, and my social circle consisted of exactly one other person—Matt.

But something tickled the back of my mind. Before my dad left, my parents used to talk about how they wanted to spend more time teaching me and Matt the history of the Hmong, and our traditions and customs. They'd wanted us to know our cultural roots. My dad said that, even as our branches grew, our roots did, too, soaking up all our experiences. Maybe . . .

"It's in the roots," I said.

Miv and Zhong both looked at me suspiciously.

"How do you know?" Zhong asked, eyes narrowed.

"I don't. I just have a feeling."

"That's reassuring," Miv said. "Is this like the time you just had a feeling you should eat that two-week-old cookie? You had a very *different* feeling after—"

My face went hot. "Not like that! This time I'm *sure* it's the right choice."

Zhong didn't look entirely convinced, but she said, "Now that you mention it, it sounds like what I learned in school about the cycle of reincarnation. The roots are the part of our soul that will always remain *us* regardless of how many times the plant has withered and regrown. The trunk is our current form, and the branches represent a higher state we can achieve when our soul is finally allowed into the realm of our ancestors. If you're certain the ax is in the roots, I guess we'll have to trust your feeling."

I appreciated her saying that. I gave one last longing look at the brightly painted *branches* door. Then I grabbed the *roots* doorknob and twisted. It swung open easily to reveal a tunnel.

"Why did it have to be roots?" I sounded pitiful even to my own ears. But if this was the path I had to take to save my brother, then I had to get moving.

The floor was firmly packed dirt. Thick, fibrous roots pushed through the walls. More tree-shaped lanterns hung from the ceiling, so it wasn't as gloomy as it could have been. The light spirits stared as we passed, their large eyes narrowed warily. They probably didn't get many visitors here, much less living mortals. The tunnel curved, so there was no telling how long it was. There were a lot of doors, though, most of them wide open. It felt awkward to be trooping through what was most likely Yeng's living space.

"Is the arborist a nature or guardian spiritfolk?" I asked Zhong.

"Both, probably."

I peered through the first door into what looked like a completely normal room. A stuffed chair sat beside a fake fireplace (we were still inside a tree, after all—well, *underneath* it, anyway—and everything was super flammable) and an end table stacked with books. I tilted my head to read the spines. *Home Remedies for Frog Spirit Warts. Yoga for Snakes: No Limbs, No Problem. A History of Fashion for the Perpetually Broke. Twilight.*

The next room's walls were completely covered with mirrors. A dozen mats were spread out over the floor. I guessed we'd found Yeng's yoga room. A calendar with a bright X on it marked her next session.

The rooms got increasingly weird after that. One was completely dedicated to rainbow-themed stationery. It was like a unicorn had exploded in there. Another was filled with clothing racks organized by profession and time period, like DASHING PIRATE, 12TH-CENTURY CHINA or IMPERIAL NAIL CLIPPER, 4TH-CENTURY ITALY.

There was also a truly impressive shoe closet, where I

traded my sandals for a pair of sturdy boots. I figured Yeng wouldn't notice, and we were almost the same size. Zhong tilted her nose in the air and pretended not to see.

At last we reached the end of the corridor, which opened into the biggest room yet. It was a library, filled wall-to-wall with books. Instead of dirt, the floor was checkered tile that had faded and cracked.

"This isn't so bad," I said, even though I wasn't much of a reader. It also smelled a little musty, like it hadn't been dusted in a couple of centuries.

Zhong, though, looked like she had walked into the Sky Father's heavenly garden. If she'd been a cartoon, there would have been hearts in her eyes.

"This is amazing!" She spread her arms wide, like she wanted to hug the shelves.

"It's cool, I guess," I said. A library was a lot less menacing than what I expected, given Yeng's warnings.

Zhong was too happy to even try to look annoyed with me. She rubbed her fingers along the dusty spines to try to read the titles.

"There's the exit," I said, pointing to the other end of the library. A narrow wooden door stood open, leading who knew where, but it looked like the fastest way through.

Something hard hit my shoulder blade.

"Ow!" I spun around. A book lay on the ground behind me. "Zhong! Why are you—"

"What?" she asked. She was standing right next to me. It couldn't have been her.

Puzzled, I said, "Someone threw a book at me."

We squinted into the dark corners of the library.

"I don't see anyone," Miv said uneasily.

"Who's there?" I demanded, and then gasped as a book flew off the shelf and came hurtling at my face.

I ducked as the book shouted, "In the mortal realm, a full moon occurs every twenty-nine-point-five days!"

"What?!" My eyes widened as the first book lifted off the ground by itself.

"Some oranges stay green even when ripe!" it declared before flinging itself at me.

"Aah!" I dodged, falling onto my side. My elbows skidded painfully across the tiles. Miv jumped onto my face, smacking me with his paw to make me get up.

The second my feet were beneath me again, I ran. More books left their places on the shelves to fly at us. One hit my leg. Another my shoulder and arm. A third jabbed me in the cheek, narrowly missing my eye, and they all shouted random facts.

"One bolt of lightning can toast one hundred thousand pieces of bread!"

"Only two percent of the global population has green eyes!"

"Sarcasm makes you more creative!"

Zhong shrieked as a book smacked into her nose. "We're being pelted with knowledge!"

"Run faster!" Miv said, hiding beneath my hair.

We sprinted across the floor, arms raised to protect our heads.

The corner of a book stabbed the back of my neck. "Because of a genetic defect, cats can't taste sweet things!"

"Really?" I asked Miv, even as I slapped the book away.

"Not now!" he yowled back.

A particularly thick book slammed into the back of my leg. I fell with an *oomph*. My palms slapped the floor, stinging.

"The T. rex probably didn't roar. Scientists think it hissed or rattled like a rattlesnake!" the book said.

"Stop ruining *Jurassic Park*!" I shouted at it.

Zhong reached down with one hand to haul me up. "Keep going."

I struggled back to my feet, limping. The door was just a few paces away.

A book behind me shouted, "The god of thunder, destruction, and wrath was defeated by Shee Yee with his celestial ax!"

I almost tripped again when I spun back around. A book tried to whack me in the temple with its cover. I swatted at it, but that didn't help much. Books surrounded me, each shouting to be heard over the others. Their hard corners and sharp edges dug into my skin. I really didn't want to die by a thousand paper cuts.

Then, suddenly, they all flew a few feet away. I groaned in relief and peeked out from between my arms. Zhong stood next to me, holding a stack of flaming paper—some of her talismans—that she'd lit with the lighter in her other hand. The books, apparently understanding the danger, had backed off.

"Come on, let's go," she said to me, sounding breathless. A bruise was forming above her left eyebrow.

But I had to find out something first. "Which one of you mentioned Xov and Shee Yee?"

All the books began talking again at the same time.

"A single elephant tooth can weigh up to nine pounds."

"Queen Elizabeth II refused to sit on the Iron Throne because it was foreign."

"Shee Yee, the grandson of the Sky Father, was especially fond of goat cheese."

There! I snatched the thin blue book. It fought me, trying to snap my fingers between its covers, but I clutched it to my chest. The other books closed in again, but Zhong dropped the last of the paper talismans, now ashes, and waved her lighter in the air threateningly. Then we darted out the exit door and slammed it shut behind us.

22

~

Past-Life Highlights Reel

 I collapsed against the wall to catch my breath. Who knew books could be so deadly?

The blue volume struggled in my arms, mumbling random facts that I couldn't make out. One corner of its cover dug into my neck.

"Ow! I'm not going to burn you," I said. I ran my fingers down its spine. To my surprise, the book began to settle. "I just need you to tell me about Shee Yee and Xov."

After a few more strokes, the book went limp. It even snuggled into my arms.

"I bet those books feel pretty neglected," Zhong said. Her short hair stuck straight out from her head, and she was covered in bruises. She looked like she'd wrestled a dozen poj ntxoog.

I smiled and petted the book's cover. "Too bad Miv isn't this easy to calm down."

"Hmph!" Miv said, jumping off my shoulder.

Zhong slid to the floor, wincing as she checked her legs for more injuries. I probably looked like I'd been in battle, too—and lost—but I'd worry about that later.

I gently opened to the book's first page. "Please," I asked it, "can you tell me about Shee Yee and Xov?"

The book wriggled out of my hands. It didn't stray far, only enough to give itself room to flip through its own pages. Suddenly, the wall beside Zhong's head melted away, replaced with a vision of a darkened sky. It was like the book had turned the wall into our own private movie screen.

"That is so cool," I whispered. The book straightened its spine proudly. I sat down next to Zhong like we were settling in at a theater, and she grinned back at me. A wave of nostalgia slammed into me as I thought of all the times Matt and I had watched movies and shows together. Maybe this one would help me save him.

On the "screen," Shee Yee was riding across a flat landscape. He had brown skin, and his thick black hair blew over his shoulder in a classic hero shot. The beautiful spirit creature he rode had the legs and body of a horse but the head and wings of an eagle. Secured to the back of its saddle was a shining silver weapon—the lightning ax.

Shee Yee wore a black shirt with a band of embroidered stars along the sleeves and collar, silver and red sashes tied around a trim waist, and flowing black pants cinched at the ankles. The hem of his outer robe billowed behind him like a cape. He had a sharp jaw and keen eyes. He notched his bow and pulled the string taut as he scanned the sky.

A monster emerged from the clouds. It was a demon bird with three heads. In its claws, it held a mortal child. The child's wails were drowned out by the wind as the demon soared high above Shee Yee.

With almost languid ease, Shee Yee took aim and fired his arrow. Aided by his magic and some helpful wind spirits, the arrow spun through the air and pierced clean through the first bird head, then the second and the third. The demon scattered into black smoke, releasing the child from its talons.

Leaping from his saddle, Shee Yee caught the child in midair and landed nimbly on the ground. I almost laughed at how exaggerated his heroics were. That couldn't possibly have happened.

But then I saw Zhong's face. She was completely rapt.

"Wow," she murmured. I realized that she was basically seeing her idol in action.

But it didn't feel real to me. And if it was, then . . . *Awkward.* Shee Yee was a flashy, acrobatic, deadly warrior. Trained by the Dragon Emperor and possessing all the magical gifts of the gods, the blessings of the spirits, and the fighting skills of Bruce Lee.

I was just . . . me. I wasn't even in seventh grade yet. How was I supposed to live up to *that* when I hadn't even been enough for my own dad?

The scene changed to show a seated figure. The lightning flashes around him were too dramatic to see him clearly, but I knew it had to be Xov. He was nothing but a man-shaped silhouette shrouded in black storm clouds that rumbled ominously. From his throne in the Sky Kingdom, he watched as Shee Yee hunted down each of his demon offspring, one by one, until at last, the shaman warrior had slain them all.

Enraged, Xov descended from the Sky Kingdom to confront Shee Yee.

"Did Xov actually care about his demon children?" I asked.

"Certainly not," the book said. "They'd killed their mother when they were born, and then they tried to kill Xov. He escaped them by opening the door of the Sky Kingdom and unleashing the flesh-eating, blood-drinking horde onto the world to spread death and chaos."

"So, it was the principle of the matter," Zhong said.

"Absolutely," the book agreed. "By killing his offspring, Shee Yee had dealt Xov a grave insult, and Xov couldn't let it stand."

Their battle was a collision of thunder and lightning, devastating the Spirit Realm. They leveled mountains and boiled lakes. But at last Shee Yee split Xov's thunder spear with his lightning ax. The shaman cast gold chains around Xov's wrists, ankles, and neck. With his magic, he forged a cage of silver around the fallen god. And around that, he constructed a wall of ivory. Three seals of binding to ensure that Xov couldn't escape.

The last of Xov's children—not a demon, but one born of spiritfolk—had stood by his father's side against Shee Yee. As punishment, he was sentenced to be his father's prison guard for all eternity so he would never forget the price of the god's cruelty.

The scene vanished, and the book slammed shut.

Zhong looked crestfallen that there wasn't more, and when she reached for the book, it snapped at her fingers. She scowled.

"Was that it?" she asked. "That was incredible."

"Yeah . . ." I said, not as certain.

I mean, Shee Yee was cool and all, if a bit too flashy, and Xov was terrible for subjecting the realms to the vicious appetites of his demon children. But it felt really weird to admit that my former self had been so amazing. Not only did it seem wrong to take credit for something a previous version of me had done, but it would also mean having to admit that I was a serious downgrade.

"Is there anything else you can tell us about those seals binding Xov?" I asked the book. I thought about Shao's warning and also the dream where I'd visited Xov's cage. The old god wanted me to free him . . . probably just so he could torture me for what Shee Yee had done.

The book perked up and spoke. "Each seal of binding was accompanied by a curse, to strengthen it. The first went:

"Bound in ivory, silver, gold,
The god of wrath will prison hold.
By victor's hand the gate undone
When sky bridges earth for love of sun."

"Unfortunately, the other two curses have been lost to time." The book sounded genuinely upset that it couldn't offer more help.

"No, this is great. Thank you!" I'd already heard Xov recite those same lines, but I didn't want the book to feel bad. "I just wish I understood what it meant."

"Well," Zhong said, straightening her shoulders and lifting her chin, "the first two lines are obvious. The third line, I think, is talking about Shee Yee."

"Because he was the victor against Xov? Does that mean he's the only one who can release him?" Did that mean *I* was the only one who could release him? My shoulders bunched up around my ears at the thought . . . before I gasped in realization. "That's why he sent poj ntxoog after me! And why he wants me alive."

I thought about my dream outside his prison. He'd been certain I would come to free him. But his mind must have rotted after being locked up for so long, because there was no way I was getting anywhere near him. The curse was to keep him contained. It wasn't some prophecy for me to fulfill. Right?

No wonder Shao had warned me to stay away from his

prison. He could have been a little less cryptic about it, but I guess he'd been too busy barbecuing us at the time. Yeah, I was still kind of mad about that.

"He's not going to get his hands on you, Pahua," Zhong said, which chased away some of my anger. "That last line is confusing, though. *When sky bridges earth* . . . What could that mean?"

I ran my fingers along the book's spine. Its pages rippled like a contented cat, which made Miv hiss. "Maybe *sky* means the Sky Kingdom? Could it be referring to those stairs that Shee Yee destroyed? It's not a bridge, but it does connect the earth to the sky. . . . Maybe they need to be repaired?"

"Maybe," Zhong said, looking mildly impressed. "But then what does *for love of sun* mean?"

"The sun is just a lantern that the Sky Father orders carried across the heavens every day," I said, recalling my dream in Ntuj's garden.

"It's more than that," said Zhong. "It's a celestial object. Who knows what its full powers are."

I stood and brushed dust off my leggings. "Well, Shee Yee made the curse confusing on purpose, right? So it could never be broken."

Just the idea of being pulled into a dream with Xov again made my knees feel like rice porridge, but no matter what he tried to do to me, I'd never be able to free him. Shee Yee had made that impossible. My former self might have been a bit careless about what he did with his powers, like smashing the stairs to the Sky Kingdom, or imprisoning gods (and dooming himself to be trapped in the Tree of Souls for thousands of years), but at least he'd done one thing right—he'd made sure Xov couldn't get out and seek revenge.

Miv yawned loudly as he stretched his tiny kitten legs. He pointed down the corridor with his nose. "Let's keep going."

I stroked the book's cover one more time. Then I set it on the ground outside the closed library door for Yeng to find later. No way was I going back in there to put it away.

We didn't come across any more bizarre rooms, which was kind of disappointing. "I wonder how deep these roots go."

"We're in the biggest banyan tree in the realms," Zhong said.

"So . . . deep, then."

Miv, who was once again perched on my shoulder, butted his head into my neck. "I think the word you'd use here is *duh.*"

"I'm just worried about how long we've been here. We don't exactly have all the time in the world to wander around. How deeply is the ax buried? Are we just supposed to stumble on—"

A rumbling sound cut me off. It echoed down the corridor, and the floor began to shift beneath our feet. Dirt cascaded from the ceiling.

"Oh no," I whispered. My fears about being buried alive flashed in my head like a neon sign.

Miv leaped from my shoulder and streaked down the tunnel ahead of us to find an exit. Zhong and I followed more slowly, shielding our eyes from the dust. I thought about the way Yeng had cackled as she'd sent the minor nature spirits scurrying from her garden. We were like those nature spirits now, at the mercy of the arborist or the Tree of Souls or whatever it was that controlled this place.

The ground lifted beneath me. I stumbled just as a huge crack opened in the wall. Unable to stall my momentum on the tilting floor, I fell right into it.

"Pahua!" Zhong shouted.

I reached for her, but the crack closed again, sealing me off in utter darkness.

23

Worst Memory

 I tumbled down a hole, like an animal's burrow. My elbows and knees banged into soft earth, shooting dirt into my face and up my nose.

Then my back slammed into something hard. I groaned in pain. For a few seconds, I couldn't move. I just lay there, blinking away the sting in my eyes. Then, slowly, I rolled onto my side. I ached all over. Coughing, I brushed the hair from my face and tried to see where I was, but everything was pitch-black.

The shaft I'd fallen through rumbled, showering me with more dirt. With a gasp, I covered my head, hoping I wouldn't be buried alive before Zhong and Miv could rescue me. That is, if they could get through the wall that had just closed above, leaving me stranded.

What do I do? What do I do?

I stood even though my body wanted me to curl into a ball. My hands groped at the walls, but I couldn't feel anything except solid earth. Was there enough air in here? Panic made my stomach twist.

Pretend, Pahua. Just pretend you're someone else. I tried. I tried to imagine I was a world-famous adventurer about to pull off a daring escape . . . but the fantasy kept slipping away. I was too afraid. All I had on me was my shaman sword, and what good was that? I didn't think attacking the walls would do much, but I was open to creative solutions.

The pit trembled, and I freaked, thinking the ceiling was caving in. But then light pierced my eyes. A doorway opened. I blinked against the brightness, waiting for my vision to adjust. When it did, I was surprised to see that the door led out to a forest.

The sudden appearance of trees and blue sky should've been comforting—and it was definitely better than that dark enclosed space—but I just found it confusing. Had the Tree of Souls spat me out? It was possible I had emerged from lower down the mountain. It was also possible that I was still underground and having a panic-induced hallucination.

I shook the dirt from my clothes and patted down my hair. When I drew a deep breath, the air smelled sweet, like sugarcane and coconut milk. It made me think of nab vam, one of my favorite Hmong desserts: chewy, delicious tapioca pearls and green jelly mixed with ice, caramelized sugar, and coconut milk.

Whenever we made the drive to the Asian-foods store, which was almost an hour away, we always bought two cups of nab vam, one each for me and Matt. I would make a game of how long I could make mine last, but Matt always finished his within ten minutes of getting in the car. He wasn't very good at waiting. . . .

A lump formed in my throat, and I swallowed it back down. I had to focus and get out of there so I could find the lightning ax and rescue him.

The grass beneath my feet was thick enough to be carpet. It made me want to take off my boots and dig my toes into the softness. Clusters of wild violets weaved purple trails through the trees. The sun felt warm against my face.

It all looked too perfect. As I walked, not sure where I was headed, a weight continued to drag at my stomach. I needed to find Miv and Zhong, but that wasn't all that was bothering me. When my fingers passed over a tree and the rough-looking bark felt unnervingly smooth, I realized what was wrong.

It was quiet. Much too quiet. In a forest this alive, the trees, flowers, and air should have been swarming with nature spirits. But I was alone. Goose bumps rose on my arms. I looked over my shoulder. The door where I exited was gone.

I swallowed nervously. I was still underneath the mountain. I felt certain of it. This had to be another impossible magical room, like the library.

Not even my footsteps could break the silence, because the grass cushioned my boots. I kept one hand on the hilt of my sword. Everything looked peaceful, but just because I wasn't in danger of being pelted with heavy books again didn't mean I should let my guard down.

The farther I walked, the more a certain feeling grew inside me. It began as a dread of never being able to find my way out of here and evolved into a fear that I'd been left behind. I rubbed down the goose bumps on my arms. It was all just in my head. The magic of this place was getting to me. But I couldn't shake the sudden thought that I'd been forgotten.

My hand found the chain around my neck. With a tug, I pulled the locket from beneath my collar. The leaf was still inside, green and strangely perfect. Yeng had said it would help get me where I needed to go.

I held up the leaf and rocked on the balls of my feet, anxious. Biting my lip, I waited. But nothing happened. There was no magical awakening, no sense of awareness, no sudden knowledge. It just felt like a leaf.

My shoulders fell, and I put the leaf back into the locket. What was I going to do?

A voice made me jump. "Hello there."

Through a break in the trees, a creek glimmered. As I got closer, I noticed that a wooden bridge stretched over the water. A shiver ran down my spine. It looked a lot like the bridge near school, where I'd first encountered the angry spirit. Except this one was in way better condition, with all the boards still in place. On the other side of the creek, a door stood against the backdrop of the trees, looking strange and out of place.

The person who'd spoken was a man sitting in a stuffed leather chair. He looked out of place, too. He and his chair were parked beside the bridge along with a metal bucket overflowing with fat purple plums.

"Come closer," he called out.

I really didn't want to. Unfortunately, he was the only other person here, and I needed help. Reluctantly, I approached the bridge.

"Who are you?" I asked.

The man was dressed in neatly pressed gray slacks, the kind important businessmen in movies wear when they say things like *Let me make you a deal*, or *Bring me my solid-gold toothbrush*. His black shoes were so shiny that I could have checked my hair in their reflection (except I already knew that I looked like I'd lost a dodgeball game with a mountain). The sleeves of his white button-down shirt were rolled up to his elbows. He had short black hair, perfectly styled to look like he hadn't tried very hard.

"I'm Cag," he said simply. "I've been waiting for you."

I frowned. "Roots? How did you know I was coming?"

"Because you selected my door. Which meant you would arrive here eventually."

"I don't understand."

He gestured to the forest and the jewel-bright colors too intense to be real. "When people think about their past, what do they remember? What do *you* remember?"

"Um—"

"Tell me the first thing that comes to mind."

"I got a fever and hives once after eating at Burger King." I had itched *all over*, even after taking Benadryl. But I hadn't even minded much, because my mom had stayed home with me for two whole days. She had fed me rice porridge and boiled chicken in herbs and cuddled with me on the sofa while we watched space documentaries about the end of the universe.

The man laughed, a low, delighted sound. "You're too young to be filled with so much sadness."

I shrugged, uncomfortable.

"When people think about their past, they usually like to . . . brighten it up. They tend to gloss over the shadows and the hollow spaces, smooth out the dull patches. They talk about the 'good old days.' Most souls here don't want to face the pitted and stained reality of what their lives had been. But they must take stock of everything before they can move on. So I help them."

"You force them to remember bad stuff?"

The man laughed again. "Let's say I give all their memories a fresh coat of paint and a rose-tinted finish. Sometimes it helps ease them into moving on, and sometimes it makes them clutch even tighter to their own falsehoods. Either way, I stay busy."

"What do you want with me, then?"

He perked up, sitting straighter in his leather seat. "I want to unburden you. You seek the lightning ax." He pointed to the bridge and the door waiting on the other side. "This will take you there. There's a toll to cross it, but don't worry—it's one you won't mind paying. All I require is a bad memory."

I thought about it. "That's not so terrible."

Maybe he could take the memory of that time my aunt made me hold a live chicken for her while she completed some shaman blessing. I couldn't tell her that the chicken scared me, so I just stood there until I began sobbing uncontrollably. The chicken hadn't seemed to mind. Or maybe that time I went to school sick and threw up my breakfast on the kid in front of me. For the rest of year, the other kids called me P*ahurl*.

"Not just any memory," the man said. His nose wrinkled as if he'd read my thoughts or glimpsed the memories I was thinking about. "Your *worst* memory. That's the one I need. You're very young. It will be quick and painless."

My shoulders bunched. I knew immediately which memory he wanted—the day my dad left.

A chill swept through me. I wished I hadn't left my cloak with Spike.

For a moment, I let myself think about what it would be

like to let go of that memory. It would no longer play in my head whenever I saw how tired my mom was after a long week of work. I would finally be able to stop wondering if it had been my fault. I'd stop being so angry with him.

Would that be so bad?

But it didn't feel right. Not at this point in my life, anyway. If our roots are who we are, everything we've been and done, then wouldn't cutting out such an important piece, even if it was a bad one, hurt the whole tree?

"Why do you need it?" I asked. I had to understand.

He spread out his hands, like the answer should be obvious. I was really tired of everybody expecting me just to know things. "Roots must be watered. The most nourishing memories for me are the ones that burrow deep inside others and lodge in the heart like a splinter that can't be extracted."

"Except *you* can extract them," I said.

Maybe I would be happier if I didn't have that memory anymore.

But then again, maybe I wouldn't. Maybe I'd just be confused. Maybe I'd end up wondering why I was sad for no reason.

"I can't," I said heavily. "I can't give that to you."

Cag's dark eyes narrowed. He regarded me with such intensity that I squirmed and wanted to wash my face.

But then he plucked a plum from his bucket and handed it to me. "Then, Pahua Moua, the only way forward is back."

"But I can't go back. The door closed behind me."

He didn't speak, only continued to hold out the fruit.

I hesitated. "I'm going to need clearer instructions."

"Eat the plum."

"Why?"

"Because if you don't, you'll be trapped here forever."

Well, that was a pretty compelling reason. I took the plum. It was so big that it filled both my palms. But it looked ripe and juicy, and I was *starving*.

"What's going to happen?"

He gave me a blank look.

"Right. Eat the plum," I said. "Okay, here goes nothing." I took a bite.

Sweet liquid flooded my mouth and dripped down my chin. The fruit was *delicious* and just the right texture—soft but not mushy. I took a second messy bite, savoring the taste. Then the forest and the man swirled into a blur.

The plum fell from my sticky fingers. I turned in a slow circle, the vortex of color making me dizzy. After a few seconds, the world re-formed around me.

I stood in a living room. Not just any living room, but the one in the house we'd lived in before my dad left. I swallowed thickly. What was left of the fruit suddenly soured in my mouth.

The room was smaller than I remembered. A brown leather sofa sat against the wall, faded and scuffed with age. It faced a flat-screen TV with a game console under it. A stack of games had fallen over, and a handful lay scattered on the carpet. Through the windows, the street looked just as I remembered—a cul-de-sac where the neighborhood kids rode their bikes back and forth.

My parents stepped into the room. At the sight of my dad, something tore inside me. Tears filled my eyes. I backed away, skirting a potted banana tree until I was pressed into a corner. I slid to the ground and hugged my knees.

My mom's eyes were red and puffy, her lips pressed into a hard line. She was wearing a pretty blouse with big lilacs on it. My dad had given it to her the previous Christmas. Attached to the shirt, right above her heart, was a shiny metal pin. It was a shaman's cymbal with a pair of elephant-foot spirals inside and a single stripe on top.

I knew the pin was important for some reason, but at the moment, my mind couldn't put the pieces together. I was too caught up in the awfulness of what was happening.

This was the last day my dad would be with us. My parents had just had a fight. Usually when that happened, Dad would leave for a few hours. In the morning, he'd be home again to drop me off at school and kiss me good-bye. But after this particular fight, he hadn't returned. A week later, my mom had sat Matt and me down to tell us he never would. She'd given no explanation.

In this memory, Mom didn't speak as my dad put on his coat. It was fall. A month before Halloween, and I'd been bugging him about our costumes. I wanted to be a dinosaur trainer and for him to be the dinosaur so I could walk him around the neighborhood on a leash.

Somewhere in the house, three-year-old Matt started crying.

Watching the scene replay, I sucked in great lungfuls of air, but it didn't seem like enough. My eyes felt hot, so I squeezed them shut. I pressed my hands over my ears. I wasn't here. This wasn't real. I was a ballerina in a recital. I was a detective hiding from criminals. I was a—a—

I couldn't think of anything, so I curled tighter around my knees. *It's not real. It's not real. It's not—*

A teacher said you went into the woods with some girls, came Matt's voice.

I stiffened. The voice hadn't come from the room. It had come from inside my head.

I snuck out to find you.

The words were from the day I'd freed the bridge spirit. Matt had only been out there because of me.

He'd looked so small in that big hospital bed. Mom would still be at his side, her eyes dark with shadows while her fingers worked on the charm. I thought of how Matt slurped up my dinners of ramen noodles and eggs and rice, the only things I knew how to cook, as if they were his favorite foods in the whole world. I thought of the way he reached for my hand when we crossed the street without me having to remind him, and how he always got excited about which TV or movie series we were going to marathon the next weekend, even if we'd seen them a million times before.

My pretending might have started because of the feeling that I didn't fit in, but after our dad left, it had also become a shield, allowing me to hide from the truth that I hadn't been enough to make him stay.

None of that mattered now, though. My brother needed me. I was his big sister, and it was my job to protect him. I had to get out of there and find that lightning ax. I had to get his soul back.

Slowly, I got to my feet.

Dad was still by the door, like he hadn't yet made up his mind about whether he was going to stay. Mom was gone, probably to wherever Matt was in the house. I stepped out into the middle of the room, my chin held high.

"I don't forgive you," I said loudly. My voice shook, but my eyes were dry.

Dad turned to me, the lines around his mouth deep. He didn't look the way I remembered. He seemed older, more tired.

"I know I'm only eleven, but I also know what it's like when things aren't what you want them to be. I pretend to be other people all the time. But . . . I don't run away. That's what cowards do. And while you're not there for them, I will be."

Dad took a step toward me, and everything went black.

I wavered on my feet. I was suddenly standing on the

other side of the bridge, in front of the door. I whirled around to see Cag at the other end. He pointed to his open hand.

I looked down. Cupped in my palm was a plum pit. When I closed my fingers around it, the pain from only moments ago echoed through my skull, as if I were holding a living record of my worst memory. I flinched, almost dropping it.

"A memento!" Cag called.

Frowning, I tucked the pit into the same pocket that held my gloves. Part of me wanted to throw the stone away. The memory was still in my head—Cag hadn't erased it—so what was the point of carrying the pit around as well? But it seemed that he wanted me to keep it.

Was I supposed to feel different now that I'd faced my worst memory? I didn't feel any lighter. All the anger was still there. Except . . . I guess the memory felt smaller now. Small enough to fit into my palm. Small enough that I could let it go if I wanted to.

With one last glance at Cag, who waved good-bye, I pulled open the door and walked through.

Right into Zhong.

"Ow!" she yelled as we both stumbled.

"Pahua!" Miv leaped onto my shoulder. He smacked my face with both paws. "What happened? You fell through a crack in the wall and disappeared."

"Yeah, I know. I was there." Despite my sarcasm, I was relieved to be with them again. I ran my fingers through his fur and felt instantly reassured.

"Where'd you go?" Zhong asked, peering over my shoulder. But both the forest and Cag were gone.

"Nowhere I'd want to go back to," I said, avoiding her eyes. "What about you guys?"

Zhong immediately turned away. "Like you said: nowhere I'd want to go back to."

I frowned. We were inside a lantern-lit corridor again, but as we walked, I snuck glances at her. She looked the way I felt—a little uneasy, like she'd faced something she'd hoped never to see again. I realized then the Tree of Souls hadn't targeted only me. It was testing all of us. Even Miv seemed quieter than usual.

Like Cag had said, every spirit bound to the Tree of Souls had to confront things they didn't want to before they could move on. I guess I was lucky I was only eleven.

I wondered what Shee Yee had been forced to deal with when he was here. What regrets and secret sorrows did a hero have?

I was dying to know what the tree had shown Zhong, though I would never dare to ask her. Had she seen something about her family and how she felt like she would never measure up? Or maybe about how she might fail this quest and get kicked out of her school? I could imagine how ashamed she would be if that happened, especially with her family's history of powerful shaman warriors. I'd already told her that she was amazing, but I wanted to remind her again . . . even though it probably wouldn't help.

And what about Miv? I knew next to nothing about his life before he'd found me when I was four.

The tunnel grew wider as we walked. The lamps became larger, filling the corridor with light. The walls smoothed out. The ceiling became stone instead of earth. A scent thickened the air, but it wasn't the dank musk of being underground. It smelled like jasmine.

The tunnel opened into an airy, bright room with a garden in the middle. The walls and ceiling were made of white marble tiles. At each corner, stone fountains ran with clear water.

Even though this room looked as out of place as the others had, it felt different. Safer somehow. I didn't know how I knew, but there would be no trick floors or tests to pass here.

A path was cut through thick swathes of jasmine blooms to the center of the garden, where a life-size stone statue of Shee Yee stood on a pedestal. In his hand, he held a formidable weapon.

A gleaming silver ax.

24

King Arthur Did It Better

 "The lightning ax," I whispered.

The object belonged in a museum, not a battle. The black handle shone like it had been freshly polished. Coiled around the top of the shaft, crafted to look like it was holding the ax blade, was a metal sculpture of a fearsome dragon with a sparkling ruby for an eye.

Spirals, like the one on my arm, were etched into the broad blade along with a many-pointed star. My mom had told me the star was a symbol of protection.

"It's stunning," breathed Zhong.

It was also *huge*. The weapon had to be almost as tall as I was. The blade had me convinced I stood a good chance of cutting off my own feet if I tried to use it.

"Take the ax," Miv said, nudging my foot with his paw.

"How?" I probably wouldn't even be able to lift it.

Zhong pushed my back to get me moving. "Just trust in yourself. You have Shee Yee's spirit. You can do it."

I wiped my palms against my leggings, which didn't do much other than streak more dirt on my hands. But I was nervous. Everything rode on me being able to wield the celestial weapon. My brother and Zhong were relying on me. I had to try.

I climbed onto the statue's pedestal. If the sculpture was true to life, then Shee Yee had been tall and broad with long, lean arms strong enough to carry a heavy ax. The sculptor had done an amazing job with the veins in the backs of his hands and the folds of his sashes. A heavy silver tribal necklace, a xauv, hung around his neck.

My mom used to make me wear an intricate xauv made of interlocking silver chains to Hmong New Year celebrations, and it always made my neck hurt. Shee Yee didn't look like a heavy necklace would bother him. He looked how a hero was supposed to.

Luckily, he was holding the ax down at his side. If he'd been holding it up, there was no way I could have reached it without climbing a ladder or learning to fly. After seeing the way Shee Yee had leaped from his spirit mount in the book's story, I wouldn't have been surprised if flying had been one of his many talents.

The weapon was even more intimidating up close. Every detail of the dragon was perfect, down to its sharp teeth, individual scales, and the mane along its serpentine spine.

It didn't seem like the ax had been sitting here for thousands of years, waiting for Shee Yee to claim it again. It looked . . . ready.

Unlike me. I wasn't ready to take this responsibility. But I *was* ready to save my brother. I wanted all this to be over with so I could take Matt home.

"I'm not Shee Yee," I whispered, flexing my fingers. Fear seized my insides.

Miv leaped up the statue until he landed on my shoulder, his slight weight barely there. "No, you're not Shee Yee," he said, but it wasn't with his usual insulting tone. He pressed the top of his head beneath my jaw. "You're Pahua Moua. You can do this."

I smiled, his support filling me with courage. Then I reached for the ax.

A shimmering rope wrapped around my wrist. I stilled, confused, before the rope abruptly tightened and wrenched me off the statue. I hit the ground hard, all the air squeezing from my lungs. Miv yowled in anger somewhere beside me, and Zhong shouted my name.

The marble ceiling blurred. A shadow fell over me. It was a woman in shiny scaled armor. Her hair was dark blue, and her skin was iridescent, like fish scales catching the sunlight. Her eyes were slitted and golden.

"So much trouble over one tiny shamanling." She clamped her hand around my arm and dragged me to my feet.

I wheezed as my lungs began to work again. Four more warriors surrounded us. One of them held a knife to Zhong's neck, and another was shoving Miv into what looked like a giant floating soap bubble. Miv was shouting something, but the bubble muffled his voice.

Like the shape-shifter who'd torn up my apartment, these were dragons in human form. In full armor, they were way scarier than the one wearing oversize jeans had been. The dragon restraining me removed my sword belt. Then she bound my hands behind my back and shoved me down against the base of the statue's pedestal. The other dragons all but flung Zhong next to me.

I didn't have to be a mind reader to know Zhong was thinking the same thing I was. How were we supposed to defeat five trained dragon warriors? We'd only been able to restrain the one in my apartment because of the guardian spirits, and then only long enough to convince him to leave of his own accord. I had a feeling these dragons weren't going to be persuaded to give up.

"It's as magnificent as the legends say," one of the dragons said. She stared in awe at the lightning ax still on the statue. "It will make a fine gift for our lord."

"The Dragon Emperor?" I asked, surprised. Huab Tais Zaj was Shee Yee's uncle and Ntuj's son-in-law. Since Ntuj was one of the gods *not* trying to kill me, I'd hoped that meant his son-in-law wasn't, either. And the Dragon Emperor had trained Shee Yee himself, so maybe he—

"We do not serve Huab Tais Zaj. Our lord is the Thunder Dragon, Lord Xiav. And he will make great use of your lightning ax."

Oh. If I had to have a dragon after me, I was glad it wasn't the emperor. Still, I would've preferred no dragon at all. But would Huab Tais Zaj really let Xiav keep the lightning ax? I'm pretty sure the Dragon Emperor would recognize the weapon he'd gifted to his nephew. Was it a *finders keepers* kind of deal?

Out of the corner of my eye, I saw Zhong reach for something hidden beneath the sleeve of her jean jacket. I had to keep the dragons' attention on me and buy her more time.

"Do you know if Xiav and Huab Tais Zaj are related?" I asked them.

The dragons exchanged confused glances, like they'd never thought about that before.

"Well . . ." a dragon with a blue goatee began haltingly, "his second cousin is married to Huab Tais Zaj's nephew's cousin on his mom's side, I think?" He looked to his comrades for confirmation.

They all mumbled uncertainly.

"Wasn't it his wife's aunt's niece on her husband's side?"

"No, no, I'm pretty sure it was his nephew's brother-in-law's cousin."

"That doesn't sound right."

I cut in before they got too carried away. "So, if they're

related, and I'm Huab Tais Zaj's niece, then we're practically family. Not to mention, I'm technically royalty by marriage."

The dragons considered this. "I . . . don't think it works like that," said the one with the goatee.

A soft *snick* sounded next to me. Zhong slowly stretched out her wrists. She'd gotten out of her bonds. I had to keep them talking.

"I'm sorry," I said, trying for my best *I'm small and harmless* smile. "It's just really confusing. If I'm family, attacking me is super disrespectful to your lord."

The dragons looked uncomfortable with the idea.

"And since I'm also royalty, I'm pretty sure it's got to be illegal." It was in fantasy movies, anyway. Royals could always do whatever they wanted, without any consequences.

"Maybe she has a point," the goateed dragon said. A murmur of worry passed between them.

Then the woman who'd tied me up cut her hand through the air, and the other dragons fell silent. She must have been their leader. "Enough of this. Focus! We have our orders. We must return her to Lord Xiav so she can be locked away and prevented from releasing Xov."

I wasn't sure I'd heard right. "Wait, did you just say you have to keep me from releasing Xov?"

"Lord Xiav has gained much as the Thunder Dragon. He can't have you restoring Xov to power," she continued.

"I would never!" To be honest, I was kind of offended.

"We can't trust the word of a mortal. You do have a record of locking up thunder gods, after all. And with the lightning ax, you would be too powerful. It would best serve in the hands of Lord Xiav."

"If he wants the lightning ax for himself, why didn't he just take it before now? He's had thousands of years to do it."

"Ignorant child," the dragon leader said scornfully. "This room has never before revealed itself. We don't trespass on sacred ground lightly." She nodded to one of her companions. "Take the ax."

Eagerly, a dragon with braided blue hair climbed onto the pedestal. I scooted closer to Zhong so that if he fell, it wouldn't be on top of me. No one was looking at us now, and I felt Zhong's hands behind my back. Then the sawing of a small blade that she must've hidden up her sleeve. A moment later, the rope around my wrists went slack.

Above us, the dragon rubbed his palms like he was about to dig into a big slice of cake. Then he wrapped both hands around the ax's gleaming black handle.

In a flash, he vaporized into smoke, leaving only the scent of ash. I gasped. The dragons all stared in shock. Their leader growled.

I turned to Zhong, my heart pounding. "And to think I was just about to grab it," I whispered, horrified.

She gave me an impatient look. "You're the only person who can."

"How do you know? I could end up—"

The dragon leader loomed over me. She drew her sword and I stiffened, but instead of threatening me with it, she touched the point of her blade against Zhong's chest. Zhong's hands were now free behind her back, but there was nothing she'd be able to do with a pocketknife.

"You will retrieve the ax for us," the dragon leader said to me. "And then you will bequeath it to me so that I may wield it. Do it, or I'll kill your friend."

Zhong shook her head furiously. "Don't do it, Pahua! You need that ax to save your brother."

Shee Yee's ability to transmute objects would have come in real handy right about then. I could've turned all their swords into spaghetti noodles. I clenched my fists behind me, willing something to happen. Anything.

The dragon suddenly drew back, a look of alarm on her face. I wiggled my fingers, confused. Had I actually done something?

But then she turned to her companions and snarled, "Demons!"

Right then, a pack of poj ntxoog burst into the garden. Yeng really needed better security. All the dragons drew their swords as the enemies stared one another down.

"You've got our prisoner!" a poj ntxoog shrieked, baring its claws. To my surprise, it was the demon in the sundress, which was still torn. It must not have found a seamstress yet.

"Looks like she's ours now," the dragon woman said.

"Not if we kill you," said a poj ntxoog in floral-print leggings. Its stringy black hair was tied back with a bow.

"You can try, demon, but you'll need to be able to breathe inside that corset."

One of them was indeed wearing a corset.

"It accents my waist!"

"What if we cut her in half?" another demon suggested.

Its friend jabbed it with a hairy elbow. "Idiot! Mortals can't survive that."

"No one can survive that, genius," a dragon sneered.

"Then I guess there's only one solution."

The poj ntxoog attacked. They outnumbered the dragons three to one.

The dragons were fierce warriors, though, and they held their own even against the odds. The dragon in possession of our shaman swords dropped them to join the fray. With our captors preoccupied, I dove for the weapons.

I tossed Zhong her sword and then belted mine around my waist just as the poj ntxoog in the sundress charged me. I barely drew the sword in time to block the swipe of its claws.

"Tricky little shaman," it said, snarling. Up close, its hollow black eyes were like ink stains. "How about you give me that pretty hair clip, and I'll only hurt you a little?"

"Literally no one would say yes to that." I relaxed my body, concentrating on the current of spiritual energy that was always flowing through me. My senses opened up, and

I ducked another blow, slashing my sword down on the demon's arm. Smoke spewed from the gash.

"Aaagh, not fair! Come here and let me capture you easily."

The demon pounced, and I didn't raise my sword fast enough. The creature barreled into me, knocking us both over. We tumbled across the marble floor and into the jasmine bushes.

"I want it!" the demon shrieked, clawing for my clip.

"What is your problem?" I shouted. I smashed the butt of my sword into its temple.

The demon toppled off me, its claws curled around its stringy hair. "I want it! It reminds me of something." The monster scratched at its scalp. "Don't like this place—it's itchy."

I backed away from the whining demon. Killing it while it lay curled up in the jasmine bushes didn't feel right. I searched for Zhong instead. She was fending off a demon as well. I hurried to her side and slashed through the creature's arm with my blade. The entire limb vanished into smoke. As the demon shrieked, Zhong took off its head.

"Come on," I said, pulling her behind the statue of Shee Yee before anyone else could notice that we were no longer tied up.

"Get the ax," she said, pointing upward.

"Where's Miv?" I looked around, searching frantically

for his small black form. His bubble had floated off toward one of the fountains in the far corner. "There he is!"

"No," Zhong hissed, grabbing me before I could take off. "The ax first. Hurry."

"But—"

"He's not going anywhere," she said, exasperated. "But if you want to get all of us out of here alive, we need that ax!"

She had a point. I sheathed my sword and began to climb the pedestal. But when I reached the ax, I hesitated. The dragon had vaporized after touching it.

People kept saying I had Shee Yee's spirit, but it still didn't feel real. What if the ax didn't recognize me? I wasn't anything like the shaman warrior. I was just a kid who'd only ever been good at pretending to be a hero. Seeing the book's vision of Shee Yee had driven that point home.

"Take it!" Zhong shouted, frantic.

I peered around Shee Yee's stone arm. Although the dragons had lost one of their own, they had cut the poj ntxoog's numbers in half. The battle would soon be over.

Okay, Pahua, I told myself. I closed my eyes and imagined how Shee Yee must have felt receiving such a powerful gift from his uncle. Maybe he hadn't even been surprised, like getting celestial gifts was no big deal to the son of a goddess. *You can do this. Just take it.*

Before I could talk myself out of it, I gripped the ax. Cold energy crackled through me, burning my hands. I gasped and released the ax handle so quickly that I almost fell off the pedestal. I grabbed Shee Yee's arm just in time. The skin on my palms smoked faintly.

"I can't do it," I whispered, my stomach dropping. I looked down at Zhong. "I can't do it."

She looked just as confused as I felt. "That can't be right. You *have* to be able to wield it. No one else can."

I flexed my hands, wincing at the pain. The tips of my fingers bore the delicate lace of frost.

Spiritual energy. The lightning ax must require a lot from the wielder, and I had plenty. But even though I could now sense it within me, I hadn't had time to practice how to control it. Like Zhong had said, my energy was all over the place, and I wasn't sure what would happen if I tried to focus it into my hands. I could hurt myself or worse. So what I needed was . . .

I dug into my pocket and withdrew the neutralization gloves. *Please work,* I thought as I pulled them on. Warmth soothed my stinging palms.

"Hurry!" Zhong said.

Okay, let's try this again, I told myself. I wasn't the hero Shee Yee was, and I couldn't do all the fancy magical things he could—at least not yet, if ever. But all I needed to be was enough for my brother. I'd been watching out for him his entire life. That wasn't going to change now.

Bracing against more pain, I gripped the handle.

The gloves grew warmer. A tingling sensation spread from my hands to my shoulders, as if a current was passing from the ax to me, merging seamlessly with my own spiritual power. On my arm, the spiral symbol of the gods rose against my skin.

To my amazement, the ax began to shrink. It went from being a massive weapon meant for a hero of Shee Yee's stature to one that fit comfortably in the much smaller hands of an eleven-year-old. It was even light enough that I could lift it easily. Now that it was half its original size, the ax didn't look nearly as terrifying, but it was still beautiful.

I felt like Arthur pulling Excalibur from the stone. I'd done it! Triumph soared through me as I jumped down and landed clumsily next to Zhong.

She beamed, clapping me hard on the back. "Nice job!"

The room began to shake. Zhong's grin vanished. Cracks snaked down the walls and broke open the floor, swallowing an entire fountain. Marble tiles rained down on us. The remaining dragons and poj ntxoog abandoned the fight and scattered.

"What's happening?" I shouted, taking cover beside the statue again. "Why is the room falling apart?" Whole shrubs of jasmine disappeared into the earth. For some reason, I felt especially sad to see those destroyed.

"Maybe because it no longer has a purpose," Zhong said. "The ax has been found."

A chunk of rock scraped my arm, drawing a bead of blood. It was definitely time to get out of here. I searched for Miv's bubble again, but it wasn't where I'd seen it last. It must have floated elsewhere. Shielding my eyes from the dust, I stood, searching the quickly vanishing garden.

"Miv!" I shouted, jumping over widening crevices. I didn't see him anywhere, but if his bubble had popped, and he'd fallen . . . He was so small, so easy to miss. "Miv, where are you?"

"Pahua!" Zhong shouted. She was pointing at the exit.

The poj ntxoog had given up on trying to capture me. Instead, they were now fleeing for their lives. Gripped in one of their massive paws was a small black kitten. Miv flailed his legs and clawed at the hand that held him, but the demon's grip didn't loosen.

"Miv!" I shouted, and raced after them.

The poj ntxoog were already in the corridor, though, and I was at the other end of the garden. I raised the ax. Lightning crackled up the grip into the blade, which began to glow a brilliant white.

"No!" Zhong shouted, grabbing my arm. "We're still underground. You'll bury us alive."

I jerked away from her in frustration. But I knew she was right. The walls were already coming down around us. If I used the ax, we might not get out in time to save ourselves, much less Miv.

We darted around chunks of ceiling and leaped over cracks that opened into black nothingness. By the time we reached the corridor, the poj ntxoog and the dragons were gone.

"No, no, no," I whispered as we raced through the tunnel.

The crash of the garden room imploding shook the ground. A plume of dirt and dust shot down the tunnel behind us. Up ahead, a door stood open to where the demons and dragons must have fled. Zhong and I burst through it.

I gasped and stumbled to a stop. We were outside, for real this time. The Tree of Souls loomed over us. The white cloths whispered incomprehensibly at the back of my mind. I blinked in confusion and looked over my shoulder at the door. Stairs made of roots descended into the dark.

We were right back where we'd started.

25

~

Stranded

I turned, about to dive back into the tree, but the door slammed shut in my face. "Hey!"

"You're not going to find him in there."

Yeng sat cross-legged on a patch of grass nearby. She was playing a game of pick-up stones with . . . the tree. Roots that looked eerily like fingers drummed the grass as they awaited their turn.

"Where is Miv?" I demanded.

The lightning ax crackled at my side. Bolts of energy sang through me. Sparks leaped from my gloved hand to the earth, scorching a patch of grass. I was bruised and dirty and exhausted, and I needed to find my best friend.

"So much for not wanting to cause destruction, eh, little shaman?" Yeng said, eyeing the burned grass. "How quickly your mind changes when you've had a taste of power."

I swallowed the angry words rising in my throat. She

was right, I realized. I had to be very careful with so much power at my fingertips. Suddenly uneasy, I set the ax down against the tree.

"Did you see where the demons went?" I asked, still urgent but more politely this time.

"They were shown different ways in and out." She spat sap on the ground. "Allowing dragons and demons into the Tree of Souls . . . Only the gods would dare such a thing. But the trespassers will get their due. Invading sacred ground invites ill fortune."

"Where's Spike?" Zhong suddenly asked. She scanned the boundary for her spirit horse. "They didn't hurt her, did they?"

"She took off the moment she sensed the dragons. The only one around here with some sense," Yeng said. "Bah! You're cheating."

The roots had sprouted a sixth finger. The game was a simple one that I'd taught to Matt just last year. You scatter a bunch of pebbles in front of you, keeping one in your hand. Then you toss up the pebble, quickly scoop another from the ground, and catch the first stone in the air before it can hit the dirt. You keep every new pebble you pick up, so the more you collect, the harder it gets until you have to throw and catch a whole handful while still trying to grab more. The extra finger had helped the roots win.

"Why would Spike leave?" Zhong asked, getting Yeng's attention again.

The woman tossed a stone at the roots. They zipped back into the earth like a pouty kid storming out of a room.

Yeng got to her feet and brushed off her dry palms, flicking bits of peeling bark from her knobby fingers. "Dragons and horses have a long-standing rivalry, mostly about who's the best mode of transportation for the Spirit Emperor. Dragons are flashier, but they're shifters with a realm of their own, and horses think that should disqualify them. The horses have a monopoly on travel through four of the six realms with Equestrian Rentals, so the dragons think they should get to keep the royal posts. Over time, it's gotten quite ugly. One horse even set the royal dragon hotel on fire once. It didn't do much damage, because dragons can summon water. But you should have seen how angry—"

"Um," I cut in, trying not to sound as impatient as I felt. "So, you don't know where the demons might have gone? They took Miv."

"I did tell you that a cat spirit had no business in the Tree of Souls."

I slumped to the ground, cradling my head. At my side, the lightning ax hummed. The seams on my neutralization gloves had begun to fray. The weapon's power was too great. I would have to find a set of sturdier gloves until I could train myself to control my spiritual energy.

"I hope Spike comes back," Zhong murmured, twisting the bracelet around her wrist.

"She might, once she thinks it's safe," Yeng said. "The

dragon-horse rivalry is bad, but you're lucky it's not like the one between monkeys and grasshoppers. Those two groups would start a war right outside the Tree of Souls if they had the chance. They haven't stopped hating each other since a monkey once sat on a grasshopper princess." She dropped her voice to a whisper. "And I don't believe for one second it was an accident."

I was barely listening. I traced a gloved finger over the intricate metalwork on the ax. It must have been crafted in Zaj Teb, the Land of Dragons, by one of Huab Tais Zaj's weaponsmiths. Here I was with a celestial weapon in my hands, when I'd never truly believed I'd get this far. It had only cost me my best friend.

Tears welled in my eyes. I wiped them away, because Yeng was watching me. Zhong was walking the boundary, searching the clouds for a sign of Spike. The sun was setting. Soon it would be impossible to spot anything in the sky, much less a horse. We had exactly one day left, and without the horse spirit, there was no way we were getting back to those elephant tunnels in time. All our effort had been for nothing.

Yeng sighed. Then she kicked my foot with her red rubber boots. "Are those my shoes you're wearing?"

I wiped my nose. I was too miserable to even be embarrassed. "I needed something sturdier."

"Well, at least you left me your sandals. The shoes of

Pahua Moua, granddaughter to Ntuj. I could probably trade them for something."

"Isn't there any way you can help us?" I pleaded.

"What do you think I can do, girl? I watch after a tree."

"It's not just any tree."

Yeng patted her gnarled hand against the bark of the Tree of Souls. "No. Not just any tree."

The white cloths glowed faintly in the twilight. From a distance, the banyan probably looked like the universe's biggest Christmas tree.

"Anytime a mortal soul enters the Spirit Realm, I sense its arrival," said the arborist. "Where it goes after that, I can't tell, but I know when they cross the border. I felt it when your bridge spirit arrived. She died young, but her spirit lingered in the mortal realm for centuries, filled with anger and sadness. There were too many roots knotting her to her former life. She should have come to me, to face herself in the Tree of Souls and await reincarnation. But she didn't. I have felt part of her slipping back and forth across the border since then, and she never returns alone. She's brought other mortal souls with her, souls that do not belong here yet."

"We know where she went." I rose to my feet, leaving the lightning ax in the grass. I could still feel it thrumming through my skin, so powerful and yet so useless to me right now. I needed a different kind of help, and I would beg Yeng if I had to. "She's in the tunnels beneath the Spirit Realm with the souls she stole from my brother and other kids. We need to get back there by tomorrow night before they're turned into demons. Please. There has to be something you can do."

Yeng waved her hand airily, like I hadn't just told her that lives were at stake. "You don't get something for nothing."

Suddenly, begging was the furthest thing from my mind. I clenched my fists, and my face grew hot with anger. "What's wrong with you? You're surrounded by mortal souls all the time. You have to listen to every terrible thing they lived through, but you don't care about any of it. How can you be so heartless?"

I was breathing hard, and my pulse thundered in my ears. I'd never confronted a grown-up in this way before, and part of me felt ashamed. The arborist was an ancient being with a sacred purpose. Like Shao, she deserved to be treated with respect and deference. My mom would ground me for a month if I ever yelled at her like that.

Yeng lifted one eyebrow, which crinkled the bark of her forehead. Then she squatted, as if she intended to sit. A root rose from the earth to meet her, providing an instant seat. With daytime fading fast, our only light came from the spirits bound to the tree.

Zhong, who'd heard me shouting, wandered back. Her arms were crossed tight, her shoulders bunched around her ears. I thought maybe she was upset about Spike.

But then her lips pinched like she was sucking on a sour

gummy as she spoke to Yeng. "You're one of the oldest spirits in this entire realm. There has to be something you can do. Just tell us what you want."

I remembered then that I wasn't the only one who had something to lose. Zhong's future as a shaman warrior, and her family's pride, depended on us being able to defeat the bridge spirit. I swallowed my anger and nodded in agreement.

"Mortals," Yeng said with an exasperated sigh. "I was mortal once, too, you know."

Surprised, I tilted my head, taking in her bark skin that was slightly peeling in a dozen places.

She noticed and snapped, "I need a good exfoliation, okay? Pay attention. Like I said, I was mortal once. Not only that, but I was in love."

Zhong straightened her shoulders, eyes brightening with curiosity. I tried to act interested as well, even though all I wanted to do was storm down the mountainside. I hoped there was a point to this story—it was hard to tell with Yeng.

The arborist's pale, watery eyes glazed over. "Ka was kind and sweet and all the things we're not allowed to be if we want to survive in a world built for the ruthless. We used to take walks together through the mountain rice paddies. Our parents would scold us for ignoring our chores. But what did we care? We were young.

"Then one day she went into the woods and came back with a story about meeting a beautiful princess who'd promised to take her away to a palace in the clouds. I was cursed with the ability to see through enchantments, and I knew that whoever that princess was, she had cast a veil over Ka's eyes. When Ka went to meet her again, I followed. I saw that she was no princess at all, but a goddess. Nhia Ngao Zhua Pa."

Yeng said the name bitterly, years of built-up resentment in her voice.

"When I tried to convince Ka that she was a fraud, the goddess became enraged. She trapped me inside the banyan tree." Yeng pressed her hand to the root that had become her seat. Her fingers fit neatly into its grooves. "It took me years to find my way out, and by then, it was too late. Ka was dead, and I was forever bound to the Tree of Souls."

"I'm sorry," I said. "That was cruel."

Yeng shrugged like it was no big deal. "The past is the past. But it can teach us a thing or two about how to move forward. I believe you learned that during your time in the tree as well."

"But what I need to know right now is how to move from here to the bridge spirit."

She rolled her eyes. "No one appreciates a lesson anymore. My point, little shaman, is that the world will not mold itself to suit your needs and morals, quaint as they are. Life is unfair. Don't come crying to me about it. I get enough of that from the spirits here. If you want help, you'd better be ready to pay for it."

"Then what do you want as payment?"

"I'm not talking about me. I want nothing. And I've already given you a gift, haven't I? I can't do any more than that."

I could have ripped out my hair. Why hadn't she just said that at the start? I pulled out the locket. "This wasn't any help when I was inside the tree."

"You found your way out again, didn't you?" Yeng said, rising from her seat. The root sank back into the earth. "That's proof enough it helped."

Without even a farewell, she stepped over the root and left us standing there, stranded at the top of a mountain.

26

~

Trust-Fall, Extreme Edition

"This is all my fault." Zhong sank to her knees in the grass. "The moment I learned that the bridge spirit was strong enough to steal mortal souls into the Spirit Realm, I should have called Master Bo and turned the matter over to an experienced shaman warrior. I just . . ."

"You didn't want to give up. You wanted to prove yourself," I said, still glaring after Yeng.

Zhong nodded. "I can't stand the thought of not being a shaman warrior. I don't want to be anything other than"—she waved a hand at herself: the shaman sword, the bottomless backpack with all her supplies, the buttons like badges of honor on her jacket—"this."

I understood. And it wouldn't have mattered anyway if she had called her mentor. Even a shaman master wouldn't have been enough to face the bridge spirit—Shao had said as much. Once I'd felt the bridge spirit's power for myself in that tunnel, I knew he was right.

No one stood a chance without the lightning ax, and since I was the only one who could wield it, this was no one's responsibility but mine. It had to be me.

Except I was stuck on the top of a mountain, far from where I needed to be, and my brother was running out of time. I rubbed my eyes. There was no use crying.

I reached down and hefted the ax. It was a good thing it wasn't heavy, because I had a feeling we weren't going to find a village with an equestrian-rental agency anywhere nearby. We had a lot of walking ahead of us. I couldn't just sit here and give up, not when Matt was still waiting for me.

There was a flash of movement at the edge of my vision. I turned to look and caught a glimpse of someone with stringy black hair and a dingy yellow dress before they disappeared behind thick branches.

"Hey!" I yelled, and began running after it. I heard Zhong shout and follow me.

I leaped over roots and skirted around branches so thick they might have been trees themselves. Luckily, the light from the white cloths was enough to see by. I held the ax at my side, careful not to cut off my leg as I ran.

The poj ntxoog was having a hard time navigating the banyan tree's root system with its backward feet. Suddenly, a crossbow bolt shot past me and buried itself in the demon's calf. It fell, crashing into a snarl of roots.

Within seconds, Zhong and I were on it. Before Zhong could take off its head, though, I shouted for her to stop.

"It'll know where Miv is," I explained.

Sometime between our fight in the garden and now, the sundress demon had tried to run a plastic yellow comb through its stringy hair. The comb seemed to have gotten stuck, because it dangled next to its face. The gash on its arm where I'd cut it still leaked smoke but had begun to heal.

"Where's my friend?" I demanded, smacking the handle of the lightning ax against my gloved palm. In movies, people do that with baseball bats when they want to look tough.

"Taken to camp with the others," the demon said, wincing and examining its leg.

"Then why are you here?"

"B-because of the tree. It feels . . . weird." The demon looked up through its hair at the forbidding banyan. Its hollow black eyes were wide with something that I might have called awe if it had been anyone else. "But not a bad weird."

"What are you talking about?" Zhong asked impatiently, but actually, I thought I understood.

"The demon used to be mortal," I explained. "Its spirit should have ended up here at the Tree of Souls, but it never got that chance. And somehow, the banyan still calls to it." I stepped back from the poj ntxoog. "I thought you said demons couldn't remember what it was like to be mortal."

"They shouldn't be able to. . . ." Zhong sounded uncomfortable with the idea that she might have been mistaken.

Come to think of it, the demon hadn't tried very hard to capture me in the garden. Maybe this demon was different from the rest?

"What's your name?" I asked it.

The poj ntxoog looked surprised. Then it winced as it tried to move its leg. When it spoke, its voice was thick with pain. "The others call me Hluas."

I repeated the name, a little clumsily with my poor Hmong. "Huh . . . Huh-loo-uh?"

"It means *young*," Zhong translated. "Is that just a name, or are you the youngest in the group?"

"One of the youngest. C-can you remove this?" It gestured to the crossbow bolt.

"We will if you agree to take us to your camp," I said.

The demon shook its head quickly. The comb stuck in its hair smacked its cheek. "I can't do that. The others will kill me if they think I helped you."

"*We'll* kill you if you don't," Zhong said. She had her shaman sword in one hand and her crossbow in the other. She pointed both at Hluas.

I didn't argue with her, but I didn't like it. The idea of killing the poj ntxoog bothered me now that we knew it had a name and it felt a connection with the Tree of Souls. Could it ever turn mortal again?

I put my hand on Zhong's arm so that she'd lower her weapons. Yeng had said I couldn't get anything in this world without giving something up. Like I'd been telling Zhong this whole time, threats weren't always the right answer.

I reached up and tugged the clip from my hair. I felt Hluas's eyes on me, confused, as I ran my thumb over the *P* and the few remaining rhinestones. It was scuffed and ugly, but still, something tightened in my chest.

I held it up. "If you take us to the camp, you can have this."

"Pahua, your mom gave you that," Zhong said. "You can't give it to a demon."

"I can if it helps us get Miv back. Back in the room with Shee Yee's statue, Hluas said my hair clip reminded it of something. I'm betting it has to do with when it was human."

Zhong glanced between me and the hair clip, looking torn. "Just because you've figured out what it wants doesn't mean you have to hand it over."

"It's okay. My best friend is more important than a piece of junk." It hurt me to call it that, because it was much more than an old plastic hair clip. It was the first gift my mom had given me after Dad left. She'd never been good with words, so I think it was her way of telling me that she wasn't going to leave as well.

But right now I didn't have a choice. I held it out and waited.

The demon looked like it wanted to snatch the hair clip out of my hand. "I . . . I can't be seen helping you."

"Then we'll be sneaky about it." To be honest, we really couldn't spare the time for a side quest. Matt's hourglass was running out. But I couldn't just turn my back on Miv, either.

They were the only two people who'd always stuck with me, and even when they'd teased me, they had always been on my side.

Hluas's fingers twitched eagerly. "Okay."

It swiped for the hair clip, but I pulled it out of reach. "You can have it when we get to the camp."

"How do I know you're telling the truth?"

"We don't have to prove—" Zhong began, but I cut her off again. She glared at me.

"To prove that we'll keep our word, I'll help you pull out that bolt." I handed the hair clip to Zhong, who tucked it into the pocket of her T-shirt dress. Then, with my gloved hands outstretched like I was approaching an angry stray dog, I slowly lowered myself to the ground beside the demon.

"Try anything and you're smoke," Zhong said to Hluas. She raised the crossbow again while thrusting the sword beneath the demon's jaw.

My nose wrinkled at the demon's smell. It reminded me of that time our teacher volunteered me for cleanup duty after a field-trip lunch and I had my first close encounter with one of those big metal dumpsters. The greasy, rotting food stench had been stuck in my nose for days.

Holding my breath, I gripped the crossbow bolt. The demon whimpered in pain. I counted to three in my head and then yanked it free. The demon howled in my face. Its breath was so bad that it made me long for the frog back-wash. Smoke curled into the air from the wound.

"Do we need to bandage it?" I asked.

Hluas groaned, long and pitiful, and then shook its head. "It'll start healing on its own."

"That's a cool power to have," I said appreciatively.

"Okay, demon, now which way to your camp?" Zhong asked.

It gestured behind us, toward the gradual downward slope of the mountain. "I came here by storm spirit."

I realized Hluas wasn't gesturing at the landscape, which was too dark to see. The poj ntxoog was indicating something in the sky. It was hard to make out at first, but what might have been a mini thundercloud churned in the air just past the branches.

"Is this a trick?" I asked.

"I doubt it," came a rough voice. We all turned to find Yeng reemerging from the Tree of Souls, her garden hoe resting against her shoulder. "I do my best gardening at night, but I'm never going to get anything done with all the racket you're making."

I stood up and tossed the crossbow bolt to the grass. "We found—"

"I know what you found, foolish child. I'm looking at it, aren't I?"

"But the demon says it got here by storm spirit. I thought nature spirits were good."

"Then you're an idiot. Spirits are just like anyone

else—good or bad or both. Their nature isn't determined simply by what they are."

"Storm spirits won't carry *us*, though," Zhong pointed out.

"I wouldn't want them to," I said. I was afraid they would either drop me to my death or carry me off to their masters.

"No, a storm spirit won't. But it did just give me an idea for how to get you off my mountain." Yeng nodded to two wind spirits playing tag in the banyan tree's branches. She let out a piercing whistle that made my ears ring. "Wind spirits are cousins to storm spirits. Not as wild, but just as strong."

The wind spirits blew toward us, lifting the hair off my shoulders. Zhong looked uneasy about being carried by literal *air*. I reminded myself that Spike had gotten help from the wind spirits as well, and she was way heavier than two kids.

Hluas limped to its feet and made a gesture at the sky. The storm spirit approached with a low rumble.

"Remember," I said. "No tricks if you want that hair clip."

The demon nodded eagerly. It looked relieved to get off its injured leg as it dropped onto the storm spirit. I half expected the demon to fall through and hit the ground again. But of course, it didn't. The little storm spirit was like a roiling gray beanbag chair.

"Go on, then," Yeng said, making a shooing gesture at us. "The wind spirits will carry you as a favor to me, but don't expect them to make a habit of it. They can be fickle."

That was reassuring. The wind spirits twirled around us in the shapes of sea turtles, rustling our clothes.

"How?" I asked.

Yeng gave a dramatic huff. "Shee Yee was never this slow on the uptake."

My face went hot. Shee Yee had also had the guidance of his godly family, whereas Zhong and I were figuring all this out on our own.

Without a word, Yeng made a large root lift out of the ground. "Climb up. That might help. Then just fall, and they'll catch you."

I wasn't sure I liked this idea. Still, it was our only option, so we had to try. Zhong and I clambered onto the root. It wasn't any higher than my kitchen counter, which I'd climbed onto plenty of times to get to the top shelves. But I'd never intended to fall off.

Once we were on the root, I had to close my eyes or I'd lose my nerve. *Just fall.* I could do that. I clutched the lightning ax to my chest. This was like the group exercise my gym teacher had made us do last year where we had to fall backward and trust our classmates to catch us.

My classmates had caught me. But then they'd let go before I got my feet on the ground. I'd flailed and taken down Hailey Jones with me. I'd accidentally elbowed her in the face.

"Aren't you on a tight deadline?" Yeng asked, sounding annoyed.

Right. I drew a deep breath and let myself fall. It was like dropping onto a mountain of the softest sofa cushions in the world. I opened my eyes, amazed to see the wind spirits twisting around my legs. Then one of them changed into the form of a donkey, large enough for me to ride. Sitting on her own wind spirit, Zhong looked just as dumbstruck.

"Is this okay?" I asked Yeng. "You helping us, I mean?"

"I'm not helping you," she said. "I'm just getting you off my mountain. If you happen to go in a direction that benefits you, that's not my concern."

I smiled. "Thank you. I won't forget this."

"See that you don't."

"Okay, Hluas," I said. "Show us the way."

The demon wiped snot from the corner of its nose and nodded. Our wind spirits followed the storm spirit as we slowly rose into the dark sky. My stomach dropped, and I had to close my eyes again.

"Hopefully their camp isn't too far," Yeng mumbled as she turned away. "Those wind spirits won't hold you for long."

"What?!" I asked, my eyes popping open again in alarm.

But it was too late. The arborist had disappeared beneath the branches of the banyan tree as we flew ever farther into the night.

27

~

Don't Take Me to Your Leader

 The wind spirits weren't as fast as Spike had been. But still, everything felt pretty wild when you were riding on a donkey made of air.

Hluas didn't get too far ahead of us, although we were only able to spot the demon because its storm cloud kept flickering like a dying lightbulb. With only the roar of the wind in my ears, it was impossible to talk and too dark to see much beneath us other than silvery treetops. So I looked up instead, watching the stars dart across the sky. Unlike in the mortal realm, these stars weren't fixed points. They danced and chased one another from one horizon to the other and played . . . connect the dots?

Zhong waved her arm to get my attention. Then she pointed ahead. Our wind spirits were descending, following Hluas down into the forest. A faint orange glow lit up the branches from below, like from a campfire.

As the trees grew closer, I realized Hluas was taking us much closer to the camp than I would have liked. I held my breath as the firelight flickered past the shadows of trees. The storm spirit rumbled as it wove around the branches and then deposited Hluas on the ground. The demon grimaced in pain.

A moment later, our wind spirits followed. The leaves rustled, and a few branches snapped off. I winced at the sounds we were making. A tree spirit poked its head out of its trunk and waved.

"You hear that?" came a gruff voice.

My heart beat faster. We were *way* too close to the camp. Once our feet were on the ground and the wind spirits had swept back into the air, Zhong gestured wordlessly for me to follow her. We crept slowly deeper into the woods to put more space between us and the demons.

"No, but I do *smell* something," came another voice.

"It's just your armpits. Put your arms down before you take out the whole forest."

There was a round of grunts that I realized was demon laughter.

"I'm pretty sure I do smell something, though," the same demon said. "Smells like mortals."

Oh no, Zhong mouthed as we moved more quickly.

Hluas had turned around and was limping after us. But then it stopped and glared angrily at Zhong. "The hair clip. You promised."

"Keep it down," Zhong hissed.

The demon's lips pulled back over its teeth again, this time in a snarl. "You promised," it repeated much too loudly. "Give it to me, or I'll shout for my friends."

"What was that?" one of the demons said. There was the sound of shuffling, like they were getting up.

"Just give it to Hluas," I whispered frantically.

Zhong thrust her hand into her pocket. Then she flung the plastic hair clip through the air. As it flew toward the demon, a flower spirit jumped up and down and called out, "Ooh, pretty!"

Zhong and I both hissed at them to be quiet. The flower spirit pouted and stuck out a purple tongue.

Hluas caught the hair clip. Its teeth flashed in triumph. Then it turned and limped off into the trees, in the opposite direction from camp. Now that it had what it wanted, it was surprisingly quick as it vanished into the thick undergrowth.

Just in time, too, because one of its companions came crashing through the forest not a second later.

Zhong drew her sword as I raised the lightning ax. She muttered some choice insults in Hluas's direction that sounded like "cabbage breath" and "stick it with my sword next time."

"I told you!" the demon shouted, pointing at us. It had pink curlers in its hair and wore a nightgown with lace cuffs at the wrists. "Mortals. Just in time for dinner."

My eyes widened as more of them appeared. There were

five in all. I recognized them as the ones who'd survived the battle with the dragon warriors. That meant they were good fighters, which also meant we were in big trouble.

A demon in a gleaming pair of fake leather pants that looked incredibly uncomfortable bashed its fist into Curler Demon's head. A punch like that would have knocked out a normal person, but Curler Demon just snarled and jabbed its sharp elbow into its companion's gut.

"You idiot!" Leather Pants said. "These aren't just any mortals. It's the shaman brat. And that other one."

"Hey," Zhong said, sounding offended. I gave her a look to remind her that now probably wasn't the time.

"How'd they find us?" another demon said, scratching its greasy head.

"Who cares?" Leather Pants said. When it stepped toward us, the leather squeaked like a dying toy mouse. "Our master will be so pleased. Tie her up."

"What about the other one?" Curler Demon asked.

"We can have her for dessert."

A cheer went up among the group. Before they could get any closer, though, I held out the lightning ax. It glowed white, illuminating the entire space. Energy crackled down the handle and sparked across the ground. The demons paused.

"You guys used to be mortal, but you also *eat* mortals? Doesn't that seem kind of gross?"

One of the demons shrugged. "If we eat enough mortals, we might become mortal again."

"That doesn't make even a little sense." I thought the opposite was more likely to be true. The more they behaved like monsters, the less human they became.

"Also, you taste good."

They tried to get closer, but I lifted the lightning ax higher. "No one's eating my friend. And you aren't taking me to your master, either. But you *are* going to tell me what you did with the cat spirit you took from the Tree of Souls."

"Too late for that one," one of the demons said. It was picking its sharp yellow teeth with what looked like a small bone.

My stomach did a serious double backflip. Even though I was afraid of the answer, I made myself ask, "What do you mean?"

"Storm spirits carried him away. He's with our master now. You cannot save him, shamanling."

I shouldn't have been so relieved to hear Miv was Xov's prisoner, but at least the demons hadn't eaten him. What mattered was that he was still alive.

"*Now* do we get to eat them?" Curler Demon asked.

The flower spirit, who'd been watching the entire exchange, cut in. "They'd probably give you heartburn. Have you ever smelled a poj ntxoog with heartburn? Phoo-eey. It's all singed fur, smoke, and ashes."

Leather Pants only growled and ripped one of the curlers from the other demon's hair. "Don't you ever listen? We're not eating both. We have to take the shorter one back to our master. Just squish the other shaman so we can have some gravy with our dinner."

I cleared my throat. Now that I knew Miv wasn't here, there was no reason for us to stick around. "Or you could let us go, and we'll bring you back some nice juicy steaks? I think I saw a restaurant just down the mountainside."

Two of the demons began nodding enthusiastically. "And mashed potatoes?"

"And spaghetti with eyeballs?"

"I'll have to check on those eyeballs, but sure," I said, slowly backing away.

Zhong began to follow suit, but Leather Pants shouted, "It's a trick, you idiots! Grab them now!"

There was a second of confused mayhem, with one of the demons muttering, "But spaghetti . . ." and the *squeak-squeak* of those shiny leather pants. Then the group charged us with flashing claws and snarling teeth. The flower spirit squealed in fear and vanished under a rock.

I focused my senses on the current of spiritual energy flowing through me. It wasn't easy to relax while being attacked by five hideous demons, but eventually my body's reflexes took over. The lightning ax hummed through my gloves, but the part of me that had Shee Yee's instincts told me not to use it.

I ducked a swipe of claws and swept the legs out from under one of the demons. It fell, tripping the one behind it. I leaped over them both, smashing my foot into a nose. But then that demon snatched my ankle, slamming me down hard.

My head smacked the ground. Pain lit through me, and lights burst behind my eyes.

"Pahua—agh!"

I couldn't see, but it sounded like Zhong was in trouble. The demon dragged me through the underbrush, probably back toward its camp. Twigs and leaves caught in my hair and scraped the side of my face. The ax snagged on a root and was nearly wrenched from my fingers, but somehow I held on.

"Zhong!" I shouted, trying to shield my head. There was no reply, only the grunts and snarls of the demons. The one gripping me jerked harder, like it was trying to take off my leg. But my fear for Zhong cut through the pain.

With a grunt, I twisted around, squinted through the foliage slapping my face, and smashed the handle of the ax into the demon's fingers around my ankle.

"Ow!" the demon roared, and let go.

In an instant, I was on my feet again, darting toward my friend. My eyesight seemed fuzzy, though, and everything spun a little. I stumbled, my shoulder colliding with a tree. I reached up and winced as my fingers found a lump on the back of my head.

"Come back here!" the demon yelled behind me. The sound of its heavy steps grew closer as it darted for me. I shoved myself off the tree, ducking to avoid its claws. It collided with the trunk as I hurried ahead.

I'd already gotten Matt and Miv kidnapped by evil spirits because I hadn't protected them well enough. I wasn't going to lose Zhong, too. I blinked rapidly to focus my vision before finding her.

To my relief, she was still standing, but she didn't look like she was doing very well. She was facing off against the other four demons, her shaman sword raised. Her left arm hung at her side. As I neared, the light from my ax illuminated her torn jean jacket sleeve, dark with blood.

Her gaze flicked to mine as I stumbled forward, still a bit dizzy. I was almost there. But the demons saw her moment of distraction and lunged, their claws flashing.

Panic shoved all my instincts aside. I leaped in front of Zhong and slammed the lightning ax into the ground.

28

~

Smoke and Ashes

 White light burst from the ax in a shock wave of energy. It was so bright that, for a second, the entire forest lit up like daylight. Lightning crackled over the earth, shooting through the demons and up the nearest trees. All five demons were instantly vaporized. Plants disintegrated into ash. The tree in front of me exploded into flaming cinders.

I gasped and ducked as a falling branch nearly crushed us. Embers floated down, flaring red like deadly snowflakes.

"Smoke and ashes," the little flower spirit whispered. They were shaking as they peered out from behind their smoldering rock.

"Pahua . . ." Zhong whispered. The shock in her voice mirrored my own.

I dropped the lightning ax. Its glow faded, but its shining metal surface continued to reflect the red light of its destruction. I sank to my knees within a charred and smoking half circle. It wasn't very big, maybe the size of my room, but still, I hadn't meant for this to happen.

Two dandelion spirits with all their seeds missing covered their faces with furry green hands. Mushroom spirits shook ash flakes off their big red-capped heads. Fire spirits appeared, making little exclamations of surprise as they circled the branches that were still burning.

"You destroyed one of our oldest trees," came a soft, clear voice. A tree spirit, larger than all the others, emerged from a nearby trunk that had been scorched down one side. Moss speckled their long body of braided bark. Mushrooms that looked like stacked plates grew out from their shoulders and down to their elbows. They wore withered purple flowers in their hair of tangled leaves and twigs. When they coughed, soot flew from their mouth.

"Nyom!" Other nature spirits scurried out from where they'd been hiding and gathered around.

Nyom? She was the nature-spirit queen Nplooj had told us about! I felt sick knowing that I'd destroyed even part of her home after how nice her siblings had been to us.

My eyes stung as they filled with tears. Zhong crouched beside me, resting her hand on my shoulder.

"Your arm," I said, wiping at my nose. "It's bleeding."

"It can wait," she said. I could tell by the strain in her voice that she was hurting.

Overhead, there was a rumble like distant thunder. The

enormous crab cloud that we'd first seen over the valley had scuttled across the sky and was now almost directly above us. Moonlight traced its shape. It must have seen the smoke from the fire.

"Get out," the nature spirits growled. Some of them picked up pebbles and small bits of debris and pelted my legs. "Get out of our forest!"

Zhong shoved herself to her feet, gripping her injured arm. "Stop it!" she shouted. The smaller nature spirits backed away warily. "She didn't mean to do this. The demons were going to kill me. She was protecting me."

"She's right," Nyom said, her soft voice carrying over the angry ones.

At once, a hush fell over the gathered nature spirits. They scurried aside as the tree spirit approached. She towered over us.

I didn't know what to say. I could only go with "I'm sorry. It was an accident."

"Even accidents have consequences. You must fix this, young shaman."

"I don't know how." I bowed my head, ashamed. The locket Yeng had given me dangled a few inches lower, and I felt its coolness against my skin. That gave me an idea. I pulled the necklace out of my shirt.

"What is that?" Nyom asked. The little curls of wood that formed her eyebrows drew together.

I opened the locket to reveal the leaf. It was starkly green even in the dim light. All around the clearing, nature spirits gasped as they sensed immediately what it was. Gently, I removed the leaf from the locket and held it out to the tree spirit.

"The arborist said that this is the only leaf the Tree of Souls has ever grown. Will it help restore what I destroyed?"

Nyom took the leaf with reverent care. "It will do that and more. This is a powerful gift, young shaman, and I accept it, along with your apology."

The tree spirit sank to her knees with the creaking of dry wood. She sifted her fingers through the earth, searching for the moist brown soil beneath the ash. Then she placed the leaf into the hole and covered it again.

When Nyom looked up, she was smiling. "Ours will now be a sacred grove," she told the nature spirits. They cheered, all their animosity suddenly forgotten.

Zhong touched my shoulder again. I rose, my fists clenched at my sides. The nature spirits might have been appeased, but I didn't feel any better. A part of me had known not to use the lightning ax, but I'd done it anyway. What kind of hero would do that?

"Child." The tree spirit sensed my distress and clasped my hands. Her rough tree-bark skin scratched against the silky cloth of my gloves. "We all must make mistakes before we can succeed. No hero emerges into the world fully formed, not even Shee Yee."

"How did you—"

"The trees are always listening. And unless I'm mistaken, you have a brother to rescue and very little time left."

My eyes filled with tears again. "But how can I save him when I couldn't even defeat the demons properly? I'm not brave, and I'm not a good fighter. I'm only good at pretending, and that doesn't help when real lives are in danger." My words were a whisper, like I was one of the spirits bound to the Tree of Souls releasing my regrets.

Zhong made an exasperated sound. I looked over to see her wearing an expression like she thought I was a complete idiot. "For someone who's pretty good at figuring people out, you're completely clueless when it comes to yourself."

I flushed, embarrassed, even though I wasn't sure what she was trying to say.

"I made the mistake of going into the Bamboo Nursery," she explained, "and you're the one who got us out. You've saved our lives more than once, and that wasn't pretend. This?" She gestured to the trees. "Yeah, you messed up. But be glad it was a mess-up you could fix. Considering you didn't even know what a shaman warrior was a few days ago, you're doing really great. If you were an apprentice at the school, the shaman elders would be super proud."

I blinked. Was I hearing her right? "You . . . You really think so?"

"I wouldn't say it if it weren't true."

That, at least, I believed.

"Now if only we could get some divine assistance from your relatives," Zhong said, looking up at the sky.

That would definitely be welcome right about now. I craned my neck, too, watching the crab cloud's pincer snatch at silvery wind spirits. I waited, wondering if I'd get some kind of sign that the Sky Father was listening. The gods weren't all-seeing—otherwise they wouldn't need to rely on servants to find me—but I figured Ntuj must have a way of keeping tabs on people.

Nothing happened, of course. No help would be coming from Shee Yee's grandfather, because he and the other gods had never intended for me to exist in the first place.

But I *was* here.

Though I had Shee Yee's spirit, I wasn't him. And maybe, if I stopped pretending to be other people long enough, I could finally figure out what it meant to be *me*.

"We need to bandage your arm," I told Zhong.

I knew she had to be in serious pain, because she didn't even argue when I opened her backpack and started rummaging inside for bandages. My fingers closed around a box with a huge red plus sign on the top. It figured Zhong would carry a whole first-aid kit. I helped her take off her jean jacket.

"The blood doesn't bother you?" Zhong asked me. Her lips were pressed tightly together, her face paler than usual.

"I've cleaned a lot of Matt's scraped knees and elbows," I explained. "They weren't this bloody, but it looks like your scratches aren't so bad." Luckily, the demon's claws hadn't gone too deep. The denim had taken most of the damage.

"All shaman warriors are trained in basic first aid, but not all of them can handle seeing blood," Zhong said.

"Normally, I would offer you a healing fruit," Nyom said as she watched me wrap bandages around my friend's arm. "But the tree that grows them was . . ." She gestured to one of the nearby trees. It wasn't destroyed, but some of its branches were singed. The low-hanging fruit looked roasted.

"Sorry," I said again, wincing. I returned the first-aid kit to Zhong's backpack and exchanged it for the flashlight. Zhong wouldn't be needing her jean jacket anymore, so I put that in her backpack as well.

Something cool and wet struck my cheek. I looked up to find the crab cloud scratching its giant fluffy shell and releasing a gentle spray of water from its armpits. The nature spirits cheered again as the scent of fresh rain washed away the stink of smoke.

Nyom pointed to the lightning ax, which still lay in the dirt. As the raindrops struck the blade, the metal sang a strange chorus of notes. "You wield a dangerous weapon. Now you know its destructive power. You cannot use it so carelessly."

I didn't want to touch the ax again, but I knew I had to pick it up. We'd gone through so much to get it, and I needed the weapon to defeat the bridge spirit and save my brother. But now I also understood the responsibility I'd taken on by removing it from Shee Yee's statue. He had known it was not a weapon to use lightly, which was why the ax had remained tied to his saddle in the book's story. It wasn't to be swung unless absolutely necessary.

"That's not where your real strength is anyway," Zhong said.

I tensed. "Then what *is* my real strength? Shee Yee's spirit?"

"Weren't you listening to what I *just* said? We didn't get this far because of Shee Yee. It's because you, Pahua Moua, try to see the truth of people. It can be a little annoying when I just want to fight whatever's attacking us and you're trying to reason with them, but even so, it seems to be working okay."

"You're doing it again," I said, giving her a crooked smile.

"What?" she asked, frowning.

"Complimenting me."

She rolled her eyes. "Then I'll stop. You're being stupid and wasting time. Now grab your ax."

Still wary of the weapon, I reached down and lifted the ax. Its power thrummed through me.

"Give it here," Nyom said, reaching for it.

"No, don't!" I said, holding the weapon out of her reach. "It'll hurt you."

Nyom smiled. "It won't. I don't intend to use it. I only want to make a modification that will help lighten your burden."

Warily, I extended the ax without letting go of it. Nyom touched the gleaming handle, and the weapon began to glow again. For a moment, I was filled with fear that it would explode and destroy what was left of the clearing. But then the light faded. In my gloved hands, the ax had transformed into a beautiful decorative comb, like the kind Asian princesses wear in their hair. The silver dragon now coiled above a row of gleaming metal teeth. Its red eye flashed.

"When you have need of the weapon, just press its ruby eye." She took the decorative comb from my palm and fixed it gently in my wet hair, right where my old hair clip had always gone.

"Transmutation magic?" I asked, reaching up to skim my fingers over the cool metal. The gloves were so thin that I had no trouble feeling every detail. "But how? It's a celestial weapon."

Nyom gestured to the ground. I didn't need the flashlight to see that the leaf she had buried had somehow taken root. A vibrant green shoot was already pushing through the wet earth. "You gave us a celestial gift. Powerful roots make the whole forest stronger."

"Pahua," Zhong said, "let's go."

I nodded grimly. We had to get back to the tunnels beneath the Spirit Realm, where Matt was trapped with the bridge spirit. It was a long way to go, but if we could find a town and get in contact with Spike, we might have a chance.

"We'll have to come back for Miv," Zhong said. "After."

Nyom nodded. "You will need to get there quickly."

I didn't like the idea of leaving Miv with Xov. In fact, it made me feel sick just thinking about it. But Xov wanted me alive, which meant he would probably keep Miv as a prisoner until I could find him. My brother didn't have that kind of time.

"Can you tell us where the nearest town is?" I asked.

Nyom shook her head, and my hopes sank. But then she said, "We will send you to your destination. You'll find the trees a much faster way to travel."

"You're going to help me?" I asked, confused. "After what I did?"

The tree spirit ran her bristly fingers down my cheek. "Someday, you will be a powerful shaman. Perhaps even greater than Shee Yee. We would benefit from having an alliance with you." She gestured to the green shoot again. "See? The good fortune begins already. Now come."

Yeng had been right. The leaf would help get us where we needed to go.

Nyom led me and Zhong out of the small crater and into the forest until we were once again surrounded by healthy green trees. Before us, the bark of a trunk split open, revealing a doorway. It wasn't like the door into the Tree of Souls. This looked more like the hollow in the tree back home.

When we were pushed inside, the flashlight wedged

between us, it felt like that one, too—uncomfortable, scratchy, and way too tight. *Squashed banana,* as Matt had once said.

Nyom waved her fingers. "Tell Nplooj hello for me."

The tree sealed itself, and everything compressed around us.

29

~

Dragon, Meet My Friend
the Water Buffalo

 I would have screamed if I'd had the breath. Traveling by tree was like being forced through a straw, squeezed beyond possibility.

Then the pressure released, and the tree spat us out onto a bush. I groaned. My whole body ached. Slowly, I rolled onto my side and reached up to make sure the magical comb was still in my hair. It was.

"Let's never do that again," Zhong said. She sounded muffled. She was lying facedown in the dirt, her rear in the air and her enormous backpack sitting on the back of her head.

I laughed and then wished I hadn't, because it hurt. "Ow. Yeah. Good idea."

When I could finally take in the forest around us, the flashlight revealed decidedly different trees than the ones we'd just left. These grew less thickly and had flowering shrubs around their roots. Also, the ground was dry, which meant we weren't beneath the crab cloud anymore. The air smelled crisp and fresh, without a hint of smoke.

I forced myself to stand and stumbled a few feet away. I spotted the remains of an old cooking fire and gasped.

"We're back at our campsite!" I shouted. My body was still trying to recover from being nearly squeezed to death, but the pain wasn't enough to dim my excitement. We were in the forest with the hidden tunnel entrance. We'd made it! Now all we had to do was go rescue Matt.

Zhong dug her fingers into the grass and mumbled something I was pretty sure wasn't allowed in any school, much less a shaman one. The bandage around her arm was spotted red.

"You're bleeding again!" I rushed over, but she waved me away.

"It's fine."

"But—"

"Hello, mortals."

I swung the flashlight around to find the source of the voice. Sitting in a nearby branch, legs swinging in the air, was Nplooj. Her twig-like fingers were stroking the flower growing over her ear.

"Nyom wanted me to receive you," she said. "And she said something about her healing fruit getting broiled?"

"Here's a gift," called another tree spirit with a mossy green cap. It was the spirit I'd rescued from the charging water buffalo. They tossed me a plump mango. As I watched, the mango's skin peeled back on its own, revealing the juicy yellow flesh beneath. "For the trial ahead of you."

They threw another one at Zhong, who wasn't looking. The mango smacked her wetly on the side of the head, and she glared.

Remembering the last time I was offered fruit, I hesitated. The plum pit was still in my pocket. But because Nplooj was watching and waiting, and because I still felt truly awful about what I'd done to Nyom's trees, I took a tentative nibble.

The flesh was sweet and delicious. A surge of energy swept through me. Feeling more confident, I took bigger bites, reminded of how little I'd eaten that day. With every mouthful, the aches in my body subsided. I shone the flashlight at Zhong and gaped. The bruise on her forehead from where a book had struck her was fading.

In wonder, she lifted her injured arm, flexing it. There wasn't a hint of pain on her face.

I checked my own wounds. Every scratch, bruise, and cut from the last two days had healed. My mind felt clear, as if I'd had a whole night's sleep. Even my hunger disappeared.

"Thank you," I said, bowing deeply. "You've been extremely kind, and I won't forget it."

Nplooj waved. Then the two tree spirits vanished into the dark.

~

It didn't take us long to reach the edge of the forest.

We got close enough to see the broad plain past the trees, which looked just as it had before, even in the moonlight—swathed with muddy water and occupied by a herd of water-buffalo spirits. One was sleeping right by the hidden tunnel entrance.

"How do we get past them?" I asked. I really didn't want a repeat of last time.

"Create a diversion?" Zhong suggested, shrugging off her backpack. I handed her the flashlight so she could see inside it.

I didn't know what she could possibly be carrying that would be an effective distraction for deadly six-horned beasts. Maybe she could play them a lullaby on her qeej. Or use her paper talismans to bind the buffalo spirits long enough for us to slip past. Or we could just trick the entire herd into entering her bottomless backpack.

Zhong put her jean jacket back on now that her arm was healed. The blood on the ripped sleeve was still a little unsettling. As she rummaged through the rest of her stuff, the pins on the front pocket glinted, reminding me of a question I had.

"Your first-year pin," I said. "It would have one stripe on it instead of three, right?"

"Yeah," she said distractedly. She pulled out a can opener, squinted thoughtfully at it, and then shook her head and kept digging.

"My mom had a pin like that. It was a gift from her sister." I'd completely forgotten the memory until now. My mom had tried to refuse it, saying it was too important for her sister to give away, but my aunt had said she didn't want it anymore.

Zhong raised her eyebrows at me. "You said your aunt is a shaman. She must have spent at least one year at the school." After saying this, she dove into her backpack again. Nearly her entire head disappeared into the thing. "Seriously, why didn't I prepare for water-buffalo spirits? I'll have to plan better next time."

As Zhong muttered to herself, I rubbed my temple to block the headache trying to form there. Aunt Kalia couldn't have gone to Zhong's school. She was just a regular old shaman. But why else would she have had that pin? My stomach felt like it was doing somersaults. What did it mean?

Something rustled in the branches overhead. I tilted my head back to peer through the foliage, expecting to see a tree spirit.

A shining pair of slitted golden eyes peered back.

My heart lurched, and I gasped as a huge body crashed through the branches to land in front of me. The dragon was long and slender, with blue scales and four sets of clawed feet. It had an impressive snout, two spiraling horns curling over the back of its head, and a blue mane down its serpentine spine. It rose over me, poised like a cobra about to strike. When it spoke, it was in the voice of the dragon leader from the Tree of Souls.

"You're going to pay for making us hunt you halfway across the realm," she said, her voice a low growl. Sharp teeth as long as my fingers gleamed in her mouth.

"Are you kidding me?" I asked, almost too incredulous to be scared. Didn't these minions ever give up?

A moment later, more bodies descended from the sky, stripping leaves from the branches and sending nature spirits scrambling into the night. It was the other three dragons who'd survived the fight with the poj ntxoog. *Great.* I'd had enough of demons and dragons.

The thing was, though, the dragons were beautiful. I'd daydreamed about what they might look like, and the reality far surpassed anything my imagination had ever come up with.

Each of the dragons was blue. (Maybe Xiav, whose name meant *blue*, only allowed dragons of that color to work for him. Even gods have to pick a theme, I guess.) But when their scales shifted beneath the moonlight, they shimmered in every shade of the rainbow. My mom used to say that rainbows were the glimmering bodies of dragons in the sky.

Maybe someday I'd be able to convince Xiav that I wasn't

a threat to his power, if his dragon cronies would just let me save my brother in peace first.

"How did you even find us?" Zhong asked. She slung her backpack over her shoulders and backed up against a tree. She had the flashlight in one hand and her sword in the other.

For a second, I almost reached for the enchanted comb in my hair. But I didn't want to go there yet, if ever. I'd caused enough destruction for one night.

I drew my shaman sword instead.

"Lord Xiav's spies are everywhere," said the leader, "even among your sweet little nature spirits."

I made a face and a mental note to inform Nplooj. Nyom would need to know, too. We couldn't be allies if their friends were reporting everything I did back to Xiav.

"Where are you hiding the lightning ax?" the dragon asked as the others closed in to prevent any escape.

I kept my back to the tree so the dragons couldn't sneak up behind me. "A place where your master will never get his hands on it."

The dragon bared her teeth. "You're very young. That means Lord Xiav has a *lot* of time to show you all the ways he can make you talk."

From somewhere behind me, past the trees, I heard a low grunting sound. An idea struck, and my pulse kicked up. I raised my sword and said loudly, "Are all dragons as pathetic as you and your Lord Xiav? I wonder why Shee Yee didn't cut off your heads when he had the chance. Maybe it's because you're not worth it. I bet you're the Land of Dragons' rejects."

"Pahua . . ." Zhong whispered with a meaningful glance over her shoulder.

I know, I mouthed. Her eyes widened in understanding just as the dragon snarled.

"You *will* learn respect, mortal fool." She lowered her face to mine. Her head was the size of a huge watermelon, and her breath smelled like Matt's dirty laundry.

I made an exaggerated gagging noise and practically shouted my next words. "And you need to learn dental hygiene!"

"Yeah!" Zhong yelled. "And, like, floss sometimes!"

I shot her a look like *Really?* Even the dragons seemed confused. Zhong gave me a helpless shrug. She could fight demons all day, but trash-talking bad guys was not one of her strengths.

"*Hygiene* is a big word for such a puny creature," the dragon said.

"Only to someone dumb enough to try to take the lightning ax again after it vaporized your buddy. Are dragons related to dinosaurs? Are tiny brains a family thing?"

The dragon's golden eyes narrowed. Its silence made me nervous as it drew back. Then it slowly coiled its body in front of Zhong.

"Hey!" I shouted as loud as I could. The snorting behind

me had grown louder. *Come on, come on.* "What's the matter? You afraid of me?"

"What's that sound?" one of the dragons said, peering around us to squint through the trees. "Something smells like . . . cow?"

"We passed a water-buffalo herd, remember?" another dragon said.

The dragon leader ignored her companions. Instead, she rose over Zhong, her mouth opening wide. I could tell Zhong was afraid because of the way the flashlight trembled. But her eyes remained focused on the dragon, as fierce as ever.

"Leave her alone!" I began stomping my feet and banging my sword against the tree. This *had* to work. *Please, please.*

"Why is she doing that?" one of the dragons asked.

Then, finally, a rumbling sound came from behind me. The ground began to shudder. I flattened my back against the tree and tried to make myself as small as possible. Zhong lowered her sword and did the same.

"Hey, pea brain!" I called to the leader. "Tell your blue boss that if he sends any more worms after me, I'll vaporize you like I did those poj ntxoog."

The dragon sneered. "What are you—"

"Horns!" shouted one of the dragons.

A look of confusion spread through the group before an enormous water buffalo barreled past my tree. Its horns scraped bark, and I winced as splinters of wood went flying. Two of the dragons leaped into the air, twining through the branches to escape those deadly projections. The other two snarled and twisted as the buffalo spirit tried to gore them. A moment later, a second water buffalo collided with one of the dragons, smashing it against a tree with a vicious *thud*.

Zhong swung the flashlight into the trees behind us. The coast was clear. "Come on!"

We dashed through the forest toward the hidden tunnel opening. It wasn't far. Behind us, the dragon leader screamed in frustration.

"Come back he— *Oof!*"

I winced. She'd probably just gotten head-butted by a six-horned water buffalo. I couldn't say I felt very sorry for her.

"There!" Zhong pointed the flashlight ahead, illuminating the ferns that shielded the entrance from view. The coast was clear, as the water buffalo now behind us were playing volleyball with the dragons. I dove beneath the plants, sliding right through the hole into the pitch-black of the tunnels.

30

~

Sibling Reunion

 Grunting, I landed hard on my bottom. I got up quickly before Zhong fell on top of me. She joined me a breath later. Her backpack scraped along the wall, showering dirt over our feet.

For a few seconds, we remained perfectly still, waiting. When we didn't hear anyone following, we breathed sighs of relief.

"We lost them," I said, brushing roots from my face.

"Hopefully that's the last we see of them."

I doubted Xiav would give up that easily, but I had a feeling he wouldn't try anything again for a while. And anyway, he was the least of my problems.

In silence, we retraced our steps from only a day earlier. It was unbelievable how much had happened since then. I felt like a completely different person. Before long, we found the fork in the tunnel.

Zhong motioned to my comb. Even though I was nervous about wielding the lightning ax again, this confrontation was why we'd gone through all the trouble of retrieving the weapon in the first place. I had to be prepared.

I pulled the comb from my hair and rubbed my gloved fingers over the gleaming silver. My thumb pressed the red gem of the dragon's eye. With a flash, the lightning ax transformed, once again a deadly weapon in my hands. Its power surged into me, sending my spiritual energy shooting through my limbs.

I nodded to indicate I was ready, and we continued. Part of me wanted to slow down, to delay the inevitable. But I knew I had to get to my brother as quickly as possible, so my body hurried along.

"So, what happens after you complete your quest?" I asked when the silence became too unnerving.

There was longing in Zhong's voice when she answered. "The shaman masters will take me to the school's guardian spirit, who will tie a silver string around my wrist as a blessing. It'll be proof that I've been promised a place as a shaman warrior once I graduate."

"It'll happen," I said firmly. "I'll make sure Matt gets a bracelet to protect his spirit, and you'll get your blessing to become the best fighter your school has ever seen. And then—"

I realized with a start that I wasn't sure I'd ever see Zhong again once this was over—or whether she'd even want to stay friends after this. She would be busy with shaman stuff, and I would have Matt to take care of. The thought made something tighten in my chest, but I decided that would be a question to ask later. First, we had to make it through this alive.

"Then . . . ?" Zhong prompted when I didn't continue.

I gave her a small smile. "And then I figure out where the poj ntxoog took Miv and rescue my best friend."

"If you think you're doing that by yourself, you're delusional," she said, a little too quickly. "You're going to need my help."

Some of the tightness in my chest loosened. "Most likely, yeah."

The walls eventually transitioned from stone and dirt to elephant-head engravings. Tusks still protruded from the walls and ceilings. Many of them were cracked from the last time we were here. We edged around them carefully, avoiding the debris on the ground as well.

Even though I knew what to expect this time, the bridge spirit's power still hit me like a punch to the gut. I gasped and staggered back. Zhong bumped into me, and we steadied each other, sharing grim looks. Gripping the lightning ax tighter, I let its power ground me. Then I clenched my teeth and kept walking.

A high, girly voice broke the heavy silence. "Have you come to stay with me?"

The bridge spirit's words echoed all around us. I

shuddered as the fine hairs on my arms stood up straight. As we continued, the spirit's presence grew heavier. I closed my eyes and sucked in a deep breath. The power of the lightning ax chased away the menacing energy.

Zhong swayed on her feet. I caught her before she fell against a stone tusk. "You okay?"

"I'll be fine," she said. She'd drawn her sword and her crossbow. She was ready to finish this as well.

Looking at her, I suddenly felt a burst of such intense gratitude that I wanted to hug her. "Hey, Zhong. Thank you for being here with me. I wouldn't want to do this with anyone else."

She frowned. "Are you trying to tell me good-bye before we've even tried anything?"

"What? No! I just meant that I wouldn't pick anyone else to have my back." This was where Miv would have interjected with *That's because you don't know anyone else.*

Worry for him cut through me, but as terrible as it sounded, I couldn't think about him right now. I had to focus on rescuing Matt.

"Oh," Zhong said, still sounding suspicious.

I would have laughed if our situation weren't so serious.

A minute later, the tunnel ended abruptly. What spread out before us caught me completely off guard. The cavern was enormous and lit by rows of torches on the walls, which went back as far as I could see. Directly ahead, though, stood a partition half the height of the space. It was made entirely of elephant sculptures.

These weren't just elephant heads, though, like in the tunnel. They were full, life-size statues. The elephants were perfectly stacked so that the heads of one column met the heads of the next, their tusks intertwined in a glinting mesh of sharp points.

All this was only a brief distraction, though. In front of the elephant wall, a large expanse of cracked, pitted stone formed a courtyard. In the far-left corner of the courtyard, the bridge spirit sat on a crumbling bench, surrounded by the spirits of all the stolen children. There had to be over a dozen. My eyes found Matt immediately. He sat directly to the bridge spirit's right. She was running her fingers through his hair.

"Look who's come to stay with us," she said in that eerie singsong voice. Her power gathered all around me. The lightning ax crackled, warding off whatever magic she was spinning.

As one, the children's heads turned to look at us. Their eyes were completely black, like poj ntxoog. They were already starting to transform.

"Matt!" I shouted.

His expression didn't change. There was no sign that he recognized me or had even heard me. He looked bone-white and ghastly, which I told myself made sense, since he was only a spirit. But in his lap, his fingers had elongated and light patches of fur had begun to grow across his knuckles. The sight made me want to gag. Were we too late?

"Stay with us." The children spoke as one in flat, lifeless voices.

I wanted to smash the ax into the courtyard floor. But I had to be careful to not destroy the children along with the bridge spirit.

Even though she felt so much more powerful now, she looked exactly as she had at the bridge. Her hair was a dark, tangled mess, like it hadn't been combed for weeks. Her nightgown, which she adjusted to cover her dirty bare feet, was gray and stained at the hem. She ran her fingers over the children's cheeks and cooed at them like they were her dolls.

"Get away from my brother!" I yelled, starting forward. Lightning crackled down my arms. The blade of the weapon began to glow.

"Pahua, don't!"

My head jerked up at the shout, and my eyes went huge. At the very top of the wall, trapped within a cage of deadly tusks, was a tiny black cat.

"What is he doing here?" Zhong asked, voicing my own question. She didn't look so great with the bridge spirit's power working on her, but she was still standing.

The poj ntxoog had said that Miv was taken to their master. I'd assumed it was Xov, but they'd never actually said that they served the old thunder god. It must have been the bridge spirit all along.

"You have to get out of here!" Miv shouted. "You can't—" Even with the distance between us, I could see the way his glowing yellow eyes widened when the tusks began to grow. The tip of one slowly extended until it pressed into his throat, cutting off his voice.

"No!" I looked between my best friend and my brother.

Zhong nudged me with her elbow. "We're doing this together, remember? Go get Miv. I'll keep the bridge spirit busy. She's the one I'm after anyway."

"But the kids . . ." I began.

"I'll be careful." She slung her backpack off her shoulders, looking relieved to be free of its weight. Then she unzipped it and pulled out a stack of paper talismans for spirit-binding. "I knew these would come in handy for something."

Grateful, I nodded and found Matt's small face again. I wanted to hug him so badly. *We're going to get you out of here. Wait for me just a little bit longer, okay?*

I slid the ax into my sword belt. Then, together, Zhong and I charged the courtyard.

"This is not how we play," the bridge spirit said. She stood, her face twisting with rage. As if in response to her anger, the children rushed forward to meet us, their unnaturally long fingers curled into claws.

Zhong didn't break her speed as she slapped a paper

talisman onto the forehead of a child spirit running straight at her. A wisp of black smoke seeped out from the talisman, and the child collapsed onto the stone ground, unconscious. I assumed Zhong knew what she was doing, and the child's soul was only subdued, not injured.

I tried to dodge the children, not wanting to hurt them. They were fast, though. One spirit, a boy around Matt's age, grabbed my wrist. To my shock, he nearly pulled me off my feet. He was much stronger than he should have been. Somehow I twisted free, but then I almost collided with a girl spirit trying to tackle me. I punched her in the nose.

"Sorry!" I shouted.

The spirit fell back, but she didn't cry out or make any sign at all that I'd injured her. She only shook her head and got up again. So. Creepy.

I bolted around her before she could grab me and nearly ran face-first into the wall of elephants. In the torchlight, the statues gleamed yellow, like aged bones. Even though the thought made me shudder, I grabbed the first tusk and began to climb. The entwined tusks made it easy—it was like climbing a tree with dozens of easy-to-reach branches . . . if those branches were actually spears that could impale me if I slipped.

I would be the first to admit that I'm not exactly the best at gym. I wasn't even halfway up the wall before the muscles in my arms and legs began to burn. Still, I kept going. Miv's yellow eyes were staring down at me, bright with terror. It shook something inside me to see him that way—my oldest and bravest friend.

"Don't worry," I called. "I'm going to get you down."

A few seconds later, I finally reached the top. I was breathing hard, and my pulse was pounding in my ears, but I'd made it. Then I glanced down.

I really shouldn't have done that. I wasn't afraid of heights, but still, vertigo slammed into me. I squeezed my eyes shut for a moment before forcing my gaze upward, toward Miv. I'd glimpsed just enough of the courtyard to assure myself that Zhong was still holding up. She'd been a blur of movement, dodging and taking down the kids like a real warrior while making her way closer to the bridge spirit. She hadn't been kidding when she said fighting was her strength.

Miv spoke very, very softly, mindful of the tusk pressing into his small throat. "Don't," he whispered. "Just leave me."

"Why would you say that? You're my best friend. I'll never leave you. In fact, I dropped in on a whole camp of demons to find you. You would've been really impressed."

"Listen very carefully to me, Pahua. You have to—" He squeaked as the tusk grew another fraction, cutting him off.

The sudden movement startled me. I nearly lost my footing. I drew a deep breath to calm my nerves. Then I studied the mass of sharp bony tusks caging him like overgrown thorns. He was Rapunzel trapped in a tower, and I was here to rescue him, hopefully without falling like the prince did in the fairy tale. Miv was wedged so tightly between the tusks that, even as a kitten, there was no way he could get free without my breaking through.

I reached for the lightning ax at my waist. Miv's eyes filled with something I couldn't name. It looked like he was trying to tell me something.

"I know," I said. "This is a dangerous weapon. But I'll be careful. Trust me."

Lightning crackled along the grip up to my arm. The metal glowed a brilliant white. Instead of swinging the ax, I pressed the blade against one of the tusks enclosing Miv and willed the lightning to cut through it.

White energy speared the tusk, snapping it in half. Triumphant, I repeated the motion with the next tusk, and then the next, until I could reach around Miv and gently . . .

The elephant sculptures began to tremble. An ominous sound, like an approaching thundercloud, shook the cavern. Beneath me, I watched with growing horror as more and more tusks fractured and snapped. Then, with a groan, the entire wall exploded.

Lights and pain swirled around me as I was suddenly airborne.

And everything went dark.

31

~

God of Thunder,
Destruction, and Goth

 I was floating through empty space. It felt like that place between the Echo and the mortal realm that was neither here nor there.

Someone else was with me. I couldn't see them, but I sensed them in the cold air that wrapped around my neck like an icy hand. My skin stung with pinpricks of frost, even though I was still wearing the neutralization gloves.

"Miv?" My voice didn't echo. Instead, the darkness seemed to swallow it up. "Matt? Zhong!"

My body hurt like I was being slowly pulled apart. What was happening? I groped at my wrist and found that the protection charm Zhong had tied there, the one that was supposed to keep my spirit tethered to my body, had disintegrated into loose threads.

My heartbeat sped up. Did that mean my body was still

back in that cavern? And my spirit was here? How was I able to feel things? Where was I?

The cold hand around my throat tightened. I gasped, shivering. From nowhere and everywhere, a voice emerged in the darkness.

"What did I tell you, defiler? You would willingly free me from my prison."

I had freed Xov? That wasn't possible. He was locked away behind three seals of binding: the gold chains, the silver cage, and the ivory gates. I hadn't done anything except break a few elephant tusks on a wall.

And then it hit me. The tusks had been smooth and yellow, not at all like stone. Because they'd been made of ivory.

Oh no. Dread filled me, chilling me from the inside. *Oh no. Oh no.*

No wonder the bridge spirit had seemed so much stronger than she'd been in the mortal realm. It hadn't been just her I was sensing. It had also been Xov, extending his power from within his prison.

But what about the curse on the ivory seal? Shee Yee had ensured that the gates could never be broken. . . . And yet, somehow, they had.

"Yesss," the voice hissed. "You're beginning to understand now. I've been waiting for you for a very, very long time."

I shook away the daze. I couldn't waste time yelling at

myself for falling into Xov's trap. I had to focus and distract him long enough to figure out how to get out of here.

"You know you've been replaced, right?" I said. "The Thunder Dragon is doing your job now."

Xov's power squeezed around me, like a giant rubber band made of ice. I couldn't move my arms. "Xiav isn't a dragon. He's a peacock. He'd rather color-coordinate his house staff than rain down destruction."

"When you put it that way, Xiav sounds like a way better option," I said. "What have you been doing in your prison for thousands of years? Shouldn't you have taken up a few hobbies by now?"

"I'll have you know that I'm accomplished at crochet, cross-stitch, and embroidery. But don't try to distract me. It won't work now that I finally have you. My fool son should have brought you to me long ago, when you were younger and could be more easily shaped to my will. But he played his part in the end. He drew you right into my trap, like a cat toying with a mouse."

His son? The blue book from the Tree of Souls' library had mentioned that the gods made Xov's remaining child his prison guard. In the story, there had been a brief flash of a boy with black hair and bright eyes, but—

"Son . . ." I whispered, the revelation like a shock of lightning running from the top of my head all the way to my toes. The curse wasn't *for love of sun*. It was *for love of* SON.

I'd only ever heard the words spoken out loud. Because of the part about sky and earth, I'd assumed it had meant the celestial object.

Wait. . . . *A cat toying with a mouse?*

Xov's son was *Miv*?! My legs quivered with the knowledge. I remembered what Yeng had said about the person who'd trespassed at the Tree of Souls. *Shee Yee was magicked free with a power greater than my own.*

Miv had some of his father's divine magic! That explained so much, like why he could cross between realms without a neutralizer or protection charm. And how he'd been able to resist the sleep enchantment in the Bamboo Nursery. He hadn't wanted to be in the same room as Shao, because Shao would have known who he was. And after what Miv had done the last time he was at the Tree of Souls, it was no wonder he hadn't wanted to face the arborist.

The betrayal was like an ax chop to my chest. My eyes grew hot, and I squeezed them shut. The conditions of the curse stated that only I could free Xov, and now that I'd done it with Shee Yee's weapon, that last line finally made sense. *When sky bridges earth for love of son.*

It was talking about lightning. When lightning strikes, for that brief moment, the sky and the earth are connected. And I'd used it to free Miv, Xov's son, because I loved him.

It had all been a trick. I gasped for breath, the truth rising around me like a wave.

"It was a stroke of fortune," Xov continued, "when that pathetic spirit from the bridge slipped into the Spirit Realm with traces of Shee Yee's energy on her. I had my demons seize her before she could get to that annoying arborist. The girl went with them willingly, because she was so very angry. So very lonely. Such an easy soul to manipulate. Just like you. What makes *you* angry, fake shaman?"

His words were like a hook at the end of a fishing line. They sank into me, snagged the anger I rarely thought about, and reeled it up to the surface. A sudden fury seized me, clouding my thoughts. I was angry at my dad for abandoning his family, at my mom for always leaving me to care for my baby brother, at the kids at school for making me feel like I would never belong, at every single person who'd ever seen my sadness and didn't care.

And now, at Miv for being the one friend who'd always been there for me, but only as a ruse. A lie. He'd *used* me. Being angry felt so much better than being sad.

Through the red haze, though, part of me knew that it was Xov's power making me so angry. He was manipulating me, just like he had the bridge spirit.

"Get out of my head!"

"I can make all your enemies pay. I can bring you the satisfaction you deserve."

"The only enemy I have is *you*!"

He hissed in annoyance. "You're going to open the last

two seals. You *will* free me from the prison you constructed, even though you are not what you once were. You have become so weak, Shee Yee."

Hearing that name helped to clear my head. Because even though I was still trying to figure out who I was, there was one thing I knew for sure—I would never be Shee Yee.

"You've made a big mistake." My voice began small, but it grew stronger the more I spoke. The electrifying current of my spiritual energy surged within me, filling me with warmth against Xov's icy aura. "My name is Pahua Moua. I'm a shaman-in-training. And you don't have any power over me." My body strained as I pushed against his grasp.

On my arm, the spiral symbol blazed bright and golden. The lightning ax materialized in my hand. I didn't know how it could possibly be there with my spirit, but I wasn't going to argue. I must have unconsciously summoned it somehow.

Xov's hold broke, his power thrashing around me in a cruel blast of chilled air. My stomach lurched as I fell, but it wasn't far before my feet touched down on something solid. The ground was smooth gray stone, leading into blackness in all directions. The sky overhead was just as gray. Wherever this place was, I was still trapped with an angry god.

The cold swirled violently into a cyclone of ice. Then all that twisting power came together to form the shape of a man.

It wasn't a complete shape, though. He was fuzzy at the edges, like an overexposed picture. Whatever power he could project from behind the two seals still binding him was barely enough to hold his form together. But even unfinished, he was intimidating.

He was much taller than a normal adult, with broad shoulders and a long, thin body. His head kept blurring, as if a kid were smearing it with paint. When the lines did sharpen, the face they revealed was surprisingly handsome—lean cheeks, a pointed chin, and a broad nose. His eyes, though, were black and cruel.

"Who are you supposed to be, Kylo Ren?" I asked, gesturing to his clothes. A xauv that looked like three silver bands hung from around his neck. Silver chains and the spiral symbol of the gods hung from either side of the necklace. Beneath the xauv he wore a long black robe, like he was going for a Sith-lord vibe.

"I don't know who that is," he said, annoyed. He waved his hand. The robes were replaced by a simple black suit. His hair, which had been long, was now cut short around his ears. The silver necklace remained, though.

"Okay," I said with a grudging nod. "That outfit has a more modern villain vibe. Why black, though? Is there a rule about villains having to dress like they're going to a funeral?"

He ignored the question. Despite the royal-goth look, the makeover did help him appear more human. But aside from the fact he kept flickering like a glitchy video game, there was no mistaking him for a normal man. His aura was still ice-cold and overwhelmingly powerful.

I'd be lying if I said I wasn't scared. But to get back to my brother, I had to stand my ground. And not pretend to be someone else. This time, the only person who could save me was me.

I focused on my spiritual energy, feeling the way it coursed outward from my chest, and tried to imagine all that power channeling into the lightning ax. The ax already glowed, but now it looked like a star about to go supernova. I raised the blade and lowered my center of gravity. Even with the celestial weapon and access to all of Shee Yee's battle knowledge, I still wasn't sure I had what it would take to defeat a god. Fighting wasn't my strength, after all.

How had Zhong put it? *You try to see the truth of people.*

Xov's lips stretched into a smile that would have made me shudder if I weren't already terrified.

He opened his arms like he wanted to give me a hug. I lifted one eyebrow. Then he brought his hands together in a thunderous clap. A roar shook the ground and reverberated through my skull. It made me want to drop the ax and cover my ears.

A storm cloud appeared overhead and from it a silver spear descended into Xov's hands. It shone with blinding light and was crowned by a vicious arrow-pointed tip. Along the length of the spear were engraved scenes of destruction: the earth cracking open, volcanoes spewing ash and lava, ocean waves cresting over the coast to swallow whole cities, tornadoes ripping up trees from the roots.

Xov wasn't just the god of thunder. He was also the god of destruction and wrath. Before his imprisonment, he had been an executioner for Ntuj.

It didn't exactly make me feel confident.

"You will release the final two seals," he said.

"Yeah, I don't think so. And as soon as I save my brother, I'll find a way to fix the third seal." Lightning crackled through the shaft of my ax. The blade glowed white and hot.

For only a second, uncertainty flashed over Xov's face, and his form flickered again. Then his black eyes narrowed, and he said, "Let's see if you're any good with that ax."

He attacked, lunging with his spear. I dodged and rolled, letting my Shee Yee instincts take over. Xov was unbelievably fast, though. His long, lean body worked in perfect rhythm with the spear. He twirled the weapon over his head and then slammed it down. I barely got out of the way in time. Where the spear head struck the ground, lightning flashed, cracking the stone. Thunder followed, splitting through my head.

He grinned at my surprise. "Did you forget? I'm the thunder god. And you're just a pale echo of Shee Yee."

See the truth of people. . . . Figure out his motive. What was there to figure out? He'd unleashed his demon children on the three realms just to save his own skin. And now he wanted revenge because he'd picked a fight with Shee Yee and lost. Maybe Xov was just a terrible being, no reasons needed.

Thunder rumbled through the darkness as he spun the spear in a wide arc. I lifted the ax to block it, but the force of his swing nearly knocked me off my feet. I staggered. Xov flipped the spear with lightning speed and attacked from the opposite direction.

This time, I couldn't keep my balance as the butt of his weapon smashed into my shoulder blade. I crashed to the ground, bitter dirt coating my mouth.

32

~

Truth and Lies

 At this rate, I wasn't getting out of there in one piece. I had to think. Find a weakness.

"How pathetic," Xov said, clicking his tongue. "What would your mother Gao Pa say if she could see what you've become? Squandering the divine power she passed down to you."

Maybe it was my imagination, but at his mention of Gao Pa, I swear I caught the sweet scent of jasmine. I recalled all the times I'd smelled a trace of that light fragrance during this quest. Had she been helping me all along?

Then I thought of my own mom, waiting for Matt to wake up in a sterile hospital room. I was doing this for my family, and in return, they gave me the strength and motivation to keep going. Did Xov have anyone to love and love him in return?

"*I've* squandered my power?" I said, standing.

With a patronizing twist of his mouth, Xov waited for me to catch my breath. He was mocking me.

"You're the one who picked a fight with your brother's grandson," I said. "Was it just for your ego? Or did you actually care about the demon children he killed?"

Xov scoffed. "Why would I care about that mindless lot? They murdered their mother, and I would have been next."

"And your one life was worth more than the lives of all the mortals they killed when you opened the door between realms?"

"Of course," he said, as if I'd asked a ridiculous question.

It was obvious that the most important person to Xov was himself. If I could make Xov angry by wounding his pride, he might lower his guard enough for me to get an advantage.

"You must have been so humiliated when you were defeated by a half-mortal shaman," I said, my hands tightening around the ax. Before, in the cave, I'd had to be careful about using it. But here, with nothing around us, I didn't have to worry about destroying more trees or hurting anyone else.

Xov's eyes narrowed, his pupils flickering red. "He was an unworthy rival—nothing but a trickster, like that useless goddess Nhia Ngao Zhua Pa."

"Or he was better than you." My words were joined by a

bolt of lightning from the ax's blade, arcing toward Xov in a dazzling white streak.

He blocked it, his spear absorbing most of the blow. But he grimaced, too, as sparks of white energy seared his hands and danced up his arms. His features blurred and flickered. After a moment, he re-formed, looking even angrier. His eyes began to burn like hot coals.

My satisfaction at being able to hurt him didn't last long. He attacked, the sharp end of his spear moving so fast that it would have taken off my head if not for the spiritual energy guiding my reflexes. I dodged and nearly fell again.

"No wonder you want revenge," I said as I jogged backward, avoiding another swift strike. "You're the laughing-stock of the gods."

A low growl escaped Xov's lips, and he lunged. I ducked awkwardly but managed to slam the butt of my ax into the back of his leg.

"Argh!" He fell to one knee. His form flickered again as he turned and sliced my shoulder with his spear.

Pain shot through me. I rolled, deflecting another blow with my ax before regaining my feet. Gasping, I clutched my throbbing shoulder and backed away as he advanced on me.

Flashes of lightning split the darkness, followed by the crack of thunder. It made concentrating on his next attack harder.

"But the Sky Father is your brother. Why would you try to kill his grandson?" I said through my teeth, breathing hard. "Maybe you had something to prove." Compared to Ntuj, Xov would always be second best. His own son, Miv, had said it himself when we were in the Echo: *Hard for a little brother to compete with the creator of all realms.*

Xov roared as he thrust again with his spear, but I blocked it. Lightning leaped from the ax blade toward Xov's head. He almost didn't move in time. The ends of his hair crackled. The stench of burned hair made my nose wrinkle, but I'd nearly had him.

I spun the ax in my hand as smoothly as if I'd done it a thousand times before and aimed for the head of his spear. For a heartbeat, I thought I might have succeeded in unsettling him enough to get the upper hand. But then Xov twisted away, ramming his elbow into the back of my skull.

My vision went black with pain for a second. I stumbled, but somehow, I didn't fall. Squinting through my watering eyes, I quickly turned to face him again, ax raised.

"I must admit I didn't expect you to last even this long," he said scornfully. His eyes glowed an even deeper red, his anger practically simmering through the air. He swung his spear around his shoulders and over his head with such incredible speed and agility that I couldn't help but admire it. He was a terrible person, but the guy had skills.

He attacked again, faster now. It was all I could do to

block before Xov spun away to stab from another direction. My foot slipped out from beneath me. With a gasp, I fell.

I hit the ground hard and barely got my ax up in time to prevent the spear from stabbing my chest. I panted, eyes wide. Electricity shot from the ax to the spear, but the thunder god was ready this time with his own lightning. The two powers collided between us with a thunderous *crack* that made my teeth ache and my hair stand on end. The air felt thick and charged.

Xov grinned, all teeth. On his thin face, it looked skeletal. I couldn't believe I'd just been admiring his fighting skills.

He bore down on his staff. I groaned, the strength of the ax's blade the only thing keeping me alive. If it were any other weapon, the metal would have shattered by now, and the spear would have found my heart. Unfortunately, I was still pinned, and I couldn't see a way to escape.

"You might have Shee Yee's weapon, little girl, and maybe even a fraction of his skill in battle. But you don't have his experience or his strength. You're just a child playing at being a hero."

I gritted my teeth, fighting against the sour taste of fear at the back of my throat. I'd tried my best, but it hadn't been enough. Not against an ancient god, even one whose powers were limited by his prison.

"If you kill me now, you'll never be free," I managed to grunt. "The gods will make sure Shee Yee is never reincarnated again. They won't make the same mistake twice."

His grin transformed into a snarl as he realized I spoke the truth. Then he abruptly flipped his spear and smashed the metal rod into the handle of my ax. The weapon flew from my hands, skidding several feet away. I started to scramble backward, but he quickly pressed the butt of his spear against my throat to keep me pinned.

"Give me your oath that you will lift the final two curses and release the seals. Otherwise, I will destroy your friends."

My friends . . . While I was stuck here, Zhong was still at the gates, fighting the bridge spirit.

And Miv . . . I didn't know what he was doing, but he was no longer my friend. He had betrayed me. Pain shot through my shoulder again.

Then I remembered something Xov had said. *My fool son should have brought you to me long ago.*

So why hadn't he?

You're not Shee Yee, Miv had told me back at the Tree of Souls. *You're Pahua Moua.*

Had Miv known all along that I would be no match for Xov? No shaman warrior, just a dreamy girl. Had the quest been an elaborate trick to get me to retrieve the ax and release his father?

It didn't make sense. Miv had been by my side for *ages,* always giving me confidence when I most needed it.

Also, he *hadn't* taken me to Xov. He'd been carried away by demons. Maybe Miv understood what Xov didn't—that I *wasn't* Shee Yee.

And I didn't have to be in order to be the hero my brother needed.

Unleashing the bridge spirit had been my own fault. If I hadn't done that, Xov never would have found me. Miv had kept his identity a secret from me all these years, but he hadn't betrayed me. Not really.

I might have been lying to myself to make me feel better. I might have been grasping at any straw of hope I could find. But it was better than holding on to all my anger and sadness until it twisted me up inside and made me as bitter and evil as the bridge spirit.

Shivering, I pressed my arms against my sides and felt something through the pocket of my dress. Slipping my hand inside, I closed my fingers around the plum pit. All the pain from the memory of the last time I'd seen my dad flickered through me.

I still didn't know why he left us. I only knew that I hadn't been enough.

But I'd been enough for Matt, who'd never once complained about being stuck with me. And I was enough for my mom. I'd even been enough for Miv. Xov's son was supposed to have betrayed me, and instead (I hoped) he had seen and appreciated me for who I really was. He loved me. And that had been enough to make him stay.

Cag had called the plum stone a memento. I don't think he'd meant for me to carry it around forever, though. That wasn't moving on. But he'd given me the chance to let it go.

"Destroy my friends?" I said to Xov. "Not in this lifetime!" I flung the pit at his face.

He caught it with one hand, his lips twisting into a sneer. And then he froze, his eyes going blank as whatever magic was inside the pit drew him into its depths. Maybe the pit was forcing him to relive his worst memory, the way the plum had for me. Maybe that meant he was suffering his defeat and imprisonment at a half mortal's hands all over again, or some other terrible moment from a long life spent in his older brother's shadow. Whatever the case, it only lasted a couple of seconds before he wrestled back control of his mind.

It was just enough time for me, though.

I rolled away and retrieved the ax. I wrapped both hands around the handle. Then I sat up and swung as hard as I could.

The weapon glowed so bright that I had to close my eyes and trust the ax to find its target. The blade bit into Xov's spear, and the silver staff snapped in half.

"Nooooo!" Xov bellowed. With a crack of thunder, the spear vanished. Xov's body began to dissolve as well. His edges melted away like an ice cube's on a hot sidewalk. "This isn't over!"

The nasty smells of ozone and burned metal were suddenly replaced by the teasing scent of jasmine. A sweet wind swept around me, scattering the last of Xov's form. The sound of thunder retreated, like a dissipating storm.

I felt a pressure at my wrist. When I looked down, the tattered remnants of Zhong's talisman had been repaired. This time, silver threads were interwoven with the red ones.

Then my vision went black, and I faded into nothingness.

33

~

True Strength

 I awoke with a jolt. The ceiling of the cavern came into focus overhead. I was back in my body again, the lightning ax at my side.

"Pahua!" Miv pounced on my face.

I shouted his name, but it was more like "Mmm!" because I was being smothered by fur.

"You're alive!" He eased up enough for me to see his large cat's eyes. They were filled with anguish and fear.

Part of me was still angry with him for not telling me the truth, but most of me was relieved to see him. I squeezed him into a hug, more grateful than ever to have him at my side, knowing that he'd had a choice, and he'd chosen me.

"Did he . . . ?" Miv began. I knew what he was asking, mostly because he wasn't clawing at me for squeezing him. He wanted to know if his father had revealed Miv's true identity.

"Yes," I said. "But let's talk about it later, okay? How long was I out? What's happening?"

I released the cat spirit and sat up. My entire body ached in protest, reminding me that I'd been blasted from the elephant wall. My head throbbed. There was no way I could've survived that fall without breaking anything. Honestly, I don't think I should have survived at all. Yet somehow I had.

Maybe my being the Sky Father's granddaughter meant I was harder to kill? It was possible, I supposed. Otherwise I'm not sure my spirit could have withstood Xov's attacks for as long as it did.

"You were out for a few minutes," said Miv. "When the wall exploded, the spirits were too confused to attack at first. Zhong was able to move the unconscious kids out of harm's way. But you have to get up now. She needs help."

I eased myself up again, slower this time, and looked at the ivory gates. An enormous hole remained where the tusks had been, and remnants littered the courtyard. Stalactites had shaken loose from the cavern's ceiling, and they, too, lay shattered among chunks of elephant statues.

"I'm sorry," Miv said, sounding miserable. "This is all my fault. I never wanted you to get hurt."

"I know you didn't, and it's not just your fault. It's mine, too." I scanned the courtyard, and my stomach dropped when I found Zhong. She was being wrestled to the ground by three spirit children. The bridge spirit stood over her, trying to snap the protection charm off Zhong's wrist. Matt lay nearby, unmoving.

Panic shot through me. It felt like my heart was trying to climb up my throat. I grabbed the lightning ax and surged to my feet. Pain rocketed through my right leg, and I nearly fell again. It didn't feel broken, but my ankle was definitely sprained. Somehow I still remained standing.

At my wrist, the braided red-and-silver charm reminded me that I hadn't hallucinated the fight with Xov. That knowledge gave me the strength to limp toward Zhong and Matt.

The cavern trembled again, shaking loose more debris from the ruined wall. Rocks tumbled into the courtyard and almost crushed Zhong's backpack, which someone had tossed out of her reach. I hobbled over to it and, while keeping one eye on the bridge spirit, dug inside for more paper talismans.

The bridge spirit fixed her dark gaze on me. She said something to the remaining two children at her side. Counting the three holding down Zhong, there were only five left. As Miv had said, the unconscious ones had been dragged to the far end of the courtyard, away from the falling debris.

The two kids rushed me. I held up the lightning ax, but I didn't swing it. Energy crackled from the blade to the earth, spiking across the stone to snap at the children's feet. They stopped in their tracks.

I edged ever closer to the bridge spirit, the ax raised threateningly. But I couldn't risk turning my back on the kids, which meant I had no choice but to deal with them. I lowered the weapon, and the children attacked. I managed to knock one out with a talisman to the forehead. But the second one, a boy, leaped onto my right side and nearly dragged me down. I must have injured my rib, because a sharp pain in my side shoved the air from my lungs.

Then a screeching ball of fur flew past me, clawing at the spirit boy's face. The kid immediately let go of me as he tried to tear off the furious black kitten. I'd certainly missed having my brave best friend fighting at my side.

The bridge spirit screamed in rage. Her hair whipped above her head. The dingy nightgown snapped against her legs as if an invisible cyclone were swirling around her. Her power slammed into me, making me stagger. After my battle with Xov, I could tell that much of her strength came from him. When I'd felt it the first time, the bridge spirit's energy had only been a tangled mass of anger and sadness. Now it physically hurt.

I smacked a paper talisman onto the forehead of the spirit Miv was trying to scratch to death. The child went limp and collapsed. Two of the three children holding down Zhong released her as the bridge spirit directed them toward me instead. With a yowl, Miv launched himself at one of them. The other child rammed into me. My body lit up with pain, but I elbowed the girl in the face, loosening her grip.

"Sorry," I mumbled, before slapping a talisman on her.

Miv and I subdued the other spirit quickly, and then I

hurried over to Zhong. The bridge spirit had gone back to trying to wrench off Zhong's charm, and I realized why. She wanted to steal Zhong's soul.

With the same battle cry I'd heard Zhong use, I swung the ax in an arc. Lightning shot from the blade and went right over Zhong's head and into the bridge spirit, blasting her across the ruined courtyard. She slumped to the floor, motionless.

Once the bridge spirit's energy no longer restrained Zhong, my friend was able to wrench free of the last child. I reached her just in time to disable the kid with a talisman before he could do any damage.

Zhong collapsed onto her back, breathing hard. She had a giant bruise on her jaw and a scratch at her temple that was lightly bleeding. Another tremor rocked the cavern. She shielded her face from the rock dust raining down on us.

"You okay?" I asked.

"Never better," she said. "Took you long enough."

"Sorry, sorry."

Matt was lying a few feet away. I rushed to his side as quickly as my injuries would let me. A talisman was fixed to his forehead. I cast Zhong a grateful look as I knelt over him. My eyes welled with tears, and I pushed the dark hair from his temples. He always hated it when I did that.

"Will he be okay now?" I asked Zhong in a trembling voice.

Zhong nodded. "Good as new."

"I'm sorry I put you through all this," I said to Matt's spirit, my throat tight. "But the next time you open your eyes, you'll be home. I promise."

I turned to face the bridge spirit. She had risen to her knees. Her nightgown was more tattered than ever.

When she saw me, she screamed, *"You can't take them away from me!"*

She rose unnaturally to her feet as if pulled by puppet strings. Her black eyes swirled with fury. Something glittered near her foot. For the first time, I noticed a nearly invisible string tied around her ankle. It led toward the gate into Xov's prison.

As long as the bridge spirit was tied to Xov's power, she would have control over the children's spirits. I had to destroy her if I wanted to save Matt and the others once and for all. I gripped the lightning ax and stepped toward her.

The ghost continued to scream her rage. Her power battered me from all sides. It tore at my skin like needles, drawing tiny flecks of blood all over my arms and face. I gasped at the pain, but I didn't stop. Once I was close enough, I lifted the ax. Its energy crackled all around me, forming a protective shield against her energy.

Her screams grew more ragged, more desperate, as she saw she had no effect on me. I raised the lightning ax high over my head, poised to strike.

And then I hesitated.

This didn't feel right. I remembered my first impression of the ghost girl at the bridge. I'd felt sorry for her.

What was it Xov had said? *She was so very angry. So very lonely.*

I knew about loneliness. That was why I'd tried talking to her in the first place. It had only been a few days ago, but it felt like forever. She had struck me as just a little girl, younger than Matt. I'd thought then that maybe all she needed was someone to acknowledge her sadness rather than pretend she wasn't there. To see the truth of her.

I set down the ax.

"Pahua, what are you doing?" Zhong yelled from somewhere behind me. But she sounded far away.

I knew about loneliness, but I didn't know what it felt like to be lost in the woods, abandoned by the parents who should have protected me.

The ghost hadn't stolen the kids' souls because she was evil. Yeah, she'd been angry, but her emotions had been amplified and manipulated by Xov, just as mine had been.

She'd taken the children because she was lonely.

Without the protection of the lightning ax, I was vulnerable to the spirit's power. It lashed me and I winced, hurting all over. But I didn't back away. Instead, I stepped right up to her and put my arms around her.

The bridge spirit stiffened in surprise. She hissed, her

power clawing at me like a feral animal. I held on tight and bent close so my words would reach her ear.

"I'm so sorry," I whispered, surprised at the way my eyes began to sting. "I'm sorry for what you went through. It was terrible, and it shouldn't have happened."

The bridge spirit thrashed, small fists pounding against my stinging sides. I sucked in a breath from the pain, but I didn't let go.

"You should have been taken care of and protected. You deserved so much better." I poured into the words my own frustrations—with people who saw my differences and thought they made me inferior, with my dad, who was supposed to have loved me but only let me down.

Suddenly, the bridge spirit's screams of anger transformed, becoming a long keening wail. I tried to pull back to see her face, but now she was the one hugging me, bawling into my dress. Tears filled my eyes, too.

"I know it feels impossible," I said, "but you have to let go. It's the only way to move on."

The bridge spirit only cried harder, her small shoulders heaving with each sob. When Matt was younger, he used to cry because he missed Mom after a long day without her. I would wrap him in a blanket and let him sleep in my bed with me so he wouldn't feel alone. Since I didn't have a blanket now, I settled for hugging the girl tight and stroking her back the way my mom did when I was sick.

I let her cry for as long as she needed. Eventually the bridge spirit's sobs began to calm into hiccups. When she finally released me—just enough to look up at my face—it was with wide, fearful eyes.

"What's your name?" I asked.

She seemed a little panicked. "I . . . I don't remember."

"It's okay," I said quickly. "You'll get a new one, anyway. It'll be even better than the last."

She hiccuped and bit her lip. "I'm scared," she whispered.

"It *is* a little scary, but that's because you don't know what's going to happen next. I do, though, because I was there recently."

"Really?"

"Yep. A woman is waiting to take care of you. She's a little grumpy, but she's got a good heart and a pretty cool garden. You won't ever be alone."

Although the girl still looked uncertain, she seemed to relax a little.

I took her hands in mine. "It's okay to be scared. But it's going to be all right."

She released a shaky breath. Then she closed her eyes and leaned into me. I hugged her again, and she squeezed back, her head tucked against my shoulder. Finally she dissolved into mist, leaving nothing behind but a gleaming strip of white cloth. After a second, that vanished, too.

I smiled. Yeng had her now and would make sure she had a place on the banyan tree.

"Pahua, look."

Zhong was turning in a slow circle, watching the spirits of the other children fade. They didn't leave white strips, so I could only hope that meant they were returning to their bodies in the mortal realm. When I looked, Matt had gone, too.

Another tremor rocked through the cavern, stronger than the last one. More tusks broke from the wall. The thunder god was angry that I had severed his connection to the bridge spirit.

I stooped to pick up the ax. "We'd better get out of here before Xov brings down the whole cavern."

"Xov?" Zhong repeated, confused.

"Oh, right. I have some bad news to tell you, but let's wait until we get back to the surface."

Zhong frowned, but she didn't argue. Miv, to my surprise, was on her shoulder. A stalactite fell and shattered across the courtyard—close enough that we all jumped.

That was a sign we needed to leave. Right now.

We made a run for it, dashing back into the tunnel. The walls trembled all around us, raining dirt into our hair. We forged on. Even now, I felt Xov's power trying to wrench me back. His voice echoed in my head.

This isn't over.

34

~

Time for Those Long-Overdue Talks

 Leaving the Spirit Realm turned out to be a lot less complicated than entering it had been.

I filled in Zhong and Miv on what had happened when my spirit left my body and how I'd been tricked into breaking the first seal on Xov's prison. I described how I'd paid him back by using the lightning ax—now an innocent-looking dragon comb over my right ear—to destroy his spear.

Zhong looked dubious, as if she thought I was making up the story. I couldn't blame her—it was pretty crazy.

After some emergency mango first aid from Nplooj to heal my ankle, Zhong's face, and various other injuries, we returned to the nearby town to try to contact Spike again. I was eager to get back home. Hopefully, my brother had woken up by now, but I wouldn't be able to relax until I saw him for myself.

Suab Nag was especially put out to be woken up in the

middle of the night, but to our surprise, Spike was already there, waiting. She even still had my cloak and backpack.

"I meant to return for you," she explained as I hung my backpack from her saddle alongside Zhong's. "But Suab Nag has had me filling out paperwork all evening for the unusual trip."

"That miserable donkey," Zhong muttered, which made Spike whinny-laugh. Suab Nag had gladly seen us out the door and then locked it with a grumpy *Harrumph*.

"I'm glad everything worked out," Spike said. She stood still as I climbed clumsily onto her back, settling behind Zhong. "The tree spirits don't usually let outsiders use their pathways to travel. They must have really liked you."

I winced. It was more that they liked the gift I gave them, but it had gotten us where we needed to go. I swore never to travel by tree again, though. Not enough legroom. Or arm-room. Or existing-room. Speaking of being squished, Miv was smooshed between me and Zhong, but he didn't complain this time.

"Thanks again for the ride," I said to the spirit horse. "I hope it doesn't mean more paperwork." I held on to Zhong's waist as Spike stomped her hooves and then leaped into a full-out gallop. My eyes widened, and my stomach felt like it'd been left behind.

"I don't mind," Spike called. Wind spirits dashed around us in hazy shapes. "You need to get back to your brother, after all, and this is the quickest way."

Not having to wait in Crossroads traffic was a relief, as was not having to agonize about what would happen if the eagle demon spotted us again.

With the help of the wind spirits, we ascended ever higher into the sky. We flew above even the crab cloud.

When Spike heard me whisper "Wow," she slowed her breakneck pace so that we could observe the shifting stars without worrying about being ripped from the saddle. The constellations waved to us as we passed. Far in the distance, I thought I saw a team of white birds carrying a palanquin that bore a shining silver lantern.

"I get to be the first to congratulate you," I said to Zhong. "For completing your quest."

"Technically, you did most of the work at the end there." Fortunately, she didn't sound too upset about it. "But it had to be that way."

"You could have defeated the ghost girl just as well," I said.

"Yeah, I could have defeated her. But you're the only one who could have *saved* her."

I opened my mouth and then closed it again, not sure what to say to that. Feeling embarrassed, I asked, "Will you let me know when you get the guardian spirit's blessing back at school?"

Zhong beamed and nodded, putting to rest my uncertainty that she wouldn't want to stay friends after this. "We'll exchange contact info. Don't forget."

"Also, um—"

When I hesitated, Zhong jabbed me with her elbow and said, "What?"

"I still need to restore the ivory gates, and I don't know how." I'd majorly messed up. This mistake couldn't be fixed as easily as the damage I'd done to the trees in Nyom's forest, but hopefully it wouldn't be impossible, either. One fight with Xov had assured me that he couldn't be allowed to go free.

"I'll do some research," Zhong said, "and ask the shaman masters about it. I'm sure they'll have some ideas."

"Thanks," I said, relieved. Zhong's school would have information and resources I couldn't possibly get on my own.

I did, however, have an expert on Xov sitting right in my lap. When our eyes met, Miv understood that it was time to talk. Now that the wind wasn't trying to yank him off the horse, he climbed onto my shoulder. He pushed his head against the side of my neck, and I sighed with contentment.

"Miv," I began, keeping my eyes on the stars. It helped to pretend that we were just having a normal conversation. "If you're the son of a god, then why are you a kitten?"

Zhong's head snapped up from where she'd begun fiddling with the pins on her jacket. "What?" she demanded.

Miv ignored her. "Because when I escaped my post as my father's prison guard, the gods put a curse on me."

If Zhong could have jumped to her feet, she would have. Instead, her ears flushed with color. "You're Xov's son?! I knew it! I knew we couldn't trust you from the moment we first met!"

"Calm down," I told her.

"Less moving around back there, please!" called Spike as her hooves dusted the tops of clouds.

Zhong's shoulders relaxed, but I was sure she still wanted to strangle the cat spirit.

"Will you tell me your real name, at least?" I asked him.

He hesitated, then finally said, "My mother was a leopard spirit. She left me at the doors to my father's palace when I was a child. Xov called me Mos, which means *soft*. It's not a name I think about fondly. I'll stick with Miv, if you don't mind."

I shook my head, quietly glad he preferred the foolish name I'd given him. "Are you going to be stuck as a kitten forever?"

"For as long as the gods see fit to punish me, I guess."

If the Sky Father ever dropped into another of my dreams, I promised myself I would put in a good word for Miv.

"So, are you the one who freed Shee Yee's spirit from the Tree of Souls?" Zhong demanded, trying to glare back at him.

I could tell Miv didn't want to answer her, but I nudged him, and he sighed. "Yes. Xov commanded me to do it, because only the 'victor's hand' could free him. Being forced into this form robbed me of much of my former power, and freeing Shee Yee took every last bit of what I had left." He looked down at his small paws. "I never really recovered. After that, it was years before I located you in the mortal realm."

"How did you even find me?"

"I pulled some favors and had someone seek out Shao."

My eyes narrowed. "Is that why Shao tried roasting me to make sure I wasn't an evil spirit?"

He cringed. "It might have been. . . . But Shao has always been unreliable, especially when it comes to Shee Yee."

A trace of my annoyance with Shao returned, and I poked Miv's cheek for playing a small part in what had happened.

"Unbelievable," Zhong muttered, her knuckles white around Spike's mane. "I should have trusted my gut about you."

"Give him a chance," I said. Then, before Zhong could explode at me, I quickly asked Miv, "Xov said you should have taken me to him when I was younger. Why didn't you?"

"Because you surprised me." He flopped onto his stomach, his small body draped over my shoulder. I rested my hand over his back, afraid the wind would snatch him away. "I initially sided with my father because I wanted his approval. I thought that by helping him escape his prison I would finally earn his love. But the more time I spent with you and your family—in the beginning, with your dad, and then after, seeing the way your mom worked so hard to support you and Matt, and the way you always took care of your brother—the more I understood what love really is. I couldn't let my father destroy you the way he destroyed everything else."

As the cat spirit spoke, I ran my fingers through his soft fur. The last remnants of my anger with him melted away. Even Zhong looked less angry when she glanced over her shoulder at us.

"And then everything with the bridge spirit happened," Miv went on, "and I knew that the demons coming after you were sent by my father. I figured if you got the lightning ax, you would at least have protection from him. But then he kidnapped me in order to set a trap for you, and . . . I'm sorry, Pahua. You have to believe me when I say I never meant for any of this to happen."

"I do believe you," I said, and I felt him relax against me. My gloves grew warm, indicating that we were crossing between realms. "But no more secrets, okay?"

He nodded. "Promise."

The threads of my gloves were frayed, and the seams were coming apart. Four fingers had holes in them. I wasn't sure how much longer they'd last. Strangely, I was okay with that. It meant I'd have to rely on my own spiritual energy from now on, which I would learn to control as soon as I saw that Matt was safe. I'd have to get him a protection charm as well.

Gradually, the sky changed from black to the dusky blue of the mortal realm. The sun was just setting, a lazy orb on the horizon, and none of the clouds were shaped like enormous crabs.

Familiar buildings took shape below as Spike descended. I directed her to the hospital, and she dropped us off right outside the main doors. Just like when we'd emerged from the elephant statue, no one noticed our arrival on a magical flying horse.

As I wiped off my clothes—I was still coated in dust from being in the tunnels, and there was a tear in my leggings—Spike and Zhong said their good-byes. I wasn't sure how it was that Spike was visible to Zhong in the mortal realm. Maybe it had something to do with their contract. Then, with a blast of wind, the horse was gone.

We found a restroom first to ensure that my appearance wouldn't alarm my mom too much. Thanks to the tree spirits, all my injuries had healed, at least. I splashed my face with water and tried to use the dragon comb to tame my wind-tangled hair.

As Zhong watched me in the bathroom mirror, she cleared her throat and said, "I've been thinking. You should consider coming with me. To the school, I mean. Not right now, but, like . . . later. Once you've thought about it. The shaman masters can help you with Xov's seal, and in the meantime, you'll be assigned a mentor who can teach you how to control your powers. And I'll help, too, like I said."

The suggestion came as a surprise. Me, join Zhong in her

shaman-warrior community? A few days ago, it would've seemed like an impossible idea. But after nearly being turned to stone, almost drowning in frog backwash, getting pelted by books, and surviving an encounter with an angry god . . . shaman school sounded pretty cool. And with Zhong, I would even have a real friend there.

"I'll definitely think about it," I said with a smile. First, I had to make sure my brother was safe.

Zhong tugged at her jean jacket to scan the pins on her front pocket. She gently removed one that looked like a rice stalk and handed it to me. "In the meantime, here's your first pin."

"What does it mean? I eat rice?"

She rolled her eyes. "The school didn't give me this one. My mom did. She said it's a symbol of growth."

"Thank you," I said. "Are you sure you want to give it up?"

"It's fine. I'm making space for all the marks of achievement they'll give me once I get back," she said, admiring her reflection. I laughed as Miv rolled his eyes.

Out in the lobby, the clock showed that even though we'd been in the Spirit Realm for two days, we'd only been gone from the mortal realm for a little over six hours. That was great news, because I hadn't wanted to worry my mom. But my heart still hammered as we made our way through the hospital to Matt's room.

"I'll wait here," Zhong said, leaning against the wall outside the door.

I flashed her a grateful smile for sticking around a little longer, and then, with Miv tucked against my neck, I pushed open the door.

Inside, Matt was sitting up in bed, stuffing a spoonful of rice porridge into his mouth. At the sight of me, his eyes lit up. My own began to burn as I rushed across the room to his bedside.

"You're awake!" I said, pushing away the retractable tray and bowl so I could pull him into a hug.

"Hey!" he said grumpily, even though he hugged me back. "I was eating that. I'm hungry."

Miv jumped off my shoulder and onto the top of Matt's head, settling into the mess of his hair. I blinked the tears from my eyes and drew back so I could brush my fingers over his forehead. His skin was cool, and I felt nothing unusual inside him. His spirit was back, safe and sound, and the connection to the ghost girl was gone. Relief made my limbs so weak, I had to sit down on his mattress.

Matt reached for his tray and rice porridge again, and then paused. After a moment, he stroked my hand. "Mom says you were worried."

"Of course I was. Where is she, anyway?"

Just then the bathroom door opened, and my mom stepped out. "Pahua! I thought I heard your voice."

As I'd expected, she looked like she hadn't left Matt's side since I'd seen them last. Her clothes were rumpled, and her hair was still messily tied back. But she looked happy, too, now that Matt's mysterious "illness" had passed.

"They want to keep him here for observation while they run more tests, but otherwise, he seems to be completely recovered," she said as she gave me a hug. Matt smiled as he proceeded to shovel more rice porridge into his mouth.

I nodded, my throat tight, and pressed my face into her shirt. I was happy that my brother was safe, but there was so much more I needed to do to ensure that he stayed that way. I had to make myself stronger so I could protect him and Mom. I had to repair the ivory gates. Lord Xiav would probably come for me again, and Xov had said this wasn't over. I needed to be ready.

But first, there was something I was dying to know.

"Mom, I have to ask you something," I said once she'd released me.

I moved aside so she could sit on the edge of Matt's bed in my place and smooth down his hair. It was sticking up in the back where he'd been lying on it. Miv jumped from his head to the tray and then onto the bed before settling into the blanket.

"Sure," she said, smiling faintly as she watched Matt eat.

"Do you remember that old pin Aunt Kalia gave you?"

Her smile wilted at once, and a guardedness crept behind her eyes. I frowned at her reaction. She was probably going to try to lie to me, but I was tired of being kept in the dark. Which meant I would have to be truthful as well about everything I'd learned over the last few days.

But not right now. Not in a hospital room with Matt next to us, an apartment in need of cleaning up, and my shaman-warrior friend still waiting in the hallway.

"Why are you talking about that all of a sudden?" she asked, her voice lowered.

"Because I . . . I had a dream about it. So I want to know what the pin means." It was just a little lie, and I'd clear things up later, when we were back home. My mom had once said that the Hmong believe that spirits sometimes try to tell us things in dreams. Miv's head popped up from the blankets; he was also curious about my mom's answer.

Matt seemed to sense the tension in the air, because he stopped eating and glanced between the two of us. Mom didn't notice, though. She sighed and fidgeted with the small red charm pouch that hung around her neck.

"The pin was . . . It was from a shaman school your aunt used to attend when she was around your age. She had to leave the school, and she never got over it. It was a painful memory for her, so she gave me the pin, along with all her old student supplies."

"Did . . . Did Aunt Kalia want me to go to that school as well?" I asked.

Mom's eyes grew wide. "How did you . . . ?" Then her shoulders slumped a bit, and she admitted, "Yes. We used to fight about it, but it wasn't a decision that either of us could make for you. I wasn't even sure if you . . . if you *could* go to the school, but Kalia insisted that she'd divined from the spirits some great future waiting for you." She shook her head, rubbing her eyes. "It's not that I don't think you're meant for great things. But I wanted to wait until you were older so I could ask you if it's something you'd even want to do."

Some of the anxiety tying my stomach into knots eased a little. "I think . . . I do want that."

"We'll talk about it more once we get Matt home, okay?" Mom said.

"Promise?"

She reached out and cupped my cheek. "I promise."

I nodded. It was amazing how much better I felt just knowing that she was willing to talk about something she'd always kept secret. Maybe I could even convince her to talk about why Dad left. Someday.

She lifted the collar of her T-shirt and gave it a sniff. "Do you think you could go home and get me a change of clothes? I'm feeling kind of gross."

I nodded before leaning over the bed to hug Matt again. "Love you," I said before planting a kiss on his cheek.

He laughed, relaxing now that the tension had passed, and said, "Love you, too, dummy."

Those were the sweetest words I'd heard in days. Miv jumped onto my shoulder, and I gave Matt one more glance before heading into the hallway. He was happily digging into a cup of Jell-O.

When I bounced over to her, Zhong straightened off the wall. "Everything good?" she asked.

I smiled. "Yeah, I think so. For now, anyway. Thanks for waiting. Could you, maybe, help me clean up my apartment? It's probably still a wreck."

Zhong's nose wrinkled. "I should have escaped while I had the chance." Then she smiled and pointed at my shirt. "Did your mom give you that?"

I looked down and was surprised to find a small flower tucked behind the pin Zhong had given me. It was a single jasmine blossom. Bemused, I removed the flower and twirled it between my fingers. The scent of jasmine teased my nose.

I smiled as well. "Yeah. She did." I wondered if I would ever meet Gao Pa, even if it was only in a dream. I hoped so.

But I wasn't in a hurry to meet any more celestial relatives. For the first time in ages, I didn't feel like pretending I was a shaman-warrior princess. For now, I was more than okay with just being me.

Glossary

Something I've always found interesting about the Hmong language is how a word completely changes meaning depending on how it's spoken. Hmong is a tonal language, so each word must be spoken with a particular tone, similar to different pitches in music. Unfortunately, there's no current system in place to describe Hmong tones with written words, but I hope you'll feel inspired to look up more information about tonal languages and how fascinating they are!

cag ntoo   (kah thohng) the Hmong word for *roots*.

ceg ntoo   (kay thohng) the Hmong word for *branches*.

cev ntoo   (kay thohng) the Hmong word for *trunk*.

choj   (kaw) the Hmong word for *bridge*.

dab neeg   (dah nehng) literally translated, the Hmong word *dab* can mean *monster/ghost* or even just *creature not of this world*, and *neeg* means *person/people*. However, when the two words are used together, the phrase *dab neeg* means Hmong folktales or myths, traditionally told orally.

Dab Qhov Txos (dah qaw tsaw) the spirit of the stove. A house spirit that lives in the fireplace used for cooking. They are generally helpful, but can cause illness in the family if offended.

Dab Teb (dah thay) the Spirit Realm, where mortal souls go after death. Living mortal souls can also get lost there when they're frightened out of their bodies—for example, due to an accident or shock—requiring a shaman to retrieve them.

Dab Txhiaj Meej (dah TSEE-uh muhng) the spirit of the front door. A house spirit honored with prayers that are annually renewed by a shaman or someone who knows the ritual ceremony. During the ceremony, the shaman drapes a strip of red cloth over the door so that the spirit will bless the family with prosperity.

Dab Xwm Kab (dah soo kah) the spirit of the altar. A house spirit that some consider a minor god of wealth. Caring for the family altar can gain its favor, but the spirit can also cause illness if the altar is neglected.

Echo one of the six realms. It is a copy of the mortal realm, a safe haven created by the gods for spiritfolk fleeing the growing dominance of mortals in the mortal realm.

Elder Gods the Council of Elder Gods is made up of the four oldest and most powerful of the Hmong gods: Ntuj, Huab Tais Zaj, Nhia Ngao Zhua Pa, and Xov, who was replaced by Xiav after his imprisonment.

Gao Pa (gow pah) Ntuj's youngest daughter and Shee Yee's mother.

hluas (huh-LOO-uh) the Hmong word for *young*.

Hmong (hmuhng) an ethnic minority with many different tribes, customs, and dialects. The Hmong originated in the mountainous regions of China, and then migrated across Southeast Asia. A variation of "hmoob."

Huab Tais Zaj (HOO-uh thahy zhah) Dragon Emperor of Zaj Teb, the Land of Dragons. God of rivers and lakes. All rivers originate in Zaj Teb, where Huab Tais Zaj ensures their continual flow throughout the six realms. He is the Sky Father's son-in-law. He trained his nephew (by marriage) Shee Yee to become a master swordsman, archer, and rider, and also taught him how to use magic, including transmutation and shape-shifting.

koj xiam hlwb lawm los (kaw SEE-uh hloo luh law) Hmong phrase that generally means *Have you lost your mind?*

miv (mee) the Hmong word for *cat*.

mos (maw) the Hmong word for *soft*.

nab vam (nah vah) a Hmong dessert made of tapioca pearls and green jelly mixed with ice, caramelized sugar, and coconut milk.

Nhia Ngao Zhua Pa (NEE-uh gow ZHOO-uh pa) a shape-shifting goddess and the progenitor of all shape-shifters except dragons. She's the most meddlesome of the Elder Gods, because she's a trickster and loves to prey on selfish mortal men. She features prominently in many Hmong folktales as a tragic heroine or damsel, because she's good at hiding her true nature behind deception.

niam tais   (NEE-uh thahy) the Hmong word for an aunt on your mother's side. It's also a polite way to address an older woman you don't know.

nplooj   (blohng) the Hmong word for *leaf.*

Ntuj   (thoo) the Hmong word for *sky*; the Sky Father, the creation god and most powerful of the Hmong gods. He was the firstborn son of the first man and woman after they emerged from the core of the world. He lifted the sky and created four pillars to hold it up. He then fashioned two celestial lanterns—the sun and the moon—and ordered them carried across the sky to divide the days.

nyom   (nyaw) the Hmong word for *grass.*

poj ntxoog   (paw zohng) a demon typically associated with vengeful spirits who were either kidnapped by other demons or who can't move on. They often take the form of young women with tangled hair and backward feet, although they aren't exclusively female.

shaman   Hmong shamans are gifted with the ability to communicate with spirits and travel through the Spirit Realm via ritual ceremonies. They are spiritual leaders called to the profession, typically through dreams or sickness.

Shao   (shau) a mortal who tried to follow in Shee Yee's footsteps and dared to enter the gods' home in the Sky

Kingdom. He was blessed with immortality and the powers of an oracle. At the same time, he was cursed to help any traveler who sought his advice.

Shee Yee (shee yee) a grandson of Ntuj; the first and most powerful Hmong shaman. His father was a mortal, and his mother was Gao Pa, the youngest and favorite of Ntuj's daughters. His given name was Tong (tawng), but he was renamed Shee Yee once he mastered his skills.

six realms consisting of the mortal realm, the Echo, the Spirit Realm, the Land of Dragons, the Sky Kingdom, and the realm of the ancestors.

Sky Kingdom where the Elder Gods live and oversee the other realms.

spiritfolk any non-mortal spirit, including beast, nature, and guardian spirits.

suab nag (SHOO-uh nah) the Hmong phrase meaning *the sound of rain.*

Tree of Souls where all mortal souls go after death in order to await reincarnation.

xauv (sau) a traditional Hmong necklace made of silver interlocking chains in varying and intricate designs. The word *xauv* means *lock.*

Xiav (SEE-uh) the Hmong word for *blue*; the blue thunder dragon who replaced Xov on the Council of Elder Gods.

Xov (saw) the Hmong word for *thread*; Ntuj's younger brother; the god of thunder, destruction, and wrath. In the beginning of the world, for a brief time, he also held the position of official executioner for Ntuj. He fathered the world's first demons. When his horde of children chased him across the Sky Kingdom, he opened the door to the other realms to save himself, thereby unleashing his murderous offspring upon the world, along with disease and strife. He was ultimately defeated and imprisoned by his great-nephew, Shee Yee.

Yeng (yehng) the immortal arborist who cares for the Tree of Souls. She was once mortal but was trapped within the tree by Nhia Ngao Zhua Pa, and she remained there for so long that she became a part of the tree itself. A variation of *yeej*.

Zaj Teb (zhah thay) the Land of Dragons (literal translation).

zhong (zhawng) variation of the Hmong word for *forest*, traditionally *hav zoov* (hah zhohng).

Author's Note

When I was a month old, my mother, barely in her twenties, bundled me up and snuck me and my five siblings out of our village home in Laos and into the jungles of Southeast Asia. For aiding the United States during the Vietnam War, the Hmong were forced to flee the mountains, on foot, and cross the Mekong River into Thailand to escape persecution and death.

After spending several years in a refugee camp, my family immigrated to the US when I was three, and we settled in Wisconsin. While my local Hmong community tried hard to hold on to their customs and traditions, I grew up desperately wanting to fit into our small American town. Like Pahua, I spent a lot of time wishing I could be someone else.

I was raised on Hmong superstitions and folktales; shaman customs and Chinese wuxia movies; fairy godmothers, glass slippers, and happily-ever-afters. But as someone straddling two very different cultures, I felt like I didn't fit into either one. Everything from books to TV to movies to magazines told me that being who I was meant I couldn't go on epic adventures or discover magic or ride off into the sunset.

I've matured since then, and now I know that representation matters, representation matters, representation matters. Being me is enough and always has been. It's my hope that Pahua's story will show all the kids out there wondering if they belong that they do.

They do, and no matter where they come from or what they look like, they can be heroes, too.

I owe a lot to my family for always believing in me and never trying to dissuade me from writing as a (wildly impractical) career choice. My mom and brothers used to tell dab neeg, oral Hmong folktales, when I was young. My brother would scare (and delight) me with stories of poj ntxoog, girls who unknowingly fell in love with ghosts, and water spirits who drowned unsuspecting villagers. These were the first stories that inspired my imagination and made me hungry for more—not just more Hmong mythology, but anything I could find about the supernatural and the fantastical.

While the mythology in this book is inspired by the stories I grew up with and the research I conducted, as Zhong tells Pahua, the tradition of oral storytelling and the lack of historical records means there are a dozen different versions of every tale depending on the storyteller, and nothing presented here should be taken as cultural fact. The Hmong are a varied people spread across China and Southeast Asia (and the world!), with different customs, beliefs, and dialects depending on the region.

Our stories have always been fluid, which used to be frustrating to me when I was figuring out who I was and where I fit. Now I'm incredibly honored to count myself among those storytellers.

Mom, I'm sorry it took me so long to write about our myths and folktales, and I hope I've made you proud.

In addition to my family, this story wouldn't have been possible without a whole host of wonderful people. My deepest thanks go out to:

Suzie Townsend, for being my very own fairy godmother and helping me to chase dreams and pursue the impossible. And to Devin Ross as well for sprinkling her magic over this book and then venturing off on new adventures to spread that magic elsewhere.

Stephanie Lurie, for believing in Pahua's story and then casting her own brand of editorial magic and making it even better than I could have hoped.

Rick Riordan and Disney Hyperion, for the opportunity to share Pahua's story with readers. My daughter discovered the Percy Jackson books first many years ago and then introduced me to them. They've reshaped how I imagine mythological retellings, and it's not hyperbole to say Pahua's story might not exist if not for the way his books have inspired me and so many others.

The copy editors; creative director; production people;

marketing, publicity, and sales team; assistants; and every person who leaves their mark on a book but not their name. I see and appreciate you so much.

The parents, booksellers, librarians, and educators who put books into the hands of children and encourage whole new generations of readers and writers.

Every reader who has picked up one of my books and lost themselves for a few hours within its pages.

Shveta Thakrar, who is always a light in dark places.

Mindee Arnett, who's been with me every step of this wild journey called publishing.

My fellowship—Emily, Audrey, Lyn, Imaan, Myra, Patricia—who've been with me since even before that.

And again, my family, for carrying me through a jungle, across a river, and then an ocean, so I could write these words that will never be enough—thank you.

Don't miss the next

PAHUA

adventure

Pahua and the Dragon's Secret